At Medeleni

A Summer in Moldavia

Ionel Teodoreanu

At Medeleni

A Summer in Moldavia

Translated by Eugenia Farca
Introduction by A.K. Brackob
Illustrated by Alexandra Maxim

CENTER FOR
Romanian
STUDIES

The Center for Romanian Studies

Las Vegas ◊ Chicago ◊ Palm Beach

Classics of Romanian Literature

Volume II

ISSN 2693-1796

Published in the United States of America by
Histria Books
7181 N. Hualapai Way, Ste. 130-86
Las Vegas, NV 89166 USA
HistriaBooks.com

The Center for Romanian Studies is an independent academic and cultural institute with the mission to promote knowledge of the history, literature, and culture of Romania in the world. The publishing program of the Center is affiliated with Histria Books. Contributions from scholars from around the world are welcome. To support the work of the Center for Romanian Studies, contact us at info@centerforromanianstudies.com

Library of Congress Control Number: 2021949310

ISBN 978-1-59211-110-7 (hardcover)
ISBN 978-1-59211-292-0 (softbound)
ISBN 978-1-59211-295-1 (eBook)

Contents

Introduction

A t *Medeleni: A Summer in Moldavia* is the first volume of Ionel Teodoreanu's acclaimed trilogy, *La Medeleni*. The story ranks among the best loved novels in Romanian Literature; almost any Romanian can tell you about the three principal heroes of the story — Dănuț, Olguța, and Monica. In his three volume work, Teodoreanu follows his heroes through the innocence of childhood to adulthood, as they experience the tragic years of the First World War. In many ways, the characters are representatives of this generation which grew up in one world and then had to come to grips with the new one that arose from the flames of war that engulfed Europe between 1914 to 1918. Of the three volumes, the first [*Hotarul nestatornic*], which presents the heroes in their childhood, is recognized as Teodoreanu's finest work.

lonel Teodoreanu was born in Iaşi on 6 January 1897. He grew up in a family of intellectuals. Like his father and his older brother [Al. O. "Pastorel" Teodoreanu (1894-1964), also a well-known writer, poet, and satirist], he studied law and became a lawyer. He made his literary debut in 1919 in the short-lived journal *Însemnari literare*, edited by George Topîrceanu and Mihail Sadoveanu. With the reappearance of *Viaţa Românească*, Teodoreanu came under the guidance of G. Ibrăileanu who considered him to be one of the most promising young writers of the post-war generation. In Iaşi, under Ibrăileanu's leadership, he actively took part, along with Topîrceanu, Sadoveanu, Mihai Codreanu, Gala Galaction, Tudor Arghezi, Otilia Cazimir, and others, in the most vibrant cultural movement of inter-war Romania. As Topîrceanu later recalled, "it was with these people, in an atmosphere of cordiality, esteem, enthusiasm, and Moldavian indolence that *Viaţa Românească*, issue by issue, month after month, was produced. And its publication was eagerly awaited by thousands of readers from all social strata — its well to do subscribers who never paid for their subscriptions, teachers and intellectuals of our country, priests, and, above all, students, twenty of whom would chip in to buy a single copy and then pass it around until it fell to pieces. And that is how the eyes of educated Romania of those days... were riveted on Iaşi." It was in this environment that Ionel Teodoreanu wrote and published his classic work, *La Medeleni* (1925-1927).

Teodoreanu is the Romanian novelist who best handled the theme of childhood, presenting it in a subtle psychological context, while at the same time retaining its innocence and charm. These qualities made *La Medeleni*, especially the first book, a novel which appealed to readers of all ages. It is not, however, an autobiographical account as many have concluded. "When the first volume of the trilogy La Medeleni appeared, entitled *Hotarul Nestatornic*," Teodoreanu later recalled, "the opinion of the reading public, in agreement with that of the literary critics, decreed that it is nothing more than a romantic autobiography of my childhood... No one thought that the explanation of this novel is extremely simple: *Hotarul Nestatornic* is not an autobiography of the author's childhood, but a stage, the first, in the lives of the three heroes... These personages have some characteristics borrowed from real living people, but their souls, their individuality, is nothing more than an expression of the soul of their creator. In Medeleni, Olguţa, Monica, and Dănuţ are virtual expressions of my soul." The world of childhood presented in *At Medeleni: A Summer in Moldavia* is a reflection of upper middle class life in Romania during the early decades of the twentieth century. It depicts the innocence of childhood soon to be shattered by the world, a world which itself, one that will soon be devastated by the ravages of the great war and its aftermath. Although it is not an autobiography, the author's experience of having grown up in such a family in Moldavia during this time served as the basis for his literary creation.

At Medeleni ranks among the classics of Romanian literature. Despite his success, Teodoreanu abandoned the childhood theme in most of his later literary works and never again attained the same level of literary success. Although he lacked the wit of his older brother Pastorel, who spent time in communist prisons for his sarcasm, Ionel Teodoreanu was also a devoted patriot who never compromised himself or his work after the Soviet armies forcibly installed the Communist regime in Romania. He died in Bucharest at the age of 54 on 3 February 1951.

My sincerest gratitude goes to the translator, the late Eugenia Farca, for her excellent work on this volume — a story which she has always loved. For too long Romanian translators have gone unnoticed, in part because of the isolation of the country, and one of the intentions of this series is to make their work known outside of Romania. For many years, Eugenia Farca was among the finest translators of Romanian prose into English. This volume of *Classics of Romanian Literature* is dedicated to the late Academician David Prodan. *At Medeleni* was a story dear to his heart.

A.K. Brackob

Part I

I. Potemkin and Kami-Mura

With old-time solemnity, two peasants greeted the future owner of the estate. The sweep of the vast hats wrapped Dănuţ in the epic wind of glory. He stopped in the middle of the road like a gladiator acclaimed in the arena, heel planted on the body of the vanquished, with his kite as a shield, and the cord as a pear wrapped tightly around the fist he had just jerked back.

"Won't that huge thing knock you down, master?" asked one of the peasants.

"Knock me down?"

Dănuţ had gone through four years of elementary school. He was a middle school pupil on his holiday.

"Hadn't we better help the young master to fly it?" put in the other peasant, approaching the kite.

"It certainly is big," he marveled.

"As big as the windows of the gentlefolk."

Dănuţ felt proud to own the kite and humbled to be less tall than it was. Instinctively — very much like a small woman shunning the vicinity of the

"He stopped in the middle of the road
like a gladiator acclaimed in the arena"

tall pines — he stepped away gravely, then took a few steps along the road. The kite stood arrested between the two peasants.

"Stop, master," said one of them, "the wind isn't blowing that way! Turn back." It was an order, even though the tone was soft as if imparting considerate advice.

Dănuț hesitated for a moment: he scanned the skyline, knitted his brows with dignity as if dreading over deep-going concerns, over responsibilities... and submitted. He passed by the tense kite at a gallop and went running, letting out the cord between his fingers. The reel behind him was rolling and tossing like an epileptic rat.

"Let go!" he yelled from a distance, tugging at the cord for all he was worth.

The kite fell head first; Dănuț fell on his back. Meanwhile, one by one, then in groups, the village children, bare-footed and artless, gathered around close to the considerable incident taking place on the road.

"Never you mind, master; I'll make it all right for you," one of the peasants said to soothe him, brushing off his clothes gently, as if handling a priest's stole, to shake off the dust.

"There! That's because you haven't stretched its tail," Dănuț sighed, haltingly, hardly able to control his tears.

"Now then, master, if you only handle it gently, you'll get it started! That's how it is with restive horses!... Look at it!... You pull it... try it... ease it for a while... then draw the bridle again... Only listen!"

Pouring forth melodious wrath, as if of many cellos, the kite buzzer hummed with the leaps and bounds of the kite whose tense arching quickened with the life of the transparent winds. The tails swung with feminine grace in the distance, coaxing the power of the winds.

"Ups-a-daisy!"

Dănuț felt a twist in his chest; he half stretched out his arms as if to assist the flying thing above and, all a-quiver, he put his head to one side. The little girls swayed gently as if starting a ballet movement, the boys stood taut, ready to dash forward.

Like a dolphin on the billows, the kite had turned a somersault... and, growling, had stiffened again, challenging the sky. The tails undulated behind with the grace of falling stars.

"Hey! Hey!" exclaimed the children.

Dănuț's eyelashes fluttered. He was smiling.

The cord flowed swiftly skyward. The kite soared above the village, higher than the hills, higher than the sun and the swallows. The children scanned the sky for it, shading their eyes, with their other hand spread out.

"There it is!" a small boy burst out.

"Shut up!" another snubbed him.

"Well, what? Picking on me, are you?"

"Hush!" the others silenced them, with knitted brows.

The silence was once again untroubled save for the muffled humming high up.

Dănuț felt the cord with his fingertips as one does the cutting edge of a sword.

"Take hold of it firmly, master. I'm holding it, too..."

Squeezing against the peasant, Dănuț gripped the cord, but becoming aware of the deep vortex high up, he drew one hand away from it and, groped behind, seized the man's arm. The hand on the arm gripped hard, the one on the cord but gingerly.

"Hold on tight, master! Don't be afraid!... With both hands, like a man!"

As if in enmity, Dănuț put his back into it and tugged, his face puckering. The sky did not fall in... In his hands an athletic cord vibrated, filling his muscles with manliness... His eyes were shining as if intoxicated.

"You can go now."

"So long, master," the peasant joked in all seriousness, pretending to go. The cord burst out of his hand.

"Come back! Come back! Don't leave me! Save me!" Dănuţ shouted as if flung, dragged, seized by the panic of being drawn into the air high up.

"I'm here!"

A lively trot could be heard from behind.

"My lady bids you come to the Mansion without delay."

"Why?" Dănuţ huffed at the man in the carriage.

"We're going to the station, master. It's time to go," the man replied, scarcely able to control the horse.

"Be careful!" the children shouted, darting out of the way of the frightened horse.

The dust on the road and fell like a wrestler knocked down and raising himself in turns. The ring of children drew close to Dănuţ.

"What are we to do?" the latter asked, pinning his hopes on the peasant... "Shall we take it down?"

"Let it be, uncle!... Don't take it down, master!" the children pleaded in a choir, looking first at the peasant, then at Dănuţ.

"We'd better take into the yard and tie it there."

"That's it! That's it!" Dănuţ rejoiced, ready to jump up and put his arms around the savior's neck.

Headed by Dănuţ, the procession of the little ones walked to the gate of the yard, keeping pace with the kite high up... With the dogs barking and the servants coming up from all sides, the yard was now a pandemonium.

"Come on, Dănuţ, the train is due to arrive soon," Mrs. Deleanu, ready to leave, her hands over her ears, urged the boy from the carriage.

"Wait, mother, can't you see that I'm busy!" Dănuţ retorted, tugging at the cord of the tethered kite as if to test it.

"Ready, master! It will not escape us now because the oak is holding it."

"Are you done, Dănuţ?"

"That's all very well, but who will keep watch over it?" Dănuţ said anxiously.

"We will, we will!" protested the grateful of children.

"I will!" a little boy somewhat taller than the rest of them decided ponderously, trying to sound convincing.

Quite prepared to face the dogs, he entered the yard and took his stand stiffly by the oak around which the kite's cord was wound.

"What do they call you?" Dănuţ inquired suspiciously.

"Maranda's son, with all due respect!" came the martial answer.

"And what else, little fellow?" Mrs. Deleanu asked in her gentler voice, coming down on the carriage step.

"Gheorghiţă, madam!"

"And aren't you afraid the dogs might eat you?"

"Me?"

"Don't you budge from here, Gheorghiţă," Dănuţ ordered.

"Listen, my dear, you must speak nicely to him, not the way you just did. Here, offer him some sweets!"

"There!... here you are," Dănuţ softened his tone, watched by Mrs. Deleanu.

He thrust the small box of violet sweets to the boy, offering them as is done in the towns. Gheorghiţă hesitated, but the lady's prompting determined him to take them. He quickly got hold of the box. Dănuţ indignant and at a loss was left with the lid in his hand. "It's alright, Dănuţ, let him have the lid as well... And this is for you for a drink, and thank you," she added, addressing the peasant.

"Long life to the master, and may he grow up big and strong!" the peasant said with a bow as the carriage started on its way.

Kneeling on the cushion, his chin resting on the drop-head, Dănuț looked for a long time with melancholic envy at the dwindling figure of Gheorghiță. And the children perched all along the gate gave the same look to the sentinel by the oak that held the kite.

Not master of the field, Maranda's Gheorghiță stroked the taut cord as a string... and disregarding the goodies in his closed fist, sat down on the ground, leaned on the trunk, and crossed his arms, gazing up at the sky like a young man in love.

***

"Please don't trouble yourself, Mr. Șteflea."

"I beg your pardon! Please excuse me! You know, the heat..."

The low-ceiling room buzzed as if it had been the flies' national day. The station master, his coat half on, was vainly, unseeingly, boxing with his fist the cursed hole of the other sleeve behind him. Finally finding its way through the blue alpaca tunnel, the station master's hand swooped down on Mrs. Deleanu's gloved hand. With a fat man's heroic bend, he kissed the glove, and remembering the handkerchief on his head, he pulled it away in embarrassment.

Dănuț felt all-a-quiver as if he had been in a store filled with mysterious toys. His eyes were riveted on the slow turning of the punched paper tape on the small wheel of the telegraph. He knew that the tape was the secret cable's way of taking the words up and down from high up in the sky... and he found it incredible.

"Will it arrive on time, Mr. Șteflea?"

"Of course, my lady? It'll be here in no time," the station master said panting.

"Come outside, Dănuț."

Waiting on the platform were a bunch of geese tied together, a striped knapsack, and a summer morning of fair complexion between two chestnut trees.

"Let me have a look at you, Dănuţ... My goodness! The state you are in!"

The smart sailor suit put on for the first time that morning had gone through a wreckage on the road. The sandals sent up dust, like smoke, at every movement and the socks hung thick-lipped, exposing ankles that were whiter than his legs.

Mrs. Deleanu sat down on a bench with Dănuţ, an architectural problem before her. She raised her hat veil and took off her gloves. Dănuţ felt as if he had been put back together.

Impertinently coquettish, as required by a childishly turned-up nose, the white beret came down towards the nape of the neck, a little to one side, exposing the whole forehead; the ribbons were fluttering marine-like, the blue bow was flowering again; with the anchor right in front, between the two wings of the collar.

"A bride is all he wants!" the station master marveled emotionally, coming up with a small register under his arm, his red cap over a handkerchief that hung on either side of it.

"Is it coming?"

"It is."

"Dănuţ! Dănuţ!"

With a satisfied resignation, as if he had been saved from suicide, Dănuţ allowed himself to be pulled back. At the whirling horizon of the rails, he has seen a black, inimical point, as the hole of a charged revolver.

They waited awhile, looking at the quivering rails... Terribly angry with the station, the engine went past it...

"Goods... goods... goods, third class... third... third..." Dănuţ was reading aloud, screwing up his eyes and tightening his grip on Mrs. Deleanu's hand.

"There is father, mother! Can't you see him?! Papa! Papa!"

At the window of a compartment, Mr. Deleanu's hands were shaking their gloves towards those on the platform... At the wagon's door, Olguţa's dark tresses were fluttering. The train had hardly stopped when Olguţa jumped out of the carriage, joyful, familiar, just as she had jumped from her bed onto the carpet in the morning.

"Good heavens, Olguţa! You'll be the death of me!" Mrs. Deleanu cried out, running towards her.

Olguţa kissed her hand in passing and ran up to the coachman.

"Moş Gheorghe! Moş Gheorghe! Here I am!"

Next after Olguţa, the luggage came down, being passed on to Ion through the window, then Mr. Deleanu, good-humored, in a soie-ecrue suit, his panama hat down on the nape of his head, ready to joke, to challenge people; after him, with quiet movements and big eyes, the eyes of a girl in love, scanning and breathing in her holiday, came Monica.

"Are you glad to come to live with us, Monica?" Mrs. Deleanu asked her, taking her in her arms from the last carriage step and kissing her cheeks.

"Yes."

The round-brimmed straw hat with a black ribbon, held under her chain by an elastic band, slid down her back, hanging from her neck. Mrs. Deleanu smiled at the uncovered hair; it was golden like the patches of sunlight which the children chasing butterflies find in the forest grass, smiling under their hat, instead of the butterfly they had thrown it over.

"Well, children, did we forget any of the luggage?... Good!... Everything is alright then! Very good! I'm in such good spirits!" Mr. Deleanu's face was aglow; he rubbed his hands as he did after winning a lawsuit. He used the same gesture to signify joy and anticipation and to wash his hands.

Dănuț pouted: nobody took any notice of him, nobody looked at him! He closed his eyes and wished he was invisible.

"Mother, where is my hat?" panted Olguța, rushing up from the horses.

A grandfather's head appeared at the window of the train, gold-rimmed glasses on the tip of his nose.

"A young lady's hat has been left in the compartment. Isn't it yours?"

"It is!" Olguța claimed it resolutely.

"You might thank the gentleman, Olguța... Here you are! What else have you left behind," Mrs. Deleanu asked her, eyeing her from head to toe.

Dănuț came into Olguța's line of sight. She chuckled and whispered something into Monica's ear.

They both giggled.

"Puffy face! Humpty-Dumpty!" Olguța addressed Dănuț.

The two-week holiday in the country had puffed up Dănuț's cheeks, suggesting a new nickname to Olguța. Awakening from his gloom and withdrawal, Dănuț looked askance at his sister and with the hands that had held the kite's cord, slapped her on both cheeks, removing the pale hue resulting from her studies for the exams.

"Bravo! A gallant cavalier!" the old gentleman intervened from the window of the departing train. "My respects, Mr. Iorgu!" came a voice from the window in the next wagon.

"Vus tis di Iankl!... A ghiten weig."

On hearing the irreproachable jargon, the windows of the second class carriage filled with Semite heads (like the windows of the café on Stefan cel Mare street)... and with amiable greetings. Was there a shopkeeper in Iași who had not been or was not the client of Mr. Iorgu Deleanu?

"Children! Children! Please," Mrs. Deleanu interfered, saving Dănuţ, just in time, from Olguţa's fist and foot.

"I'll teach you a lesson!" Olguţa threatened.

"Leave him alone, Olguţa, why speak to someone so badly brought up?" Monica comforted her, taking her arm.

The two started off together alongside Mrs. Deleanu... Dănuţ soon caught up with them.

"You... You are girls!" he snarled at them, choking with indignation.

"That's not true!" Olguţa wounded by the insult said putting her foot down.

"There's no question about that, you are a boy," Mr. Deleanu put in. "Our only little girl is Monica. Isn't it true, Monica?"

"I am also," Olguţa protested. "But I won't allow him" — and she pointed fiercely at Dănuţ — "to insult me."

"Nothing but fire, our young lady," Moş Gheorghe, mustache and eyes smiling, whispered to the man who was loading the suitcases into the cart.

"Peace be with you!" Mr. Deleanu ordered laughingly. "Who's coming with me in the dog-cart?"

"I am!" Dănuţ put in promptly.

"I am!" Olguţa said as if she were pushing her brother aside.

"I said I would first!"

"What's that got to do with it?"

"It has."

"I'm not talking to you."

In the meantime, Mrs. Deleanu got into the carriage.

"That's all very well, but isn't anyone coming with me?"

"I am, aunt Alice," Monica offered.

"You two are coming with me in the dog-cart."

"He should go in the carriage," Olguţa insisted, frowning.

"Come with me on the box," Moş Gheorghe whispered to her.

Olguţa cheered up... but quickly put on a martyr's face.

"You go in the dog-cart. I have no use for it!... I am being left aside, I know that," she said pretending to sigh, as she climbed into the box.

And pulling the whip out of its stand, she lashed the horses.

"Gently, young lady! They'll overturn us."

"Moş Gheorghe, drive as fast as you can. Don't let them catch up with us. Do you hear, Moş Gheorghe?" Standing between the old man's legs, Olguţa was fretting and fuming.

***

"Greetings, Mr. Iorgu."

"Well, how are you, Mr. Şteflea? Well and hearty, I see. And in good spirits."

"Yes, thank you. What with my duties... Mmm..."

Astride the *bihunca*, Dănuţ was all restless and angry; and there was also restlessness in the hooves of the horse left standing behind while the carriage was on its way.

"Come on, Papa, please... Quick!"

"Wait a bit, why all this hurry? You're not the President of the Court of Cassation, are you?"

"God help him to become that!" Mr. Şteflea wished wholeheartedly.

"Do you have a case there?"

"Not quite yet," he confessed modestly.

"Only at the Court of Appeals, as a man of my station will."

"A helping hand?..."

"If you would!" he dared to ask.

"Oh well! We'll talk it over some time!"

Dănuț was quaking at the knees; the carriage was out of sight now. He felt a bitter lump in his throat, remembering how Olguța had climbed into the carriage box. Such a feeling of distress came over him that under his closed eyelids, his imagination rushed him into the carriage beside his mother, that he might cry and be comforted... The place was filled by Monica!... Dănuț spurred on the wheels of the dog-cart.

***

Monica's legs did not reach the carriage floor. They hung about, but she did not swing them. Nor were the tips of her diligently polished shoes striking her suitcase on the seat in front of her. Monica's hands were resting quietly on her knees, drawn close together; her fingertips alone rose at times... and came down again, soon to go up and drawn apart.

On each side of the road, sun-colored cornfields tossed about now alight, now shaded... And now and then so many poppies spread out that one would have thought all the pictures of Little Red Riding Hood in the children's story books had set off to color the fields, leaving blank pages behind.

"How well black suits her," Mrs. Deleanu thought, but immediately raised her hand to her mouth in superstitious fear. Monica was scarcely ten and already had to put on morning clothes three times. This was the last time for she no longer had anybody to mourn for... The black dress she had put on after her grandmother's death had been made by Mrs. Deleanu.

"What color do you like best, Monica?"

The little girl's eyes gave Mrs. Deleanu a serious look.

Aware of the look directed at the mourning dress, she looked down with her eyes which were the color of brown honey. She blushed and big tears slid down her face... Her little hands gripped the dress as they would a doll in danger.

"Little girl, I didn't mean to hurt your feelings."

She took the girl's grieved head on her knees, murmuring sweet words such as are uttered to charm away the sorrows of children and young people in love.

The fields resounded with the laughter of tiny voices. Deep sunlight was making a gift of itself to the earth.

"Forgive me, aunt Alice, I won't do it again. I like blue," Monica whispered, clothing the crops where her holidays began with the blue of the sky where her grandmother dwelt.

***

"Don't you smoke a pipe, Moş Gheorghe?"

"My little girl knows everything!..." the old man said shaking his head. "I do smoke when I have the time. Everything at the right time."

"But why aren't you smoking now?"

The old man raised his shoulders. How could he smoke? His dark, calloused palms covered protectively the little white fists that clutched the reins tight — two nut shells covering the tender walnuts.

"Who will drive the horses then, my little lady?"

"Who?... I will!"

"God bless you!"

"Don't you have any tobacco?" Olguţa asked, imitating the old man's pronunciation.

"I'll buy some."

"Moş Gheorghe," Olguţa said shyly, looking at him sideways, her dark eyes like two swallows' heads thrust out of their nest.

"I brought you a packet of tobacco... You see I've kept my word, Moş Gheorghe!" she reproved him seriously.

Olguța had promised the old man a packet of tobacco and she hadn't forgotten. The packet was a metal box with first-class tobacco that Olguța had bought with her pocket money in autumn and which she had kept in her little cupboard for a whole year.

Olguța had no grandparents.

The old man's lively, waggish face filled with tenderness. His small eyes puckered up and glittered; his untidy mustache trembled. Clasping in one hand the reins held fast in Olguța's hands, he fumbled with the other in his breast pocket and drew out a field carnation — a red star — which he stuck in the little girl's dark tresses to ward off the evil eye.

***

Dănuț heard nothing but the mat tick-tack of the hooves striking at the same pace with his heart deep down into the depths of the earth. Under the wheels of the dog-cart, the road sent up whirls of dust behind them... Dănuț closed his eyes.

...It was a night as dark as hell when the dragon rushed fiercely in pursuit of the runways. Prince Charming's horse rode like the wind but the dragon was as quick as thought. Prince Charming felt behind him...

Dănuț felt fear creeping down his back; he opened his eyes. He had turned into a dragon, but had only felt the fear of Prince Charming... If Prince Charming had cut the dragon's head, who would have gone in pursuit of Olguța?... Dănuț started off again, this time astride the dog-cart...

Mr. Deleanu was holding the reins but it would never have occurred to him that it was not himself that drove the horse. How could he have driven it? The carriage, the horse, the reins and Ion, who was holding Dănuț lest he should fall, were all Dănuț himself, who had turned into them all. With clenched teeth, closed eyes, and a knitted brow, Dănuț was rushing in pursuit of Olguța, wheels rolling, hooves going tick-tack.

Dănuț could turn into anyone and everything; he could be anywhere at any time. He only had to close his eyes... He could have done any amount of harm, had he wanted to! But he was merciful! Dănuț was proud of the power hidden within him and also terrified of it. He had once been angry with his mother for pulling his ears and putting him in time-out. Dănuț had killed her... had regretted and had quickly brought her back to life, for who would have forgiven him if his mother had died? Nobody suspected Dănuț's secret, not even the doctor who knew him inside out. Beneath Dănuț's eyelids, deep down where tears come from, there was something hidden, something like a sleep full of dreams; as soon as he closed his eyes he was above everyone, even above his father and mother. He would make an express of his mother, a general or a great dignitary of his father, a page of Olguța... or perhaps a kitchen maid.

When Moş Gheorghe had told them the story of Ivan and His Bag, Olguța had asked the old man to give her a knapsack like Ivan's.

"Were I St. Peter, I would give one to you, my little girl!"

"Give it to me, Moş Gheorghe!"

"Where will I take one from?"

"Give it to me, Moş Gheorghe!" Olguța was flushed with anger. Dănuț had kept silent, with a smile he alone knew the reason for. Later, by candle-light, Dănuț had felt his brow, looking at it in the strange depth of the mirror. He had even caressed it as if it had been a gift. That was Ivan's knapsack, which could hold the whole of hell and earth. Dănuț had been very glad to find that nobody, not even Olguța, had such a knapsack. And nobody knew that he alone had it when he closed his eyes...

Dănuț suddenly felt the wind and the sun in his hair.

"What is it?"

"Stop, master, stop... the young gentleman's hat has fallen off."

The beret was rolling on the road, its ribbons fluttering. Ion jumped down to retrieve it.

"Aren't we starting out again, Papa?" Dănuţ queried, alarmed at the thought of a new halt.

"Hold the reins, Ion... In a hurry again, are you? Oh my! Just a moment for me to roll a cigarette. And this is for you."

With a childish smile, Mr. Deleanu thrust his hat over Dănuţ's head, leaving him headless, like an entrance hall peg.

"Oh..." he yawned noisily, stretching his arms lazily.

Dănuţ raised the panama hat gloomily and stared at his father, who was rolling his cigarette, with the eyes of a woman misunderstood by her husband.

***

"Woo! Woo! Woo!"

"Who's doing that, Moş Gheorghe?" Olguţa asked, imitating the sound.

"The horses, my young lady, they've drunk too much water."

"Ah!... They've got frogs in their bellies."

***

Monica stroked Mrs. Deleanu's hand.

"Aunt Alice!"

"What is it, Monica?"

"Nothing, aunt Alice," Monica smiled and breathed in deeply.

"Is there anything you want to tell me, Monica?"

"No... It's beautiful, aunt Alice."

"Little girl!... Take off your hat so the sun can kiss you."

"Aunt Alice, those are chamomiles!" Monica recognized the flowers that were being trodden on in the schoolyard.

The chamomiles were smiling in the sunlight; they were on holiday too.

"What are those over there, aunt Alice?"

"Sweet woodruff!"

"And those?"

"Sweet peas!"

"And those?"

"Indian cress!"

"Sweet woodruff," Monica murmured those syllables that trembled with sunlight like a verse the bees had left on the children's lips.

They were silent.

Sweet pigeons, unseen, could be heard cooing all around the carriage. The horses were nodding placidly as they trotted up the climbing road... Blue butterflies fluttered about... Morning glories were drying their dew-drenched petals in the sun... The road, with its rustling and fragrances, was taking Monica — golden-haired, pale-faced, with her pigtails down her back and her hands, clasped together — towards a sky not far off.

Where the road joined the blue horizon, St. Peter might have appeared in a white robe, holding the heavy keys that opened the gates of heaven in one hand.

***

"I'm hungry," Olguţa complained.

Moş Gheorghe had long been waiting for this.

"Hush!" he whispered in Olguţa's ear. "I have something!"

"Let me see?" Olguţa pleaded in a low voice.

Moş Gheorghe took a small paper bag from his pocket.

"What do you have there?" Olguţa asked, fretting.

"Some sugar icicles," he sighed melancholically.

"Monica! We have sugar icicles!" Olguţa shouted, joyfully.

"It seems that you want me to give your salary to the dentists, Moş Gheorghe," Mrs. Deleanu reproved him in jest.

"Why not let the children eat sugar?... Didn't I give it to you when you were a little girl?"

Mrs. Deleanu smiled. It was true... She also... But that was so very long ago.

"But will you give me some now?"

"Well, it is for the young lady to decide."

Olguţa was crunching the misty diamonds strung upon a string. The feast began. On the box, Olguţa crunched, sucked and swallowed, and started it all anew. In the carriage, Monica was nibbling gently, looking ahead. Mrs. Deleanu sucked awkwardly the vanilla-flavored icicles that pricked her cheeks. She was thinking of the holidays of yore. Moş Gheorghe plucked at his mustache and smiled. Olguţa didn't forget about him; she forcibly stuck a piece into his mouth. The old man stealthily and most carefully slipped it into his pocket, like a precious gift.

"Moş Gheorghe, I feel like having a raw cucumber... with salt and pepper, you know!" Olguţa said crunching away at the sugar.

"Wait until we get home! I'll prepare it, the way I know!"

"Moş Gheorghe, can we also buy some carobs at the pub? It's so long since I ate some. They don't have any carobs at the pastry shops. Can you hear me, Moş Gheorghe?"

"I hear!"

"And are we going to buy some?"

"We'll buy some, of course."

"And we'll eat them."

"If you'll give me my teeth back, I'll eat too, little one."

"Moş Gheorghe! Aren't you going to eat some carobs? Let's stew them then!"

A horse's neighing behind them heralded the approach of the dog-cart. The carriage horses gave a warlike neigh. Olguța turned around, looked, knit her brows, and took hold of the whip.

"Moş Gheorghe! Don't let me down! They are catching up with us!"

Moş Gheorghe dearly loved the horses — those drawing the carriage as well as the one drawing the dog-cart. And yet the competition started briskly — as in the old days when the gentlemen were fierce in their anger as well in their joy and when the coachmen whirled their whip and struck the gates with the leaders' shaft to brighten the hearts of the gentlemen that heard the ladies scream. Moş Gheorghe remembered and Olguța knew about it from him.

"Giddy up!" Olguța yelled.

Moş Gheorghe only smiled; the whip whistled, serpent-like. The horses lengthened their trot, shaking their heavy manes, their long tails fluttering. Eight hooves beat like drums calling soldiers to battle.

"Look behind, Monica!" Olguța prompted, shouted aloud as if to be heard above a storm.

Monica knelt on the cushions and looked over the drop head of the carriage.

"Is it drawing near?" Olguța asked.

"It seems to be," was the hesitating answer.

"Is it drawing near?"

"It seems it is," said a fearful Monica.

"Is it drawing near?" thundered Olguța, taking the whip out of Moş Gheorghe's hand.

"Yes, it is!" Monica said in terror.

With the long, slim body of a dragonfly, the dog-cart came up level with the carriage, well-nigh outstripping it.

"Hurry up, children! Hurry up! I'm fearfully hungry! And thirsty too!" Mr. Deleanu said while the dog-cart passed by at full speed.

A serene Dănuţ was looking straight ahead, the corner of his eye taut. He thus showed Olguţa his contempt and could at the same time take a glimpse of her prolonged defeat.

"How good is to be a man!" Dănuţ thought, insatiably breathing in the tobacco flavor given off by his father's coat and also breathing in with conviction the smell of coarse tobacco coming from Ion's hands and breath behind him.

"Stop, Moş Gheorghe!" Olguţa decided in a whisper.

"Whoa, my lads! Whoa, my children!"

The dog-cart was speeding on through the dust, like a wheeled sled.

"Alright! Alright! You gallop as fast as you wish! We're not going to kill our horses," Olguţa threw the magnanimity of pity after them like a murderous stone.

The horses stopped, but they panted hard. Their breaths were still running, causing them to fret even when they no longer ran.

Those in the carriage stood up, watching the dust raised by the dog-cart on the road. Olguţa, full of thoughts, was twisting the whip in her hands... The transparent heat genie filled the air with bodiless dancers. And suddenly, like the melancholy of mown hay when the sun is at its twilight — the melancholy of sad, gentle angels — the fragrance of melilot enwrapped them.

"I'm done for! Dying of thirst!" Olguţa complained, breathing deep as she threw into the carriage the armful of melilot she had sturdily plucked.

"Don't fret, we'll soon be on our way," Mrs. Deleanu quieted her, wiping the sweat from her perspiring cheeks away with her handkerchief.

"Here is my contribution, aunt Alice!" Monica said, coming up with an armful of green herbs interspersed with yellow sparks, and on her cheeks field colors, she had plucked together with the melilot and the corn flowers in her hair.

Going around, behind the carriage, to climb in on the left, Monica suddenly stopped as if a nasty thought had beset her. A black dress, an arrested carriage! To her mind — the mind of an unhappy child — all carriages were going to the churchyard; all stopping carriages were waiting for the procession to start on its way…

"Aunt Alice, the carriage has no number!"

"Of course not! Private carriages have no number."

"You have no number!" Monica whispered to the carriage, her little hand patting it joyously.

With Monica's help, Mrs. Deleanu laid the bunches of melilot on the drop-head of the carriage in an orderly fashion… The horses started off… Faithful bees for long followed the heap melilot that had been their home… Fragrant little stars glowed in the sunlight, lightly touching the heads in the carriage.

"Aunt Alice!"

"What is it, Monica?"

"Is it long until we get home?"

"We'll be there in no time!"

"A pity!"

"Are you sorry, Monica?"

"No, aunt Alice!"

She was glad, of course. And yet!… She felt as if she would never come down from the carriage which had no number and had melilot on the hood of it; the carriage of her holidays.

"What's that sound, Moş Gheorghe?" Olguţa asked, scanning the sky, her hand shading her eyes.

"The dogs barking!"

"Nonsense! The dogs! Up there, Moş Gheorghe!"

"Bless it! It's master Dănuţ's kite."

"Aha!" Olguţa murmured.

"Don't fret, I'll make you a finer one!"

"I have no use of it!"

The horses stopped, pulling hard at the harness, and went over the gate threshold at a trot, below the whistle of a kite, near which a small sailor kept guard. A sailor? And admiral with, on his lips, the smile of him that received the sword of the defeated Napoleon.

The white houses scattered about the yard, with the one in the middle, deep and looming over them all, appeared in Monica's eyes like a bright monastery that had no towers and no monks.

The horses stopped at the house steps snorting... The frail many-colored morning glories yawned on the terrace amid the rustle of the green vines.

"I'm hungry!" Olguţa cried out, petulantly. "Where are you, baba?"

Following the sound of her voice, with the enormous face and body of a eunuch, with a white shawl and apron, laughing, with a belly rising and falling and a toothless mouth gaping, her open arms folding in the whole yard, the cook came down the steps.

"Here is the old woman! And a good thing you're here at last, for the chickens are roasting on the spit. God bless them!"

***

A wet sheet pinned at the corners of the open window was curving gently and coming back again, turning the heat that softened the apricots in the orchard into a breath of wind.

There was nobody in the girls' room... Anica had rushed in, bare-footed, leaving on a chair Monica's light suitcase and had gone out banging the door after having mirrored her smile — the smile of a young gypsy — into the oval glass of the mahogany wardrobe.

And now the suitcase that bore her grandmother's initials sat alone. Waiting in it to see Monica's new place of residence were her grandmother's portrait and a doll dressed in black.

Monica, seated in the dining room on a chair with two pillows under her, was eating nicely as her grandmother had taught her. With the napkin hanging from the front of her dress, without stretching her elbows on the table, with mouth closed, and seated upright…

If her grandmother had entered the girls' room, she would have put on her glasses and without touching with her finger the wardrobe or the little tables beside the walnut beds, she would have seen that there was not a speck of dust anywhere, nor any flies, and she would have sighed lightheartedly; she would have smelled the waxed floors and the cool fragrance specific to the peaceful old houses, where apples and quinces winter, and she would have shaken her head in kindness and tenderness.

She would have most carefully leaned over the nearly covered beds and, lifting the corner of the quilt, she would have seen the linen sheets washed by a diligent laundress and the melilot and lavender left in the linen cupboard from last year, and she would have reverently covered up the corner she had turned up, and if she had also opened the wardrobe and had seen the dolls waiting to witness the excitement of the little girls who had been awarded prizes for the third-grade exams, the grandmother would have lifted her glasses from her nose, would have wiped them, and she would have made the sign of the cross before the icon of the Holy Virgin on the wall, and another sign over the room, and slowly, very slowly, she would have left the room… for Monica could now enter it.

There was nobody in the girls' room now.

"And now the suitcase that bore her grandmother's initials sat alone.
Waiting in it to see Monica's new place of residence
were her grandmother's portrait and a doll dressed in black."

***

"Allow me to take off my coat, children; I can't bear it any longer!"

Taking off the soie-ecrue coat, Mr. Deleanu remained in his soie-ecrue short with a low, soft collar. When he raised his arms, he shook them and the sleeves slid down. He kept this personal tradition from long ago when the barristers wore gowns at the bar. And he also kept the gown in the hope that Dănuț would put it on one day to plead... By then it might be that the "cretins" would understand — cretins were all those who were against Mrs. Deleanu's professional views — that a robe lends wings to words, and would reintroduce it. If not, in the cupboard where it hung, it would remind Dănuț of the old days.

Mr. Deleanu loved his profession "like a mistress" — those were his words in a pleading at the Court of Cassation (he had uttered the illegal words passionately, arrogantly to wake up a sleeping counselor) and he wanted Dănuț to think so and say so. If Olguța had been a boy!...

"Well, Dănuț, you're in middle now! A big boy. You can decide. Are you going to be a barrister, like your father?"

Mrs. Deleanu raised her shoulders.

"Let him eat his dinner first! Dănuț, your elbows are on the table again!... Look how nicely Monica is eating. And she's younger than you!"

Olguța had withdrawn her elbows with a smile. Dănuț blushed and gave Monica and Olguța a fierce look... The horror of comparisons with Monica had lasted for a year since Monica and Olguța had been acing the elementary school exams together. Who on earth had discovered Monica! Olguța, of course! It was she who, to the cook's despair, also brought home the kittens abandoned next to their fence. That was not so bad! But he couldn't stand Monica! The usurper! Olguța's ally! The blonde!... Dănuț had been waiting for a long time to pull her pigtails properly!

"Just wait!" he thought in anger. And again he escaped and ran out to his kite.

Olguţa's eyes were spying on him from under her eyelashes. After a time he became aware of it. he riveted his eyes on hers.

"Why are you looking at me?"

"Me?" Olguţa queried, wondering candidly.

"Yes, you," he replied, determined to have it out with her.

"I'm not looking at you! I'm looking at Monica!" Olguţa argued, now looking at her friend. "Isn't that so, Mother?"

"You looked at me," Dănuţ said in a huff, changing the tone of his voice and pointing with his finger menacingly.

"What of it? Am I not allowed to look?"

"Alright! We'll see!"

"Will you please be quiet." Mrs. Deleanu reproved him, her eyes looking as if she was ready to pull his ears.

Olguţa hid her mouth with her napkin to hide her joy.

"You be quiet as well."

"I'm not doing anything!... I very nearly choked," said Olguţa breathing hard.

"Come now!"

In vain Mr. Deleanu passed his napkin over his face; everybody saw that he was laughing. Mrs. Deleanu shrugged and resigned, giggling as well. The laughter spread around the table, mocking Dănuţ's gloom. He rose from his seat, threw down his napkin, and made for the door.

"Where are you going, Dănuţ? Did you finish? Did we rise from our seats?... Will you please come back!"

"I don't want to!" Dănuţ mumbled.

"You don't want to sit down? Good! Very good! You go stand in the corner then... Do you hear me, Dănuț?" Mrs. Deleanu concluded scathingly, energetically.

A round-shouldered Dănuț made for the corner... A solemn silence was reigning the dining-room... Meeting Monica's frightened, tearful eyes riveted on her, Mrs. Deleanu smiled kindly.

"Do you want me to forgive him, Monica?"

Monica nodded forcefully.

"Come back to the table... And thank Monica! Yes, do it!"

"Thanks!" Dănuț's lips trembled sarcastically, putting a lifeless hand into Monica's hands.

"And now eat your apricots!"

Dănuț bit into half an apricot and waited... to get over the lump in his throat so that he might swallow it... With the pit inside it and a freshly landed wasp on it, the other half remained on the plate with the other apricots whose lives had been spared.

"It's been a nice dinner. I am going to have a nap!"

"You go take a nap as well, Dănuț!"

"Why, Mother?"

"Because it's good for you."

"Come and have a nap with father, Dănuț," Mr. Deleanu comforted him, yawning delightedly.

"What about the kite outside?" Dănuț whined.

"It'll be waiting for you."

The joy of flying the kite in full sunlight turned into the bitterness of forced sleep.

"To the Devil with sleep!" Dănuț cursed in his mind the menace of children's afternoons.

"Did you finish, Monica?"

"Yes, aunt Alice, thank you!" Monica answered folding the napkin and shaking sparse crumbs off her dress.

"Come and see your room."

Head bent over her plate, Olguța was painstakingly eating apricots, with the intentness and ascription she would have put into learning a piece of poetry by heart.

"You too, Olguța. Come on, finish up!

"I'll be coming directly. I have only four more apricots left," she pleaded.

"I'll be waiting for you in your room. Don't go out!"

"I am telling you I'll be coming!"

"Alright!"

Once she was alone, Olguța listened intently... When she was confident that nobody was returning into the dining room, she looked long at Profira. Profira turned towards Olguța her flat face that looked like a white pansy. She waited while shaking a napkin.

"Profira... listen carefully... You must bring me right now a pair of scissors, a pencil, and a piece of paper!" said Olguța, tapping her finger on the table every time she uttered one of the things she wanted.

"What for?" the woman inquired, unable to see the reason for it all.

"That does not concern you. It's what I want!"

Waiting for Profira, Olguța rested her chin on the edge of the table, spread her elbows, her hands holding her cheeks, and thought hard.

"Did you bring everything?"

"I did!"

"Did you, by any chance, ask my mother to let you have them?" Olguța suddenly asked in alarm.

"Of course I did!"

"Oh no Profira! And you expect me to trust you from now on!"

"Why not? Here is what you asked for."

"And what did mother say?"

"She said I should look for those things in her room, which I did. Here they are."

"Ah! Good... I think!"

Olguța smiled. Leaning over the table, she began to write on the dainty paper which Profira had taken from Mrs. Deleanu's notepaper box. She wrote with big letters, spacing them, pressing hard on the paper, and sticking her tongue out whenever she had to make curves.

"Good!"

"She went out, determined, with Salome's dark eyes, in her hand the open scissors — the scissors of the Parcae."

"A terrible devil!" Profira exclaimed with admiration, biting into an apricot.

***

Dănuț's room was dangerously near the girls' room. The frontier post was the closet door, the key for which was on the other side.

The side that was in the girls' room had a stand from which hung straw hats, silk ribbons, a tri-colored hoop, a net with many colored balls in it, and two little pin-striped coats.

The side in Dănuț's room was adorned on its upper part with a panoply of billiard cloth consisting of a Eureka rifle spreading on its target — white cardboard with red circles around a blue center — with the little sticks that had been fired and a pad of sticky stuff; two crossed tin swords with scabbards studded with spots of rust and hollowed out in the duels fought with

Olguţa; and a whistle attached to a red cord, which gave a stuttering sound and tasted sour.

Below the panoply, divided by a sword that hung vertically as if figuring the backbone of war, two uniforms were crucified: one of a Japanese admiral, with a cap but without trousers, named Kami-Mura, the other of a Russian admiral, which had been christened Potemkin. The Russo-Japanese war was in fashion at the time.

Olguţa sided with the Russians, Dănuţ with the Japanese. For which reason, the decoration — a ribbon from Mrs. Deleanu's garter sewn for eternity by Profira on the breast of the Japanese admiral — which had been torn off, cloth and all, was prudently preserved in the admiral's pocket, the admiral now being decorated with "the star of the lining." On the other hand, the cap of the Russian admiral has been crushed under Dănuţ's fist. Olguţa had stuck the cardboard archipelago with Arabic gum and had sewn the crown fast with string, at the same time decorating the cap with strange golden embroidery. She had promoted her cap to the rank of Admiral-in-Chief and had inaugurated the event crushing in her turn the cap of the Japanese admiral, which she had done more calmly and more methodically than Dănuţ had done. Mrs. Deleanu had fixed the cap and Dănuţ had generously promoted it to the rank of Admiral-in-Chief-in-Chief, "which," Olguţa had said, "was impossible."

And the epilogue of the Russo-Japanese war was as follows:

"What do you say now? You were defeated," Dănuţ in the uniform of the Japanese admiral, said to Olguţa.

"That's not true! Papa will vouch for it!"

"Oh well, Olguţa. There's no denying it! The Russians were defeated; it's in the papers."

"The Russians were, not I."

"But aren't you Potemkin?" Dănuţ countered defiantly.

"Me? I wasn't and couldn't."

"How's that?"

"Girls don't join the army. I'm a girl, Papa will vouch for it... Apart from which, the Japanese were just lucky, because they're cowards."

"That's a lie!"

"A lie? Why are they yellow then?"

"What do you mean, why?" Because they're yellow; that's what Japanese are like.

"I'll tell you; they're yellow with fear. They all have jaundice... And if you want to fight, fight me, not the Russians," Olguţa had concluded, her head held high.

At the dinner given in honor of both admirals, Mr. Deleanu had read the following communiqué:

> *Potemkin and Kami-Mura*
> *Are to dreadful battle gone;*
> *Weighty guns and nimble steel*
> *Flash and thunder on and on.*
> *Sabers flash and cannon boom*
> *Through parlor, hall, and dining room,*
> *Raging up the giddy staircase*
> *Even to the smallest room!*
> *But, woe! parental fires descend;*
> *Nipponese and Muscovite*
> *Each in his own corner penned*
> *Wordily pursue the fight.*
> *Still by Admiral-in-Chief*
> *(Your cap, Potemkin, what a state!)*
> *Kami-Mura is outranked,*
> *Now a mere subordinate.*
> *Then, lo! A sudden field promotion,*
> *Admiral-in-Chief-in-Chief*

Kami-Mura — and his cap
Crumpled now beyond belief.
Kami-Mura has prevailed —
To Dănuţ the victory?
Not at all, Olguţa cried;
Not a boy, a girl is she.
She cannot be overcome
Or reduced to vassalry
Since she never could have been
A proper Admiral-at-Sea.
Mark the proverb, Kami-Mura:
Great trees fall to beaver bites,
But the teeth in question are
Not the teeth of Muscovites.
What avails your victory,
Bold commander of the seas?
In the end, you must succumb
To the jaundice, Japanese!

There was a fleet in Dănuţ's room. The basin fleet made by Moş Gheorghe out of big nut shells, with matched for masts, waxed tissue paper for sails, Dănuţ's lips for wind, and Olguţa's lips for cyclones.

And there was also a pool fleet: frail little boats loaded like Noah's Ark with living creatures made of hollow celluloid. And last of all, there was the pond fleet bought by Uncle Puiu from the "Universal Department Store" in Bucharest: one single vessel as long and thick as a loaf of bread, with a propeller, flag, cannons, funnels, and tin sailors paralyzed on deck.

***

Dănuţ banged the door so hard that plaster fell on his shoulders. He shook it off, shaking his chestnut locks with Samson's biblical move.

"You wait!" he said shaking his head.

Catching sight of the last coronet awarded for coming up top in his class, which hung above his head, he snatched it from the nail and threw it on the floor, kicking it.

"That is why I learn, to be persecuted! Only wait… I'll show you!" He shook his fists towards the girl's room.

He detached the rifle from the target, slipped in the rubber arrow, and shot… The cap of the Russian admiral quivered and was marked by a little dark hollow.

"Bang!" the arrow stuck to the door like a fish… Dănuț removed it. There was a dark round mark left on the door. Bang!… bang!… bang!…

"What's all this noise? What are you doing, Dănuț? Aren't you sleeping?" It was Mrs. Deleanu's voice on the other side of the door.

Dănuț was silent. He hung the rifle up again, tiptoeing… He picked up the coronet, kicked the leaves that had come off it below the cupboard, and hung up the remainder of his glory on its nail.

"Are you asleep?"

Dănuț fluffed his pillow and stretched out.

***

"Look, Monica… This is your room, yours and Olguța's. Do you like it?"

Monica pressed Mrs. Deleanu's hand.

"Such a pleasant smell, aunt Alice."

Mrs. Deleanu picked her up and lifted her as high as she could…

"Can you see something there?"

"Yes… Oh! Thank you, aunt Alice!"

On the wardrobe, she saw a silver tray covered with melilot.

"Now tell me which bed you want to sleep in."

"Which did Olguţa chose, aunt Alice?"

"Leave Olguţa out of it," Mrs. Deleanu said caressingly. "Choose which-ever you want. The one close to the window on the one by the door?"

"It is all the same to me, aunt Alice."

"Alright, then I'll choose the one by the window for you. I'll have Olguţa closer to me so I can hear her," said Mrs. Deleanu smiling.

The door of her room and the door of the girls' room faced each other, being divided by the silence of a long hallway.

"And now let's unpack... Where is the key?"

"Here it is, aunt Alice!" Monica raised her head and took the silver chain from under her dress front to offer it.

"What is this, Monica? What a nice little cross!"

Next to the little nickel key, there was a copper cross with a crucifix in relief.

"Do you like it, aunt Alice?"

"Very much... Do you have it from your mother?"

"I don't know... Grandmother gave it to me... Aunt Alice..."

"What is it, Monica?"

"Please take it!" the little girl pleaded with burning cheeks as she took off the chain, "I want to give it to you, aunt Alice!" she insisted, her eye-brows raised, very close to tears.

She forced the chain into Mrs. Deleanu's hand.

"Thank you, Monica," she said soothingly, stroking her hair, "but such things should not be given away, little girl. It's something you have from your parents... I'll only keep it safe for you."

"I can give it to you," Monica said quietly and gravely, looking down.

"Do you love aunt Alice so much?"

"Yes."

"Aunt Alice also loves you very much... as much as she loves Olguţa and Dănuţ."

"I know," Monica whispered.

"Why isn't Olguţa coming? Will you go and see?"

Mrs. Deleanu blinked... it took a long time to open the suitcase with the little nickel key, fumbling around with the lock.

"I can't find her, aunt Alice," Monica said in alarm, entering the room.

"Oh well, she'll come. She must be at Moş Gheorghe's place! Look, Monica! I put grandmother's portrait on the bedside table... If you want to hang it on the wall I'll give you another frame."

"No, no, it's all right where it is, aunt Alice."

"I put your things in the wardrobe... Look, the upper shelves are yours..."

"Aunt Alice," said a frightened Monica, "didn't you find a doll in the suitcase?"

"I did," said Mrs. Deleanu with a smile. "I put it to sleep. Look..."

From the semi-darkness of the shelf, she took a small bed where two dolls with hats on slept.

"Is that for me, aunt Alice?" Monica could not believe her eyes.

"Of course, Monica... And here is a wardrobe with dresses for your dolls."

Monica hesitated, with stretched-out arms. "What about Olguţa?"

"She has plenty of toys!"

The door handle let out the sound of a firing gun, the door banged open and closed, pushed back by Olguţa's left hand...

"What is it? What is it?"

Olguţa threw herself on the bed, bouncing delightedly on the squeaking springs that had been used only for a year.

"Is that how one enters a decent house?... And with dirty shoes on the bed?... Terrible, just terrible."

"I'm done for!"

"Where have you been?"

"At Moş Gheorghe's place."

"And what else did you do, Olguţa?" Mrs. Deleanu asked, being suddenly struck by the look in Olguţa's eyes.

"Didn't I just tell you? I was at Moş Gheorghe's place!"

"Olguţa you're up to something again!..."

"Come on, confess, Olguţa!"

"I did what I had to do!" Olguţa said in a defying voice.

"Olguţa, stop being silly! Is that the way you reply to your mother?"

"I put the scissors back in their place," Olguţa said, concluding in words the avowal she had started in her mind.

"The scissors?!... Who gave them to you?"

"You did... Of course! You gave them to me." Olguţa's face cleared up as she had the happy feeling of the guilty one who suddenly discovers an accomplice sharing the responsibility after having perpetrated the deed by themselves.

"I did? Olguţa, be sensible! Well, you will better get undressed now. And quickly!"

"Mother, my sock is torn!"

A shoe in one hand, Olguţa rejoiced as she arched her big toe through the tear that grew ever larger with the help of the rosy toe.

"I am glad to see it... Leave the sock alone, Olguţa! Take it off!... Shall I help you, Monica?"

"No, thank you, aunt Alice. I can manage."

Her arms bent back, Monica unbuttoned her dress... Olguța's sock flew violently in the air... Slipping down, Monica's dress revealed the little body with burgeoning breasts. Aware of Mrs. Deleanu's eyes, she covered herself again, lowering her chin.

"I'll be going now... Undress, Monica."

"Mother, it's so pleasant to be in pants!" Olguța boasted, jumping down from the bed to look at herself in a fencing position in the mirror.

"You imp, go to bed!... I'll see you in a bit, Monica."

***

Closing his eyes, Dănuț opened Ivan's knapsack... Dănuț is a pasha or a sultan. Doesn't matter which! His head is wrapped in a turban from under which his mustache comes up like a yataghan, together with a pair of fierce eyes... Two long teeth jut out of a sneering mouth. The teeth had been borrowed from a vampire.

Dănuț, the sultan, was so awe-inspiring that Dănuț opened his eyes and turned to one side... Olguța's voice could be heard from the girls' room. Dănuț closed his eyes angrily!... The sultan is seated on a golden throne. Two black women on the right and left of him with teeth like whipped cream over iced coffee, swing big, colored fans. Below the throne, thousands of turbans bent down to the ground are lined up. They all kneel before the sultan. Alone two naked blackamoors, dark and thick-lipped, stand up straight, waiting, hands clasped on axes. Nobody speaks. The sultan raises a finger... A stallion comes up, prancing and snorting... The sultan makes a sign... The blackamoors knot Monica's plaits to the stallion's tail... Monica bites into an apricot. She doesn't care! Well, well, the sultan will show her!... A hundred thousand whips swish the horse...

The blackamoors take hold of Olguța. Olguța kicks and makes faces at the sultan. So that's it? All right! A blackamoor raises his ax... Olguța is frightened... She had no one to defend her brother Dănuț... And indeed, at the head of an army, like Michael the Brave, Dănuț comes up, kills the sultan and the blackamoors while the turbans scamper away, and Olguța and Monica are saved. They kneel and kiss his hands. He takes them up on his saddle and is off...

Sleep was at bottom of Ivan's knapsack.

***

"Are you asleep, Monica?"

"No."

"Neither am I."

Olguța raised her legs and tapped her bare soles with her hands.

"Hear that, Monica?"

"Hear what?"

"I'm tapping my soles..."

"Why?"

"I don't know... Do it, too...."

"What are we going to do?"

"Shouldn't we sleep?"

"Why sleep?"

"Aunt Alice wants us to! I'm trying to sleep!" Monica said apologetically.

"Stop trying... Nobody knows. Mother is asleep...."

"Monica?"

"What?"

"Nothing..."

Olguța yawned in boredom. Her eyes scanned the white ceiling, counting the cracks in the paint.

"Would you like to be a fly, Monica?"

"A fly?"

"Yes, a fly. I would love it. I'd walk on the ceiling head down."

"I would like to be a grown-up," Monica said dreamily.

"So would I," Olguţa said, hastening to catch up with her. "What would you do if you were a grown-up?"

"I don't know!" Monica floundered.

"I would become a coachman like Moş Gheorghe! And I'd overturn Humpty-Dumpty from the carriage."

"What do you have against Dănuţ?"

"Me?... Nothing! He has something against me!"

"That's true!" Monica consented. "He hit you; it's not over!"

"He hit me?" Olguţa flew at her.

"Yes, this morning!"

"It had skipped my mind... If mother had not defended him I would have shown him."

"Do you know how to fight, Olguţa?"

"Don't you?"

"No."

"I know very well!"

"And do you like it?"

"Of course... Do you want me to show you?"

"No."

"They kept their peace," Olguţa sighed.

"Monica, why don't you cut off your plaits?"

"Why should I cut them off? Grandmother liked them... She plaited them!"

"Yes… I believe you, but they are not good for fighting. They can be used against you."

"Why should I fight?"

"You never know!"

"And whom could I fight?"

"Humpty-Dumpty… No, you are right," Olguţa said, changing her mind. "I wouldn't allow him to…"

Olguţa got up, leaning on her elbow and moving her leg in the air.

"Monica, do you have any muscles?"

"I don't know."

"I have!… Look! When I flex my leg!… Monica, I can't sleep any longer!"

She jumped off her bed and skipped about the floor, inspecting the room.

"Monica!" she suddenly cried out, the tone being like that Columbus is presumed to have had when discovering America.

"What is it?" asked a startled Monica.

"Nothing!" Olguţa replied quickly, closing the door of the stove.

She sat down on the chair on top of Monica's dress, meditating.

"Listen, Monica, I'll tell you a secret."

"Tell me."

"Oh! Not that way," Olguţa said, shaking her head and sitting down on Monica's bed.

"You must swear first not to tell anyone."

"I won't tell!" Monica said stubbornly.

"Don't be angry. I believe you, but you must swear…."

"Will you swear?"

"I won't swear because I won't tell," Monica said stubbornly.

"Won't you swear?"

"No."

"Alright."

Olguţa rose from the bed. She walked about the room, shunning Monica... Finally, she sat down on the edge of the bed.

"Are you cross, Monica?" she said tenderly.

"No, but why won't you believe me?" Monica seemed more tractable now.

"If you're not, please swear... Please, Monica... As a favor to me! Come on, Monica!"

"Alright, I'll swear."

"Good for you!... What will you swear on?"

Looking around the room, Olguţa's eyes rested for a moment on the bedside table. Monica noticed Olguţa's look.

"On Grandmother's portrait?" she asked, big-eyed.

"No, not that!" Olguţa said in her defense. "Swear on your doll."

"Repeat after me: I swear on my doll, Monica" she began hurriedly. "That I shan't tell anyone." Olguţa continued, beating time with her forefinger.

"...that I shan't tell anyone," Monica repeated, nodding.

"...what Olguţa is going to tell me."

"What Olguţa is going to tell me!"

"Wait a minute!" Olguţa continued with a frown. "Say after me: And if I tell..."

"and if I tell," Monica repeated in disgust, shaking her head.

"...let my doll die."

"...let me doll die. Have you finished?"

"Just a moment, that's not right… Say it once again!… And if I tell… Are you going to say it?"

"…and if I tell," Monica said with a sigh.

"…I will allow Olguţa…"

"…I will allow Olguţa…"

"…to break the head of my doll Monica."

"…to break the head of my doll Monica," Monica repeatedly indignantly.

"Say amen now!"

"Amen"

"Make the sign of the cross."

"I did."

"And now I'll tell you the secret!"

She kept silent and smiled.

"Are you going to tell me, Olguţa?"

"I am! Just wait. I am going to tell you. Get up and come with me."

She took Monica by the hand and walked with her to the door of the stove.

"You won't tell, will you?" Olguţa insisted, trying to extract a supreme promise.

"How can you, Olguţa?"

"Open and look in," Olguţa gave her leave with a wide gesture.

"Was that the secret?"

In the cool shadow of the stove, there were two preserve jars with white caps on.

"What? Perhaps you don't like it. Don't tell, Monica," Olguţa gestured with a bellicose finger.

"She took Monica by the hand and walked with her to the door of the stove."

"Did you sleep well?" Mrs. Deleanu asked, entering the room, Profira following her with a tray that held a jar of rose leaf preserve.

Monica blushed and looked down.

"It's so hot, mother dear," Olguţa confessed, raising her arms.

"She didn't let you sleep, Monica?"

"One can't sleep in this heat," Olguţa decided, turning the spoon in the preserve jar.

"You have insomnia?"

"What is insomnia mother," Olguţa asked, suspicious of the word and the accompanying smile.

"It's something that's not for you... You better tell me straight out why you didn't sleep."

"I don't have insomnia. He has!" Olguţa threw the new word at the door of Dănuţ, who was sleeping soundly...

***

The door opened gently, the handle not making a sound... Because they were walking on tiptoes, the shoes squeaked, reproved by a "tzz" well known to Dănuţ. Mrs. Deleanu produced that sound (creasing her nose and shaking her head in lively fashion) when small or more serious matters got on her nerves and she had to control herself... For example, because the thread wouldn't get into the eye of the needle, or because the lamp had smoked for some time without her noticing it, or when a badly brought up guest ate cheese with his knife...

"He's asleep... Walk quietly."

Without any shoes on, Profira walked as if she had shod with long boots and she caused the floor to resound. Long ago the children had nicknamed her "St. Elijah's Saint."

"Tick-tock, tick-tock, tick-tock, bang…" said the clock on the wall without taking the order to keep quiet into consideration.

It struck four-thirty…

"Shall I wake him?"

"Mrs. Deleanu hesitated, balancing the fact that she was endangering the night's sleep against the good afternoon sleep."

The roller blind did not jerk up as it usually did when Dănuţ pulled it; it went up gently, accompanied by Mrs. Deleanu's hand until it had reached the sky basking in the sunlight that came in between the leaves of the apple-tree facing the window.

Dănuţ kept in check a superior smile… The eyelids he was gazing at with closed eyes, decorated the gray silk wrap of a sleep that had hardly come to an end with torturous orange chrysanthemums scattered down from the light.

The sleep-like illness made Dănuţ invulnerable and caused him to be spoiled by his parents. For which reason Dănuţ liked to be ill and to keep his eyes closed after waking.

Mrs. Deleanu sat down on the edge of the bed with a sign… Her presence scented differently the heat coming in from the orchard.

"She's looking at me… Ha-ha!… peek-a-boo, here I am." Dănuţ's mind cried out, skipping about in its hiding place within the warm, happy body, as if in an attic where ripe grapes were hanging lazily.

Dănuţ's lashed quivered; he blinked…

"Come on, lazybones!… Get up, sleepyhead," Mrs. Deleanu urged him, pushing up Dănuţ's curls away from his face.

Dănuţ stretched and gave a sincere yawn, opening his eyes.

"Open your mouth wide!… Quick or it will drip!"

The spoonful brought to Dănuț over the glass of water where it was re-flected, entered the open mouth and got out again with great difficulty, be-ing caught between Dănuț's lips from which it came out perfectly clean. Mrs. Deleanu took Dănuț's head in her arms, raising it to help him drink the water from the glass, as she would have done to a convalescent not yet in good health.

Dănuț calmly accepted the reward of his sleep.

***

The silk blouse clothed in poppy red Olguța's summer agitation. She hur-riedly buckled on the black lacquer belt which divided the blouse from the checkered skirt at the waist.

"Finished!" she said, delighted to have been ready before Monica.

"Wait, Olguța, you don't have your socks on."

"Looking at herself in the mirror over her shoulder, Monica was button-ing her mourning dress at the back."

"Have you seen my socks, Monica?" Olguța asked looking for them in irritation even under her pillow.

"Perhaps Profira took them."

"I'll show her!... I don't allow her to mess with my things!... I'm not a child!..." Olguța grumbled, throwing herself on the bed again.

"I'll let you have a pair... See if they fit," Monica said, putting the socks at the head of the bed.

"I don't want anything. I won't accept!... I won't budge from the bed until I get my socks!... There they are, Monica! I found them... Thank you."

The socks Olguța had thrown were hanging over the hats on the stand before the door.

"Are you ready, Olguța?"

"In just a minute."

She pressed her palms right and left of a parting she had made without looking at herself.

"Look at me! Is everything all right?"

"Why don't you comb your hair in the mirror, Olguţa?" Monica asked, making a straight parting.

Olguţa submitted with docility under Monica's hands. Monica combed Olguţa's hair neatly, smoothing the strands at the temples. For a moment, she kept between her hands a neatly combed head — an enormous Ceylon coffee bean roasted to excess… Olguţa looked at herself in the mirror.

"Let's see, who is the tallest?"

"The red blouse suits you. You are beautiful, Olguţa!"

"You are taller! But I am sturdier," Olguţa comforted herself spreading out her shoulders and puffing out her breast in the mirror.

"Pull your sucks up, Olguţa."

"Let them be! Come on now."

In front of the door, she suddenly turned around, struck still by thought.

"Listen, Monica, you must know that something is going to happen to-day."

Monica raised her shoulders, while her finger arranged the elastic of the hat under her chin.

"I don't know anything about that," she said.

"I'm telling you!" Olguţa assured her.

"Alright, but what's going to happen?"

"Something is!" Olguţa said, frowning enigmatically.

"And what can I do about it?"

"There's something you can do!"

"Me?"

"Of course," Olguţa said insistently, looking her straight in the eyes.

"What can I do?"

"You must side with me!"

"Why?"

"Because you are my friend."

"Of course…"

"It's a promise then?"

"Yes, Olguța," Monica said with a sigh.

***

Dănuț ran through the house. His hands were itching, having waited to hold the kite's cord for so long. And yet, after banging the door of the entrance hall, ready to run out, he slowed down his pace… and sat down on the steps of the sun-warmed veranda. The kite was there, Dănuț here… Before playing, Dănuț rejoiced at the thought of playing. He was looking forward to it. Saturday and a Sunday were great times to play, just like the rest of the week… During school time, Sunday was the long-awaited holiday of the week. Saturday was the eve. While Sunday's joy was always saddened by the gradual approach of the nastiest day of the week — Monday, a black-letter day in the calendar after the red-letter day — Saturday's joy was protected by the approach of Sunday, which separated it from Monday. Dănuț had come to value Saturday more than Sunday… He seemed to be somewhat afraid of Sunday.

"He knows!" Olguța thought looking at Dănuț seated on the steps. She took a good bite of her buttered bread, asked Monica to hold what was left, and went down the steps, her hands free. Monica followed her, holding two slices, not daring to bite from hers. They passed by Dănuț, touching him with their shadows. Dănuț turned his head away.

"Coward!" Olguța murmured the word for her benefit. It was a word which she had lately learned from a piece of patriotic poetry, and which her father had explained to her.

"It's a promise then?"
"Yes, Olguţa," Monica said with a sigh.

"What is the meaning of the word coward, Papa?"

"How can I explain it to you? You see, if someone slaps your face and you don't respond, you're a coward."

"Which means that I was a coward, Papa."

"Why?"

"You see, Papa, when mother slapped me with her slipper you know where?" Olguţa had countered, looking at him with raised eyebrows.

"That's something else," Mr. Deleanu had said with a laugh.

"And if I had slapped her too?" Olguţa had dared to ask, but rather shyly and unconvinced.

"You would have been a bad girl and Papa would have been cross!"

"I don't understand. Explain it once more."

Olguţa had ultimately understood that a child can only be a coward among children and he mustn't be one.

"Come along, Monica. We have no business here!"

Dănuţ felt somewhat uneasy after the girls passed him. It was only then that he realized that something was amiss… something — ah! he didn't hear the kite buzzing device. Heart thumping, Dănuţ made a bee-line for the oak.

Below a sky that was godless and kiteless, Dănuţ read the note through which ran the cord that hung down from the oak.

This is for the slap at the station, Humpty-Dumpty

Olguţa Deleanu

Dănuţ's heart dropped, being cut through like the kite's cord… Weary with grief, he sat down at the foot at the oak. This time, Ivan's knapsack was full of tears.

"Leave the kite alone, Dănuţ… Come and have something to eat," Mrs. Deleanu called to him from the top of the steps. "Can't you hear me, Dănuţ?…"

Mrs. Deleanu went down the steps… "Are you hurt, Dănuţ? Why are you sitting here like this?…"

"Ah! That's what Olguţa needed the scissors for."

Mrs. Deleanu was deeply moved by some kind of tears. Dănuţ's tears at present were those kind of tears… Olguţa's spiteful behavior sickened her.

"Come with mother, Dănuţ… Don't you trust mother?"

Dănuţ was waiting for a miracle.

Mrs. Deleanu put her arm around her shoulders and directed his steps toward the house.

The further Dănuţ got from the place where the kite had been, the more often he raised his hands to his eyes. Blind and shaking with sobs, he stumbled on the steps as if he had been on the threshold of a prison.

***

A piercing voice sounded the alarm in the orchard: "Miss Olguţa, Miss Olguţa!"

"Ah!... I'm here!" Olguţa answered, preparing to face the beginning of it all.

"Miss Olguţa, my lady is asking you to come in," Anica said, panting from running, her hands holding her breasts.

"Tell them I'm coming."

"Not so, Miss!" she shook her head in fear. "My lady ordered that you came at once… or else I should take you there forcefully," Anica added, lowering her head in embarrassment.

"You wouldn't dare!... Go and tell them I'm coming," Olguţa ordered.

"I'm going then!... But do come, Miss Olguţa," Anica begged.

Olguța waited until Anica's red kerchief was no longer in sight. "Let's go now!"

Olguța was striding ahead like a hero. Monica was following like a martyr.

***

"Miss Olguța has said she would be coming directly," Anica said fulfilling her errand in a low voice, with eyes that were as near to those of a gazelle as possible.

"I am waiting for her... She knows what to expect!" Mrs. Deleanu said dryly.

Mr. Deleanu stifled a burst of laughter.

Mrs. Deleanu reproved the guilty one's father with a look and crossing her arms, raised her shoulders in revolt and lowered them in despair. Mr. Deleanu was a barrister to such an extent that he could not pass sentences even on children, especially on Olguța.

The tribunal of parental retribution began its proceedings on the veranda under the shelter of a vine full of song, shade, and sunlight.

His heart as heavy as the lock of a deserted church, Dănuț was standing behind the osier armchair where the wrath of his mother, now sitting in judgment, was seething.

Leaning back in his armchair, Mr. Deleanu, with his legs crossed, was looking up, thinking impatiently and with curiously about Olguța's plea. The amber cigarette holder with an unsmoked cigarette was waiting on the table for the moment when proud of Olguța, he would get to smoke it. Olguța came up the veranda steps by herself. Catching sight of Dănuț behind the barricade, she frowned and shook her locks.

"I'm here!"

"I can see that."

"I know why you asked for me and I am right."

"Do you think so?"

"I am sure of it."

"Keep quiet then."

"If that's how it is, I'm off."

"I invite you to stay… and be polite."

"Alice," Mr. Deleanu put in, "let her put forward her case."

"No need for it, she has enough barristers."

"But she must have a judge as well," Mr. Deleanu insisted meaningfully on this abstract noun, as he sometimes described it.

"Alright, judge her."

"No!" he drew back… "You know, I…"

"I know…" Mrs. Deleanu said. "Have your say," she added, addressing Olguţa.

"I shall be silent!"

"Olguţa, don't irritate me."

"I shall be silent!"

"Dănuţ, say what she has done."

"I have forgiven her," Dănuţ mumbled hoarsely, gloomily.

"No, I will have no forgiveness," Olguţa flared. "I am right. He struck me first. Isn't that so, Monica?"

"That is true… I saw it at the station."

"You see?" Olguţa said triumphantly.

"You're lying," Dănuţ said in revolt.

"It is you who is lying."

"That's not true."

"It is!"

"You insulted me!"

"And you struck me!" Olguṭa flared out, ready to take her revenge.

"Why did you call me Humpty-Dumpty?"

"Because you are."

"Me?"

"You, Humpty-Dumpty!"

"She must get me another kite, mother!" Dănuṭ whined.

"Take it!" Olguṭa said with a Mephistophelian smile, pointing towards the sky.

"I've listened long enough. Leave it to me, Dănuṭ!" Mrs. Deleanu put in protectively.

"Of course! Everybody is against me!"

"Olguṭa!"

"I am right!"

"Alright... You'll go to your room — where you'll remain all day — and you'll write "I am right" a hundred times and "I am not right" two hundred times. Tomorrow morning you'll come to tell me who is right in front of Dănuṭ. That is if you want me to allow you to play and to give you sweets."

"Keep to my room until tomorrow morning?... Me?..."

Olguṭa's voice climbed the steps of the scaffold, implanting the flag of revolt on the last step.

"Yes! You... and right now!"

"If that's so, I'll move away!"

"Move?!"

"Yes!"

"Where to, please?"

"To Moş Gheorghe's place. He doesn't persecute me because I am right and I'm not a boy!"

Mr. Deleanu lit his cigarette. Olguţa had lost her case brilliantly.

"You must obey mother, Olguţa…"

Olguţa frowned.

Mr. Deleanu made a skillful pause so that the sentence to follow should acquire an independent value… He sent a pleasantly scented roll of smoke towards Olguţa and added: "When your father asks you to…"

Olguţa entered the house holding her head high and sneezing.

"That's how you spoil the children."

"Alice…" Mr. Deleanu said, twisting his mustache, "all anger, all irritation apart, isn't Olguţa a little devil… an angelic devil?" He had Olguţa's eyes when he smiled.

"That's so," Mrs. Deleanu said with a sigh, hardly controlling a glimpse of secret pride. But she quickly stroked the head of the defeated Dănuţ.

Monica whispered approvingly, ready to imitate her: "It's nice of aunt Alice to do that."

"Dănuţ dear, I will buy you a bigger kite. I'll write to the "Universal" department store directly. Now take Monica by the hand and play with her!"

Dănuţ unwillingly took the shy hand of the one who was to replace the kite and rushed off into the orchard.

Mrs. Deleanu rose from her armchair and made for the door. In passing, she stroked the impertinently curved brow of the head that leaned on the back of the armchair.

"I should put you in the corner too," she said with a gentle smile.

"A pity it is impossible," Mr. Deleanu said, smiling wistfully as he shook the cigarette ashes off himself.

***

Olguța left her room, closing the door noisily. She made for the opposite door unhesitatingly, treading energetically on the soft carpet. With her finger curved, she knocked twice, properly, coldly, on the door of Mrs. Deleanu's boudoir.

"May I come in?..."

She knocked again hurriedly and violently.

"Ow!"

She angrily sucked at her sore joint... She knocked again, this time with her fist.

"...Can't I come in?" she uplifted the slanting handle....

She rushed into the room.

"I am here to..."

The room was empty.

"I see!" Olguța said, enlightened now.

She made for the small drawing-room... One of her feet slid on the well-waxed floor, very nearly causing her to fall. She looked at the floor fiercely, thinking of Anica who turned the floors into mirrors and went back. She dashed and slid down the red glaze... Bang! Her hands struck the drawing-room door.

"What is it?"

"I tripped!" Olguța panted, her hand on the outside door handle.

"Did you get hurt?" Mrs. Deleanu was immediately on alert.

"No," Olguța answered, recovering her dignity.

"What is it you want?"

"I am here to ask for paper, ink, penholder, pen, blotting paper... and black lines!" She had taken a new breath to add her last invented requirement.

"What for?" Mrs. Deleanu asked, absent-minded, holding the pages of a half-read book.

"To write a hundred times that I am right."

"And two hundred times that you are not right!" Mrs. Deleanu added, putting her book down.

Olguța's hand passed over her forehead to brush away the strands of hair that has slid over it. Mrs. Deleanu opened the drawer of her rosewood cabinet. Taking out a pencil case of Japanese lacquer, she fumbled on the narrow shelves, with the movements of a pianist, to find what she wanted. A curved petal came down from a red peony. Olguța picked it up in its flight, made a little pouch of it which she filled with her breath, and struck her forehead with it: Bang! Mrs. Deleanu was startled by the noise.

"More pranks!... Here is a beautiful penholder!"

Olguța's forehead creased.

"… and a new pen," Mrs. Deleanu added.

"One more, please," Olguța claimed, holding out her hand in continuation with the attitude of a young waiter not content with the tip he had received.

"Here is another one… This one a Klaps," Mrs. Deleanu explained.

"I can't write with a Klaps."

"Please finish! What do you want? Tell me!"

"An aluminum pen," Olguța said triumphantly, nevertheless keeping the Klaps.

"Here is an aluminum pen! Be done with it!... Take the ink pot too. And see that you don't drop it!... What else do you want, Olguța?" Mrs. Deleanu asked in a temper, seeing that the girl was not leaving.

"Paper."

"Oh! I have no paper," Mrs. Deleanu answered curtly while closing the box that held the note paper.

"I shouldn't write then?"

"You dare!... Go to your father and tell him to give you sheets of paper... as many as you want!"

"Mother, I can't open the door."

Mrs. Deleanu put down her book on the cabinet energetically and did the job of a doorkeeper for her majesty, the punished one.

***

"Papa, mother sent me to you ask for some sheets of paper."

"What for, dear child?" Mr. Deleanu asked, folding the paper.

"I'm being punished. Remember?"

Olguţa put the inkpot on the table, collected solicitously the ashes at the end of the cigarette in her palm, and blew them towards the vine on the veranda.

"Come with me to my study for it."

"And black lines."

Olguţa held out her hand to take the crystal inkpot.

"I'll take it," Mrs. Deleanu offered courteously.

"Thank you, papa."

Olguţa took the newspaper under her arm as if it were portfolio and obligingly followed Mrs. Deleanu.

The oak desk was covered with law books like Mrs. Deleanu's heart, and inside it was full of goodies for the children.

"Here you are, Olguţa, from your mother...!"

He held out to her a full pad of white paper and also black lines with spots of ink on them.

"And this from me — help yourself..."

He offered a box full of mint sweets as green as the leaves in spring.

"...on the condition that you obey your mother and no longer annoy her."

"But I am right, Papa," Olguța defended herself as she crushed a sweet between her teeth.

"Olguța, when your mother is right... you can't be right too!"

"Why are you laughing, Papa?" Olguța queried.

"I thought of something!"

"I know!"

"Olguța, let the grown-ups know... You just play!... That is, go and write what your mother has commanded..."

"Papa, are you cross with me?"

"No, Why?"

"I was right then. Thank you, Papa!"

***

Dănuț entered the orchard holding Monica's hand like a gloomy husband bringing home the wife that had been discovered to be unfaithful. Monica was following him, looking up... The horizon was red as if a basketful of cherries had been overturned, coloring the sky and people's faces.

Dănuț knew he had to take his revenge but did not know where to begin. He seemed to have got over his anger and that angered him.

"Why do you walk so slowly? Can't you walk faster?" he addressed Monica angrily, walking faster.

Monica quickened her pace to follow him. They walked fast as if it threatened to rain and they had no umbrella.

"Where are we going, Dănuț?"

"That's not your business!"

"He's upset, poor thing!" Monica pitied him.

"Do you know what? Let's run a race, Dănuț!"

"No."

"What do you want?"

"That's what I want!"

"Are you mad at me, Dănuț?..."

"Why don't you answer?..."

"Don't you want to talk with me?"

"No."

"I'll be going then."

"You stay here!"

"Forcibly?"

"Yes."

"Why's that? Won't you allow me to go?"

"No, I won't."

"What does it all mean?"

"It means!"

"You're badly brought up."

"So you're insulting me!... I'll show you!"

Violently, he took hold of her plaits and pulled. Monica closed her teeth tight; her eyes got blacker under her drawn eyebrows...

"Do you want to beat me?" she panted.

"Yes," Dănuț burst out, not knowing how to give a trashing to someone who speaks instead of striking and shrieking.

He gave another pull at her plaits, clumsily this time... Before he realized that her plaits had slipped out of his hands, his finger felt a sharp pain...

"Oh!"

Monica let go.

"You bit me!" he threatened with his fists.

"And you scratched me!"

Facing Monica's eyes and hands, Dănuţ took a step back. Another Monica defended the Monica that had been there before.

"I don't fight with girls!... Go home and tell them I've given you a beating," he defied her, pale-faced, from a distance.

"I don't tell on anyone… as you told on Olguţa. Instead of siding with Olguţa, I pitied… I deserve this." Monica sighed as she wiped her eyes with her sleeve.

"Are you sad?" Dănuţ said, now disarmed, seeing her tears.

"Don't speak to me again."

For a long time, Dănuţ gazed at the blond plaits that rose and fell with Monica's steps… She was soon out of sight.

"We should have played horses together," he sighed only just aware of what wonderful reins Monica's plaits would have made and how difficult it would be for him to have them in his hands from now on. "I was a fool…"

His finger was stinging. Monica's teeth had left a little painful crown… "not to have given her a thrashing!"

"Why did she call me a tattle-tale?" he cried out angrily stomping his foot. "I'll show her! That blonde!" Dănuţ addressed a ripe apricot because, apart from Monica, apricots alone were fair in the orchard.

The twilight was red.

***

With her fingers, Olguţa took the last mint sweet out of her mouth and put it on the blotting paper. She then slipped the now aluminum pen that tasted like an unripe grape, dipped it into the ink, shook the pen holder on the blotting paper, and wrote the title of her imposition:

"Olguța is right."

She underlined the title with such energy that the line, which had been inked all through at first, finally turned into two thin rails as if the express train that had filled the space in between had gone off the rails. Olguța contemplated them with satisfaction. She dipped the penholder into the ink again and began to write the statement in beautiful handwriting. The red protrusion of the tongue that issued at an increasing length between the lips, accompanied the black curves of the pen, the speed of which was increasing. After the tenth affirmative statement, Olguța frowned at the thought of the two hundred negative statements that waited their turn in the black cradle of the crystal inkpot... There was a smell of ink.

Olguța put down her penholder and began to twist her nose.

She picked up the penholder again. With the tip of the pen, she put two straight quotation marks below each word of the last affirmative statement. And beneath those quotation marks, more quotation marks and more. The movement delighted her. It was as if she scratched the sheet of paper. The paper was gradually filled to the bottom with a play of violent mosquitoes.

Olguța was not pleased. She put down her penholder and again twisted her nose. She also took the mint sweet and put it into her mouth. She started a Swedish drill with her fingers, stretching and closing them in turn...

With a sound specific to castanets, the fingers struck her palms. The mint sweet exploded between her teeth. The penholder rose horizontally into the air whence it came down to a clean sheet as if inspired:

"Olguța isn't right two hundred times."

Olguța cast a pitying look at the representative of two hundred negative statements as if it had been a dumb plenipotentiary. She had deliberately made a spelling mistake, omitting the apostrophe.

She looked proudly at the properly written synthesis of the two hundred affirmative statements.

"Olguța is not right one hundred times."

Under them, she drew a line, made a deduction, and wrote:

"Olguța is not right a hundred times."

So she had done away with one hundred negative statements. Good! But there were a hundred left... Well, if that is how things were...

"Olguța is not right a hundred times, but Humpty-Dumpty is not right at all."

Olguța breathed deeply as she gazed at the epitaph of the imposition... The door opened quietly. Monica entered the room. She was staring at the floor, her hand over her mouth.

"Come see what I wrote, Monica!"

"Olguța, I betrayed you," Monica said, forgetting to take off her hat.

"Who? You?"

"Yes, I did."

"I don't believe you!" Olguța said, shaking her head.

Monica sighed.

"I went in the orchard with Dănuț."

"Did he give you a beating?"

"No."

"What did you do then?"

"... We walked..."

"No, you didn't betray me!" Olguța denied Monica's statement. "You sided with me when I asked you. You can walk with him in the orchard. She shrugged her shoulders in unconcern and changed her tone. But see that he doesn't hit you... He knows that you side with me," she imparted to her confidentially.

"Yes, he knows!" Monica sighed.

"Did he tell you?"

"No... I know!"

"Of course. Right you are."

"Yes."

"Did he tell you anything?"

"… No. I'm not going to talk to Dănuț any longer."

"Why?"

"Just because."

"Very good," Olguța said approvingly. "You are my friend."

"Yes, Olguța. I promise you that from now on I'll be only your friend."

"Good!" Olguța accepted Monica's statement. "You didn't what I've written."

"What? You finished it already?" Monica felt reassured.

"You don't like it?"

"I didn't say that… But I wanted to help you write it."

"But I don't want you to!… That's what I wanted to write."

"Did aunt Alice see this?"

"That's how I want it done!" Olguța countered.

"Olguța, do me a favor… I have done you a favor. You see, I took an oath for your sake."

"And what shall I do?" Olguța said, half consenting.

"You look on."

"No, I won't."

"Put the blotting paper down."

"Tut-tut!…"

"Well, do something! Come on, Olguța, let me start."

"Do you know what?"

"…?"

"I'm going to write alongside you."

"I don't want you to."

"But I want it that way."

"Why, Olguța?"

"Because there is nothing for me to do! You write "Olguța is not right" two hundred times and I write that I'm right."

"Let's start."

"Monica, I have no penholder," Olguța wailed while she allowed Monica to take the penholder.

"See, Olguța? Let me do it all."

"As you wish! I will be waiting for you to finish."

She walked up and down the room, more and more quickly. She stopped by the stove, opened the little door, gave a short audience to the preserve pots, and closed the door.

"Listen, Monica, did you number them?"

"I didn't."

"How do you know how many lines you wrote then?"

"I count them in my head."

"Aha!"

"Do you want me to put down the numbers?"

"No... Tell me when you come to the twenty-fifth."

"Why?"

"You'll see!...."

She bent over Monica's shoulder checking...

"Right! The twentieth?"

"Yes."

"Write fifty at the beginning."

"Olguța!"

"Do as I tell you!"

"What about aunt Alice?"

"She's not going to check… Write a very big fifty… Good! You have another twenty lines to write and that will amount to my hundred."

***

"What are we having for supper, Mother?" Dănuț asked Mrs. Deleanu on entering the drawing-room. The loneliness bored him.

"Are you hungry, Dănuț?"

"I'm not sure… But I have nothing to do!"

"Why don't you play with Monica?"

"She went to join Olguța."

"Go to her too."

"To join Olguța?!"

"Alright! Take a book and read."

"What book shall I take?"

"Dănuț!… You're a big boy! Listen to music if you don't want to read."

"How irksome to be a big boy!" Dănuț yawned as he plumped down on the divan. Because of Olguța and Monica, he had to endure until supper the punishment of a Beethoven sonata… He was suddenly tempted to conclude a peace initiated by himself, but he kept himself in check. "When you're a big boy…" he said to himself.

"Mother, let me have a handkerchief."

"Oh! Dănuț, worse than savages! Here is my handkerchief. Why don't you have one?"

The sonata was resumed. Dănuț stuck his mother's handkerchief into his pocket, over his own.

"When I'm a grown-up I won't allow my wife to play the piano," he decided, noticing Mr. Deleanu's absence.

And because he was no longer listening, the Sonata to the Moon sounded in him for later memories...

The silvery moment of the evening sky had appeared outside, with the melancholy of sunless and moonless shadows — the moment when nobody dares to light the candles under the eyes of the day that still see.

***

"Hurry up, Monica," Olguța said impatiently.

"Patience. There isn't much left."

Olguța had misnumbered the negative statements as well, compelling Monica to put a persuasive fifty before every fifteenth line.

"I say, Monica," Olguța said in agitation after an uncomfortable hesitation, "I'll give you my doll."

"Because I helped you write this?" Monica said pointing contemptuously at the sheets covered with the deluging parading letters. "I have two dolls!... What will you do without a doll?"

"It's not because of what you did for me, but because I don't need a doll. Did you finish?"

"I did... But it's not right, Olguța! What will aunt Alice say?"

"Don't worry... Look for a ribbon."

Olguța rolled back the sheets.

"Did you find one?"

"Yes."

"Now make a nice bow; you know, as you did for the prize."

"Why, Olguța?" Monica said, as with her fingertips she puffed up the bow of the doll.

"Mother will see that the bow is well made and will be pleased...."

"Because I don't know how to make bows... and she'll forget to check!"

"You're so artful, Olguța!"

"That's the way when... you have parents," but the last words were left unsaid.

"When what?"

"Nothing... it's my way of saying things."

"You are being called to supper," Anica said from the doorway, her eyes on the elaborate red bow.

"By whom?" Olguța asked peremptorily.

"By madam!"

"Who is asked?"

"You, miss."

"How did she put it?..."

"Say how she put it."

"How could she put it, Miss? She said you should come to supper."

"Monica, you go by yourself. I'm not going."

"Why not, Olguța?"

"Because she didn't ask me, although I completed my punishment."

"You're starting again, Olguța?"

"Please, Monica! I am doing what I have to do. Go and tell them that I'm not coming because I wasn't asked," she said emphasizing with her hand and foot.

"And what are you going to do?"

"I'm going to wait to be asked!"

***

"Aunt Alice, Olguța asked me to ask you whether she can come to supper."

"Of course she can… Go and ask her to come, Anica."

"Girls are the devil!" Anica thought without herself proudly as she ran back to the girls' room.

Mr. Deleanu turned his face from the light to smile; he had recognized the touched-up phrase.

They had supper on the veranda. As if a revelry was about to start, unseen crickets tuned their fiddles; the frogs cleared their throats…

"I'm here."

Olguța handed out the roll as if it had been a pretext for the bow.

"Well done, Olguța!" Mrs. Deleanu praised her. She had given in.

Olguța gave an unassuming, blasé smile.

"And now, because you're a good girl, you'll tell us nicely and straight out, who was right. Was it you or Dănuț?"

Olguța looked deep into Mrs. Deleanu's eyes.

"You were, mother dear."

"Come to supper, children, the soup is getting cold!" Mr. Deleanu burst out noisily, fearing that a new lawsuit was about to begin.

"Tell us straight out, Olguța. Are you sorry for what you did?" Mrs. Deleanu asked, the soup ladle in her hand.

Olguța sighed, "I'm sorry… on account of the kite."

Around the lamp with the rosy globe, moths began to turn, like delicate vehicles at the last round point of a road.

The white pansy face of big-bodied Profira was dreaming as she listened to the music of the soup spoons. Her crossed hands rested horizontally on her belly.

"Dănuț, don't slurp!"

Again!

"Why can't you eat nicely, Dănuț? Show him how one should eat the soup, Monica."

With blushing cheeks, like a fiancée kissed in front of her parents, Monica tilted the tip of the spoon towards her lips, letting the soup flow in smoothly without a murmur.

"Now do it the same way!"

"Meow!..."

The hungry modulation of a cat was heard veraciously in the summer night.

"Away!" Mrs. Deleanu muttered towards the darkness under the table, giving a kick.

An innocent cat took the blow, instead of Olguța. Mrs. Deleanu's napkin wiped a smile that had rays of soup.

The uninvited guests at the meals taken in the open began to gather. The first to come was Ali, the reddish, jolly pointer. He came to lie beside Mrs. Deleanu whom she regarded with hungry deference. He was full of ticks and fleas. He sniffed and quivered, he sneezed; he turned his neck like those wearing strangling collars; he turned his head now to one side then the other; he lapped up flies and swallowed them as if he had suffered from tonsillitis; he rubbed his behind against the ground; his muzzle was at grips with his tail; his tail with the floor; the floor with his legs.

"Go away, Ali!"

Shaking and fawning, full of kind talk, but taking too loud — bow-wow — he came and sat by Dănuț.

The plates had been changed and the smell of the roast now rose from them... Drawn by that smell, the mastiffs in the yard — with the eyes of outlaws and the shyness of doves — appeared in their dark coats on the steps... and did not dare... Protected by the legs of those seated at the table;

the cats came together more closely, silent, a cold tremor going down their spine.

"Patapum, left! Patapum, right! Patapum, left! Patapum right!" Olguţa ordered, standing on her chair, without keeping count of things forbidden.

A black ear over one eye and a brown ear spreading over the nape of his neck; with a crocodile muzzle; with a large breast and crooked legs; with the rocking walk of an athlete in a dress coat, Patapum, the basset, the rogue of rogues and Olguţa's hoy, had put in an appearance. Nobody knew where he was in the daytime. He hid like a tragedian tanned too much by the sunlight.

He went up straight to Olguţa as if aware of the laughter he was giving rise to. He stopped by the legs of Olguţa's chair, tilting his head to one side as if saying "I beg your pardon?"

"Patapum, at the ready."

Patapum sat up soldierly fashion.

"Patapum, sit!"

Patapum fell on his back.

"Patapum, up!"

Patapum came alive again, swishing his tail.

"Patapum, snap!"

Making a wry face, as if taking cod-liver oil, Patapum swallowed the offered fly.

"Well done, Patapum!"

After making a pirouette, Patapum stood on his hind legs with half Olguţa's roast between his hilarious teeth.

Monica was rearing with laughter, big tears falling on a surprised roast. Mrs. Deleanu laughed, her eyes on Monica; Mr. Deleanu laughed, his eyes on Olguţa; Olguţa laughed, holding Patapum in her arms; and the rosy lamp smiled at them all.

A dignified Dănuţ held out a piece of roast to Ali, the only one serious that he could address — and who obeyed him.

"Oh!" Olguţa gave a shrill cry and jumped down from her chair, her hands covering her ears.

Rejected from her arms, Patapum rolled down until he was under Ali's nose, who looked down on the old scoundrel in disgust.

Olguţa covered her ears with her hands and thrust her head into Mrs. Deleanu's arms to hide.

"What is it, Olguţa? What's happened?... Come on tell us, Olguţa!..."

"Did the cat get your tongue, Olguţa? Is that possible!"

"It's gone!" Olguţa cried out, her voice muted by Mrs. Deleanu's dress.

"Who's gone?"

"The bat!" she cried out, quivering in her mother's arms.

The silence was broken by a shrill meowing.

"Where is it?"

"It's gone," she said, heaving a sigh of relief.

Mrs. Deleanu closed her eyes, a tremor of fear going through her. The flabby ghost with long hair had flown away — a dark streak of lightning against a tremulous evening star.

"Come on, Olguţa. It's gone... It's certainly gone."

"I don't believe it!"

"Olguţa, don't be childish!"

"Is it gone, Papa?" Olguţa asked, looking out from the corner of her eye.

"Yes, of course. It's gone!"

Olguţa jumped up, her eyes riveted on Dănuţ's eyes.

"I was sure you'd laugh! I won't allow you to make fun of me! I'm not afraid of anyone!"

"Except bats!" Dănuţ whispered blandly, his legs taut under the table.

"Bravo, Dănuţ!" Mr. Deleanu said approvingly.

Dănuţ's outer self stood motionless for fear his inner self might be laid bare.

Olguţa frowned for a moment and then burst out laughing.

"You're right!... A good thing it's gone!... Why am I afraid of bats, Papa?"

"Ask your mother."

"Mother, do you know why I'm afraid of bats?"

"How should I know," she said shrugging her shoulders and looking aslant at Mr. Deleanu.

"Why did Papa send me to you then?"

"Ask him!"

"I know," Olguţa said, shaking her head knowingly.

"Why, if you please?"

"Shall I tell you!"

"Yes."

"Because you are also afraid of bats."

"Don't be cheeky, Olguţa!"

"I'm afraid of bats too!" a still pale-faced Monica confessed.

"Of course you are, you're my friend."

"What a fool Monica is!" Dănuţ thought, with a kind of respect, however. Nobody knew he had been afraid too; nobody except the cats under the table, whose tails had been trodden on.

"Dănuţ, fold your napkin!"

Monica had folded Olguţa's napkin so it was a disappointment for Dănuţ's eyes. Moreover, Olguţa's eyes were on the lookout. So Olguţa hadn't forgotten that he had been witty at her expense. Dănuţ focused on his napkin.

"Let's talk in French, mother," Olguţa proposed, looking at Dănuţ.

"Of course," Mrs. Deleanu consented, surprised by the suggestion, but well pleased.

"Can I leave the table, mother?" Dănuţ asked, gathering up his courage.

"Why should you, Dănuţ? Stay here with us, we'll all talk!"

Dănuţ blinked, swallowed hard, and obeyed. It was the beginning of Olguţa's revenge.

"Olguţa, que fais-tu en ce moment?" Mrs. Deleanu began.

"C'est trop simple, maman! Pose-moi une autre question... plus difficile; n'est-ce pas, mon frère?..."

"Est-ce-que tu as mal a la tete, mon frere?... Dis vrai? Si c'est oui, que je ne te derange plus!"

"Leave me alone!" Dănuţ mumbled, another blush coming over his face.

"Voyons, mon petit, dis cela en francais, au moins!. Dănuţ comment dit-on en francais: leave me alone?"

"Laisse-le tranquille, maman, il ne comprehend pas!" Olguţa said, contempt in her words, her tone, and the movement of her lips.

"Sois plus amiable, Olguţa!"

"Mais puisque je dis la verite, maman!"

Mr. Deleanu bit his lips. His heart leaped to hear Olguţa going into polemics in a language she had only recently learned, mostly by listening to it, with the right accent too and off-handedly.

"The temperament of a barrister!" he thought regretfully.

"Olguţa, tu n'as pas raison," Mrs. Deleanu said in Dănuţ's defense, controlling her smile.

"Qu'il le prouve!" Olguţa said with the adequate gesture.

Dănuţ knew as much French as Olguţa, but he didn't dare to speak. He felt uneasy, just as he did when he had to recite poetry in a drawing-room full of guests.

"Allons, mon petit, responds!" Mrs. Deleanu summoned him.

Blood rushed to Dănuț's head. Gathering up his strength, he grabbed a phrase he had heard Mr. Deleanu say from his beclouded silence and he launched at Olguța in French.

"Je m'en fiche!"

"Alors va te coucher!" Mrs. Deleanu concluded sharply.

Dănuț set off. The hallway was dark. He went back to the veranda and sat down on the steps among the shepherd dogs who did not know French but could bite… With a viola's voice, Monica had entered the enemies' camp in her turn.

"Patapum, comment font les avocats?"

"Bow-wow!"

"C'est bien! Patapum, comment font les magistrats?"

Patapum closed his eyes and laid down as if he'd taken a narcotic.

"Come on, Monica!… Patapum too knows French," Olguța said aloud as she walked past Dănuț, holding Monica's hand.

Dănuț on the steps among the dogs clenched his jaw tight and was patriotically silent in the Romanian night.

"What are you thinking of, Alice?"

"Oh, of nothing… We are getting old… The children are growing…"

"Yes…."

"Before long the house will be empty… and we'll be older…"

"What can we do?"

"Nothing. Except raise them and look at ourselves in the mirror ever more seldom…"

"From now on mirrors are only for them, just as we are."

They were silent for a while.

"Olguța and Monica put your coats on. And you too Dănuț."

"Put your coat on too, Alice. You might catch a cold!"

Something seemed to have started in the sky or on earth. Though there was no wind, no foliage rustling.

The frogs were silent for a moment. From the silence of their troubled hearts that had suddenly stopped beating, the mire drum let out its sad, homely complaint. And then the frogs started croaking again, but differently, for coming off the horizon, with an amphora of coolness on its bare shoulders — the shoulders of a full moon — the true night was approaching slowly.

***

"Did you like what I did to him, Monica?"

"Poor Dănuț!" Monica thought, seeing him in her mind alone on the steps among the dogs. But aloud, she said: "Doesn't Dănuț know French?"

"Of course he does!" Olguța defended her brother. She felt hurt as she shook her body into the white nightgown falling about her.

"Why doesn't he want to speak then?"

"That's how boys are… fools! Monica, will you please button me up at the neck?"

"What? Is Dănuț a fool?" Monica said in surprise as she slid Olguța's button into the collar buttonhole.

"Did I say that?"

"Yes. You said boys were fools."

"Of course."

"How is it then?"

"He's not a fool… But that's what boys are like."

"Won't you put your slippers on too, Olguța?"

"Nooo! It's pleasant like this. Take them off too. Isn't it different to be bare-footed?"

"How nice it is, Olguța," Monica said with a smile as she stepped bare-footed in the moonlight.

"You see if you obey me!"

"What are we going to do now?"

"Have a pillow fight!" Olguța said, in proof of which she threw a small pillow at Monica.

"Don't you say your prayers, Olguța?" Monica asked guardedly.

"After the pillow fight!"

"No, I'm going to say my prayers now."

"I'll do it too then!"

Monica knelt on her bed and prayed in her mind with her eyes closed: "Our father who art in heaven…" Olguța did it aloud and standing. She stopped to straighten the icon which had tilted when the pillow fight had been inaugurated.

"Would you like to be the Savior's Mother, Monica?"

"…in the name of the Father, of the Son and the Holy Ghost, amen… What did you say, Olguța?" Monica asked, turning her face away from heaven where her grandmother was.

"Let's have a pillow fight! Name… Father… Son… Ghost… amen!"

***

Dănuț knew why Ali was sleeping on the carpet in his room instead of sleeping on the veranda outside. But nobody must know what Dănuț knew, or that Ali snored in his room, coiled up on the carpet like a continent of fleas. Truth be told, Dănuț himself felt rather awkward to know what he knew because, knowing it, the fear of the night and of loneliness, though unavowed, stared him in the face, ready to come to him, like someone whose name is called.

"I'm going to undress," Dănuţ told himself to pluck up the courage as he stood up noisily from the edge of the bed.

He began taking off his clothes with the unnatural movements of actors reproducing small everyday gestures on the stage. The sound of pillows clashing and of two voices laughing came in from Olguţa's room.

"How nice it will be to be married!" And he suddenly found himself at a loss thinking that he, Dănuţ, was to become a grown-up... He raised his eyes and, tilting his head back, looked up to the place where Dănuţ's head would be — actually Dan's head — many years hence... He found it difficult to believe!...

This means that a foreign person, a giant, was to gobble up Dănuţ, and with Dănuţ inside him make the others believe that he was Dănuţ... Strange... And where would Dănuţ be?... Dănuţ would be nowhere...

"I don't want that!" Dănuţ bristled up... as if facing death and the grave.

No, not that way! Dănuţ would be inside him, like a small wooden egg in a big egg... It isn't the same thing... For the giant would be Dănuţ... How is that going to be? Both small and big?... Dănuţ's head now reached the waistcoat pocket where father's watch was and at the same time, the giant's head was Dănuţ's own head! Strange! It was as if the head would be held in one's hands, and the head would think separately — how could that be? And the headless body would also think... Very strange!...

"Was father also small once?... Of course, he was..."

This means that he was once a child of Dănuţ's age, the brother of Dănuţ and Olguţa if he still existed, and now he was only Dănuţ's father... But where's the other one? Has he disappeared or was he within him? Would he find the other one if he cut father in two? Of course not!... There was a skeleton, a heart, lungs within the body... Dănuţ had learned at school about everything to be found in his father's body. Where was the other one then?

"Is it possible that I should be it?"

Dănuț blinked. He was dazed.

… He was father's child… and mother's child too! Strange… that a single person should be the child of two people. One plus one makes two… That is certain! He had learned arithmetic… Why is Dănuț the child of his father as well as of his mother?...

How are children made?

"Will I produce children?"

Dănuț looked at himself in the mirror in fear.

"I'm a boy!" he thought a quiet himself down as if he had deluded himself, as he would have deluded someone younger than himself and more ignorant…

"Olguța will have children," Dănuț decided as a punishment.

"Olguța!... Olguța was his sister!... Why?... Because she also belonged to father and mother… Impossible!... Olguța was mother's child and Dănuț was father's child… Mother was a woman… How can a woman produce a boy?... Was it the father who had produced Dănuț?... But tomcats have no kittens… only she-cats have!... That's different!... Doesn't mother say that Dănuț is her boy? Can mother tell lies?... Why is the mother a woman?... She has long hair. Father has a mustache!... The mother wears a dress!... Father could put on a dress!"

Imagining him in a women's dress, Dănuț smiled.

Father is a barrister… Mother is a woman… Will Dănuț be a barrister too? He found it hard to believe!...

How can his father speak for an hour without reading?... Does he learn it all by heart? Impossible!... Poetry alone can be learned by heart!... Father is very clever… Dănuț is afraid of Olguța! He had come up top in his class, but Olguța is very clever... He can't compete with her... Is Dănuț a fool?... That's what Olguța believes, but it isn't true!... How can Dănuț be a fool when he knows what Olguța is like and what he is like!... He can't talk to Olguța... What then?... That is something else! Dănuț knows he's not a fool because he has Ivan's knapsack. Olguța doesn't know that Dănuț is clever... even very clever!... Olguța could only listen to what Dănuț thinks... What a pity!... He can only speak to Olguța.

Dănuț suddenly looked at himself in the mirror. Was he speaking or was it someone else? He touched his hands, one hand touching the other. He moved his fingers, his arms.

So he — Dănuț — was his own master. Dănuț's master. He ordered and he obeyed... Just as Dănuț had to obey mother and father... He could make himself do anything! He could tell his hand: "Stretch out!" And his hand stretched... If he had told it: "Scratch Dănuț!" it would have scratched him!... No... did it refuse to obey?... Because he had no means of compelling it... But he had! Employing the other hand... No! neither of his hands were willing to scratch him... Why?... Because he could not punish them... Oh yes, he could... He could bite them!... But the teeth were unwilling to bite Dănuț!... That was it! The hands that wouldn't scratch Dănuț were his hands!... Could fingers think?...

"What is this, Dănuț? You're looking at yourself in the mirror instead of sleeping? Come on!"

Mrs. Deleanu in her kimono was going on the night rounds quietly like all those who do it.

"Did you brush your teeth?"

"I did."

"Are your hands clean?... Let me see them... Dănuț, Dănuț! What are nail brushes for?"

"For yourself, mother, Olguța would have answered." That is what Dănuț told himself, blushing.

"Come to me in the morning to have your nails cut. Do you understand?"

"Yes."

"And now go to bed… Dănuţ!… What is this!" Mrs. Deleanu was aghast on finding Ali… "Go away, Ali!"

Ali opened his eyes like those of a pious monk found by the mother superior in the nuns' quarters, and made his winding way towards the door."

"What is he doing here?"

"He came by himself, mother!"

"I believe you! That would be the limit… Why didn't you drive him out?"

"… I forgot."

"Luckily I remembered… What are you doing here?"

"We have no matches, mother!" Olguţa's head popped in; she was on the lookout in the open door that led into the corridor.

"You go about bare-footed? Olguţa!"

"I can't find my slippers! I'll show Anica!"

"You better go to bed!"

"What are you doing in my room?" Dănuţ asked angrily.

"I'm talking to mother! This is my mother's house. Why don't you drive mother out?"

"Leave him alone, Olguţa!"

"Did you send Ali out, mother?"

"Is that the reason why you're here?… Go to bed! Quickly, Olguţa!"

"Do dogs have bugs, mother?"

"What? Did you find any bugs?" Mrs. Deleanu asked in fear.

"No. I'm just asking!"

"You'll drive me mad, Olguţa!"

"Why, mother dear?"

"Let Dănuț go to sleep, please!"

"I won't let him? He doesn't let me!"

"Olguța!"

"Well, I'm going… Mother dear, the kimono suits you so well!"

Mrs. Deleanu turned her head towards the window for her smile to go where the butterflies come from.

"Good night, Dănuț!"

She kissed the boy's forehead, blew out the candle, and went out, leaving Dănuț with the moonlight… and with something that had not yet entered the room… But Dănuț's heart could feel it coming, silent, dumb, sharp like the flight of a bat.

…A thought in his head, he started reciting it aloud, a deafeningly loud voice, like a parrot, the whole dialogue with Olguța and with mother. "You're a fool! You're a fool! You're a fool! Go and give Olguța a beating! Aren't you ashamed of letting her make fun of you?... Make fun of you…!"

While another thought, simultaneously with the other, was whispering serpent-like… "In the cemetery, the vampire is rising from the grave. Its face is yellow; its black eyes are burning; its teeth and ears are growing every longer. And the vampire comes unheard in the moonlight… In the cemetery, in the cemetery… You can't hear it coming…"

He opened his eyes, the fear-inspiring moonlight filled the room… He wrenched himself away from the pillow and quickly turned his head. There was nobody behind, but it may have gone and have come back again…

"Vampires seek young men's blood…"

"Young girls' blood!" another of Dănuț's thoughts cried out.

"In the cemetery, the vampire is rising from the grave.
Its face is yel-low; its black eyes are burning;
its teeth and ears are growing every longer.
And the vampire comes unheard in the moonlight…
In the cemetery, in the cemetery… You can't hear it coming…"

He made the sign of the cross. He had gone to bed without saying his prayers. He paled in the pale moonlight.

***

Olguța left the spoon in the jam pot and pushed the pot into the stove. Monica got into bed. Resolutely, Olguța set off towards the door between their room and Dănuț's room, whence the knocking had come.

"Who's there?"

"I am."

"Who's I?"

"Me, your brother."

"I don't believe it!"

"I have to tell you something."

"Say it."

"Open the door."

"What for?"

"For me to tell you something!"

"And what will you give me if I open it?"

"Say what you want."

Olguța frowned. She was at a loss.

"Don't open it, Olguța!" Monica prompted.

"Why shouldn't I open it?"

"Open up, Olguța," Dănuț's voice was heard to say loud, intently.

" Give me your gun…"

"I'll give it to you."

"Swear…"

"On my honor."

"Say I swear."

"Open, Olguţa, I swear on my honor."

Olguţa turned the key, pressed the door handle, and upon opening the door, suddenly stepped on the threshold.

"Where's the gun?"

"Take it."

Olguţa took the gun but did not let Dănuţ cross the border.

"Humpty-Dumpty!" she challenged him, gun in hand.

"You can call me that! I don't mind!"

"I won't call you that anymore then."

"As you wish."

"But what do you want?"

"Olguţa… I want to make up."

"You want to make up?"

"Yes."

"You really want to?"

"I really want to."

"Come in then."

Dănuţ breathed deep.

"I want to make up with you too, Monica."

"I'm so glad, Dănuţ. Let's kiss."

They kissed each other enthusiastically. Dănuţ hurriedly, in the air; Monica kissed him on the nose by mistake.

"What shall we do?" Olguţa sked.

"Give him some too," Monica tried to persuade Olguţa.

"You think I should give him some?"

"Yes, Olguţa, why shouldn't you?"

"What do you two want to give me?" Dănuț asked uneasily.

"But will you swear?" Olguța asked.

"Haven't I sworn?"

"For the gun only."

"Alright. I swear!"

"Repeat after me: I swear…"

"Aren't you sleeping, children?" Mrs. Deleanu asked a second time at the end of the corridor.

"Monica, say we're sleeping; she believes you!"

"Not yet, aunt Alice!"

"Good night, Monica. Olguța, you should know I can hear you!"

"I swear… Come on, Olguța," Dănuț whispered.

"Wait a bit, I must find… Let me have cramps…"

"Let me have cramps…"

"That's a curse, not an oath, Olguța," Monica said in fright.

"Yes? Very good. Repeat after me… What did I say?"

"Let me have cramps…" Dănuț repeated benevolently, making a face.

"…and stay in bed all through the holiday…"

"…and stay in bed all through the holiday…"

"…and be dieted by the doctor…"

"…and be dieted by the doctor," Dănuț repeated anxiously.

"Without any sweets…"

"Without any sweets…," he sighed bitterly.

"…if I tell anyone…"

"…if I tell anyone…"

"…what Olguța…"

"…what Olguța…"

"...will show me..."

"...will show me..."

"Amen!"

"Mind! And now, here is your gun back."

"Why, Olguța?"

"It's a toy! I have no use for it."

"I won't accept it. I've given it!"

"I'll keep it for Monica then... You'll put it into the dolls' bed. Do you hear, Monica?"

White rays of moonlight shown on the carpet where three bare-footed children in long nightgowns — one with fair plaits, two with brown locks — gathered around a pot of jam.

All three ate with the same spoon under the gaze of the same grand-mother, from the preserves of the same giants — down on the carpet.

II. The White Cottage and the Red Dress

Moş Gheorghe, the chief stable man, had his quarters at the mansion of the masters of the estate: a tall, well-whitewashed room with a bed with clean linen on it, windows as big as the big icon of the village church and food that Anica brought him from the menu of the gentlefolk.

But Moş Gheorghe also had his own household; a cottage that was on the outskirts of the village — not very far from it and close to the mansion — and not so very near to it wither; the distance a shepherd dog kept between the flock and the shepherd.

"Why must you have a house, Moş Gheorghe?... You have no children; Mother Anica, God forgive her, is no more; your horses are here; I am here and so is Olguţa! Why all the trouble?" That was Mrs. Deleanu's kind reproof.

Moş Gheorghe's brow creased and there was an awful smile in his screwed-up eyes.

"Well, well!... The old man knows!"

On a sloping piece of land behind the cottage, was an orchard with plum and cherry trees, which came down from the blue sky in fragrant garb in the spring; farther down there was a field, where the summer wheat came out like Easter procession from church.

"Moş Gheorghe, you no longer have the strength for it. I'll send the villagers to plow for you."

"God forbid, my lady! And God help you; give me only the oxen and plow."

The priest alone entered Moş Gheorghe's cottage, and also a wedding party when a larger space was needed, and Olguţa, whenever she wanted to. But Olguţa never came unless she was asked; that doesn't mean that she didn't come often.

Moş Gheorghe had no dogs. "What for? I'm living at the mansion. Who will look after them?" But on the cottage roof, there was the nest of a stork whose bill was heard to clap in the evening.

"Because the old man has a kind heart." That is how the villagers interpreted the stork's preference for a cottage that was hardly ever lived in.

That might also have been the reason why the evil-doers did not break into the household without a dog of the man who was a veteran of the war of 1877.

***

"What holiday is it today, Mother dear?"

"Today?... No holiday at all! What's come over you, Olguţa?"

"I thought was a holiday, Mother dear!"

"Mother dear, Mother dear! You love me so, don't you? You better tell me what you want."

"Me? Nothing!... I should only like to see how the blue dress suits Monica."

Mrs. Deleanu searched Olguţa's eyes in vain. Her eyes did not disclose more than her words; to put it more plainly, because of Olguţa's eyes...

"Monica, do you want to try the blue dress on?"

"Of course she wants to!" Olguţa commented on Monica's blush intuitively, before she saw the blush.

"Yes, aunt Alice," Monica mumbled in response to Olguța's imperative. She was delighted that a guilty wish was being fulfilled and that she was not to blame for it.

The blue dress had been waiting for Monica ever since the beginning of the holidays. Mrs. Deleanu had made it immediately, but Monica had only tried it on. At the time Monica loved her mourning dress: it was not a duty but a remembrance of her grandmother.

One day Dănuț, Olguța, and Monica were playing at colors — Olguța's invention.

"What color would you like to be?... Answer quickly for if you don't you tell lies and I'll get angry!"

"Summoned at a moment's notice unexpectedly by Olguța's voice and eyes, Dănuț was at loss. Nothing of the sort had crossed his mind. What had he to do with colors?"

"Blue, Olguța!" he had decided, the color of the sky helping him to get out of the fix.

"And why would you like to be blue?"

"Because it's beautiful."

"Yes?"

"Of course," Dănuț asserted resolutely.

"Very beautiful?"

"Very beautiful!"

"The most beautiful?"

"The most beautiful."

"That's not true. Red is beautiful, very beautiful, the most beautiful."

"Blue is even more beautiful."

"You're telling lies. What do you think, Monica?"

"I don't know!"

"That means that you think as I do, and we two are right," Olguța had declared triumphantly.

So Dănuț also liked blue... ever since Monica had been waiting for the dress that was Dănuț's color. Mrs. Deleanu had not dared to give it to her, for fear of hurting her feelings. Monica had not dared to ask for it... And Monica was so very much afraid of grieving her grandmother!... Nor would she have wanted to betray Olguța.

Monica followed Mrs. Deleanu into her room. Olguța entered for a moment and made as if to go.

"Where are you going, Olguța?"

"I have something to say to Papa."

"There's something fishy about you today, Olguța!"

"Why?"

"Didn't you say you wanted to see how the blue dress suited Monica?"

"I did."

"Why are you leaving then?"

"Because..." she smiled, "Mother dear, I have seen Monica in knickers before! I'll be back by the time she is dressed."

***

When she paid visits, Olguța never entered a room before knocking on the door. A single door was the exception from this rule, namely Dănuț's door which she kicked when she didn't want to get in but wanted to get him by surprise.

Olguța knocked discreetly at the door of Mr. Deleanu's study.

"Come in!"

"I've come to see you, Papa."

"Alright, my little darling... You want something perhaps?"

"No, Papa! I've come to see you!"

"Here is a chair, Olguţa. Sit down."

"Like a client, Papa?"

"My little darling... If I had clients such as you I'd win all my cases."

"Do you lose cases, Papa?"

"Of course. I lose some, like everyone else."

"If I was a judge, Papa, you wouldn't lose any cases."

"Why not, Olguţa? Father isn't always right."

"Yes... only mother is!"

Mr. Deleanu looked at the window, keeping his face away from Olguţa's eyes. When he turned around he was very serious.

"I always know when you laugh, Papa!"

...?

"Because I also feel like laughing."

They both laughed.

"... And do you love Father?"

Olguţa frowned.

"Why do you ask me. As if you didn't know!"

"I know, of course I know, but I like to be told too."

"I don't."

"Why, Olguţa?"

"Well... I don't know..."

"Want any sweets?"

"Yes, please... Why don't you smoke, Papa? Is it because I'm here?"

"No Olguţa. I forgot... Do you want me to smoke?"

"Yes, Papa. Smoking suits you."

Mr. Deleanu screwed a cigarette into the cigarette holder. Olguța struck a match and carefully offered him the conic flame.

"Why is a pipe nicer than a cigarette, Papa?"

"Because you like it better."

"Eh, Papa! That's something else! Don't you like pipes?"

"I like them."

"Why don't you smoke a pipe then?"

"I got used to cigarettes… And it's not the right thing. With a pipe you only puff; you don't breathe in as I do," Mr. Deleanu said, smoking voluptuously.

"And do you still have a pipe?"

"Yes. I've got several."

"And what do you do with them?"

"I keep them for nothing."

"For nothing?"

"Oh well, I give one to a friend occasionally."

"Do you love me, Papa?"

"No!"

"You do."

"As you wish."

"But do you love me more than you love your friends?"

"Undoubtedly."

"Give me a pipe too then."

"A pipe?"

"If you love me Papa."

"What do you want to do with a pipe?"

"I want to keep it… for beauty's sake!"

"Alright, Olguța... Come here... Choose one to your liking."

He opened a drawer full of various smoking utensils.

"Here you are, Olguța. This one is pretty and it's small — meerschaum. The right thing for you. Do you like it?"

"I like it, papa. But I want a big one."

"Choose a big one them!"

"Is this good? I received it from a Frenchman who tuned pianos in Iași... He's dead, the poor man. What a decent fellow! An excellent pipe."

"I'll take it, Papa. Thank you, Papa. I'll remember."

"Don't bother, Father's darling. They're all yours. Don't you know Father gives you anything you like?"

Olguța stroked his forehead and hair.

"What fine hair you have, Papa! So silky! I'll be going now."

"Listen, Olguța. Why not come to the woods with Father. I'm taking Dănuț too. Maybe mother is coming as well. We will go for a ride in the buggy."

Olguța passed her hand over her forehead.

"It'll wait for another time, Papa. Today I'm visiting Moş Gheorghe, with Monica... He invited us, you know," she said, looking down.

Mr. Deleanu stroked his mustache... looked Olguța up and down... and opened the drawer with the pipes again.

"Take another pipe, Olguța. You should have one as well."

Olguța looked at his forehead and smiled.

"You're so clever, Papa! Thank you, I have no use for it!"

After Olguța left, Mr. Deleanu took his forehead between his hands and thought for a long time, his heart aching as he accompanied his child over the threshold of life, far away.

"One-day Olguța will be grown up. Poor Olguța!"

***

Monica left the drawing-room in her black dress, walking slowly, with controlled joy, in the wake of Mrs. Deleanu.

From Mrs. Deleanu's room, she returned in the blue dress, walking first. But the girl who had entered the room had not come out of it. She hung on the stand in her black dress. Monica had not merely changed a dress, she had changed a season. Her eyes as well as her hair had another luster.

When the sky is blue all the clear lakes would be blue were it not for the tousled sunlight.

Monica's hair, plaited in two pigtails, hung down her back. And Monica had on a blue linen dress, with a neck just low enough for a child, and her head with eyes and mouth, and the stem of her neck, to show to advantage.

The dress reached above the knees. Mrs. Deleanu did not make clothes with the children's growth in mind, but only to adorn their age at a given time, for children's knees can be as sincere as their face, and they are as beautiful and as much alive.

Dănuț was dressed in the same way... He grew quicker. Mrs. Deleanu had a great deal of work on her hands for every age to have its neat dowry for every season of the year. And yet the cupboards were not full of jackets that were too tight and of dresses that were too short. The jackets and dresses that had been left behind by the growing children clothed other boys and other girls in needy households.

Monica was not another Olguța. She was on a par with Olguța. For which reason the blue dress was the first to come up in a new grove on the verge of which the shadow of a black dress had passed.

"Look at yourself in the mirror," Mrs. Deleanu invited her at the inauguration of the dress while raising the roller-blind of the drawing-room window.

The light of noon guided the picture of the spring mornings in the mirror. Monica looked down.

"Isn't it a sin, aunt Alice?" Her joy was tinged with fear.

"Little girl, it isn't a sin. And if it were, aunt Alice would take it upon herself."

"How kind you are, aunt Alice!"

The door handle was pulled sharply down.

"Here I am!"

"Don't bang…"

"…don't slam, don't… I love you so, Mother dear!"

"Olguţa!"

"Was I cheeky?"

Mrs. Deleanu laughed.

"You see, Mother dear!"

"Keep quiet! You better look at Monica."

"Let me look at you," Olguţa inspected Monica turning her towards herself. "Very good, I like it very much!... You do things so well, Mother dear!"

"Thank God! I've at last heard some praise from you."

"I'm in a good humor, Mother!"

"You'd better let Father be in good humor when he pleases. You must always be."

"Why?"

"Because you're a child."

"Perhaps… but today I'm in very good humor. And you, Mother?"

"I am too if you don't make me dizzy!"

"Today is a holiday, Mother; I'm telling you!"

"I've told you before that it isn't, Olguţa!"

"I believe you... but it is very much like a holiday! Are you going to undress now, Monica, or are you going to remain as you are?"

"Leave her alone, Olguța! Why do you want her to take off her dress?"

"I don't want her to. I would have been surprised if... Look at me, Mother!"

"What do you want?"

"Me? Nothing. Only that you should look at me."

"Alright, I'm looking."

"Not into my eyes! Look at me, you know how... As you look when we're going to the theatre... Inspect me."

"Well?"

"Can't you see anything?"

"I can see that you've stained your dress! When did you stain it?"

"You see!... When did I stain it?... Do you know, Monica?..."

"Neither do I!... Mother dear, isn't it a pity that I have a stained dress?"

"A pity for the dress."

"And not for me?"

"Why did you stain it?"

"Me?"

"Who else?"

"It's the soup's fault."

"Olguța!"

"Do you want to punish me, mother?"

"Do tell me what you want."

"And you'll give it to me?"

"Tell me what you want."

"I'm not asking for anything. But why should I have a stained dress? I don't want to have a stained dress."

"Keep quiet, please! I understand now... You saw the new dress in the wardrobe."

"Yes, when you look out Monica's dress." Olguţa was directing the dialogue towards victory.

"Why are you telling lies, Olguţa?"

"I'm not telling lies."

"Quiet!... Didn't you know I made a new dress for you?"

"I knew."

"Why did you say that you only saw it now?"

"Of course! It's only now I saw it's ready."

"And do you want to put it on?"

"Good. You're right. But I am only asking you to answer my question straight out."

"Right-o, I will answer."

"You want to put on the new dress. Is that it?"

"Yes," Olguţa consented cautiously.

"So why didn't you just say so, like a good child: Mother, please let me put on the new dress?"

"Because you wouldn't have consented."

"How do you know?"

"I know. You would have replied that it isn't a holiday today and I would stain it."

"Olguţa, Olguţa! Tell me why you are so artful...."

"You're silent, Olguţa?"

"I'm not silent, I don't know!"

"You see, Olguţa!"

"Perhaps you know, Mother dear!"

"Let me help you put it on."

***

"Aha!"

Dănuţ closed the drawing-room door quietly and remained outside. Monica didn't notice.

"Hmm!"

He again saw her through the keyhole looking at herself in the mirror.

"A good thing!"

The same thing the third time.

"Bravo!"

And the fourth time.

So Monica is looking at herself in the mirror! Monica, the good girl; Monica, the obedient girl; Monica... is looking too, but he is a boy! So Monica...

"But you are looking through the keyhole!"

"That's different!" Dănuţ replied to his impertinent thought verbosely.

And to prove it to her, he entered the drawing-room suddenly. Monica was looking out the window.

"Hmm!"

"Aren't you hot, Dănuţ?" Monica was ready to serve him, dressed in imperial garb.

"That's my business. Don't meddle."

"Did I do something that upset you, Dănuţ?"

"You wouldn't dare!"

"I won't do anything to you, Dănuţ."

"You're afraid!"

"I'm not afraid, Dănuţ..." Monica's cheeks were getting ever redder as her thoughts went on to say: "I pity you because Olguţa persecutes you."

"Aren't you afraid?" he said defiantly.

"No... Why should I be afraid?"

"Why don't you start a fight?"

"I don't fight, Dănuţ."

"Because you'd be defeated?"

Monica sighed... A pity she did not have the black dress on. Why had she put on the blue dress?... A pity! Yes! A pity!

"Why are you quiet?"

"You're wrong, Dănuţ!" Monica said, shaking her head.

"And you're right!"

"Don't be rude, Dănuţ."

"Go and tell on me!"

"I'm not a snitch!"

"But you're looking at yourself in the mirror!" Dănuţ countered victoriously, pointing at the bare mirror with his finger.

"I did look. Aunt Alice told me to look and I looked..."

"Hah! I know what I'm saying... Do you have anything to say?..."

"Tell me; why did you look?"

Monica further lowered her eyes and her heart was beating loudly.

"Because there was nobody here because you're dissembling because you're a hypocrite."

Dănuţ wished Olguţa could have heard him speak for so long and so well... What joy! Perhaps Olguţa was eavesdropping...

"Do you have anything else to tell me? Of course not! You're turning your back on me. That's an easy way to talk!"

Monica was crying with closed eyes while listening.

Dănuţ made for the door... There was nothing for him to do... He lingered a little on the threshold, waiting to be challenged. He was leaving Monica as one leaves after having scored a success that had won no applause — sadly.

"Dănuţ is mad at me! If that is how things stand..."

The tearful anger hardened Monica's heart. She gathered her handkerchief resolutely, punishing her dress to be stained with tears.

***

Mrs. Deleanu took two steps back.

"Be quiet, Olguţa!"

Olguţa was motionless as if at that solemn moment the new dress had been a brier bush in bloom that might have been scattered. With knitted brow and screwed up eyes, Mrs. Deleanu had the look characteristic of young generals for their armies before an assault; of sculptors for their statues before their being sent to the Gallery; of young men in love for the first envelope before its destiny is entrusted to the letterbox; and of experienced women in the mirror before putting on their evening gown...

"You may thank me."

"Thank you, Mother dear!" Olguţa could breathe freely now. She thanked her mother for having approved of the dress rather than for the dress itself. One single flaw and the dress would have been taken to the operating table!

"Come over for a kiss, Olguţa!"

Olguţa belonged to Mrs. Deleanu. That was the reward. And on top of it:

"Go to Father and show him."

They crossed each other in the corridor. Olguţa surveyed Dănuţ compassionately.

"You thought I didn't know!"

"Know what?" Dănuţ shivered.

"What do you mean 'know what?' — that you are going to the woods in the buggy."

"What of it? I'm going," Dănuţ broke out, carried away by a first victory.

"Go!... I refused," Olguţa countered sarcastically.

"You refused?" Dănuţ couldn't believe his ears.

"I didn't ask to be taken as you did. I refused to go — because that's what I want."

"Good for you, Olguţa." Dănuţ's thoughts cheered. "I'm going alone! I'm going alone!"

"Of course, if that's what you want," he said aloud ceremoniously.

"And don't be so sure you're going to drive. It's Father that holds the reins. That's what he told me! So you may whistle for it!"

"I see! That is why you refused!"

"Not in the least! If I went, I would have driven the horses. I know how to drive them. Moş Gheorghe said so!"

"Why aren't you going then?"

"Because I don't want to!"

"You don't?" Dănuţ smiled skeptically... " Why?"

"That's my business!"

"Alright!... But I want it!"

"Want what?"

"To go."

"You? Father wants it and that is altogether different!"

"And he won't take you, serves you right."

"Won't take me? I'll prove it to you! And don't you say 'serves you right' again."

"Not in the least! If I went, I would have driven the horses.
I know how to drive them. Moş Gheorghe said so!"

She took hold of his hand and pulled him towards the door of the study.

"What is it, children? Are we going?"

"Papa, you tell him... Didn't you invite me to go to the woods and I refused?"

"Yes, Olguṭa. You are paying visits today. Father will take you there another time. My! My! You're so pretty!"

"You see!"

Dănuṭ was on the threshold.

"You go in the buggy now."

Dănuṭ saw himself outside, standing before a door that had been closed to exclude him.

"You wait! I'll show you!" A Prince Charming in Ivan's knapsack prepared his broadsword to make up for Dănuṭ's humiliation.

***

Moş Gheorghe had prepared as he did for the village dance in his youth, which occasionally jogged his memory when joy found no rest or companion in his aged body. He had dressed up because he was in his own house and because "the old man's lassie" was to visit his house. He put a kerchief over the bowl full of pears picked one by one in the famous orchard of the Oṭăleanca. He took the bowl, went out into the vestibule, and placed it over an upper beam. As if from a rustic censer, the incense burning in the summer sunlight filled the room...

"Umm... There is a nice fragrance of I don't know what!... Where did you hide them, Moş Gheorghe?"

"What am I supposed to hide?"

"Bergamot pears from Oṭăleanca's orchard!"

"Is that so?"

"Of course it is!"

"Of course it isn't!"

"There they are, Moş Gheorghe! How do we take them down? Lift me, Gheorghe because you can't reach them."

Moş Gheorghe spoke to himself. He could always speak with God and with Olguţa. Their voices were company in the old man's loneliness.

There was a bitter thought in Moş Gheorghe's mind: he would not live to see the darling lassie a bride. At such a time Moş Gheorghe would have put on a bridegroom's clothes and from the dickey box would have shouted "Giddy-up, my lads!"

And the horses would have gone at a tremendous trot to fill the lassie's heart with joy. And the lassie would have turned towards the bridegroom to say to him: "That's Moş Gheorghe. He taught me how to drive horses."

And the old man on the dickey box would have smiled and would have straightened himself out: "Just wait!... She'll drive you along too, for the old man's lassie knows how to hold the reins!"

But Moş Gheorghe had one more hidden joy: after his death...

"Again, Moş Gheorghe?" Mrs. Deleanu would reprove him on seeing him standing with money in one hand and his hat in the other hand.

"Again..."

"And what would you have me buy for you, Moş Gheorghe?"

"Outstanding wares, as for gentlefolk!"

"Cotton print — it's good and inexpensive."

"Silk, my lady — it's expensive and beautiful."

"What for, Moş Gheorghe? You have no marriageable daughter."

"Just to have it... The old man knows what for!"

That's how it was every autumn when the family left for the city. Mrs. Deleanu could not understand it. Nor could the Oţăleanca woman — a shrewd, inquiring mind and such a good housewife! From her house fine tissues of every kind went to Moş Gheorghe cottage, being paid for without bargaining.

"For whom are you piling up a dowry, Moş Gheorghe?"

"The old man has someone to pile it all up for."

"Who is that, Moş Gheorghe?"

"It's a pity, woman, you don't weave with your tongue... you would weave a great deal then."

"The Braşov hope chest — a present from the old master — was almost full. That's why Moş Gheorghe did not know that the silks at the bottom of it had split. He did not dare to fumble in the chest with hands that had worked in the stables. He filled the chest, looked, and that was all! It was an account of the chest that Moş Gheorghe had not driven the horses to Iaşi for the last two years."

"Is that possible, Moş Gheorghe? You leave the horses in Ion's care?"

"That is so," Moş Gheorghe had said with a sigh. "But I am old! Death should find me in my home."

During the last two winters, Moş Gheorghe had grieved for his horses and had lighted a fire in his cottage for the chest.

For after his death...

Moş Gheorghe combed his white hair with his hands. He flattened his mustache, went out, and sat down on the porch, his eyes riveted on the gate, like those who know that they will soon go through it for eternity...

***

The buggy stopped in front of the gate which Ion had opened. Ali set off at a run, his tongue lolling.

"Anica! Where's Anica?" Mrs. Deleanu called.

"Anii-caa!" Ion roared as he climbed to the back of the buggy.

"Where are you, Anica?" Olguţa, standing on the veranda steps, yelled.

"Where's Anica?" Profira standing behind Olguṭa wondered placidly.

"Go and fetch her."

"Here I am, madam!" Anica shouted, rushed out of the house like game frightened by yelling hunters.

"Look at me."

"I'm looking, madam," Anica had stopped running and now stood, hips swinging, neck mincing.

"Listen carefully. You are to go to Moş Gheorghe's with the young ladies, and to keep the dogs away from them all the way there."

"Yes, my lady, I'll do that."

The buggy set off. From the steps, Olguṭa watched it ironically until the dust wrapped it up entirely. Monica accompanied it still further, her eyes like those of the fiancées of Norwegian fisherman.

"Let's go, Monica."

"Let's " Monica sighed.

"Let's go!" Anica put in.

"What is it you want?"

"To take you to Moş Gheorghe's."

"You to take me?"

"Madam has ordered it…"

"Ana I order you to dust the house… Come on, Monica!"

"Yes, miss!"

Anica's eyes obeyed Mrs. Deleanu, with a smile for the red dress in the sunlight, but Anica's body pinioned on the steps was preparing to do what the young miss with devilish eyes had ordered.

"Let's have a nap," Profira yawned.

Two pairs of eyes crossed each other with the two-colored dresses as their object: Anica's eyes from the steps and Moş Gheorghe's from the cottage porch.

The blue dress and the red dress put spots of color along the white road. Suddenly, the red dress stopped. The blue dress stood, hesitating. The red dress had left the road and had taken a course through the fields.

The blue dress was pointing her hand to show that the road was a shorter way to Moş Gheorghe's cottage than the field.

Moş Gheorghe smiled.

Suddenly the blue dress ran after the red dress like a blue butterfly enticed by a poppy.

Moş Gheorghe quickly set off for the orchard. He knew from long ago the red dresses never put in an appearance at the gate.

Moş Gheorghe hid in the grass below the tall fence at the bottom of the orchard and waited.

"She'll be dreadfully angry," he mumbled, smiling. "Listen to that!"

Olguţa's voice could now be heard.

"Do you like going in through the gate?"

"Yes, Olguţa, why shouldn't I like it?"

"And why should you like it?"

"How do I know? I've got used to it!"

"That's bad!"

"Why, Olguţa?"

"Because old men alone go in through the gate. I don't!"

"Do you jump over the fence?"

"Of course… But not now because I'd spoil my dress!"

"How do we manage then?"

"I know how."

Moş Gheorghe looked glum.

"Eh!... Impossible!" Olguţa exclaimed.

"What is it, Olguţa?"

"He's stopped it up!...."

"What...?"

"The hole in the fence!"

"Ah!... You see, Olguţa! If we had gone along the road..."

"Yes! Of course! To be full of dust!!... But why did he fix it?"

"I don't know, Olguţa!"

"But I know!"

"Why?"

"Poor Moş Gheorghe! The pigs would get into his orchard. Of course! He had to fix it!"

"My young lady isn't upset!" the old man mumbled in a subdued voice.

"And what are we to do now?"

"We'll go the other way!"

"And get in through the gate!" Monica smiled.

"Rubbish... Through the gate!... We get in where we can get in!"

"A good thing you've fixed the hole up, Moş Gheorghe! I've shown Monica where the pigs were getting in!"

Moş Gheorghe was panting when he rose from the porch steps to meet them.

"I'll unmake the hole! But please come in for a refreshment."

The red dress went in after the blue dress as it is fitting to do for guests.

"You see, Monica, this is green walnut jam."

"I see."

"You see! Eat first and then you'll see!... Leave the tray to me, Moş Gheorghe!"

"Impossible, Miss! You eat and refresh yourself with water..."

"And you won't have any?"

"Thank you, Miss. I'm old. I don't need such things."

"Do you want me to be upset, Moş Gheorghe?"

"Alright, I'll have some."

"Well? Did you see?" Olguţa frowned as she asked Monica the question.

"Very good. Thank you, Moş Gheorghe!"

"There is no such jam anywhere," Olguţa decided, her eyes on Monica.

"Aunt Alice makes very good jams too."

"Oh, if only you knew! Nobody makes a jam as good as this one. I'm telling you!"

Moş Gheorghe passed his hand over his mustache. The cook at the mansion was making his jams.

"Now sit down," Olguţa invited Monica. "This is a "laviţă". Isn't that so, Moş Gheorghe?"

"It is! My young lady knows everything."

"You see, Monica!"

"What a lovely fragrance, Olguţa!"

"Of course, a very lovely fragrance. Of course! Where are they, Moş Gheorghe?"

"What do you mean, my young lady?"

"Don't tell me, I know!"

"What should I tell you?"

"From the Oţăleanca?"

"Oţăleanca?"

Ionel Teodoreanu

"Of course, they're from the Oţăleanca."

Up in Moş Gheorghe's arms, as usual, Olguţa took the bowl down from up in the rafter.

"Of course, Moş Gheorghe alone has such pears."

"Is it Moş Gheorghe that has them?"

"I've been telling you."

"But you were saying they were from the Oţăleanca woman."

"That's got nothing to do with it," Olguţa said crossly.

"They only ripen at the Oţăleanca's!"

"I'll give you a towel so that you don't get messy... they're so juicy."

"And so good!" Monica added as she took a bite with her napkin under the pear.

"And so ripe!" Olguţa extolled them, looking proudly at the drops that had fallen on the towel spread over her dress.

"I picked them one by one." And in a lower voice, Moş Gheorghe added, "A pity they are from the Oţăleanca woman."

"Won't you show her the books, Moş Gheorghe? Monica hasn't seen them! You just wait and see what Moş Gheorghe has here."

"Only some old things, young lady." The old man smiled as he reverently took up the old books arranged on the table under the icon.

"Olguţa, this is from me!" Monica said joyfully on discovering the silk bookmark between the leaves of the book.

"Yes... Moş Gheorghe needed it for the book."

"Grandmother also had such a book!"

"Of course... like Moş Gheorghe."

Olguţa and Monica came close together on the bench. The old Bible opened its smoky leaves equally on the red as well as on the blue dress. Moş Gheorghe sat on a round stool at the girls' feet. The fragrance of the

Bergamot pears floated naturally over the Bible and the silence. Olguţa carefully turned a page. At the top of the following page, the first letter was burning red in a black frame, like a carnation in the pious little window of a monastery…

"You see, Monica? Read if you can."

"Can you?"

"How could I? Moş Gheorghe alone can."

"Do you know how, Moş Gheorghe?"

"I know. These are Cyrillics… It's not difficult!"

"Yes? Cyrillics?"

"Of course, Cyrillics. Very difficult." Olguţa shook her head respect-fully.

They spoke in low voices as one does at the fireside.

"Moş Gheorghe, I should like to hear you read," Monica pleaded with a movement that sent her pigtails to her back.

"Of course. Show her, Moş Gheorghe."

"Let me put my glasses on."

"Grandmother also had glasses."

"Of course, like Moş Gheorghe!"

"Olguţa, it's so pleasant here at Moş Gheorghe's."

"Of course, it is very pleasant."

Moş Gheorghe cleared his throat, sighed, and taking the Bible in his open palms leaned his head back solemnly.

"Isn't Moş Gheorghe handsome?"

"Yes, Olguţa," Monica answered in a whisper too…

"Let's listen to Moş Gheorghe…"

"And his parents went every year to Jerusalem for the feast of the Pass-over. And when he was twelve years old, they went up after the custom of the feast; and when they had fulfilled the days, as they were returning, the boy Jesus tarried behind in Jerusalem; and his parents knew it not..."

The girls, hands crossed over their knees, were listening.

"And when they found him not, they returned to Jerusalem, looking for him. And it came to pass, after three days they found him in the temple, sitting amid the doctors, both hearing them and asking them questions and all they heard left them amazed at his understanding and his answers."

"The dear child!" Moş Gheorghe sighed, his eyes nesting on Olguţa.

"And the doctors had long beards, Moş Gheorghe?"

"Long and white, my young lady."

"And they asked him?"

"And he replied to them all?..."

"He replied to them and he also asked them."

"Of course, Moş Gheorghe... And he confused them?"

"He confused them, my dear young lady. Of course, he did."

"And didn't he pull their beads?"

"He didn't, dear one." Moş Gheorghe smiled.

"That's why they killed him!"

"Yes, they killed him." Moş Gheorghe looked glum.

"Read on, Moş Gheorghe," Monica whispered.

"And when they saw him, they were astonished: and his mother said unto him, 'Son, why hast thou thus dealt with us? Behold, thy father and I sought thee sorrowing.' And he said unto them, 'How is it that ye sought me? Wist ye not that I must be in my Father's house?' And they understood not the saying which he spoke unto them."

"Of course,... Didn't they punish him, Moş Gheorghe?"

"No, my little lady. Punish the son of God?" Moş Gheorghe said in fright, making the sign of the cross.

"But they didn't know, Moş Gheorghe."

"But God knew!"

"…And Jesus advanced in wisdom and stature, and in favor with God and men."

Moş Gheorghe raised his eyes from the Bible and looked at the little girls. His heart was full of happiness. In the old man's cottage, under his eyes, three children grew up together before God, and sheltered from men… And only one of them, the poor thing, was to die on the cross; the Lord's son.

"You haven't shown the fez, Moş Gheorghe!"

"Here is the Turk's fez!"

"You see, Monica, you call this a fez," Olguţa explained.

"I know, Olguţa! Of course, I know! Grandmother had one from grandfather."

"It can't be!"

"Yes, Olguţa! It was like this one: red, with a black tassel!"

"Oh! That one was bought at Constant. I myself had one. But Moş Gheorghe's fez comes from the Turks."

"From the Turks?"

"Is that true, Moş Gheorghe?"

"It is true, young lady. I have it from Plevna."

"Have you been to Plevna, Moş Gheorghe?"

"Of course, he's been. I'm telling you! Moş Gheorghe also has decorations."

"Is that true?"

"It is."

"And is war beautiful, Moş Gheorghe?"

"The devil it is! The horses die, poor things, a pity to look at them; and the men too, poor men! May the devil take it all."

"How come you didn't die, Moş Gheorghe?"

"How could he? You'll make me mad?" Olguţa was indignant.

"I'm alive... Don't be upset, my young lady... But shouldn't we better go into the orchard?"

"Moş Gheorghe, if I were your daughter and I'd be cheeky, would you give me a beating?"

"God forbid!"

"You see, Monica! But why don't you smoke your pipe, Moş Gheorghe?"

"It doesn't smell nice!"

"But it does. I like it... and Monica likes it too."

"Alright. But let me show you something in the orchard."

"Come on, Monica... What are you doing, Moş Gheorghe?" Olguţa had seen the old man reaching for her hat and was alarmed.

"I wanted to give you your hat, lassie."

"Don't touch the hat, Moş Gheorghe!"

"I won't touch it!... But is there a fire in the hat?"

"A fire, that's just it!" Olguţa frowned slyly.

"Shall we go, Olguţa?"

Moş Gheorghe cast a look at the lock of his chest.

"Don't worry, Moş Gheorghe, it isn't unlocked. When will you show me?"

"There isn't much more time to wait, Missy." He smiled, looking into the future.

"Close the door, Monica."

When she was alone, she took the pipe wrapped in blotting paper from under the hat, polished it with her new dress, and looked about the room... Under the icon, at a place of honor, close to the holy books, Moş Gheorghe had placed Olguţa's gift — the box of tobacco. Olguţa lifted the lid, undid the red, sonorous wrapper, pressed the pipe into the fragment layer and closed the lid.

"Moş Gheorghe," Olguţa yelled while spending to catch up with them, "I know why you fixed the hole up."

",?"

"You're pretending, Moş Gheorghe. There is something behind the walnut tree. You wanted to surprise me. I know you didn't stop up the hole because of the pigs."

"What do you mean, Olguţa?"

"Don't you see, Monica? Look at the swing. A swing, Monica! Let's swing! Thank you, Moş Gheorghe."

The Oţăleanca woman had Bergamot pears but she didn't have a swing... Moş Gheorghe lit his pipe and set off for the bottom of the orchard to restore the hole.

"Olguţa!"

"Hush!"

"Olguţa!"

"Are you afraid?"

"I'm not afraid, but..."

"Hold on to me!"

Olguţa was standing on the flying bench, her hands clasping the wooden bars. All the shrill violins of the swing could be heard mewing aloud under her hands. Monica saw the sky and now the earth, now blue, bow green. She put her hands around Olguţa's legs... And the swing squeaked. Up and up again with a little blue angel at the feet of a little red imp.

"Olguţa!"

"Don't be afraid!"

"Olguţa, we're going to fall."

"I won't let you fall."

"Olguţa"

"Don't be afraid!"

"Olguţa, we're going to fall!"

"I won't let you fall."

"Olguţa!"

"Monica!"

Monica closed her eyes. Olguţa's cheeks were burning red.

"Stop it, Missy; you'll get dizzy." The old man brought back the swing from the sky with his strong arms.

"I want to ride, Moş Gheorghe!" Olguţa yelled, putting her foot down on the swing now at rest.

"I'll teach you, but rest a little now."

"It's great but I can't go on!" Monica breathed loudly, coming to life from the darkness of the waves into the light of a haven.

"I'm rested now, Moş Gheorghe. I want to do it again. Join me, Moş Gheorghe."

"Wait, I'm getting down," Monica shrieked.

"And now you'll see what I can do!" Olguţa trumpeted, rising again to the twilight clouds, the same color as her cheeks.

"You're terribly stubborn, Missy!"

Lying on the strip of carpet along the cottage porch, Olguţa was smiling and panting, her head on Monica's knees.

"I can't stand it any longer," she said, breathing hard. "I can no longer stand it! I have to tell you something, Moş Gheorghe, remind me… Put your hand here, Monica!"

"Oh! How your heart is racing!"

With those heartbeats, you could have shaken down a bunch of peonies. Monica's hand went up to Olguţa's forehead.

"Give me some water… lots of it."

"Good heavens no! Do you want to be sick?"

"Give me, Moş Gheorghe! Don't let me down!"

Moş Gheorghe was sighing as he went into the cottage.

"You're terrible, Olguţa!"

"Nonsense!"

"You are. I get dizzy."

"Impossible. That's what you think… I should like to have a big, very big swing. A swing that would take me from here to Iaşi. And then, do you know what I would do? I'd take Moş Gheorghe and drop him at Iaşi."

"You'd take him away from here?"

"When school time begins, not now. And after that I's take the school and throw it into the pond and I'd bring Moş Gheorghe's cottage to the place where the school is."

They kept quiet, each with her own thoughts. Monica imagined a swing that would take her to her grandmother, to heaven.

"Without Dănuţ?"

"Without grandmother?"

Monica looked towards the mansion. Dănuţ should be coming back soon… Joy filled Monica's heart just as a blush spreads over one's face… The swing had gone up to heaven without her.

Olguţa's energetic voice rang out:

"Listen, Monica, I would like to have a swing that would take me from Romania to America. Do you know that the biggest river on earth is in America? I'd bring it to Romania?"

"It doesn't matter. I'd make Moş Gheorghe Emperor over the whole country."

"And you?"

"I'd be the empress. But I'd go up in a swing!"

"What will you do with King Carol?"

"I don't know... I'd turn him into a statue and that will be the end of him!... Moş Gheorghe, you've let me down! Moş Gheorghe, I'm thirsty!"

"Well, here I am!"

Hidden behind the door, Moş Gheorghe lingered; he had waited to allow Olguţa to calm down a bit.

"The water isn't good, Missy. I've left the ewer uncovered and the flies have got into it. It's foul."

"Moş Gheorghe!"

"Believe me, Missy!"

"Moş Gheorghe, don't let me down."

"Some pears, Missy?"

"Are there a basketful!"

"Let's eat them, Moş Gheorghe!"

"That's what I think too!"

"They're delicious!"

"They're so sweet!"

"Better than water, young ladies."

"Water is good too, but it seems that the flies have got into it."

"You can believe the old man."

"You've caught the flies outside, for there are none inside!"

"It is as I said!"

"Let's say I believe you for pears are very good when you're thirsty for water."

"My young lady knows everything."

"What's that noise, Moş Gheorghe?"

"Some children… They're fighting as children will."

"They're fighting, Moş Gheorghe?"

"Oh well, just playing!"

Olguţa jumped up, looked, and rushed to the gate.

"Why are you hitting him? Aren't you ashamed?"

Slightly taller than Olguţa, the two peasant boys were fighting silently, merely groaning. But not far from them, a small boy, with only a shirt on, yelled and whined like a fiddler hired to accompany the fight of the other two.

"And why are you yelling?"

The small boy was silent and passed the back of his palm over his nose.

"I'll show you. Why are you fighting?…"

The two boys gave Olguţa a fierce look like two young bulls facing a toreador.

"Can't you speak, boys, when the young lady asks you?" Moş Gheorghe puts in.

"I hit him!"

"I put him down!"

"What's your name?"

"Ionică."

"And yours?"

"Pătru."

"And you, why were you crying?"

"He's my brother," Pătru explained gloomily.

"And what have you done to him?"

"Tell them to wipe his nose. See what beautiful eyes he has," Monica whispered pointing to two blue eyes and a running nose.

"Do you hear? Wipe your brother's nose!"

"Why?"

"Why is he your brother?" Olguţa asked, scowling to imitate him.

The little one's short was turned into a handkerchief, laying bare a bulging belly.

"Stop crying, little one. And you two come along with me."

"We did nothing wrong!" the boys said in fear, hesitation between the gate and the order.

"Come on! When the young lady tells you to!"

Moş Gheorghe put his hands around their shoulders gently and brought them in. Monica followed, having taken the little one by the hand. They all stopped in front of the cottage porch. Olguţa sat down with crossed legs, Turkish fashion, on the carpet, frowned, and spoke authoritatively.

"Leave them to me now, Moş Gheorghe."

Moş Gheorghe released them gently, pushing towards Olguţa. The little one started yelling.

"You keep quiet! Give him a pear, Monica. And now I'll judge you!"

The boys bowed their heads looking at each other, not moving. Taller than them all, Moş Gheorghe was smiling under his white mustache.

"Who started the fight?..."

"You did, Pătru?"

"I wasn't the only one."

"Tell me why you started the fight."

"Let him say."

"Taller than them all, Moş Gheorghe was smiling under his white mustache."

"You tell me; it was you whom I asked."

"He called me a pig," Pătru mumbled with clenched fists.

"Why did you call me a Jew?" Ionică burst out.

"Because you stole my marbles!"

"Where did you steal the marbles from?" Olguța pursued, making a wry face.

Pătru looked at Ionică. Ionică looked Pătru up and down. The two heads turned towards Moș Gheorghe. Moș Gheorghe met Olguța's eyes and looked down.

"Aha!... So you play at marbles instead of doing good work...."

"How many marbles do you have?"

"I don't have any; he stole them!" Pătru suddenly got hoarse as he flew at Ionică.

"How many marbles do you have?"

"I never counted them."

"How many did you have, Pătru?"

"He knows because he stole them from me!"

"Take out the marbles!"

Ionică turned his head towards the gate, ready to run off.

"Do as the young lady bids you, Ionică. She's your mistress," Moș Gheorghe advised.

Ionică gave a big sigh, raised his shoulders, his waist under the red girdle getting slenderer, and took out a small, knotted bundle — a childish purse — from which came the sound of marbles knocking against each other.

"These are the only ones I have."

"Let me have them."

Ionică's brow creased as if with old age.

"Undo the knots, Monica."

Ionică's eyes were riveted on Monica. Ionică's fists clenched more tightly with every knot that was being undone; no use for the knots of the handkerchief and the lumps in his throat… Pătru took a step aside.

Pătru's brother begun blabbing again.

"Give him another pear, Moş Gheorghe, give him two. To shut him up. Do you hear, boy?"

Monica handed Olguţa the bundle with the motley marbles on her joined palms.

"Go into the cottage and divide them into two portions."

"Don't let her, Moş Gheorghe," the two boys shouted, with one voice, prepared to rush in after Monica.

"You wouldn't dare!"

"So, Moş Gheorghe gave you the marbles!"

"He gave them to us," they declared.

"To you, of course. But why did he give them to you?"

"For us to play with," they said proudly.

"And is that what you did?"

"Of course!"

"Of course?… Did I start fighting or did you? Tell me that!"

Ionică's bare heels dug into the dirt. The big toe of Pătru's foot rose as if at a loss.

"So that instead of playing with the marbles, you stole them from each other!"

"He stole them from me."

"The marbles are mine. Tell her so, why are you lying?"

"You stole them from me!"

"It's my turn to speak now… So you stole them and fought for them… And so, Moş Gheorghe takes back the marbles because you didn't obey him. Is that so, Moş Gheorghe?"

Moş Gheorghe blinked, with three pairs of eves riveted upon him.

"Welll!…" he sighed, his eyes on Olguţa.

"What do you say now?"

Pătru sighed. Ionică scratched the nape of his neck.

"So you're silent. Alright. I will speak now… What grade are you in, Pătru?"

"I don't know!"

"You don't! Ionică will have your marbles if that is so. Tell me, Ionică, in what grade are you?"

"In the fourth," he hastened to answer.

"And am I not?" Pătru quickly put in.

"So you're in the fourth grade, just like me. Good. I'll now ask you a question: the one who answers immediately will get Moş Gheorghe's marbles. Do you hear?"

The boys stiffened as if preparing for a race.

"I'm ready, Olguţa," Monica announced, showing her closed fists.

"I'll be ready too in no time… How much are fifty-three multiplied by seventy-one? Well?"

Big-eyes, Monica, Pătru, and Ionică were looking at Olguţa with open mouths. Moş Gheorghe shook his head in admiration.

"Once three is three. Once five is five." Pătru and Ionică had started reckoning aloud, turning their backs on each other and writing the figures in the air.

"Do you know, Olguţa?" Monica whispered under her breath.

"Do you?"

"Good heavens, Olguța!"

"I don't know."

"Nor do I."

"Do you think they know? The silly things! Look how they rack their brains!"

"If only I had a slate and a piece of chalk!" Pătru complained bitterly.

"I will go to the village and bring back the sum," Ionică offered.

"So you don't know. You're in the fourth grade and you don't know how to do multiplication... You shouldn't have graduated third grade."

The boys listened to her submissively, in fear.

"So I alone know. Now, will you tell me whose marbles are those?"

They sighed, full of bitterness.

"They're mine because I'm the only one who knows. Let me have them, Monica."

"You won't give back the kerchief either?" Ionică asked shyly as if in fear.

"Let him have the kerchief, Monica. And now go! What are you waiting for?"

"Let's go!"

"Pătru, are you going to fight in the future?"

"Why should I fight?"

"What about you, Ionică?"

Ionică gave a sigh that was very nearly a sob.

"Come here!... Come on or I'll get angry."

The boys came nearer, with bent heads.

"Stretch out a hand, each of you!"

Pătru's fist swallowed up the marbles. Ionică looked at them as if saying good-bye to them rather than welcome; his eyes went first to his palm, then to Pătru's fists.

"Give me six pears, Monica."

Monica chose six pears, joined the stems in a bunch, and handed them to Olguţa.

"Here are two pears, Pătru and in future don't be a fool and lose your marbles for Ionică's benefit. And to you, Ionică, I give four Bergamot pears such as you have never eaten before. Put the marbles where they were before — no, I won't take them back from you — eat your pears. And be a good boy or I'll get angry!"

"Thank the young lady, you bears!"

"Thank you, Miss!"

"Thank y... M...!"

"Kiss her hand, for she's done you justice."

The hands of Justice on the porch of Moş Gheorghe's cottage received the kiss of the two litigants.

"Give me your hanky, Monica!"

"Here it is. Why?"

"They've smeared my hand," Olguţa smiled modestly as she came down from her pedestal.

"Anica is coming to fetch you, Missy."

"Anica again!"

"You're asked..."

"I know. What are you doing here?"

"You're asked..."

"I know. Come along with me."

Anica followed Olguţa into the cottage.

"I've lost my hanky. Look for it." Olguța shut the door, leaving Anica inside.

"Lock her in, Moș Gheorghe!"

"When should I release her?" asked Moș Gheorghe, amused.

"When we reach the gate of the house."

"I'll do that!"

"Moș Gheorghe, you forgot to remind me!"

"About...?"

"You see!... Moș Gheorghe, why don't you put carrot slices in the tobacco as papa does?"

"I will do it, Missy!"

"Do put carrot slices because carrots preserve the moisture," she explained seriously.

"When are you coming again, young ladies."

"When you want us to come, Moș Gheorghe."

"Well, I want you to come back whenever."

"We'll be coming tomorrow then."

"I put the fence right as it was, Missies," Moș Gheorghe said, blinking meaningfully.

"The pigs will get into the orchard!"

"Let them. The old man has a swing now."

"There is no handkerchief here, Miss Olguța."

"Look for it!"

Having reached the threshold of the mansion, the red dress and the blue dress signaled to Moș Gheorghe.

"You may go now," Moș Gheorghe said with a smile, releasing Anica.

"Where are the young ladies?"

"Go and look for them. It's your job!"

Moş Gheorghe set off behind them all. It was a clear evening. The evening star shone bright and friendly like the one that had shone over the Bethlehem manger.

Moş Gheorghe looked back. Ox-drawn carts and men with sickles, spades, and axes entered through the gates of village cottages in the evening.

A fairy tale had entered through the gate of Moş Gheorghe's cottage and had left the cottage the same way.

Above Moş Gheorghe's cottage, an angel or a stork said a prayer.

***

"Did you have a good time, Monica?"

"A very good time, aunt Alice. A pity Dănuţ was not with us."

III. Herr Direktor

"Do you hear something, mother?" Olguţa asked as she took a bite from a big plum.

"What am I supposed to hear?"

"Listen intently, mother!"

"Tzz! I can hear Dănuţ slurping the melon and I shouldn't hear him. Only crayfish are eaten that way when you don't know how to eat them any other way."

Mrs. Deleanu would have Dănuţ use a different silencing device for each dish. For which reason, when he felt his mother's eyes looking at him intently that she might hear with them, he would chew the soup and get burnt or would swallow the roast without chewing and choked.

Olguţa signaled to Monica with her foot under the table. Monica sighed neutrally. Dănuţ had only just begun the juicy ridge in the middle of the watermelon. He melted the frozen mouthful between his tongue and his palate, wiped his lips, after swallowing twice, raised his eyes towards Olguţa.

"Why won't you let me eat in peace?"

"Me? Hmm! It's our mother who reproved you."

"Yes, you deafen me with your plums and they don't tell you anything."

Olguța eyebrows rose at an unnatural angle.

"…I can hear you eating every day, as mother says. I'm used to it. We were speaking of other things."

The eyebrows returned to their place. Satanically, Olguța bit noisily from another plum. Dănuț's cheeks took on the color of the watermelon, mimetically it seemed.

"Listen, Papa! Can't you hear?"

They all turned towards the door and listened. Olguța's eyes were screwed up with attention like those of a short-sighted person. The bellowing of the oxen — deep, enormous — resounded, covering the chirping of the crickets and the grasshoppers, just as in church the bass voices cover the fragile murmur of the sopranos.

"Can't you hear, people?" Olguța insisted stubbornly.

"An ox-like oxen!" Dănuț declared sarcastically.

Olguța looked at him, shook her head energetically, and smiled forbearingly.

"Speak nicely, Dănuț. I told you before."

Napkin in hand, Olguța stood up solemnly like the head of the jury about to give the verdict.

"Herr Direktor is coming in his car, I tell you. Who bets on it? Can't you hear! Bah! How do the oxen below? Is that how they do it?" She was consulting Dănuț with due deference.

Forgetful of the melon and the insult, Dănuț rushed out with his napkin hanging from his neck, following by Mrs. Deleanu and Profira.

"I'm sure, Papa. Why don't you believe me?"

"I believe you, Olguța," Mrs. Deleanu said with a smith a smile as he shook his napkin. "You have a musical ear, like your mother."

"Are you making fun of me, papa?"

"No. Olguța, but tell me: how can you tell the sound of a car horn from the cattle's lowing? For the cars in our part of the world can be counted on our fingers!"

"Because I don't like them, Papa."

"You don't say!"

"Yes, Papa, I side with real horses!"

"And not with Grigore? He's a motorist!"

"With Herr Direktor, that's different."

"Who's Herr Direktor, Olguța?"

"Another Papa of yours, Mrs. Deleanu answered her from the threshold."

"You heard what Papa has just said, Monica. You should love Herr Direktor!"

"I don't know him, Olguța."

"What's that got to do with it? I know him. And you're my friend."

"Why do you call him Herr Direktor, Olguța? Is he German?"

"Nonsense! He's father's brother. It's my joke, but he likes to be called that. You should call him Herr Direktor too."

"Is he the head of a school?"

"How can you say that?... I wouldn't stand him if he were."

Seeing the heart of the melon Dănuț hadn't finished eating, Olguța started implanting toothpicks into it.

"He's the manager of a very big company... I don't know of what kind... Something having to do with electricity and with Germans."

"Does he look like uncle Iorgu?"

"No. I don't know who he looks like! He doesn't look like Papa at all... You'll see. I love him."

"So do I," Monica consented diplomatically... "What do you have against Dănuţ's melon?"

"He insulted me. I am taking my revenge."

Like the seven arrows in the Virgin Mary's biblical heart, the symbolic toothpicks wounded the heart of the melon that stood in lieu of Dănuţ.

"A pity for the melon," Monica said, trying to move her to pity.

Another toothpick went deeper into the melon.

"Aunt Alice might get angry!"

Another toothpick followed recklessly.

"Let's go out, Olguţa. I'd like to see the car!"

"You'll see it all right. There's plenty of time. We have an echo at Medeleni, that's why I heard the horn... Monica, I think you are artful!... Of course, like me."

Having achieved her vengeance. Olguţa rounded it off by eating a plum in jubilation.

"Will you allow me to take out the toothpicks, Olguţa?"

"As you wish. I am finished."

Monica weeded the pierced heart of the melon and collected the tooth-picks on her plate.

"Thank you, Monica."

Without any appetite, but enthusiastically, Olguţa ate the melon which Dănuţ had cleared of seeds and Monica of toothpicks.

***

With hearts fraternizing in the same remote geological era, cattle and peas-ants looked upon the scarlet carriage — unheard of, without any horses to draw it — God forgive me! — going uphill at full speed, its belly full of drums beaten by all the devils, squirting out behind a stinking smoke as if from hell — pah! And the Christian fellow inside — God shield us! — instead of eyes has black glasses, like the blind, instead of reins, a wheel on a spit, instead of a whip and of "heigh-ho, beast!" an ox's bellow in his hand.

The peasants crossed themselves, their eyes now on the monster, now on the church. Pressed against their mothers, the children trembled in fear lest — "May-the-cross-kill-him" — it kidnap them, and whined as they spied on the brute with women's eyes.

Moş Gheorghe had seen the unholy things on wheels before. He spat once again: "Poor Master Costache, forgive him! Such a thing to enter his yard!... I'll teach the young lady ride alright!"

The fowls lined up on the road danced before and in the wake of the speeding red thing...

Finally, whirring, roaring, hallowing, wrapped in dust, huge on its pot-bellied wheels, the Moloch of kilometers stopped in warlike fashion before the mansion steps. The dogs were barking and yelping as they did when facing a bear. All the servants were out in the yard.

"Welcome, Grigore!"

"*Guten Tag*, Herr Direktor!"

"Uncle Puiu! Uncle Puiu!" Dănuţ shouted his napkin in his hand like a petition.

Dressed from head to foot in a motorist's armor — round diver's glasses with rims of brick-colored rubber, a duck helmet, and a duck overall hermetically closed at the neck and the wrists — Herr Direktor descended phlegmatically through the door at the back of the car, raising the jointed bench. He stomped his feet to take the numbness out of them, stretched his arms, yawned, uncovered his face, letting the glasses hang from his neck, put his monocle on, frowning, rubbed his hands that had not been touched by the dust or the sunlight... and bent smilingly before the mansion steps, looking like a British admiral careered in a small Danube port.

"It's good to see you!"

The dark glasses had also fallen from the driver's face — on account of Anica. The Berlin mechanic, dispatched together with the car, rounded off the picture. He also had been made in Germany's factory that turned out fair-haired men with blue eyes and Gretchen-like cheeks.

Anica looked down bashfully.

Herr Direktor, holding Dănuț in his arms, became emotional. He seemed to be toasting with a cup of champagne.

"Kulek, dieser ist mein Sohn."

"Und ich bin sein Vater," Mr. Deleanu added modestly, as he came down the steps.

"Das ist guuut!"

Shaken by the giant peals of laughter of beer drinkers, Herr Kulek slapped his knees with his fists, bending and rising as if in imitation of the trepidations of the cars.

"You disgrace me, Grigore," Mr. Deleanu said jokingly as he kissed him.

Mrs. Deleanu protested: "It is you two who disgrace me."

"Aren't you my son, Dănuț?"

"You're a bachelor, Herr Direktor," Olguța called to him from the veranda.

"You're the same little imp!"

"Didn't even greet me, Herr Direktor!"

"My apologies, young lady."

He went up the steps and kissed her hand.

"You can also kiss my cheek, Herr Direktor. I won't object."

He sighed as he took her up in his arms: "Oh! You're very heavy."

"I have got muscles."

"You don't say!"

"Yes indeed! Humpty-Dumpty's fat; I'm sturdy."

"And the young lady here?"

Mrs. Deleanu gave her name, putting her hands on the girl's shoulders: "Monica."

"Monica?"

Mrs. Deleanu looked at him meaningfully.

"Monica is our daughter, just as Dănuț is your son, you dummy of a father!"

"It means that I have yet another niece!"

"And you can be very proud of her!"

"I'm done for! I have prepared for two nephews only. But what a pretty niece I have! Monica, is that it?"

"Olguța," Monica whispered nervously, taking hold of Olguța's hand.

"Will you allow uncle Puiu to kiss you?"

"Of course, as you kissed me," Olguța said approvingly.

"Did you have lunch, man?"

"No!"

"Let's go into the dining room then. You could have let us know, we would have waited for you."

"Impossible! What I want is water."

"Come to the table!"

"Water to wash with, my lady!"

"That's right! I forgot about your habits! Is an hour enough for washing?"

"Where do we bed the German gentleman, madam?" Anica inquired.

"The German gentleman! The German gentleman!" Olguța sang.

"Uncle Puiu, I am going to pour your water," Dănuț said insistently as he brought his suitcase inside.

"Yes, won't you? As if Anica would let you!" Olguța put in.

"I wasn't talking to you."

"You're a servant: you carry the suitcase, pour water, brush clothes... I'm talking to you. Keep quiet and listen."

Dănuț was flushed and limping, carrying the heavy suitcase.

"Do you want me to help you, Dănuț?" Monica begged, catching up with him in the corridor.

"Why do you meddle? Go and join Olguța."

Monica had no idea how rash her proposal had been. Dănuț alone entitled to carry the heavy suitcase, to pour washing water on the big sponge that looked like the tousled head of a fair-haired Hottentot, and also to pour cologne water into uncle Puiu's palms. And it was also Dănuț who brushed his clothes and saw that the trousers were folded neatly at the crease. That was a man's dignified duty and not a servant's job, as Olguța was saying. "Out of envy," Dănuț decided, and yet he felt offended.

"Are you angry, Dănuț?"

Dănuț was returning, now empty-handed, but full of a dignified pride, as if after a feat of arms. He went past Monica without replying, followed by her sad submissiveness.

"Hello, and welcome! I have some sarmale with goose breast filling for you," the flushed cook offered obligingly, coming up suddenly in the wake of Dănuț and Monica.

"Long life to Baba! You've met me with laden arms." Herr Direktor began to count the people on the veranda, Kulek included. "Baba, you have a tip from me: you've made up the big open hand. Nine, Iorgu," he cried out with the visionary eyes of a *chemin de fer* gamester, "No more luck!"

"I prepared everything for your washing."

"Ou-ia-ia You've ruined me! What a luckless family we are, Iorgu!"

"You're telling me!"

"Go out, Profira."

"Is that a way to speak, Olguța?" Mrs. Deleanu said with a frown.

"Mother dear, I've mended Herr Direktor's hand."

"Good Olguța. But it is still a bac for Baba counts for two."

"For four, Herr Direktor!"

"Let's go to lunch!"

"Let's go wash, my lady."

"Wash, and be done with it, man."

"Come on, Dănuț."

"Mind you don't forget to empty the pail," Olguța insinuated into Dănuț's ear. "And don't worry about the melon... I have seen to it."

Freshly cut, number zero, Herr Direktor's round head looked as white as a block of salt. Mrs. Deleanu claimed that it did not seem to be but actually was like a block of salt because of the too generous use of cologne water — torrentially.

"Pure slander!" Herr Direktor protested.

"Where's the proof?"

"The birth certificate, which I don't hide; the monocle which I produce; and my success with... which is well known."

"Aha! Let your hair grow and we'll know them!"

"I prefer to be slandered!"

For Herr Direktor all hair longer than three centimeters could be designated as locks: poetical and consequently baneful, uncivilized and consequently unhygienic, unaesthetic, and unpleasant. He did not even admit hair in the form of mustaches: that calamity for men even when, or especially when, worn by women.

"Herr Direktor, are you going to cut off your wife's hair when you marry?" Olguța asked.

"No — because I won't marry. Umberufen!" he added, knocking on wood as superstitious people do.

"I won't either," Dănuţ said approvingly.

"Cut off your hair then," Olguţa concluded logically and violently.

Dănuţ fell silent. He would even have married if it were a matter of having one's hair cut.

"Who is it?"

Outside the bathroom, Profira introduced herself. "I apologize," she said, "madam is asking if you have been christened..." Feeling that she would burst out laughing, she covered her wicked mouth with her hand. "For if you haven't," she continued, "we should ask the village priest to come over, that's what the mistress said."

"Tell my mistress that a pope will not be enough; she is to send me a deck of popes... That's what you are to tell her."

Dănuţ had in turn poured out water from the big pitcher over the sponge; had turned up an unruly sleeve; had handed out the towel... It was how the time for the cologne water. Dănuţ unscrewed the metal stopper.

"Who is it?"

"The deck of popes or the cartful of popes, as Profira says. May I come in, Herr Direktor?"

"You may not," Dănuţ, the bottle of cologne water in hand, replies.

"I didn't ask you, Humpty-Dumpty!" Olguţa said in a thundering voice.

"Come in, Olguţa. You two are still at war, Dănuţ?"

Dănuţ grew sulky. Olguţa took in everything at a glance and forgot the missed entrusted to her in the dining room.

"Herr Direktor, I'll show you how to use the cologne water."

"Let me see."

"Pour it out," she ordered the humbled cup-bearer.

"Do it yourself."

"You will pour it out for Herr Direktor ordered you to."

"Do it, Dănuţ."

"Do you hear? Pour it out properly; this is serious."

"I would only pretend to pour and would hurt him with the top... or would splash his eyes by mistake." Olguţa thought of plotting vengeance; instead, Dănuţ poured it out angrily but conscientiously.

"First of all, you splash the carpet, Herr Direktor..."

Separating her cupped palms, she rubbed them against each other. Acid drops rained down onto the carpet.

"...After which, you massage your head, from the eyebrows up and groan: ah ah... Do you still have migraines, Herr Direktor?"

"You imp, you'll get to know them."

"After which, dear Herr Direktor, you ask for more Cologne water, for you've used it all by now!"

Dănuţ was looking out of the window, his body a shield for the bottle in his hand.

"Can't you hear? Pour it out."

"Do it Dănuţ; we're waiting for it!"

"Right! And now you put it over your face, sigh, and rub your eyelids... Doesn't it burn you? Fff-haa." She breathed in again and again and sighed as if after a burn.

Dănuţ smiled: "Let her get burnt! She deserves it! Just wait."

Between the lattice of the artful fingers, Olguţa's eyes were on the look-out.

"You needn't rejoice, Humpty-Dumpty. I only pretended."

"And what else do I do, Olguţa?"

"You think I don't know! Let me have the bottle, Humpty-Dumpty."

Dănuț was left empty-handed.

"It is now the turn of the handkerchief, Herr Direktor. I don't have one. Let's say my dress is a hanky."

"Let's say it is… but what will Alice say?"

"Mother will say you're to blame for it."

Cologne water was gurgling over Olguța's dress.

"Grigore, you'll have to cook your dinner yourself!" It was Mrs. Deleanu's voice.

"Come in. I'm finished!"

"What are you doing, Olguța?"

"I had a stain on the dress, mother dear, and Herr Direktor said it would come off with cologne water."

"You're spoiling my children, Grigore."

"You see, Herr Direktor!"

"You better tell me what you will give me for dinner."

"Cologne water… That's what you deserve,"

"I'm sure it's a good dinner then."

"Bucharest has many good things!"

"Things that…"

"What things, Herr Direktor?"

"Dănuț will tell you… in a few years."

"Grigore!"

"I know and I won't tell Humpty-Dumpty."

"Olguța!"

"But I do know, mother dear. You go on shopping sprees in Bucharest."

"Who told you that?"

"You did, mother!"

"Me?"

"Of course. Didn't you say that papa goes on shopping sprees in Bucharest?"

"...I was joking."

"I'm joking too, Mother dear!"

"Aunt Alice, the fried eggs are getting cold," Monica announced from the threshold, looking like a shy page.

"This is the only good child in this house."

Dănuț had been forgotten by everybody. "Just wait, I'll show her" he mumbled as he nudged Monica, who had remained behind them all on purpose.

***

Herr Direktor's eye — the one with the eyeglass — made no difference between beautiful women and fine dishes. It would look at both with the same courteous impertinence while his parted lips seemed to hesitate between words and deeds.

They all sat down at their usual places around the table. In front of Herr Direktor's place setting — the only one on the table — the rosy, golden yoke of the fried egg was smoking; beside them, the sleepy, poetical corn mush seemed to be a Moldavian nickname of the sun; a little farther was the butter tattooed with a spoon and adorned with two violently red radishes, and also some cream with the complexion of a Madonna...

"Approved!"

"Stop approving and eat, man. Is this an hour for lunch?"

"And you, are you to look at me? I won't have it?"

"What will you have us do? Turn our back on you?"

"Herr Direktor's eye — the one with the eyeglass —
made no difference between beautiful women and fine dishes."

"Eat with me… Or else pay for admission!"

"Mother, my idea is that we should have a cantaloupe," Olguța proposed obligingly.

"Hmm?" Mrs. Deleanu consulted Mr. Deleanu.

"Amen. It's a red-letter day today!"

"Bring a cantaloupe, Profira. You see, Herr Direktor, I never let you down."

"That's your way, Olguța: you like to sacrifice yourself!" Mrs. Deleanu said in jest.

"Mother, tell us straight out if you like cantaloupe cooled in the icebox?"

"I like it, of course!"

"We both sacrifice ourselves then."

"Olguța!"

"My dear Alice, everything is good and beautiful in your house, beginning with you! Okay how is it that you…"

"…have any ashtrays?" Olguța finished the sentence, also taking his monocle to better imitate him.

With Herr Direktor the ashtray was one of the plates and the cigarette one of the dishes.

"Take off the monocle, Olguța!... Smoking and more smoking! Is that what you call eating, Grigore?"

"It kills the microbes and helps digestion."

"Put down the ashtray, Dănuț!"

"Let me have it, Dănuț!"

"Don't give it to him."

Olguța pulled the ashtray from a hand that stood in bewilderment between two opposing magnets and slipped it on the table.

"See what Olguţa is doing, mother!"

"Serves you right if you don't obey! And you, Olguţa, why don't you do what mother tells you to do?"

"Did you tell me something, mother dear?"

"I did. And that's enough!"

"Mother, you're only my mother while Herr Direktor…"

"What is he, if you please?"

"He's a guest… and you're the hostess."

"You're sassy!"

Profira was coming in solemnly with the sarmale; in her wake, Anica, the bearer of the cantaloupe as pale and wrinkled as the head of a martyr eunuch.

"Who wants cantaloupe must raise a finger."

Olguţa thrust two fingers toward the cantaloupe.

"You see, Monica, this is jiu-jitsu. Had you been where the cantaloupe is…" Olguţa leaned towards Monica's ear lest Dănuţ should hear too," you would have had to cut off my fingers at the palm, or I would have put out your eyes. That is how you parry. Take it from me!"

Monica raised a crooked finger meaning to take a small slice.

"Not that way. Look at me."

With her palm's edge. Olguţa cleft the air with a curt, cutting move.

Mr. Deleanu bent over the cantaloupe, inhaled its fragrance with closed lips and dilated nostrils, then looked up at the ceiling, waving his hand.

"Tell me the news!... My poor Jews again! The only ones who know how to choose a good thing; as the barrister is so is the barrister's cantaloupe. I'm going to fetch the curacao. Do you feel like a cognac, Grigore?"

"I vote against it! I'm at the second portion of sarmale. After which I'll be dead."

Dănuţ had raised his finger under the tables. What? Were they at school? Of course, he wanted to have some. There was no question about it. He felt he could eat whole melon by himself.

Yellow and scarlet juice was running down from the halved cantaloupe, like jewels from an oriental casket.

"Hmmm!" Olguţa was striking the edge of her plate with her knife in preparation.

Monica's hand, with a fan-like movement, drove away the smell of the sarmale... Dănuţ's moist lips half-opened, melting in his mouth and lungs the wafted fragrance which makes you close your eyes and distends your nostrils and your breast, like the first kiss of fiery virgins.

"Won't you have some cantaloupe, Dănuţ?"

"Of course I will, of course, I will," his thoughts intoxicated with promises ever renewed, clamored.

"No, thank you."

Why? Proud and bitter, he kept silent after that... Why? Because he wanted it so... Why?... Again and again, Dănuţ's lips were Dănuţ's enemies... Why?... Just wait!...

"I'll eat his portion," Olguţa decided.

Dănuţ swallowed hard several times, his eyes on the plate of sarmale — the deuce taken them — his heart at the gate of the lost paradise where Olguţa with teeth and knife was watching.

"Dănuţ, we have no taste for trifles... Keep me company! Sarmale is serious food."

"Yes, uncle Puiu. I feel like having some."

"Good heavens, Dănuţ! How greedy! We've only just finished lunch!"

"Let him eat as much as he wants. At his age..."

Mrs. Deleanu sighed, "Alright, alright! Give him a plate, Profira. And eat nicely, please. At least that!"...

"Humpty-Dumpty! Humpty-Dumpty!"

Olguţa's lips whispered insults as they melted lengthily the unctuous gold which, merely pressed, gushed forth streams of icy honey.

Dănuţ turned his head, crushed a tear between his eyelids, and implanted his fork into the sarmale with the gesture of suicide.

The cool fragrance of the cantaloupe floated above the heat of peppery cabbage, like a rainbow of the fortunate.

***

In the Turkish room, the five divans lined up along walls as thick as those of a citadel were spread with soft carpets made of wool with designs devised in the Orient, where idleness and the odalisques are as lovely as the tales of the Arabian nights.

At the head of each divan, there were little Arab tables with fine inlays of mother-of-pearl with icy gloss. And on each table, unfailingly, there was a copper tray decorated with willowy designs and a hookah with a long trunk for lengthy smoking.

On the floor, a carpet thicker than those on the divans, muting all sound, the sound of the bare-footed gypsy girls of yore who came in to bring to the gentlefolk a read smile bordered by white teeth and rose petal jam between glasses rimmed by the icy water inside. On the walls, panoplies of ancient weapons with scabbards decorated like the sacerdotal attire of metropolitan bishops; icons where brown faces were surrounded with gold and silver, and two portraits in oval frames: the great grandparents of the present-day children in their youth with outmoded garb and locks.

And there was yet another thing in that of the past: a Wertheim wardrobe trunk of the last type. The grandparents might perhaps have frowned on seeing the blemish, and that frown would have brought the hand jars and yataghans hanging on the walls into action... But the Berlin trunk was laden with gifts.

For which reason, in the exotic silence of the Turkish room, the portraits of the ancestors kept their places, waiting for the door to open and for the grandchildren to rush in, for the German trunk to open and for the birth of the children of these days to resound in front of the old days.

Long ago, Herr Direktor newly returned from Germany — with a monocle, completely shaven, hair cut number zero, and decorated with the half-moon of a Schlager scar — had come to Medeleni to visit his sister-in-law and her father, the now-deceased Costache Dusma, looking at him somewhat superciliously after a lunch taken under the walnut tree in the orchard with fiddlers playing and Cotnari wine served.

"In the Turkish room," Herr Direktor had answered, without taking into consideration — perhaps because of his monocle, perhaps because of the wine — the glum look on the face of the venerable old man.

"And what are you going to do with five beds, you pagan? For a glass head, and a glabrous head at that, one bed suffices."

"I'll tell you how things stand, sir. When going to bed in a five-bedroom, and the Turkish room at that, I shall dream I'm a Sultan sleeping in my harem. And it will be five! And on waking up in the morning mindful of the five burdens to carry as my dream would have it, it will be still better on seeing the five empty beds. And as long as I shall be at Medeleni, I'll thank you, sir, on going to bed and on waking up, as I would my God."

"This German fellow is no fool! Let another bottle of Cotnari be brought over. And you will sing a Moldavian song! Well said, German! You're still a Moldavian inside."

Ever since, the Turkish room, which nobody entered, had been Herr Direktor's room. The master's words were law in the old house.

***

Her head resting on the divan, Olguța turned a somersault and yet another, prepared to go on endlessly.

"What does this mean, Olguţa?"

"Somersaults, Mother dear," was the reply of the head rolling on the divan.

"Get down, please."

Olguţa began smoking a hookah.

"Olguţa, be quiet!"

"Shall I help you, Herr Direktor?"

"Impossible! A woman's hand in my chest!"

He had only just unfastened the trunk. On his knees in front of it, he pulled out the drawers one after the other. A punctilious and strategic order reigned in Herr Direktor's chest. With his eyes closed, Herr Direktor could have put on his dress coat, picking out the things needed one after the other and could have immediately undressed to put on his pajamas, his dinner jacket, or his coat.

Mrs. Deleanu was also skillful in packing chests. Hence a rivalry.

"It isn't difficult to be tidy with such a chest!"

"With such tidiness, any chest is at its best."

"Holy modesty!"

"Holy justice!"

Dănuţ's heart was racing, choking him. He kept rubbing his hands like a baccarat gamester who had put down his last penny. He had forgotten about Olguţa and everything else. Overwhelmed by the presentiment of the gifts, he was suffering... And they couldn't stop talking!... Before receiving the gifts joy turned into torture and was no longer joy. It was the same as when there were too many delicious things on the table. For example, black caviar, dry mutton sausage, pickled olives... and whipped cream cake to end up with. His greed exalted him so that he no longer felt like eating anything and ate as if in disgust but a great deal so as not to be sorry later on...

Monica knew how to organize her suitcase with her things and the dolls' dowry. But could a small room compete with a palace?

"It's like a show-case, aunt Alice."

"Good, Monica! Have you heard, Grigore? That's a good portrait of your order: mere bluster!"

"Envy interpreting the praise of sincerity! That's a portrait as well, isn't it? Thank you, Monica. I'll start with the old people. Here you are Alice, a pair of glasses for a venerable coquette!"

"You dare! Aah! A face-a-main! Thank you, Grigore. Didn't forget!"

"Like chest, like head: what gets into it never goes out of it — except when needed!"

"Napoleon!"

"...of the chests, yes. And here is your music."

"Bach?"

"No idea! I bought what you told me to buy. Bach or stockings, it's all one to me — with a slight preference for stockings. Oh! A good thing I'm out of trouble: the music gave me sick headaches."

"It must have been a different music... lighter... more Berlin-fashion!"

"That's the music that cures sick headaches!"

"The sick headaches of your head!"

"What did you say, Iorgu?"

"I regret the bachelors' headaches, dear brother... I've been left with the others... and with pyramidon."

"A nice thing to say!"

"And with Minerva, dear Alice."

"Who's Minerva, papa?"

"A lady, Olguţa."

"What a name!"

"Specific to ladies!"

"Of course, papa."

One by one, the parcels, half-unpacked by Mrs. Deleanu, were being arranged by Monica on the nearest divan. A childish excitement grew in all those present, as it does below the eaves of the houses when the birds come in spring. Dănuţ alone, hands deep in his pockets, was sullen as if shivering with cold.

"Do you remember, Iorgu, when father returned from the proceedings of the law courts in the counties?"

"Poor father! I seem to see him. Before he even took off his coat, he would call us to his study: "Have you been good, children?" — "Very good!" we would answer before mother could have her say. The only occasions when I passed for a good boy... Two tin pistols with capsules..."

"...little mint fishes..."

"...balloons, specially made for mother's ears... Do you remember, Grigore, the two lions' heads on the back of the armchairs?"

"How could I forget? Father told us they bit to frighten us and you put a bit of raw meat in their mouths to tame them. Do you remember? The meat was there a long time."

"Poor father!... Where does the bad smell come from, boys? How could the poor old man imagine that the wooden lions had become carnivorous?"

"Had the meat gone bad, papa?" Olguţa asked, her eyes sparkling with pride as she gained insight into her father's past pranks.

"Yes, Olguţa," Mr. Deleanu said with a smile. "I seem to see mother, her glasses on the nose, inspecting below the cupboards, under the desks, under the carpet... Looking at our soles — nothing!"

"And you kept silent, Papa?"

"What was I to do? I kept silent."

"And uncle Puiu didn't tell on you?"

"Treacherous brothers? Impossible."

"And what happened?"

"Mother ultimately discovered our doings! She had a nose for them! When I began to smoke — I was in the fourth grade at secondary school — I would eat a whole lemon and run about in the open air, open-mouthed and would still detect it."

"Did she thrash you for the rotted meat?"

"She couldn't catch me. I climbed on the roof and threatened to jump down unless she forgave me."

"Iorgu!" Mrs. Deleanu reproved him.

"Yes. I was like Olguţa when a boy!"

"Now also, Papa!"

"Olguţa!"

"Now, you are like me," Mr. Deleanu sighed.

"Tell us about other things that father did, Herr Direktor."

"He did what you do: annoyed mother... Poor father! When you think that out of his small salary — the salary of an honest magistrate — he managed to set money aside for gifts... and for studies in Berlin..."

The monocle had fallen from Herr Direktor's eye giving way to a look of remembrances.

Olguţa was thoughtful. She sat down on the edge of the divan. "Poor Moş Gheorghe!"

"Will you give me the scissors from the dressing case, Dănuţ?"

"What do you have there?" Mrs. Deleanu asked.

Herr Direktor put his monocle back.

"A surprise!"

"Tell us what?"

"The scissors are the first to have the floor."

"Dress materials?"

"Tzzz..."

"Sweets?"

"No."

"Books?"

"What kind?"

"I'm doing the asking. It's your job to answer."

"No use. You won't guess!"

They had all gathered around the mysterious parcel and were looking at it, frowning. Herr Direktor caressed the unrevealing paper.

"I can tell you that it comes from over many lands and seas; that it is of the neutral gender — I don't understand this; that it is grey on the outside and red inside; that it is smooth to the touch; that it's full of dainty birds which have the great quality of keeping quiet; that those they come from are ye... are pale; and that it will be fashionable."

"Eh!"

"That's all there is to it. More poetical it can't be. Guess now!"

"Be more specific!"

"What else can I tell you?... That they drink a great deal of tea in the country it comes from."

"Russia?"

"They drink vodka there."

"England?"

"You're a long way off!"

"Oh! You're unbearable with..."

"...your gifts," Herr Direktor put in.

"With your riddles!"

"My dear, a gift without an enigma is like a virtuous woman: of no interest."

"Grigore!"

"You are interesting from another standpoint."

"Here it is, uncle Puiu."

"My dear Dănuț, you've brought me my nail clippers! I've asked for the scissors!"

"Don't be finicky, Grigore. Have done with all these subtleties."

"Alright, you'll pay me for the clippers!"

"I'll pay."

Herr Direktor cut the string leisurely, made a ball of it, took off the wrapper, uncovering another paper, folded them both…

"It's a hoax!"

"As you will…"

"I believe you, Herr Direktor!"

"The kingdom of heaven will be yours. Look up. One — two — three."

Having been thrown up in the air, the Japanese kimonos unfolded and fell, with gold and red glints, like strips cut from the sky of Japanese legends.

Mrs. Deleanu, now of the same age as Olguța and Monica, knelt on the carpet to bend over the wonder.

"We're rid of the women, Iorgu. It's your turn now. With the children at the end. Fff…! It is hot!"

"Take off your coat, man!"

"May I, great lady?"

"After such a surprise, you may do anything."

"Here you are, Iorgu; genuine oriental cigarettes. They're excellent. And because there is not filter on them, I've brought you a cigarette holder!"

The amber cigarette holder, as yellow and solid as if had been cut out of the head of a pineapple, brought to Mr. Deleanu's face the smile one has to stand before a Christmas tree.

"Herr Direktor, I should like to tell you something."

"At your disposal!"

"No. Into your ear."

"Here is my ear."

"Herr Direktor, I hope you won't mind. I should like to let Monica have my kimono. I like it very much, you know, but it seems to me that she likes it even more."

"Come here for a kiss, golden mouth!"

"A kiss from me also, Herr Direktor."

"Don't you think I've forgotten you, Olguța! It's the children's turn now. The kimonos were for the ladies."

"Please give it to her, Herr Direktor," Olguța whispered. "I don't feel I should, you know!"

"Let us finish with the nuisances," Herr Direktor began covering the lower drawer with his hand. "Are you a lady, Olguța?"

"No, Herr Direktor."

"Good. You're in my lot... So the kimonos are for the ladies... You don't mind, Monica? Let's see how it suits you. One of them is smaller, that one is yours... Hocus-pocus-fillipus!"

With surprising dexterity, Herr Direktor transformed Monica in no time.

"Let me see... Oh! The Japanese ladies are lovely! I'll move to Japan!"

"Put your plaits out, Monica. That's it. Come to me for a kiss!"

"What about Olguța, aunt Alice?... I won't have it that way," she whispered in Mrs. Deleanu's arms.

"Don't worry, Monica. Olguţa has plenty of things."

"Thank you, uncle Puiu."

"Hop-la!"

Herr Direktor took her in his arms and sat her on the divan, taking a step back and looking at her up through his monocle.

"Change her hairdo, Alice. Let us make a genuine Japanese girl of her... Japan deserves it!"

"Don't you want me to, Monica?"

"Yes, aunt Alice," Monica answered. The kimono had taken her to the land of dreams.

"You must be up to the standard of the kimono, Alice, - and of the European, you have in hand."

"With such hair, it's not difficult."

"And now I'm going to open the toy bazaar! Away with the old!... We begin in the order of age. Dănuţ is the oldest. Here is a shotgun for you, Dănuţ. It is two years younger than you: nine calibers. And here is a box of cartridges. And the cartridge pouch."

A real gun! A real one. He had not expected such joy. Like a drummer in the days of Napoleon, Dănuţ's heart beat hymns of glory. Olguţa was looking at him, waiting for it.

Meeting her look, Dănuţ turned his eyes towards the window, made a tour of the ceiling, and gripped the gun tighter. Olguţa's eyes seemed to be a bugger caliber than the gun.

"Look at it, if you want to, Olguţa."

A silent Olguţa took the gun from Dănuţ's diplomatic hand into her warlike hand. The gun had become international.

"Dănuţ! Dănuţ! Dănuţ, once more!... Haven't I favored you by any chance?" One by one, the parcels were flying onto the third divan.

"And now it's Olguţa's turn. Here are riding boots and riding trousers. Your mother will make you a blouse and your father will give you a horse."

"Oh my! Kid boots!" Mrs. Deleanu marveled while fixing Monica's hair.

"What would have you? For such a gazelle!"

"Herr Direktor!..."

"Olguţa!... Help, good people! A tigress, not a gazette!" Dazed as he was by Olguţa's kisses, Herr Direktor was groaning.

"Look at this, Herr Direktor."

Olguţa took the boots in her arms and kissed them reverently on each side, as the fighters of long ago kissed their weapons.

"Wait, I haven't finished! Here are two paddle balls, a soccer ball, and more things..."

Other parcels flew, which Olguţa and Dănuţ ripped open feverishly.

"What do you say to this?" Mrs. Deleanu asked, drawing aside from Monica with studied leisureliness.

Pink, as if covered with vaporous coral, Monica sat cross-legged on the divan, her eyelashes half-covering her eyes, her shoulders bent, and her hands in the wide sleeves crossed on her knees. Shyness and the kimono had inspired the narrow gestures of the Japanese. Her abundant golden hair had been gathered in a Japanese bun kept together by Mrs. Deleanu's hair combs... Rosy dawn, with a young peach tree in bloom and on the topmost a golden bird of paradise, wrapped by the god of orchards in a little girl's kimono to keep the cold of the night out — the dream of a Japanese poet in love with peach-trees. Such was Monica — a vignette at the beginning of a legend.

"Wait a bit, children. I had forgotten. Open your mouths and put out your hands."

Herr Direktor quickly opened a little cardboard case. He rolled up his sleeves like a surgeon and thrust his hands into the case.

"Va banque!"

Plums, cherries, apricots, greengages, peaches, pears, apples, walnuts, radishes, hazelnuts, carrots, onions, chestnuts, almonds... of hard candy fell, jumped, rolled like a humorous hail of fruit and vegetables made of almond paste.

"Catch that, Papa!"

"Go after it, Olguța!"

"It hurts, Herr Direktor!"

The anarchical spirit of disorder, paradoxically arising from the trunk of perfect order had entered the Turkish room. Lying on the floor, grown-ups and children picked up the goodies for fear of treading on them.

Olguța with a carrot in her mouth like a clown's nose; Dănuț with cheeks swollen by the peach in his mouth; Mrs. Deleanu biting into a harmless onion; Monica getting entangled in her kimono and making graceful bows to the fruits as if to some dainty deities; Mr. Deleanu tripping Olguța; and Herr Direktor looking on like a delighted conjurer.

"Water for heaven's sake! I'm melting."

"What we need now is a shower. We're all mad!"

"Who's there? Come in."

Profira entered the room, blinked foolishly, and stood open-mouthed... amidst the natural peals of laughter of those on the floor.

"This is a German onion, Profira. Taste it," Olguța ordered, pelting her with onions.

"Eat, Profira! Just to see what onions are like over there," Mrs. Deleanu insisted.

The onions were wrapped in yellow tissue paper that imitated the skin. Profira took the onion and turned and twisted it with an eye to the children's disquieting smile.

"Cross yourself and eat," Olguţa advised, seeing her hesitation. "Come on, Profira. Say God help me!"

"Shall I peel it, madam… It's a tricky thing!"

"Why make such a wry face? It's as if you'd never seen an onion before!"

Profira made the sing of the cross inside her mouth with her tongue, her nostrils quivering with fear.

"Pah!" She spat into her apron, rubbing her tongue with the back of her palm.

"You've got poisoned."

"God shield us! It's medicine, madam!"

"German onion, Profira!"

"Let them keep it! I can do without it!"

"Run along and bring some water to drink!"

A carrot flung by Olguţa expulsed her. Mrs. Deleanu rose to her feet and turned into a severe housewife again.

"Gracious me! The mess we've made of this room! It's like an Istanbul bazaar."

"Let me make a turban for you, Herr Direktor," Olguţa pleaded, invented another means of prolonging the disorder.

"From what will you make the turban?"

"I'll make one with a towel."

"Approved. Let me have a shawl as well then!"

"Do you know what?" Mrs. Deleanu, distracted by the excitement again, put in, "Let's all put on a fancy dress. As each of us desires. A free hand to everyone's fantasy!"

"I'll remain as I am, aunt Alice," Monica pleaded.

"Of course, you're already dressed up. I'll be Japanese too."

"What about me, Mother?" Dănuţ asked.

Mrs. Deleanu was pondering as she put on her kimono.

"You..."

With a strange blandness in her voice, Olguţa chipped in: "He has the Japanese suit, Mother dear."

"I don't want it. Why do you meddle?"

"A good idea! Of course. You've got Kami-Mura's suit. Go and put in on."

"Why, Mother?"

"Because I'm Japanese and so is Monica."

"But Monica has a beautiful dress," Dănuţ mumbled.

"I believe you. She's a young lady. You're a valiant soldier."

"Yes, with shabby clothes!"

"Don't spoil my good mood, Dănuţ. Go and dress. That's what I want to do."

"Without my rifle?" Dănuţ was still gloomier at the thought.

"With rifle and big guns if you want. Come on, quick."

"Suggest something for me as well, Alice."

"You... You and Grigore are Turks. More precisely you are a Pasha and Grigore is the eunuch in your harem."

"My dear Alice, did you have a Mongolian ancestor."

"...?"

"Look into the mirror. You're a genuine Japanese."

The new hair-do, the dark hair, the eyes a little far apart and the dark paleness of the opal cheeks were all an exotic addition to the kimono.

"Who knows?" Mrs. Deleanu answered, smiling.

"Look!" Olguţa invited them with a dramatic gesture.

With a towel as an improvised turban around his head, Herr Direktor looked like a musical comedy Indian. The Turkish shawl on his shoulders could not neutralize the European effect of the monocle and of the smile that went with it.

"Ho-ho-ho! Look at Humpty-Dumpty!"

"Kami-Mura."

"Bravo, Kami-Mura, you're just right!"

Dănuț withdrew into a corner, hugging the wall. He dragged the rusty, clinking little sword like a shameful six-year-old, but Dănuț was eleven. The cap was too small, emphasizing the wavy circumference of the head which wore it dejectedly.

"Coffee and Turkish delight is all I need now. I have a hookah, a harem, and a eunuch," Mr. Deleanu exclaimed.

"You're Nastratin Hogea, Papa."

" I'm honored… And you, Olguța?"

"I'll put on my boots and riding trousers, turn into an outlaw and kidnap Monica."

"I was expecting that!" sighed Mrs. Deleanu for the future rather than the present. "Go and put them on."

Profira entered with the jam tray.

"Holy Moses!"

"Have we frightened you, Profira?"

"I didn't recognize you, madam."

"Why do you laugh, Profira?" Mrs. Deleanu asked, realizing that the tray was jeopardized by the volcanic upheavals of big-bellied mirth....

"Tell us, Profira."

"You won't mind, madam? It's so beautiful! Like a show at the fair."

"Well said, Profira!"

"Long life to Profira!"

"Let us drink a glass of water in honor of Profira."

"Long life to you and may you always be merry!"

"Don't you help yourself, Dănuț!... What is it you want here, Anica?"

"Ha, ha!"

In the doorway, Anica was nothing but eyes and a big smile as she took in and marveled at everything she saw. And over her shoulder, the cook's head appeared — a humorous moon with a mouth going from ear to ear.

"What is it? Have you come for the show?"

Anica and the cook, a soprano and a baritone, gave a simultaneous laugh.

Profira echoed it, looking towards them.

A whip cracked. The cook turned around, Anica took to her heels. Over the threshold now free, Olguța jumped into the room, whip in hand.

"What did you do, Olguța?"

"A mustache, mother dear. Every outlaw has one."

The soot mustache decorated the frail face of a diminutive outlaw of the kind found in folk ballads:

> His small mustache,
> A raven's feather.
> His dear eyes,
> Wild blackberries,
> His dear face
> The milk's froth.

The kid boots, the baggy trousers, and especially the red blouse with a patent leather belt were poetic licenses. Olguța might go her outlaw way amid the flowers of the riverside invaded by the poppies of Moslem fezzes.

"I vote we turn ourselves into serious people again."

"Why, Herr Direktor?" Olguța reproved him.

"I can't stand the Turkish heart."

"Olguța might go her outlaw way
amid the flowers of the riverside invaded by
the poppies of Moslem fezzes."

"Wait! Don't take off your fancy dress. I've got an idea!"

"Out with it, Mother dear, out with it!"

"Let's take a snapshot!"

"A snapshot. That's it!"

"Alright, my dear. For the children's sake, I'll do anything."

"Raise the blinds... I'll bring the camera!"

"How shall we arrange ourselves, Iorgu?"

"Why arrange ourselves! We'll stay where we are!"

"Where are you going, Dănuț?" Mrs. Deleanu asked when she met him in the corridor, sword, and cap in hand....

"Come back, Dănuț!... Or I'll be cross. And put everything on again."

Once again rallying to the armies of the ridicule, Dănuț walked on, driven from behind by his mother and the cursed camera within which the shame of the present moment was swallowed as if by a huge blotting paper, and to spread to the future.

"Join us, Alice!"

"And who will photograph you?"

"You set the camera up; Profira can do the rest."

"The idea! She will never touch the thing. She's afraid."

"Let's ask Kulek over," Herr Direktor suggested. "He knows all the ropes."

"Alright, you ask him over, Olguța."

"What shall I say, Herr Direktor?... Komen sie, Herr Kulek... nach Herr Direktor? Is that right?"

"Tell him that, Olguța. He'll come laughing. Don't mind him."

"Now sit down," Mrs. Deleanu directed. "The Turkish brothers one beside the other on the divan. That's it... Why don't you cross your legs in Turkish fashion, Grigore?"

"Here you are. Is that right? Like a Turk!"

"Monica, you sit down at the foot of the divan as you set a little while ago... Bend your head... just a little. Sit down by Monica, Dănuţ... Brr! You do look fierce! A genuine samurai!"

"Kuss die Hand, gnadige Frau. Was woollen sit, Herr Direktor?" Herr Kulek was somewhat bewildered.

"Explain please, Grigore... Olguţa, you should sit on Monica's right. That's it."

Mrs. Deleanu sat down at the foot of the divan with the children.

Mr. Deleanu turned up his mustache.

"Ruhig bleiben, bitte shon."

From the corner of her eyes, Olguţa was looking ironically at Dănuţ. Monica was looking at her sleeves, but below her lashes, she could see everything.

Breaking all records in frowning, Dănuţ turned his head from the lens, leaving to posterity the profile of a Japanese admiral with girlish curls, who prepared fierce revenge on the Japanese girl with the fair bun, protected by the smile of an outlaw with a soot mustache.

***

Mrs. Deleanu on the veranda steps spoke pointedly, trying by her serious tone to make for the lack of seriousness of her hair-do and kimono.

"Grigore, I hold you responsible! Keep Olguţa in check especially... And don't forget the bet."

Olguţa had kept the outlaw costume on, but had washed off her mustache with cotton soaked with Cologne water.

"Mother is afraid, Herr Direktor. Not like me."

"You don't say!"

"I'm serious, Herr Direktor!"

"She's afraid for you, Olguţa."

"It is all the same!"

"You'll change your mind!"

"Me? No way!"

"You. I've also changed my mind since I've had nephews."

"You're not afraid, Herr Direktor."

"I am, when necessary,... prudent."

"What does prudent mean?"

"Courage by the spoonful."

"Like a medicine."

"That's how one should be."

"I do not need it. I'm in good health."

"Why do you irritate your mother, Olguţa?"

"Because she's my mother, Herr Direktor."

A few steps ahead of the others, his gun pointing down as hunters carry guns, Dănuţ was leading his armies to battle. The hosts behind Dănuţ's imagination were never-ending. They began where the sun rises, went up and down the hills far away, spread over the plains, and only the head of those armies caught up with the valiant emperor in front, whose steps were in pace with those of the armies that followed him silently, submissively, like a giant train.

The army following Dănuţ's was made up of Herr Direktor, Olguţa and Monica. For the hunting expedition, the children had been pardoned the ritual sleep that day and Herr Direktor had put on a light-colored silk costume and had donned his colonial helmet. He had his never-failing gloves on, fully buttoned. Herr Direktor preserved the whiteness of his hands which were looked after like the hands "of..." Mrs. Deleanu said.

"Of what, mother?"

"Of a lady. That was what mother meant and could not find the word."

"Thank you, Grigore. You found the word more easily than I."

"It finds me!" Herr Direktor had smiled modestly.

"You're ridiculous, Grigore. Look! My hands are darker than yours. Sunlight means good health. Such silliness in a man!"

"My dear Alicia, I like gypsy women's hands because they're thin and dry and not because they're dark. Your sunlight I can do without. I get burned in playing cards and that's enough for me."

Monica was walking beside Olguţa. In her heart the birds embroidered on the kimono swung on a branch in bloom, sheltered from guns and hunter's eyes.

...Guided by their emperor, the armies of Dănuţ's imagination were on their way to kill a monster guarded by dragons. Dangers were lurking at every turn. The monster could steal the sun and throw the night in the way of the invaders like a thick wood. The emperor didn't care. He set the wood on fire?... Ali ran in front of Dănuţ, tail bumptiously twisted up, like a rustic mustache.

The emperor's dog had magical powers. He could grow to the size of a cow; could turn into a winged stallion that nobody dared a touch... yet still it obeyed the emperor like a dog.

The monster had dragons at the gate and a fearful mace on a peg... What of it? The emperor had a gun... Let the monster come forward!... In his cartridge box, the emperor held death for a hundred monsters and as many dragons... Herr Direktor kept the cartridges, but the monster couldn't know that.

The army behind Dănuţ — Monica excepted — was on its way to kill a legend and to win a bet on the occasion of the hunting inauguration of Dănuţ's gun.

The origin of the legend? In Costache Dumşa's house, Fiţa Elencu, his elder sister many years older, had for a long time played sultan over everyone and everything.

An ill-favored scion of a good-looking family, Fiţa Elencu was repulsive to her whole family at the turn of the century. But nobody dared even think of it for her green eyes, as green as venom, could see beyond the foreheads that bent before her. As intelligent as she was ugly, her malice exceeded the two of them added together.

When she left for Medeleni in her coach, accompanied only by books in various languages brought from abroad, the Iaşi of the gentlefolk, rid of the red-green enslavement of her tongue and eyes, sighed a sigh of relief. On the other hand, calamitous days began at Medeleni. Fiţa had been in Mrs. Deleanu's childhood and youth what locusts arc to fields of grain. A boyar of the old days had described her as a killjoy and her many daughters-in-law could not live in the same house as Fiţa Elencu. In the house of Costache Dumşa, she had lived also after his death.

A secret that has been whispered for a time and had never been repeated after, had been buried together with the youth of the then old maid. A love-affair... Was that possible?... A young man in love with Fiţa Elencu... Hardly within the bounds of possibility. Then he had an affair with a well-built gypsy girl of Medeleni. Boating on the pond, somebody drowned... Fiţa Elencu alive and a widow... A gypsy slave scourged until her body had taken the scarlet hue of her sinful lips, a hue that drew green flies, like Fiţa's eyes.

The old peasants said there was a curse on the pond.

Fiţa Elencu had a single weak spot nobody knew of Olguţa. The dark eyes of the five-year-old little girl did not drop before her green eyes. Spared by old age, the green eyes often watched the brown locks and the low, determined brow as if they were an inscription that had not yet been construed. Soon, however, an incident that had never before occurred in Fița's long life had cast its light over it.

The only teeth that old age had deprived Fița Elencu of were those grown from her gums. For Fits wore dentures. At the noonday meal, before all those seated at the table, the valet would bring the white teeth as stiff as the grin of a vampire in a blue goblet full of water.

"Naturalia non turpia."

Everybody kept silent. They all lost their appetites.

One day, Fița Elencu began a fast that lasted for more than two months — and possibly hastened her exit from the world — because her denture had been swallowed by the pond.

The valet had come with an empty goblet. He was as pale as if he had been bringing his heart in the toothless goblet.

"I have thrown them into the pond," Olguța had said bluntly, in a silence that was similar to the silence of a town buried under lava.

"Let a glass of milk be brought to my room. And you, my girl, you will come to my room after you've had your meal."

Olguța had not lost her appetite. On the contrary, she had recovered it with the disappearance of the teeth. After dinner, she had entered Fița's room banging the door ostentatiously.

"Here I am."

Fița had looked at her for a very long time, putting all the power of her eyes and mind into it, which caused Olguța to grow tall in the future, very much as a seed sprouts in the hand of a fakir.

And for the first time in their life, the toothless lips had kissed Olguța's flaming cheeks with a kind of acrid affection.

From that moment, Fița Elencu had begun to hope that another Fița Elencu had emerged in her family of weaklings. She had made Olguța her heiress.

As a reward, after her welcome death, Olguța had given the name of the defunct lady to a strange frog.

From father to son, the villagers of Medeleni had said that there was a curse on the pond and that Fița Elencu... After Fița's death, the peasants said, an inordinately big and audacious frog had made its appearance in the pond. It was a toad, of course, which lorded over the others just as green-eyed Fița had lorded over everybody. An order, a rash order, had slipped from Moș Gheorghe's lips: Olguța was to be kept away from the accursed pond. Olguța had begun to hunt the Fița in the pond where the denture of the other Fița gleamed. Her sling had been no use; nor had the skill of the hunters come from elsewhere.

The whole village now knew that Fița Elencu had turned into a be-witched toad. And, sheltered by the legend, the frogs multiplied to their hearts' content for nobody disturbed them; they abused the Lord's beauti-ful sights with increasingly load voices, the big toad among them, like an inexhaustible, diabolical cup of venom.

...They were getting near it. The pond, as lonely as if in the moonlight, gleamed freakishly in the slanting sunbeams. It smelt of mud and a rotting coolness.

...The emperor turned into Dănuț again, for Dănuț knew the legend and did not fancy facing the pond that everyone shunned by himself. He raised the gun, pointed it at the sky, and waited until the others had caught up with him. Then he set off alongside them, getting rid of the gun. It's not advisable to antagonize Fița Elencu. It's different if you're only an onlooker. Uncle Puiu doesn't mind.

Like thousands of bags of walnuts that were being shaken, the frogs' croaking sounded from among the reeds. The uproar grew pathetically. The croaking was unleashed more passionately, interrupted by lamenta-tion, moaning, and wailing — like the chanting in a synagogue.

Frogs with open mouths and astronomic eyes sat on the shore looking at the starless sky… Ali's yelping startled them without disturbing their sloth or the slothful spread of the mud.

"We must wait, Herr Direktor. You'll see her soon."

"Do you know her, Olguța?"

"Of course. I can't stand her. She's so sassy!"

"Don't worry, Olguța. I'll bring her to heel."

Herr Direktor's monocle lay in wait for Fița Elencu. Likewise a loaded gun. Moreover Olguța's sling.

When they got near them, the frogs were found to be soloists. Their aquatic barks did not gush forth volcano-like from the crater of the setting sun or the wistful paleness of the moon; it came from a flabby and scabby body, as if from a verminous old woman.

"Maybe it comes up somewhere else, Olguța."

"No, Herr Direktor, I'm telling you no. That is her throne."

Olguța's hand was thrust forward hostilely as she pointed at a willow stump that rose above the water, much farther from the shore, as if for a purpose. With a mane of duckweed, the stump looked like the body of a beheaded horse, stopped halfway on his onrush, its hooves in the water, and struck stone-still.

They lay in wait. Herr Direktor lit a cigarette. Olguța tried her sling, stretching it with a graceful gesture. Monica was listening to the mosquitos whose nearby whizzing was like the drone of thousands of violins in the sky, or so it seemed.

A male frog mounted a she-frog and together they threw themselves into the nuptial water where a quivering silver ring arose. Other frogs sprang from the water, went through the mud in elastic spurts, and then stood motionless, kneeling as if in sudden ecstasy.

From the gentle ripples, head with the bulging eyes of the drowned rose and sunk again.

Slowly, very slowly, the sun — red, round, and big — got ever farther from the pond, though still looking at it, like someone who fears he might be caught from behind.

When no words are spoken, thoughts begin to talk, quickly, strangely. Dănuț would have been glad to be assailed by Olguța. But Olguța watched the gleaming water around the willow as if it had been a door behind which a hand was pressing the handle.

"Hush!"

Nobody spoke. Herr Direktor threw down his cigarette and pressed the trigger.

"She's sure to come up now," Olguța whispered with a frowning brow.

Monica covered her ears.

Below, the water around the willow swarmed the seething mass of mauling creatures.

"There it is! Don't shoot! Wait a bit!"

The defunct Fița Elencu had bobbed up from the water… or the willow. And all the frogs, ringing in the willow with their eyes and sores, started keening in a chorus.

As bug-bellied as a Chinese idol, leprous, toothless, and goitrous, Fița Elencu faced the gun without stirring.

The bullet was released, the stone also. Bullet and stone missed their target.

The frog's drone took on howling tones, apparently driving aside both the bullet and the stone.

With a huntsman's elegant movement — very much like a greyhound's distended bound — Herr Direktor rested the gun on his shoulder and fired again. The stone followed the bullet.

A languorous and sinister Fiţa Elencu stared at them.

And suddenly, as if swallowed up, Fiţa Elencu haunted only the huntsman's eyes. There was nothing on the willow. The frogs scattered about.

"What do you say to that, Herr Direktor?"

"I have no idea... It's difficult to shoot at the water; the light blinds you... An ugly toad!"

"An ugly toad!" Olguţa sighed.

"Ugly!" Monica whispered, feeling a shiver running down her spine.

"Let's go, uncle Puiu." Dănuţ was in a hurry to leave.

"No, my dear boy. We missed the President. Let's take our revenge on the members of the Association. A prize of one leu for every frog hit. I'll keep count. Agreed?"

"Bravo, Herr Direktor! I'll show them!"

"Dănuţ, you can begin... That won't do, my boy! Aim calmly... Now shoot. You've missed it. It's Monica's turn."

"I don't know, uncle Puiu."

"You'll learn. Have no fear, Monica. It makes no noise," Herr Direktor tried to encourage her on seeing that she was covering her ears instead of taking hold of the gun.

"Monica, I'll be cross," Olguţa put in, "I'm waiting."

Olguţa's rebuke determined her. She took the gun clumsily — like women smoking for the first time — and shot at random. A frog turned over on its belly, becoming a white water lily.

"One leu for Monica... How about it, Olguţa?"

Olguţa's frog turned a desperate somersault and fell on the water showing its wounded heart to the sky with its tiny paw.

Ali was running along the shore, yelping. One shot drove him onwards, another caused him to turn back somewhat angrily, somewhat dizzily. And he seemed to be fighting the mosquitoes, he being too big and the mosquitos too small.

"Let's take a break and work out the balance sheet. Monica has two lei, Dănuț five, Olguța eight... your turn, Dănuț."

"Hush, Herr Direktor! Fița!"

There was silence on the pond, which was purplish-blue now, with evening spreading over the sky. The reeds at the farther end of the pond alone gave a dry sigh.

"Olguța you shoot. I can't see any longer," Dănuț whispered, disowning the gun.

Olguța took it from him without listening. Her cheeks were aflame as they had been on the day when she had entered Fița Elencu's room for the settling of accounts. This time no sound came from the frogs so that the voice of the toad on the willow should alone be heard.

Where did that voice come from?... From the willow or from elsewhere?... In the muted silence, in the purplish-blue shadow, the dark herds were rising from the bottom of the earth, driven by a roar of thick, smothered, jerky laughter.

"Ali, come here. Hold him by the neck."

Dănuț obeyed the epic order. Olguța put one knee down, rested her elbow on the knee, and took careful aim until her sight was inlaid in the white belly like a moon shard. The bullet spurted forth from Olguța's heart and the motionless gun... and hit a curse. Pushed by the bullet that had pierced it... like arms inflicting a curse. Pushed by the bullet that had pierced it, the body fell into the water...

The stars were coming out in the clear sky.

"Well done, Olguța! It's a masterly stroke. You deserve a hunting gun."

"I'll give you my gun, Olguța," Dănuț offered with the generous enthusiasm that great events give rise to.

"Thank you, but you keep it. I'll have a hunting gun."

"We've won the bet. That is what you have. A whipped cream cake from mother and a bottle of perfume from me."

"She couldn't get away with it, Herr Direktor. I had to kill her."

"Why, you imp?..."

"Because I was afraid of her," Olguţa said aloud so that the Olguţa of the past light hear her.

That was the epitaph of the two Fiţas.

***

A midsummer night's dream sounded musically on autumn's border. Pipers and flutes, bagpipes, mandolin and violins, cattle bells, viols and a single-stringed cello played from three darkening directions for the silver pallor that spread in a fourth direction. The moon was not up yet, the sun no longer shone. High up, a lighted spot, with a star quivering as if caught in a spider's web.

Dănuţ, with his gun, pointed downwards, opened the procession. Ali's bark heralded the victors.

...The emperor was returning from the battle alone. The armies were waiting for him farther off, like a forest prepared to bloom or to fall under the ax... The poor emperor! He alone had jeopardized his life for his soldiers and the peace of the empire. What a decent emperor! What a valiant emperor! Well done, emperor!

"Where are you, uncle Puiu? Ali! Ali!..."

Ahead of him was the cemetery on the outskirts of the village; behind him was the pond and Fiţa Elencu. But uncle Puiu was between him and the pond. Dănuţ ran back with his gun.

"Why am I not a boy, Herr Direktor?"

"God Almighty has wanted it so."

"What Almighty!"

Herr Direktor exchanged an atheistic smile with the star high up!

"Or the stork!"

"What stork!"

"Who then?" Herr Direktor asked prudently, also asking himself the question.

"Mother, Herr Direktor. I'm telling you."

"Alright, Mother and Father have wanted it," Herr Direktor amplified scrupulously.

"No, Mother alone."

"Why Mother?"

"To persecute me!"

"Nonsense!"

"Yes. Why hasn't she made a girl of Humpty-Dumpty?"

"Leave him alone, you imp. What else do you want? You're a boy now; you've got trousers."

Olguţa gave a bitter sigh.

"Why not Olguţa? What else do you want?"

"I don't know. Oh, yes, I know."

"Aren't you proud to be like mother?"

"That's quite another thing. Mother likes it."

"What about you?"

"I don't."

"Do you like boys, Olguţa?"

"Do I? I can't stand them."

"Why do you want to be a boy then?"

"I don't want to be a girl."

"What do you want to be?"

"…You see, Herr Direktor! I'm talking nonsense… because I am a girl."

"What about you, Monica?" Herr Direktor asked as he weighed her plaits in his hand.

"…I want to be like aunt Alice."

"Do you love her, Monica?"

"Yes."

"Do you love me too?"

"Of course, Herr Direktor," Olguţa assured him. "She's my friend."

They were walking along the haystacks lined up on the plain like grand cakes just out of a summer's oven.

"You are tired, Monica, aren't you?" Olguţa asked in a peremptory voice, walking more slowly.

"A little."

"And you, Herr Direktor?"

"We'll soon be home!"

"We still have some way to go, dear Herr Direktor… and I should like to ask you something."

"At your disposal."

"Promise you will do it!"

"It depends!"

"Say you will, Herr Direktor."

"You say what you want!"

"I will if you promise!"

"Say it."

"So you've promised."

"Let's say I have!"

"Let's have a rest, Herr Direktor. You see, Monica simply can't go on."

"And what will mother say?"

"She'll wait for us!"

"Whip in hand!"

"No, with fine, warm dishes because we've won the bet."

"You must tell her that."

"Of course, I'll tell her!"

"Let's sit down… But where's Dănuţ?... Dănuţ!... Dănuţ! Kami Mura, stop!"

The unbridled echo repeated the sounds.

"Uncle Puiu. I'll go to fetch him," Monica, scared by Dănuţ's loneliness, offered.

"Won't you be afraid?"

"No," Monica's lips lied, but were belied by her cheeks.

With clenched teeth and fists, Monica took to her heels, blinded by the darkness. Her pace increased in proportion to the distance separating her from those she had left behind. And her fear, a black, shrill cricket, shouted in the silence: Dănuţ, Dănuţ, Dănuţ!...

The hearts of the two fugitives striking against each other fell, as if of iron, and spurted up, exhaustingly elastic.

Hardly able to stand, Monica stopped, closed her eyes, and shouted, panting all the while: "Help, Dănuţ!..."

In his sprightly flight, Dănuţ had dropped his gun level with Monica. Monica's shriek stopped him. He turned back, picked up the gun, and took Monica to the task.

"Why did you call me?"

He held the gun by the barrel, the butt resting on the ground. He was composed, but his words were anemic, like the wings of a butterfly held by violent fingers.

Monica was speechless. She took hold of his hand and breathed deeply in the coolness of the evening.

"Let go. Can't you see I'm holding the gun?"

"Is it you, Dănuţ?"

"Of course, it's me," he said proudly in a now stronger voice. "Can't you see? What are you doing here?"

"Uncle Puiu sent me to take you back."

"Why were you running?"

"I was afraid, Dănuţ."

"Aha!"

"Please don't tell Olguţa. She gets cross."

"I also get cross!"

"Don't, Dănuţ. I'm faint-hearted."

"I knew it!"

"When I'm with you I'm not afraid."

"Ha! I believe you!"

"You're a boy; you're brave!"

"And what do you want?"

"For us to go back together."

"And if I don't want to?"

"We go home. But it seemed to me you were going back too…"

"I was just walking."

"I'll go with you, Dănuţ; wherever you want."

"Do you know what we have there?" Dănuţ asked pointing to the gun barrel.

"The village."

"No. the cemetery," Dănuţ said in a loud voice that grew ever weaker as he uttered the fearful syllables.

"Goodness gracious, Dănuţ!"

"Are you afraid?"

"Not when I'm with you."

Dănuţ subdued a sigh of relief.

"Alright. Come with me then — back."

"Let me hold your hand, Dănuţ."

Two hands were clenched together — they were near the cemetery.

They set out. Dănuţ's steps grew ever longer. The wish to run fast had again seized him.

"Don't you want to walk slower, Dănuţ?"

"You can remain by yourself!"

"No, Dănuţ... I want to go with you... But I can no longer go on... Let's walk slower, Dănuţ..."

"As you please! I'm in a hurry."

"Why, Dănuţ? Uncle Puiu is waiting for us!"

"Well, I've said it!"

...On the way, a witch had waylaid the emperor. With his bare hands — for he no longer had any bullets — the emperor had fought her. All the evil spirits in the cemetery had come to help the witch. But the emperor's hands were made of iron, like his courage. His gun in one hand, the witch's hand in the other — and off he went. The emperor was going to drown the witch in the blood of the dragon he had killed... Such an emperor!

From the great abundance of the sky, stars big and small fell in the night and over the centuries.

"Why have you stopped?"

Dănuț turned his head. Monica was gazing at the sky, big-eyed as if she had seen an angel flying. She had the same eyes when looking at Dănuț.

"Goodness, Dănuț, how lovely it is!"

That is how the first lyrical night of the moon revealed itself to Monica's heart.

"Where are they?" Dănuț said roughly, letting go of Monica's hand — it was no longer necessary now.

"I left them here, I assure you!" Monica said in her defense, bending her fingers which were stiff after being clasped by the valiant emperor.

It was downright witchcraft. Instead of the frog hunter, an ornamental old man was roasting corn cobs over a fragment fire of brushwood and corn husks.

On hearing the words, the old man bent down and turned over a roasted cob of corn. Over the haystacks and fields and perhaps in the sky also, a mythological shade wrung the neck of a dragon with tangled tongues.

"Old man!..."

"Don't you hear, old man?..."

Dănuț struck the earth with the butt of his gun authoritatively.

"Hello, old man! I'm from the mansion... Can't you hear?"

The old man turned around and blinked. With screwed-up eyes topped by white eyebrows, he looked at Dănuț as one looks at a swallow high up in the sky or at an insect wandering among the herbs.

"What?"

"Maybe the poor man can't hear," Monica put in. "Speak louder, Dănuț."

"You keep quiet! Old man, can't you hear?" Dănuț shouted. He was red in the face.

"What is it?"

"Haven't you seen a gentleman and young lady?" Dănuț roared as if talking to someone up on the moon.

The old man cast a look at the ox-drawn cart on the road and also at Dănuț's face, so glum despite the merry flames. A hand used to the fire turned a cob of corn on the other side.

Dănuț sighed a heavy sigh.

"Damn it!"

If a smile could have a shadow, the old man's smile would have covered several miles, so big and kindly it was.

"Old man, old man, can't you hear?"

"I've seen nothing."

"Are you sure?..."

Dănuț turned to Monica, "You made fun of me!"

"Believe me, I didn't, Dănuț. They were here..."

"But they aren't now!" he said stamping his foot.

"Maybe they're further on."

"Go and look for them!"

"She might be your wife, master! That's as it should be! Stop a little by the fire. Have a cob of corn."

Monica sighed.

"I'll go and look for them. Ah!..."

Dănuț turned his back on her.

Olguța had made her appearance in the cart, half of her in the light of the flames, and was signing to Monica to keep quiet and come over. Taken up in Herr Direktor's arms, Monica found herself in fragment, tickling hay prompting her to laugh, with the stars above and Olguța's whispers in her ear.

"Should I call Dănuț?"

"Let him wait."

"By himself?"

"Of course. That's what he wanted!"

Olguța halved the corn cob Monica had brought over and the three of them feasted on it.

"Have you noticed, Herr Direktor? When you eat corn on the cob it's as if you grazed?"

"Thank you!"

"Want some more?"

"No! I'd spoil my appetite."

Herr Direktor was resting on his back, looking at the sky through his monocle. The milky way spread to the horizon, like a breeze in an astral field of clover.

A gypsy band... and all the rest. A sigh accompanied Herr Direktor's secret wish.

"We must set off for home, Olguța."

"Right, I will."

"Call the old man."

"As if I couldn't drive! Come on, lads!" she urged the oxen in a dissembled voice.

"Oh well, my grandson is calling me. Stop, child! Don't start off." The old man wrapped the roasted maize stalks in corn husks and left the fire. "Goodbye, master."

"You're leaving me here alone, old man?"

"What else can I do?"

"Old man!..."

"Can't you hear, old man? I'm coming with you."

"Wait for the little girl, master. Don't leave her. The wolves will be after her. Haw!..."

The cart went on its way creaking.

"Wolves?" Dănuț mumbled. He was frowning as he drew closer to the fire.

Creak, creak... As if it spite him.

The oxen drew the cart, their pace as stately as an emperor's, their horns balancing among the stars. The cart kept creaking. The old man walked by the oxen. Dănuț was left by the fire, alone.

"Monica! Where are you, Monica?"

"Here I am, Dănuț."

"Kami-Mura!"

"Humpty-Dumpty!"

Once in the cart, Dănuț gave a sigh of relief and a well-deserved leave to the brave emperor.

"There's a moon!"

"Is that the moon?"

"Yes, it looks you, Humpty-Dumpty, when you've got the mumps."

It had come up like a transfer picture, without any linear mouth and eyebrows — a moon such as young children see in their sleep, making elastic faces — serious, merry, or sad.

To Olguța it seemed hilarious; she felt like putting out her tongue to it.

After a scrupulous examination, Monica protested:

"It doesn't look like Dănuț, Olguța!"

"Whom does it look like then? You?"

"Like a foolish pumpkin," Herr Direktor said in jest.

"Tell us what it looks like, Humpty-Dumpty. Like a golden globe?"

"Leave me alone."

"Don't be rude. Lucky for you, I'm in a good mood."

Dănuţ was not thinking of the moon. He had heard it was there and found it in Ivan's knapsack was the mistress of a grocery store bigger than that of Ermacow at Iaşi. And Dănuţ could see it putting tins of sardines into a vase paper bag, cutting red chunks of salami, opening boxes of pickled olives, holing out on the tip of a knife a fat slice of Penteleu cheese, opening a cask of smoked trout…

"Herr Direktor, I dislike the moon."

"Why?"

"Ever since we went to Slănic, Herr Direktor."

"What did it do to you, at Slănic, Herr Direktor."

"We had to take a walk by moonlight. I was a little girl at the time."

"Are you a big girl now?"

"Not quite. But I was smaller at the time. I was walking ahead, holding Humpty-Dumpty by the hand. And behind us, some young ladies were kissing the gentlemen…"

"You don't say!"

"Yes, Herr Direktor. I could see their shadows… Why did they kiss, Herr Direktor?"

"They were playing, Olguţa!"

"Is that a way to play?"

"The grown-ups' way to play!"

"Worse than children. Herr Direktor. I'll never play that way. Herr Direktor, just tell me whether you'd ever feel like kissing the mouth of a lady who isn't your relative?"

"Ah, of course not," Herr Direktor said with a sigh.

"Of course. It's sickening. Only think: Monica's my friend. You tell us, Monica, do I brush my teeth with your toothbrush?"

"No, you've got your own brush."

"You see, Herr Direktor. I tell you on my word of honor that those young ladies were kissing the mouths of those gentlemen."

"Oh my God!"

"Believe me, Herr Direktor. That is why I didn't let them kiss my cheeks... And I noticed they weren't doing it in the daytime. Only by moonlight."

"So you're not on good terms with the moon."

"No, Herr Direktor. I get angry when I see it."

"Come to me for a kiss, Olguța."

"Kiss me."

"You won't get cross?"

"No, you're a relative of mine... And you don't do what the young ladies did at Slănic."

"God forbid!"

On entering the village, a yellow tunnel pierced the night.

"We're done for, children! They have sent for us." Herr Direktor smiled, recognizing the light of the car and aware of who the car shelter.

Olguța got cross:

"Anica again!... I'd like to have a word with you, old man."

"Let's have a word."

The old man came behind the oxen, stroking his mustache.

"You'll tell them you never saw us. A gypsy girl will ask you (Olguța's voice was more subdued) — a gypsy girl who goes about with a German. You know, the German with the devil's cart."

"Leave it to me. I'll show them. The dirty folk," the old man mumbled and went ahead to walk alongside the oxen.

Herr Kulek was approaching, his arm around Anica's waist. He held the flashlight in his raised hand as he would have held a beer stein.

"Haven't you seen the gentlefolk, old man?" Anica asked absent-mindedly.

"Hum! You'll be damned, woman. Out of my sight! Go on, my pretties!"

Guffaws of muted mirth came from the hay in the cart; they were covered by the laughter of the crickets and the frogs.

Herr Kulek lighted the moon with his flashlight and went on talking to Anica as he would have talked to a deaf and dumb person of his own nation.

***

"The soup, Profira," Mr. Deleanu called from the veranda, throwing his cigarette away.

"The soup, Profira!" those in the cart called out in a choir amidst the din roused by the dogs in the courtyard and those in the village.

With one hand holding the lamp and the other the salad spoon, Mrs. Deleanu was waiting for them on the steps, as severe as the allegory of household Justice for those who are late at meals.

"Look at them! All you needed was an oxen cart! Mister motorist, is this the time for supper, and is this the way to come?"

"Out of the way, I'll throw down Fița!"

"Oh!"

Mrs. Deleanu got out of the way and seemed to dwindle. Herr Direktor's gloves had for a moment bore the fearful nickname. Ali followed the gloves out of the cart. He was fawning frantically.

"We've won the bet, ask them," Olguţa cried out, darting out of the cart into Mr. Deleanu's arms on the second step.

"Is that true?"

"Memory eternal!" Herr Direktor sang.

"Thank God!" Mrs. Deleanu said in relief. "I had a premonition: the whipped cream cake is ready."

"Hurray for the cake!"

"But you won't have it because you're naughty."

"Patapum, boom... Give it to us in Patapum's memory, Mother dear," Olguţa wailed, pointing to the ostentatious death of the basset.

"What have we got for supper?" Dănuţ asked, shaking off the hay, as a young dog shakes off the water it has been dipped in.

"Good evening, aunt Alice... Olguţa has shot the toad."

"Yes? Good evening, Monica. Are you hungry?"

"Very hungry, aunt Alice."

"Good!"

With hay in her fair and with sun-burnt cheeks, Monica blinked — a light in the light of the lamp.

"But where's Anica? Didn't you meet her?"

"She's looking for the moon!" Olguţa mumbled, nibbling at the crusty end of a loaf.

"For a honeymoon!" Herr Direktor added, shaking off the hay.

"Grigore, you won't have any cake."

"Kulek has enough for me as well."

Profira's steps made the floor to tremble. She was bringing the soup tureen.

The old man bowed, wishing them a good appetite.

"A good appetite to you also."

"Giddy-up, my pretties!"

The oxen started off, barked at by the dogs.

The steam of the soup painted wishful pictures on the faces of the famished.

No one spoke except the spoons, the crickets, and the dogs' eyes.

Part II

I. The Moldavian Environment

As if from an iced melon, a cool breeze entered through the open windows together with the sunlight. Autumn had set in.

A small basket full of grapes decorated with Bacchic leaves was a spot of light in the middle of the table.

Heaped in it were grapes the color of bright, green mornings; the color of golden noontime; the color of purple twilights; the color of midnight, purplish-grey with its unclean spirits; the color of blue nights lit by the sleep of the moon, calling to mind the memory of the days and nights gone by.

Dănuț was eating the grapes quickly and in great quantity. There were no seeds or skins on his plate — only the green skeletons of the denuded clusters. Olguța was throwing the skins into her plate vehemently, like so many insults, interested in the gesture rather than in the taste of the grapes. Monica detached the grape, her lips took its skin and while the seeds were being separated from the watery pulp, her fingers placed the skin in her plate. It was all done meditatively as if in a game of chess: the end of the holiday was near.

"Wash the grapes, Dănuț, I've told you again and again!"

Dănuţ dipped the grapes into water…

"You'll get appendicitis. Why do you swallow the seeds?"

"If only I got it." Dănuţ made the wish in his mind as he continued to swallow the seeds: school time was near.

"A match please," Mrs. Deleanu asked as she poured the boiling water into the coffee pot.

Herr Direktor took a match from his matchbox.

"Let me have the box, man. I'm not asking for the moon!"

"Impossible! Matchboxes vanish."

"Alright. I'll get my revenge by stinting on the froth."

"Here is the box, but the coffee must have its froth on top."

"Why do matchboxes vanish?" Mr. Deleanu wondered while lighting his cigarette and mechanically putting the box into his pocket.

"Because we all steal other people's matchboxes! Give me back my box."

"What box?"

"Mine."

"What? It's mine. I've taken it out of my pocket. Here you are one single box… What's this!"

Two single boxes came out of his pocket.

"You're right. Matches are a wonder. It's plain they have a penal element in their composition."

"Fire has, not the matches."

"Ever since Prometheus!"

"Naturally."

"Excellent, Grigore! When the penal code is revised, I'll propose a new offense: the Promethean misdemeanor… I'll like to do it to see the reaction of some of my colleagues: 'What's that?' 'Who is he?'"

"Who is he, Papa?"

"A valiant man, Olguṭa. He stole the fire from the gods and the gods punished him more severely than thieves are punished."

"And did he turn into an outlaw?"

"No, he died!"

"And who avenged him?"

Mrs. Deleanu smiled. "Literature," she replied.

Olguṭa frowned and was silent. Such talk accompanied by smiles angered her as if the language had been one that she didn't quite understand. Moreover, she was displeased above all by Dănuṭ's smile.

"Why do you laugh?"

"I swallowed a sour grape."

"Hmm! It suits you, that's why I asked you. You look like Patapum. Do you weep when the grape is sweet?"

Dănuṭ had made a pun, silently. When Mr. Deleanu had explained to Olguṭa that the man who had stolen the fire had been punished. Dănuṭ had thought: "He has burned his bridges." If Olguṭa had not been present, he would have made the pun out loud. That's how he had warded of Olguṭa! Dănuṭ was generally silent outside and talkative inside himself, perhaps because Olguṭa was not inside.

A violent ring of flames encircled the coffee pot.

The coffee had suddenly risen all froth and anger, like a chocolate turkey.

Mrs. Deleanu raised the pot above the flames, holding the handle, and began to collect the froth.

"I've had my fill. I'm full," Olguṭa groaned pugnaciously. "Please make some coffee for me as well, Mother dear."

"Nothing of the sort!"

"Please Mother!"

"Coffee is not for children."

"Why?"

"Because it makes one nervous."

"Why do you drink coffee then?"

"Because it helps digestion."

"Haven't I got a digestion?"

"You have, even without coffee."

"And you have nerves even without coffee, Mother dear," Olguța whispered looking at her lovingly.

"Don't be sassy, Olguța!"

"But I feel like having some coffee."

"Father will give you some in the saucer… only a little, a very little," Mr. Deleanu added, feeling Mrs. Deleanu's Neptunian eyes veering to him from the boiling coffee.

Olguța's mother sighed.

"A good thing school begins," she said. "I'll have a holiday… Dănuț, that will be quite enough. Go and wash your hands."

"Thank you, aunt Alice," Monica put in.

"You're welcome, Monica. Have done, Olguța. Go for a walk with Monica. Soon you'll have to go to bed."

Olguța sighed. "I know," she said. "Will you give me some coffee, Papa?"

Mr. Deleanu filled his saucer.

"Blow on it, Olguța, to cool it."

The brown storm in the saucer hurled a wave onto the tablecloth.

"I just changed the tablecloth today, Olguța!"

After sipping her coffee, Olguța addressed her mother: "Mother dear, why do you say you'll get some money when you spill the coffee?"

"Because it's a popular saying."

"Why are you cross when I spill some then?"

"Should I thank you?"

"Don't mention it, Mother dear! Thank you, Papa! Come on, Monica."

When they were alone, Herr Direktor began to laugh.

"Who's Olguţa teacher?"

"A very competent young woman."

"She must give that young woman no end of trouble."

"Strange to say, she doesn't. Of course, the lessons are discussions and the relations between them are friendly. Olguţa offers her tea or preserves and the teacher provides instructive talk... Actually, Olguţa learns easily and with pleasure: the only pleasant heritage from Fiţa Elencu!... I am sure that her friendship with Monica and their life together will tame her somewhat."

Mr. Deleanu sighed: "It would be a pity!"

"A pity? She's a girl, not an outlaw — think of it..."

"Yes, I know. But it suits Olguţa... If Dănuţ had been like her!"

"Dănuţ is a little foolish; he's like his mother.' Just imagine, Grigore! Such was the amiable remark offered to my face by a friend of yours from the days of your childhood... probably an old flame of the both of you."

Herr Direktor laughed.

"Who was it?" he asked.

"Miss Dobriceanu!"

"Is she still alive?"

"She's your age!"

"Poor Profiriţa! You can't be upset by anything she says. She's a large landowner in the kingdom of heaven — never to be expropriated. She greatly admired Iorgu..."

"Was it only admiration?"

"Who knows?... You and Dănuţ are not her style! She likes talkative and aggressive people; she is a lamb, but she likes toreadors! Poor girl!... Do you remember the cheeky things you used to say to her, Iorgu?"

"Yes... Poor thing!"

Herr Direktor wiped his monocle with his handkerchief, as if he had decided to fight a battle with his eyes as weapons, and began as follows: "My dears, as we have mentioned Kami-Mura and as it is time for me to leave..."

"Already?"

"If you don't show me the door, autumn will... Well, as I was saying, because my departure is close at hand, I should like to make a question that I'm quite anxious about, very clear. What are your intentions concerning Dănuţ?"

"But it's quite simple; he'll go to secondary school," Mrs. Deleanu's prompt answer.

"And?"

"Full stop."

"Aren't you overly hasty with your full stops?"

"I can't see what you are driving at."

"Just a moment... What school do you intend to send him to?"

"The boarding school."

"As a boarder?"

"How can you think such a thing, Grigore? Dănuţ, a broader! A day scholar, of course."

"Have you nothing to say, Iorgu?"

"I agree with Alice. It's as crystal clear."

"Not in the least!... How old is Dănuţ?"

"Don't you know? He's eleven."

"Alright. And he's a boy."

"A child."

"No, no! A boy, but unfortunately he'll always be a child to you."

"It's only natural. I'm his mother."

"That's fine and praiseworthy. I have nothing against it. You're an admirable mother."

"Oh!"

"And for that very reason, you're a danger for the boy's education."

"Good heavens!"

"Listen, Alice. Let's leave aside all trifling matters and speak seriously. What is at stake is the future of your only boy and the only bearer of our name. You know I love your children. Don't you?..."

"I have no children. So far God has protected me from marriage and from now on I can fend it off myself. So all my affection... and the rest, is for your children. And my only joy — others would call it an ideal, but I'm less presumptuous — is to see them turn into men... that are worthier, better than ourselves. And thank God, we're not so bad either."

Mrs. Deleanu was getting impatient.

"What about it?" she asked.

Herr Direktor lit another cigarette.

"I would ask you to believe that I am telling you has been considered and has matured for a long time in his head deprived of poetical locks... I am asking you: what is to Dănuţ if he goes to secondary school as you want him to?"

Mrs. Deleanu raised her shoulders.

"My dear man, he'll become what becomes of all children brought up in proper circumstances under their parents' watchful eyes. If you can find a more precise answer, let's have it."

"I think I can: he'll become a failure."

"Grigore!"

Mr. Deleanu smiled.

"You're in a bad mood today," he said. And yet he was somewhat worried as if what he had heard had been his own thoughts which he had put aside and which were now being uttered by someone else.

"I'm not joking and I can prove to you what I've said, mathematically, pen in hand."

"You've turned into a prophet!"

"No, Alice. It's no use getting cross. And I'm sure that Iorgu thinks as I do. What do you say?..."

"My dear Iorgu, you're a decent fellow. You love your children, your wife, but you're easy-going, a Moldavian in the full meaning of the word. And that's the whole thing in a nutshell... For example: you know the roof of your house is crumbling. Instead of putting it right — which would un-settle your habits for a time — you're perfectly able to get drunk every day to forget that it might fall on your head at any moment. Isn't that so?"

"Perhaps. Fortunately, however, the roof on our house is in good condition."

"Alright. Let's leave the roof. The button of your trousers is getting looser every day; you don't sew it because you rely on your good luck and firmly believe that good luck will see to it that the cotton that holds the button is everlasting. On the day when the button falls off you get pessimistic and write admirable stanzas to describe the melancholy of those who are ill-fated — without sewing on another button. Look at Iaşi. A city that has poets but no mayor, because the mayors are Moldavians, of course. The mayor's activity consists in endowing the city with ruins that are to an in-creasing extent poetical and melancholy, the dreams of poets that are to increasing extent devotees of the bottle, sours and penniless... Moldavian sloth, my dear, begin with the Moldavian way of doing things. Can't you see that our speech is for women and prattlers? Sweet-sounding — that's true — and soft, fearfully, depressingly soft! As if speaking from a soft bed, in front of a warm fireplace, in an undertone, between two cups of coffee with sherbet to follow and with eyes half-closed with sleep. The language of the Wallachians is vulgar, I admit. It is brutal — true. But it is lively. The words are short, blunt, as if in preparation for a fight. You have the feeling that the person uttering them has energy, a lot of energy, and nerve... And believe me, I say this regretfully for I love Moldavia... You see, even the love one bears for Moldavia is full of pity, as if for a poor old man that is frail and vulnerable. Actually, it is reflected in the Moldavians' established phrase for Iaşi, for example: "Our old city! Poor Iaşi!" Everybody pities it and all demand that other people take pity on Moldavia's old capital. Tell me now, Iorgu, aren't you the prototype of a Moldavian?"

"That's so, but we're brothers."

"We are brothers... Yes... But my Moldavian strain has received a wholesome graft..."

"The monocle?"

"Had I remained in Moldavia I'm sure I would have worn it on the seat of my trousers, as they say."

"You're piling it on."

"Not in the least... Don't you remember that I was writing poetry in the sixth grade at secondary school?"

"What of it?"

"I had already put my energy in jeopardy."

"All boys go through it."

"Especially in Moldavia… and the unfortunate thing about it is that they stick to it."

"Have you turned into a Moldavophobe?"

"No!... But I find that Moldavia is dangerous. Its essential feature, which gives rise to all the other features, is certain laziness — elegant, aristocratic, or however else you want to describe it, but in the first place, baneful. Whoever lives in Moldavia, Grigore, and I'm still alive. What do you say to that?"

"I firmly believe that you keep wondering how you've got as far as you have."

"I'm not in the habit of asking myself such questions… but you may be right."

"Of course I am. Except for Alice, all your talent and intelligence would have been a mere ferment of bitterness. I may be exaggerating a little, but I'm quite right at bottom of it. The Moldavian environment is dangerous for boys' education. Dănuț's future must not be entrusted to Moldavian good luck. At present you, we, have it in our hands."

Mrs. Deleanu shivered nervously.

"I won't be separated from Dănuț," she said. "Put that in your pipe."

"My dear Alice, it won't be so long until the time comes for military service. Whether you like it or not, they'll take him from you. And I won't mention the many other separations of parents and children, more particularly between mother and boys. They are inherent in life. There will be women, affairs, and so on — inevitably. What will you do? Will you chain him sown? No, you'll cry… For you — and especially for him — the separation should be tearless, manly. And it is also a good thing that the numberless temptations of adolescence and youth should find him a man tempered by life and not a poet anchored in his mother's petticoat… And you must know, Alice — this is from my own experience — it is the children who have grown up in life and not those who grew up in their mother's boudoir, who have a true love for their mothers. The offspring brought up in their mother's boudoir will torture their mothers in their old age with their futile misfortunes. The others can value the delicacy and secret sacrifices of the women who have brought them up because at every step they have butted against life which, as you know, doesn't waste its time on maternal solicitude and amicabilities..."

"My dear Grigore, I won't spoil count, Alice. Behind a severe mother, there is still a mother. A child knows it or feels it. That is enough: it amounts to spoiling. Severity coming from a stranger is tonic... Evidently, I don't speak of the monstrous persecutions that kill a child's heart. Thank God we can ward that off from Dănuț. I mean the severity, the sternness that children must come up against when they're young because it's the only one that shapes their energy and gives them a fighting individuality. I'll assume hypothetically that so far the severity has been faultless. But let us turn the page and look at Dănuț coming home with a broken head because he had fought other boys or had played with them... You see, you're startled. You'll be alarmed, you'll cry, you'll pity him. And Dănuț will feel the need to have a nurse for each pain, for each tribulation... But nurses are not obligatory in life or war, and even if they were, they are rare birds... Or something else. A bad mark, for instance. Dănuț will persuade you, with tears if need be, that he'd be persecuted. You'll believe him because you're his sensitive mother and because on the other hand the teachers who are men having their own life, with everything that implies, are not what mothers are, and cannot be the mother of thirty or forty children who are strangers to them... The consequence: instead of inventing a means of overcoming the bad will, inattention, or severity of the teacher, he will expect that the parents use their influence with the headmaster... That is what thaws manliness away... And listen to me, living conditions are becoming ever more difficult... The peasant uprising is a sign... Other uprisings, other disturbances, will follow — sooner or later. Civilization is penetrating our country,

assuming comical aspects, but it will ultimately penetrate our country, assuming comical aspects, but it will ultimately penetrate deeply, effectively,
and will then assume tragical aspects. Special values will be revised, barba-
rous and poetical institutions will be pulled down and the great energy of
work will overwhelm the tyranny of sloth of yesterday's masters. We will
finally have more doctors and fewer priests, more hospitals and schools,
and school life will be invaded by people who will drag civilization with
them — vulgar but energetic, brutal but powerful people. And then, my
dears, it will amount to nothing to be the grandsons of Costache Dumşa —
or perhaps that will count only in a few drawing rooms with moth0eaten
furniture and impoverished gentlefolk. Nobody will ask you who your father was. The hereditary passport allowing admittance to today's aristocratic drawing rooms and today's social life will be an outdated archaism.
Happy will be the man who, strong through himself, will be able to throw
his name, remindful of the chronicles, like impertinence in the face of the
uncouth whom he has vanquished with his fists. That is altogether different. That man will be the others' master, like his ancestors, but otherwise..."

"You forget that Dănuţ will be a rich man, Grigore."

"Not in the least... Inherited wealth is considered to be a gift of heaven
by poets, but not by people in their right mind. I don't say that dire poverty
is happiness. I leave that claim to religion with its fat priests! But unearned
wealth is as great a danger to children's hearts as poverty. My dear Alice,
my father was a man who had not risen by his own power... Have no fear!
I'm not a demagogue, no politician and no snob turned inside out. This is
what I mean: father had the experience of life. Do you know what he told
us when we were grown-up: 'You are healthy, boys, and you have a good
head. That is the wealth I'm leaving to you. If you'll turn into real men
you'll leave my grandchildren more than I'm leaving to you. But what I've
left you is enough.' That is the fruitful wealth, Alice. The other, when it is
moreover inherited, is the thing for baccarat, for champagne... and later on
for doctors. Dănuţ will be a rich man — of course and it's very good. But

the moment he will handle his wealth himself, he must be a whole man, a tempered man so that he may proudly say to himself that he would have been able to put it together as his parents had done: that he may value it rather as a proof of the worth of his forerunners, as a remembrance of them, and not measure up his meanness and weakness to it. It is for that reason that we must make a man out of him before he has become a rich man."

Mrs. Deleanu spoke slowly, hesitatingly: "Should I send him to Germany?"

"I never thought of it!"

Mrs. Deleanu took a deep breath, her face brightened. Herr Direktor frowned to hide a smile. He abandoned the cigarettes and prepared a cigar. Herr Direktor only smoked cigars after long meals with a gypsy band and other music, or after long talks, the success of which he could foresee.

He lit the cigar.

"My dears, in this respect my conviction is different from what of the upstarts, of the newly risen gentlefolk, and even of many genuine boyars who sent their offspring abroad soon after they've been weaned, that they might learn foreign languages. It is an error with serious consequences, the main one being estrangement from the national language. To my mind, everyone's childhood should be ethical. Everyone must be able to swear in his own language, without a dictionary, and be able to laugh, weep and love in the same way. When you have no childhood memories in your language, you are a pitiable mongrel, of which we have so many. Studying abroad must not make estrangement its aim; it must be the fertile graft of a superior civilization on a mind that had been ethically molded, and at a moment when it is still pervious. And as for Germany... Do you think I intend to send all my relatives to Germany because I studied there? A delusion, my dears... To begin with, Germany was not a vocation for me such as Paris is for so many rotters. God forbid! I went to Germany to learn practically, as nowhere else, as far as I know, my special vocation: engineering.

Which does not mean that I deem Germany indispensable to a good education! Germany is a country with many social qualities and many obvious shortcomings for the she-wolf's sucklings. It has been of good use to me but has not enslaved me. But that's different. I'm perfectly able to value other types of education than German ones. For a complete man, any true civilization is good. It doesn't do him any harm even to contact several civilizations. On the contrary, it opens up several real windows in the room with pained windows which is mostly our mind. We'll talk about it later. For the present what we have in mind is to mold Kami-Mura."

"Consequently?..."

"It is plain… to remove him from the Moldavian boudoir of his excellent mother."

"Are you serious, Grigore?" Mr. Deleanu asked.

"My dear Iorgu, you are too obsessed with my monocle. Here you are: I'll take it off."

"You are right, Grigore, I must say. But I sincerely confess that my wish is to see my children growing up together, under my eyes, as we have grown up under our parents' eyes… For the rest… we shall see…"

"Or more precisely, Iorgu — and I hope you won't mind my saying so — as for the rest, as God… and the first prize at the state lottery!"

"Ultimately, I won't interfere. I've said what my wish is… Alice will decide… I don't want to be an obstacle in my children's future… even if it goes against the grain."

Left alone on the battlefield, Mrs. Deleanu bit her lips while crumpling her handkerchief in her hand.

"…?" Herr Direktor looked at her through his monocle, which had reverted to its proper place.

"Speak plainly, straight out. What do you propose?"

"Thank God!... You'll give Dănuţ to me... Wait, don't be alarmed! You'll commit Dănuţ to my care."

"Be specific!"

"Specifically: I'll send him as a boarder to a school in Bucharest — which school I don't know yet, I'm speaking in principle... A German school. The Lutheran school, for example. This will be, to begin with, provisionally. I'd register him there because of the sports. With the Germans sport is compulsory. And the environment is Romanian actually. Moreover, in contact with the little Germans there, Dănuţ will become patriotic and belong to the clan of Romanians. The social stage complete on a small scale, plus the sports. What have you to say?"

"We are speaking in principle. What else is there?"

"Alright... He'll spend his holidays in Bucharest — elsewhere, in my company. In any case, not at home."

"What?"

"Wait, Alice. I'm not as frightful as you imagine. I haven't forgotten the Easter and the Christmas holidays. The summer holidays he will naturally spend with you, at Medeleni — once a year he'll inhale the Moldavian spirit in the family!"

"It's inhuman, Grigore!"

"My dear Alice, mixed wine and soda water are good but it is no use, except in a glass... On occasions such as ours, either wine or water. Do you want him to be a man? Give me the time to make a man of him. Give him to me for as long as you will send him to school; for a school year, with the short holidays... And you won't regret it!"

"Not to see him, for a whole year, Grigore?"

"When you can no longer stand it, you may come and see him, together with Iorgu — he's got plenty of suits at the Court of Cassation — but only in the parlor.

"And who will look after him? Dress him? Darn his things?"

"Eh!... Who'll blow his nose! Put his hat right! Why don't you get him married, Alice? But don't worry! I'll look after him, as much as needed and as necessary."

"And our house, Grigore?... It will be empty..."

"What about Olguţa? She's as much as five children! And Monica? A charming child; exactly what you need: delicate, quiet, pretty... And with Olguţa and Monica, you will have the pride of being twice revenged — regional and womanly revenge — on the men of my type and the Wallachians."

Mrs. Deleanu was staring into emptiness...

"And I make one more claim — a necessary claim," Herr Direktor added quickly. "You leave Dănuţ to me for the next summer holidays. We'll go abroad together: Italy, Germany, France, England — I want to give him an international appetizer... Don't worry, Alice. Obviously, I won't be a mother to him. But he'll have in me a considerate and experienced mate. He'll get used to being alone in a hotel room — a first-class hotel, of course — next to my room. He'll learn to pack his suitcase himself — a leather suitcase, with dressing-case and equipped by a bachelor competent in such matters as suit-cases. He will have to shift by himself into languages unknown to him, handle waiters, porters... He will hear good music — you see, Alice, what sacrifices I am prepared to make — so that he may learn to control the inclination to sleep in public... And in two years I'll send you another Dănuţ — more alert, more independent — who will bring presents chosen by him, out of his money, to his sisters and parents, as it is fitting for someone who comes from aboard. And you will then have time — for three long months — to instill into him the delicacy and spiritual elegance which are so necessary — the priceless gifts of the mothers of your quality..."

From Mrs. Deleanu's closed eyes tears ran down her cheeks and onto the tablecloth. At times her hands went up — in revolt or prayer — and came down again, defeated by the tears.

In the childless drawing room which autumn had invaded, silence floated and life weighed down on the inmates.

"Listen, Grigore," Mrs. Deleanu said as she wiped her eyes with her palms and not with her handkerchief, "Dănuţ... Dănuţ... Dănuţ is a child," she whispered, bursting into tears, her voice, as well as her chin, trembling.

The table cloth was burning, unnoticed. Mrs. Deleanu had withdrawn to the window. Herr Direktor shrugged his shoulders.

"Alice dear, that's our fate. We are children... until we are no more... We are men, on earth... We do what we can..."

"Grigore," Mrs. Deleanu pleaded, her hand covering her eyes. "He's not prepared for it... He's got no uniform... He's not prepared. He needs so many things... He's not prepared..."

"We'd better leave sorrow aside. It's as if we were keening over him. We're not sending him to death. We'll make a man out of him. And we'll all be happy."

Mrs. Deleanu suddenly revived.

"We must ask Dănuţ if he wants it, Grigore. It is he who must decide."

"Right you are, Alice. I mean it differently from what you think and what you wish, but you are right. He must learn to choose to abandon childhood. I'll ask him to come here."

"I'll go," Mrs. Deleanu burst out.

"Go to cool your eyes, first, Alice dear. Your eyes are red. He must not see you like that. We'll be waiting for you."

Mrs. Deleanu left the room, her shoulders stooping under the burden of the last hope.

"Now between us, men... you must admit it's a good thing that I've done!"

"You are right, my dear Grigore. The Moldavian environment is rather nerveless," Mrs. Deleanu smiled as he wiped his tearful eyes... "Poor Dănuț!" he added.

***

The soccer ball with its two bellies — one of leather on the outside and one of rubber on the inside — had swallowed up the children's kick-ball, as it was to swallow up all such balls in the country over the years. In the Deleanu home, its first victims were the shoes, which looked as if gnawed by leprosy.

"Don't you forget, Grigore. When you leave, you take the pattern of your nephew's and nieces' feet. After each soccer game, I'll send an urgent telegram... 'Send.' And you'll dispatch two pairs of shoes per head. After three telegrams, you are compromised. The whole of Bucharest will know that you have clandestine children."

"Or rather, that I have nephews and nieces whose mother is unnatural," Herr Direktor, delighted that the ball was a success, would reply.

After the shoes, the victims of the German ball were Anica and Profira. Anica and Profira had legs — Profira lazy ones; Anica sprightly ones. But the ball had wings and the forehead of a ram.

Finally, the windows: the ball never entered the house by the door. There was a piece of land facing the cemetery on the outskirts of the village; it was more suitable for soccer than the mansion yard. But Mrs. Deleanu deemed it wiser to hear Olguța, even if she broke windows, than not to hear her at all.

Herr Direktor had stated the rules of the game with explanatory demonstrations.

"That's all very well, Herr Direktor, but why isn't one allowed to strike it with one's hand?" Olguţa unwilling to accept such sportive mutilation, objected.

"Because the law is the law. It isn't to be discussed."

"I'll make another law then!"

"Why is that, Olguţa? Are you unable to do what hundreds of little Germans do?"

"Alright! I'll show them!"

And to take her revenge on the little Germans, Olguţa had sworn before Monica to strike hard this German head, which did not deserve to hit with the hand, but only with the foot.

Monica was the umpire.

Dănuţ was driving the ball, striking it with one foot as he ran and directing it with the other. Olguţa was waiting for him calmly, her eyes on the alert, like a boxer waiting for his opponent's attack in the ring. The run from the end of the yard, the ball was driven on with his feet and gradually approaching Olguţa, had exhausted Dănuţ. His temples were throbbing.

"Come on."

They faced each other at a few steps' distance. A motionless ball was waiting for the stroke that would send it flying.

Losing his composure, Dănuţ made use of a simple stratagem: he only pretended to direct the ball towards the right with his right foot, while the left foot attacked it resolutely. But Olguţa had jumped to the left and had caught the ball between her feet, clasping it. Dănuţ pushed on blindly... aimlessly. Olguţa was relaxed: she drove the ball unhurriedly, magnetizing it with the quick imperative strokes of her feet.

Dănuţ was panting as he ran after Olguţa with the despair of the unlucky... Olguţa turned her head... stepped aside at a moment's notice.,

Dănuț fell and the ball being hit powerfully, took a long spurt, and entered the goal.

Dănuț's knee was blood-red like a ripe pomegranate. Monica came at a run, holding out her handkerchief.

"Does it hurt?"

"Leave me alone!"

"What have you done to him. Olguța?" Mrs. Deleanu asked as she run down the steps.

"I've defeated him!" Olguța cried out, bringing the ball in her arms.

"Defeated him, how's that?"

"We played, Mother. I stumbled and lost the game."

"I'll throw that ball into the well, Olguța. You'll be quiet then."

"Why are you cross, Mother dear?" Olguța asked gently, examining her carefully.

"I'm not cross!... But I dislike violent games!"

"Why were you crying, Mother?"

"Let me be, Olguța! Come with Mother into the house, Dănuț dear."

"We're not sleeping this afternoon, Mother?"

"Oh well... Play with Monica for a while."

Limping, with Monica's handkerchief wrapped rounds his knee and Mrs. Deleanu's caressing hand on his head, Dănuț stepped into the future...

"Something happened, Monica. Let's go in... Wait. I'll kick it just once more."

Olguța's legs described a right angle; the ball flew up, very high up... until it came down from the angels' heaven.

"Did you see that kick? Let's go in now."

The ashtrays were full of cigarette butts; the tablecloth had grown grey in places with ashes.

Herr Direktor was smoking. Mr. Deleanu was smoking. They were both silently watching veils of the fragrant smoke describing an Oriental dance.

Olguţa took her usual place at the table. Monica huddled up close to her.

"Why don't you ask me why I came, Herr Direktor?"

"Ah! Is that you, Olguţa? Well, I'm asking you: why have you come?"

"Just because!"

"Good."

"Why aren't you asking me, Papa?"

"What should I ask you?"

"Whatever you want."

"…What have you been doing up till now?"

"I've been playing outside."

"Good!"

"Everything I'm doing today is good. Why Papa?"

"What did you say?"

"Nothing. Just a joke!"

"Good."

Olguţa looked at Monica and turned up her lower lip. Monica swept away the bread crumbs from the table.

"Do you have a migraine, Herr Direktor?"

"No!"

"Then you have one, Papa?"

"Why, Olguţa? I don't."

"I have one then."

She frowned and was silent.

"Is your head hurting, Olguţa?" Mr. Deleanu asked, finally examining her carefully.

"How do I know?"

"…Tell Father, Olguța. I can see you're rather flushed."

"I don't have one… I don't tell lies."

"Are you cross?"

"Why should I cross?"

"What's the matter with you then?"

"What's the matter with you, Papa?"

"…Nothing. I'm smoking. Thinking…"

"What are you thinking of, Papa?"

"Of you… of Dănuț.. of you all."

"Good, Papa"

There was some noise at the door. They all turned their heads that way. Profira came in, chewing. She was coming from the kitchen to have her dessert in the dining room.

"Can I clear the table, sir?" she asked, controlling a yawn, her eyes on the grapes that had been left.

"After you finish eating," Olguța answered fiercely.

"I finished."

"Go and look at yourself in the mirror."

"Go, Profira. You'll clear the table later," Mr. Deleanu put in with a smile.

Profira went out. A huge hiccup accompanied her massive steps.

"Why are we sitting here, Papa?"

"We're waiting for mother."

"You're waiting for her too, Herr Direktor?"

"I'm waiting for Dănuț."

"Shall I wait as well?"

"If you wish…"

"What do you say, Papa?"

"As you wish, Olguța."

"I'll do what you want me to do!"

"Stay here too… Why not?"

Olguța picked some grapes from a cluster and rolled them over the table.

"Does number thirteen bring bad luck, Papa?"

"I don't know, Olguța. Some people believe it does."

"But what do you believe?"

"Well… Yes and no."

"More of a yes or more of a no?"

"Perhaps more of a yes!"

"Like me, Papa… Is it the thirteenth today by any chance, Herr Direktor?"

"Why? Are you out of luck today?"

"Oh well… You answer and I'll answer after."

"It's not the thirteenth. Now answer my question."

"I'm not… but maybe others are."

"The fact is you've missed the mark. Others are in luck today."

"I know, Herr Direktor," Olguța said, just to pump him.

"How do you know? How you been eavesdropping?"

"I never eavesdrop."

"What do you know then?"

"Ask Papa."

"What does she know, man?"

"How do I know?"

"You imp!"

"What do you do when you're vexed, Herr Direktor?"

"It depends! Sometimes I swallow... at other times..."

"At other times?"

"At other times... I smoke!"

"I swallow."

"You swallow? What do you swallow?"

"Grapes, Herr Direktor," Olguţa replied calmly, crushing a tender grape between her teeth as if it had been a hazelnut.

***

In Mrs. Deleanu's room, the light of the autumn noon filtered in, subdued and soothing, through the drawn blinds.

Dănuţ rested one-handed on his mother's shoulder as she knelt beside him. He kept the leg in question stretched out. The scratched knee had been washed and bandaged with iodine. Now it was the turn of the antiseptic bandage.

A strong pharmaceutical smell teased Dănuţ's nostrils. His eyes were riveted on the bandage cover over which there was a red cross.

Wounded in the war, the soldier had fallen.

And before long his days of torment ended.

Far from the mother that had brought him up and who had loved him...

Unaware that Dănuţ was dying, "far from the mother who had brought him up and had loved him," Mrs. Deleanu was worried by the seriousness on his cheeks.

"Is the dressing too tight, Dănuţ?"

"Yes, the dressing... No. The dressing is not too tight."

"Tell mother, Dănuţ. If it's too tight I'll do it up once again."

"No, mother. It's fine as it is. Thank you!"

The dressing began above the knees and went halfway down the leg, covering it as if for a wound well worthy of decoration.

"I'll present something!"

Quite a long time ago, Mrs. Deleanu was in the habit of speaking French with Mr. Deleanu, especially when she didn't want the children to understand. The habit, now useless in words — now that the children knew French — was preserved for the secrets thoughts within.

"Are you sad, Dănuț?" she asked him, caressing his forehead.

"…"

The question had turned into a prompting. Dănuț became sad.

"Poor little guy! What a sad smile!"

Imbued with the vanity of poetic sadness, Dănuț received her caresses on the forehead and cheeks as if he had received applause.

"Do you want me to give you anything? Come on! Ask mother…"

"Don't I have to sleep today, Mother?" Dănuț asked, his voice becoming ever more irresolute as he spoke.

"Are you tired, Dănuț? Are you sleepy?"

"No!"

"Why go to bed then? Isn't it pleasant here, with Mother?"

"It is."

"Let Mother comb your hair."

Feeling he was in favor, Dănuț expressed hope within himself: "Maybe I've fallen ill."

The comb waved its way lightly through the soft, tousled hair, obeying the melancholy of the mother's eyes rather than the hands that led it for a practical purpose.

For anyone except Mrs. Deleanu, Dănuţ's hair was chestnut and curly. But strangers' eyes are absent-minded and see things conveniently: no more and no different from the eyes of the passport clerks.

"Chestnut and curly!" Which means identical with hundreds and thousands of heads through which go a barber's scissors and his cosmetics! Poor boys! You have to be a woman for people to see that you have lovely hair!

Bitterness filled Mrs. Deleanu's heart as she realized people's unconcern. For a moment, although in vain, a mother's hands protected Dănuţ's abundant locks from the scissors.

"Sit down, Dănuţ. Let Mother comb your hair nicely."

Dănuţ sat down on the sofa at the foot of the adjoining beds.

"Stretch out... That's it; Dănuţ, when you were a little boy..."

He had stretched out on the sofa, his head on Mrs. Deleanu's knees. His dusty shoes rested on the Turkish shawl and — strangely — there was no reproof! On the contrary, a smile was perceived between Mrs. Deleanu's lashes.

"Wounded in the wars..."

"Shall Mother tell you a tale?"

"Yes!"

"What shall Mother tell you?..."

She suddenly grew sad.

"Mother doesn't know any more tales for you. You've grown up, Dănuţ! Time goes by so quickly!"

Mrs. Deleanu sighed and, leaving the comb in his hair, caressed the head for which she no longer had any tales.

"Far from a mother...!"

Mrs. Deleanu's eyes knew the shades of Dănuţ's locks as she knew the notes of a Nocturne by Chopin.

Chestnut locks!... Chestnut on the outside, yes. But the flames smoldering inside! The auburn waters! The delicate copper fringes that burn along the strands!

Dǎnuț's locks were different at the end of the holidays from what they were at the beginning. In the sunny red amidst the darker strands, you felt a warmth, autumn approaching as you feel Jesus' aura in the lighted spot of some of Rembrandt's paintings.

"And curly!" Every curl differently curled. In the morning when Dǎnuț woke up — that ugly moment when people's hair is tousled and unruly — his hair was a bunch of tulips — now coppery, now chestnut-colored — which had bloomed in the gardens of sleep.

So many mornings! So many of the child's awakenings. For a moment all the past years were covered by a field of rounded golden-brown tulips...

...And now the secondary school... life... a uniform... cropped hair... Old age for some, youth for others... And the child with a girl's curls will never, never be the same.

"Dǎnuț..."

Carried away by her thoughts, Mrs. Deleanu had not noticed that Dǎnuț had dozed off on her knees. Raising his head in her hands, she gently laid it on the pillow, as if had been a flower vase.

Swish... Dǎnuț woke up. He was soared — the sound was like swords being crossed.

"What is it?"

"Nothing, Dǎnuț. Look...!"

"Are you cutting my hair, Mother?" He was alarmed on seeing the strand of hair and scissors in Mrs. Deleanu's hand.

She smiled sadly at the thought that others would cut his hair: "No Dǎnuț. I have just cut a strand... for myself."

"Why, mother?" Dǎnuț asked, yawning heartily.

"Just so… that you may see it when you've grown up… Dănuţ!"

"Yes?"

"Have you grown up, Dănuţ?"

"Yes, Mother."

"Wouldn't you like to remain as you are: a child?"

"No!"

"…with mother?"

"Yes."

"But it isn't possible, Dănuţ. Mother will give you something good."

"From the wardrobe?"

"From the wardrobe." Mrs. Deleanu smiled as she stood in front of the mahogany wardrobe that had been her mother's and her grandmother's.

…The scent of childhood's wardrobes in the room of sleep and of indulgence — the scent that brings back the past! A scene that vanished with the past… A scent that you will find in an old lane with apricot trees in bloom as you walk, hurried on by life. A strange breeze through an unknown window where a young girl's stirring face — from the house… or the past — may appear.

The scent of lavender and melilot gathered in small colored bags hanging from the shelves like delicate knapsacks of one's memories… The scent of elecampane, of Cologne water, and perfume bearing names forgotten forever, like the perfume of happiness… The piles of linen smilingly white in the violent shade of the wardrobes opened by a white hand, when in their mirror — for a moment only — a room is reflected and also a child with moist lips and fond eyes because there is chocolate in that wardrobe.

"How many am I allowed to take?" Dănuţ asked nibbling at a round Marquis chocolate tablet, his eyes on the box in his hand.

"Take them all… to keep in your room."

"Really?"

"Truly."

Dănuţ closed the box after fumbling for a while with the lid: he was flustered.

"And now Mother will put some scent on you."

Dănuţ bent his head as if he were to be crowned. The moist glass stopper wound this way between the curls, behind the ears and on the temples, wafting its way between the curls, behind the ears and on the temples, wafting a breeze as if of damp river meadows and acrid sweets.

"Dănuţ..."

"Yes?"

"Dănuţ..."

Mrs. Deleanu's hands went quickly between the shelves, turning the pile of handkerchiefs this way and that.

"Dănuţ," she whispered reluctantly, "go into the dining room. Uncle Puiu is waiting for you."

Dănuţ went out. The draft wrenched the door from his hand, slamming it. On the other side of the door, Dănuţ waited for the usual reproof: "Doors are closed, they are not slammed!" He was surprised not to hear anything and made for the dining-room, his pocket bulging with the chocolate a face...

"Here is Kami-Mura!" Herr Direktor burst out cheerfully, throwing down the cards.

Waiting for Dănuţ — for a fairly long time, Herr Direktor had played a few games of cards with Mr. Deleanu.

"But what's the matter with you, Kami-Mura?"

"I've bruised my knee, uncle Puiu."

"And you've been given a dressing... Good Sit down."

Herr Direktor turned his chair towards Dănuţ... Olguţa who had endured the torture of a reluctant silence, pressed her chin against the table, her eyes out. Mr. Deleanu's eyes were riveted on the ceiling; Monica's on her knees.

"Has mother told you why we've asked you here?"

"No."

Alright. Let's talk then, we two, like two men... like two friends. O.K.?"

"Yes," Dănuț mumbled, pressing the chocolate box.

"At your box — how old are you? Twelve?"

"Not yet," Dănuț said regretfully with a blush.

"No matter! At twelve you are no longer a child. You're a big, a very big boy. That's what you must be."

Herr Direktor's voice sounded categorical, managerial. Dănuț prepared himself for a long sequence of "Yes-es."

"You know, Dănuț, that uncle Puiu loves you... like your mother and your father..."

"Yes."

"...and that he wishes you well... very well..."

"Yes."

Olguța was fretting.

"Good, Dănuț. We will now see whether you love uncle Puiu as much as he loves you..."

Dănuț blinked. So many words addressed to him and only to him, made him dizzy. There seemed to have miles between his head and his feet. His head had gone up, as high as the ceiling: his feet had gone down, deep, very deep down, together with the floor. And over the precipice between his head and feet, the deafening train of words was running.

"Tell me now, Dănuț, do you want to be like uncle Puiu one day."

"Yes."

"...to earn money — as much as you like —to spend as much as you like, to have a car, to wear a monocle... in a word, to be your own master and when you say something to make every one before you tremble and obey you as if you were a king..."

"Yes."

"Then you must do as uncle Puiu tells you, Dănuț."

"Yes."

"Good... But because you're a big boy, and a clever and learned one, and obedient..."

A gleam of fear made Dănuț uneasy; it was like a stroke of lightning in a thick fog.

"...uncle Puiu wants you to decide for yourself... And your decision will be final. We will do as you say. Father and mother and uncle Puiu will obey you as if we were your children. But, Dănuț, you must think it over seriously and answer like a man. If you do as we believe you should, we'll love you all the more and will treat you like a grown-up, a sensible grown-up, and not like a child... Agreed?"

"Yes," Dănuț's lips alone had spoken.

"Now listen carefully!"

"Wounded in the wars — the soldier had fallen...! What's up now?"

"Starting from this year — for the holidays will soon be at an end..."

Dănuț clasped the box in his pocket tighter.

"...you'll be going to secondary school... Oh! You can't imagine, Dănuț, what it is to be a secondary school scholar. The primary school? A mere trifle! For children! A secondary school is different! Both your father and I have been secondary school scholars. And we're so very sorry we no longer are!"

Dănuț looked at Olguța from the corner of his eye but only met Monica's sad and surprised eyes.

"You'll wear trousers, with a crease, from now on. Do you hear, Dănuț? Trousers. Like your father and myself. What else could you want?"

Dănuț had started listening.

"But how do things stand? We all want you to have the best in life, the finest things. And because are no important secondary schools in Iași, we should like you to go to a secondary school in Bucharest. In the capital city of the country, Dănuț. To live in the same city as the King. On Sundays, I'll take you out of the boarding school and after... we'll have a fine lunch at Enescu's — where you'll order whatever you'd like — then we'll set out in a carriage drawn by two black horses and go for a drive along the Kisselev Road... And you should know, Dănuț, that the driver I'll pick out will get ahead King's coach! Eh! The poor King! We, with crossed legs, ahead of him, and he is our wake... You know that uncle Puiu knows about many things... And next year — after you have learned as you should so as not to disgrace uncle Puiu — we two will go for a trip abroad. By train and by ship!... And on your return, speaking so many languages, Olguța will stand agape," Herr Direktor jokes, winking at Olguța. "To sum it up, this is what uncle Puiu proposes, Dănuț: you either remain in Iași — in a tumble-down secondary school attended by bare-footed, boorish pupils, wearing ugly uniforms — or else you come to Bucharest with uncle Puiu to attend an unparalleled secondary school, to the city where the king lives, to the city where we'll have a good time each Sunday and from where, when the holiday begins, we board a train and away we go... Now think and choose... You know what is good for you and what uncle Puiu wants. Decide."

"Come on, Monica, there is nothing for us to do here."

The door was slammed... Herr Direktor lit a cigar... Dănuț looked around the room... Mr. Deleanu was looking up at the ceiling, frowning as if Jesus' betrayal had been depicted up there.

Dănuţ's eyes met Herr Direktor's cropped head and the Schlager scar; they were frightened and drifted towards the sideboard. The poor sideboard! When Dănuţ was a very little boy he would hide in the sideboard. The poor sideboard! When Dănuţ was a very little boy he would hide in the sideboard... He was a grown-up now!... And mother was not in the dining-room...

He swallowed hard and swallowed again... On a chair, alone above the world... And he had to answer yes.

He raised defeated eyes towards Herr Direktor.

"Don't be hasty, Dănuţ," Herr Direktor encouraged him. "Think it over."

There was a throbbing emptiness in Dănuţ's head.

His hand had stiffened on the box in his pocket... A wasp came from outside and buzzed under his nose. He shook his head and waved her away. The wasp settled on the grapes. Dănuţ's hand clasped the box again.

"...Ah!... So that was why mother..."

And father too, and Olguţa. They had all known except him. They were driving him away from home... They were abandoning him... Nobody cared for him... Not even mother. Not even mother!... Dănuţ had no one...

He closed his moist eyes... And suddenly, Ivan's knapsack half-opened. Like giant shades in a desert world, Barbara Ubric, Genevieve of Brabant, Cinderella, all the unhappy princesses, and empresses... rushed out of the knapsack... and among them the dog of the soldier who died in the wars — Azor.

"So that's what it is! That's what it is!"

Two tears, wiped angrily by Dănuţ's hand, ran down his cheeks and over the world of woeful shades... For out of Ivan's knapsack, Prince Charming had come forth, dark locks flying in the wind, sparkling eyes; a broadsword in one hand and a mace in the other.

Dănuț's hand thrust the chocolate box out of his pocket and onto the table.

"I don't need it! If that's what it is, I'll show you all!"

In a loud, unusually loud, and determined voice, Dănuț uttered the decisive words: "Yes, uncle Puiu, I am going to Bucharest with you. That's what I want!"

"Well done, Dănuț, well done! That's the boy! Come to me for a kiss."

"Dănuț!" Mrs. Deleanu cried out, putting her head in the half-opened door. Without coming in, as if the expectation of the result of an operation.

"What have I done?... " was Dănuț's unuttered thoughts.

Like morning dew, Prince Charming dispersed in a shower of tears on Dănuț's kissed cheeks.

"Alice! Come on, Alice! It's done! Long live Dănuț! A bottle of Cotnari wine."

"It will be all right, my dear boy," Mrs. Deleanu comforted him, clasping him in her arms as she would have done on the platform of a dismal railway station, to the shrill sound of a locomotive that was taking him away to be slaughtered.

Within a few moments, the look of the dining room was altered. Profira, stimulated by a curt order, took away the table-cloth full of ashes and bread crumbs and swept the floor, casting fierce looks at the sprightly and smiling Anica, whose hands carried plates and clinking cutlery as if there were castanets another tablecloth — a white one decorated with plain embroidery — covered the table, lending it a festive aspect. Herr Direktor was helping Mrs. Deleanu, putting right the folds and the fall of the tablecloth with the gallantry of sorts.

Mr. Deleanu went down into the cellar. Motionless on his chair, Dănuț looked serious and absent-minded like the supernumeraries when the scenery of the play, where they are just scenery, is changed.

"I'll bet you ten kilos of iced chestnuts that you have no champagne biscuits, Alice."

"Alright. Look…"

On an upper sideboard shelf, the biscuits rose in a powdered pile, like yellow oars of merriment, beside the traditional little basket of Malaga raisins and almonds.

"I've lost. I'm at your orders."

"When the iced chestnuts are in season, you'll send us a wagon-load… We'll have a feast, Dănuț! Agreed?"

"I beg your pardon?"

"Oh, nothing… Mother is talking nonsense."

A tug at her heartstrings… At the time the iced chestnuts come in, Dănuț will be in Bucharest… An empty room in the house and another in our hearts…

The sound of a kick at the door was heard.

"Open please!"

Anica pulled the door aside. Mr. Deleanu entered, panting, his hat on his head and his coat on his shoulders.

"This is for Alice and the children…"

"Introduce it!"

"Cotnari, 1848."

"Approved," Herr Direktor cried out, reading the label while his fingers were testing the solidity of the cork that wore the warlike helmet.

"Look at this, Grigore."

"I'm glad to see genuine dust on a wine bottle."

"…a Cotnari bottle," Mr. Deleanu corrected him in a heraldic tone.

"Look what you've done to my tablecloth."

Mr. Deleanu had placed the Cotnari in the middle of the table with a serviette for a bolster. The dark bottle with its wax-wrapped cork was covered with dust and the cobwebs of the years spent underground.

"Go to the young ladies' room and ask them to come here."

"Let's take our seats."

"How?"

"Dănuţ by my side," Mr. Deleanu decided, putting her arm around his neck.

"So you've driven me away!" Her Direktor protested.

"You remain there with the champagne. We, the Moldavians, will be here with Dănuţ and the Cotnari."

"I renounce Satan."

"He doesn't renounce you."

"What about Olguţa?" Mrs. Deleanu asked Monica.

"Aunt Alice, Olguţa... Olguţa says she is asleep," Monica whispered, making, "says" an inaudible as possible.

"Impossible. Olguţa must come."

"She has a headache, aunt Alice."

"I'll go and see what this is all about." Mrs. Deleanu rose from his seat: he felt there was something fishy about it...

"May I come in?..."

"Olguţa!"

Mr. Deleanu opened the door ajar, looked in, and quietly made for Olguţa's bed.

"Are you asleep?" he asked, caressing her locks.

"No," she answered, with closed eyes and clasped fists.

"Have you a headache?"

"No."

"The dark bottle with its wax-wrapped cork was covered with dust
and the cobwebs of the years spent underground."

"Then why is it you don't want to drink a glass of champagne for Dănuț?"

"I don't want it."

"Look at Father."

Dark looks shot from under her dark lashes. As if open eyes imperiously demanded a change of position. Olguța sat up. She looked without batting an eyelid.

"I am angry."

"Why?"

"Because I'm right."

"That's an occasion of joy, not anger, Olguța."

"No, it isn't. Because I am right and you're not... And I want you to be always right."

Mr. Deleanu was hardly able to control his smile. Olguța was gesticulating with her finger. It meant she was getting over her anger.

"Will you explain to me how this comes about?"

"Who am I, Papa?..." Olguța questioned vehemently.

"You? You're my daughter!"

"And who else am I?"

"Mother's daughter."

"And who else, Papa?"

"...And Moş Gheorghe's friend."

"Eh, Papa! You make me laugh and I want to be serious. Tell me, Papa."

"I've run out of answers! You tell me."

"Who's Dănuț, Papa?"

"Aha! He is your brother."

"So he is my brother?"

"Of course."

"So Dănuţ is as closely related to me as he is to you and mother. Is that it, Papa?"

Mr. Deleanu smiled. "Yes, Olguţa."

"Then, if I were as old as mother, I'd be Dănuţ's mother."

"That's so. He'd have two mothers, Poor Dănuţ!"

"I am not joking, Papa, on my honor... So I'm his sister because I'm younger..."

"No, Olguţa. You're Dănuţ's sister because the two of you are our children!"

"Of courses, Papa. That's what I was saying!... So I'm to Dănuţ what mother is. Only I'm younger and mother's older... But I'll also be older."

"Are you cross with father because he's sending Dănuţ to Bucharest?..."

"Tell me, Olguţa. You know I'm willing to listen to you!"

"Why didn't you ask me as well, Papa?"

"Are you very fond of Dănuţ?"

"Oh well!... I'm his sister. Why didn't you ask me?"

"How do I know?... That's how parents are, Olguţa. They don't trust children... And perhaps they're not right... not always."

"Are you cross, Papa?"

"No, I'm grieved perhaps, despite myself."

"I don't want to upset you, Papa. I want you to be right... Why did mother cry?"

Mr. Deleanu's hand answered the question, caressing the girl's hand.

"You're sorry too, Papa. I'm sure of it."

"As sorry as you are yourself. That's how parents are." He spoke in jest, but sadly.

"You see, Papa! You didn't ask me!"

"Do you know that Dănuţ wants to go, Olguţa? It was he who decided, of his own free will."

"I know. He does what Herr Direktor wants."

"Uncle Puiu is as vital for Dănuţ as we are. He wants things for his good… Differently from ourselves… But I think he's right."

"Is that the truth, Papa?"

"Yes, yes."

"Isn't it good enough in our home?"

"It's quite good, Olguţa… But it's better for a boy to grow up among boys… and to be properly controlled."

"It would have been better for me to be a boy."

"Why Olguţa?"

"Just so mother wouldn't have cried."

"She would, Olguţa. Mother loves both of you equally."

"I know, Papa, I know… But I don't want mother to cry."

"And would you have left father, if you had been a boy?"

"You're a man, Papa!"

"What of it?"

"…I wouldn't have left you, Papa, because I'm a girl," she burst out angrily.

Mr. Deleanu kissed her.

"Have you got over your anger?"

"Of course, seeing that you are right."

"I am, Olguţa. Barristers are always right."

"And so are parents, Papa."

"Hear, hear! That's how I want you to be: cheerful. Let's go into the dining room."

"Herr Direktor is stricter than you, Papa, isn't he?"

"Than me? I believe so — it's not difficult to be stricter than me. What do you think?"

"That's true. You aren't at all!... You needn't be either."

"No! That's what you say!"

"Yes, Papa. If you were strict, I..."

Olguța looked at his father with artful seriousness.

"I should throw myself down from the roof... as you very nearly did when you were a boy, and you would be sorry."

"Now would you?"

"But you're not strict. You can't even be angry, Papa!"

"Can't I?"

"Yes, I'm telling you! You feel like laughing when you're angry, and you want to be angrier still then..."

Mr. Deleanu laughed.

"You're like me, Papa."

"Yes, Olguța. You should send your father to the corner because he can't be a serious father."

"Nonsense, Papa! But I obey you. Do you know, I once made you angry and because you didn't reprove me I went to the corner of my own accord... You see! I'm not ashamed to admit it! But I want to know if Herr Direktor is stern."

"As stern as it's needed, Olguța. Grigore is fond of you."

"I know, Papa... Well, I'll talk to Herr Direktor myself... What are you doing here? Why don't you knock at the door, Anica?"

"The mistress is asking why you aren't coming..."

"Let's go, Papa... I'm glad you've visited me. I'll learn how to make coffee. Next time you'll pay me a visit I'll serve you black coffee."

"Alice will kill me, you imp."

"And I'll give you preserves too, Papa."

"You have preserves?"

"Of course. Look, Papa… But don't tell on me."

Mr. Deleanu's eyes were a twinkle with memories as he looked at the pots in the stove.

"That's your cupboard."

"Yes, Papa that's where I'll hide the coffee and the coffee pot!"

"And where from will you get coffee and a coffee pot?"

"You'll buy them for me, Papa… so that I should be able to receive my guests."

"And if mother catches us?"

"She'll taste the coffee… to see whether I'm a good housewife."

"And if she gets angry?"

"She'll send us both to stand in the corner!"

***

Mrs. Deleanu shook off her thoughts when they entered.

"Did you get stuck?" she asked.

"Silence!" Herr Direktor ordered solemnly. "I'll give the floor to the champagne… and also I give warning to delicate ears."

"Don't break the mirror, Grigore."

"Don't worry, Alice. Champagne bottles have a partiality for your ears! Have no care for rest, the cork will see to it."

Mrs. Deleanu and Monica both covered their ears out of a common impulse. Nevertheless, the festive burst startled them. The cork flew like a sparrow from an exuberant apricot tree that had blossomed in the bottle and was being shaken into the cups.

"Flawless!" Herr Direktor congratulated himself as he filled the cups... "Help yourselves! The fullest for Kami-Mura!"

"Fill it properly, Herr Direktor, don't persecute me!" Olguţa reproached him, her finger pointing at the actual level of the champagne below the decorative level of the froth.

"What have you got to say, Alice? Your daughter wants a full dose of alcohol."

"Give it her, Grigore. For Dănuţ's good luck!"

"Wait Olguţa, don't start. You'll soon get dizzy, don't worry!"

"Will you make a speech, Herr Direktor?" Olguţa asked, her lips covered with froth.

"Don't challenge me! You're always putting in objections..." He raised his cup as he addressed them: "Starting from today I have lost a nephew but I've received a boy on the same conditions as the Holy Virgin. I first drink to the new father — a worthy father, who christens his son in champagne and not in holy water... And what champagne!" he added as he put his lips to the blond dew. "Gaudeamus igitur."

The cups clinked together, playing the pure aria of thin crystal.

"Come on, Alice, don't be an unnatural stepmother! Touch glasses with your child's father!"

"Fill it, Grigore!"

"How's that! You've already finished it, Alice?"

"Yes, all by myself!"

Herr Direktor poured cheerfulness where much was needed. The froth climbed with a swirl. The cup rose with it as if throbbing, like a ballerina on tiptoes, carried up by the flight of unfurling veils.

"And now, my dears," Herr Direktor continued, "let us drink to the health of the son that has been set on the right way. My warmest wish is to touch glasses again in ten years, all of us now to be found here, gathered around this pleasant table. And at that time, Dănuţ, you will look at me through a monocle — as I am looking at you now — and say: 'This dodderer who couldn't produce a child in his lifetime... has succeeded in producing a man.' In expectation of that day, let us honor this day, as it is fitting we should, and let us honor all mothers!"

"You're in a good mood, Herr Direktor," Olguţa addresses him with a biscuit in her hand.

"It seems to me we both are... The champagne is good... what do you think, Olguţa?"

"It is, Herr Direktor. It pricks your tongue!"

"Propose a toast then."

"Do you think I'm afraid?"

"Let's see!" Herr Direktor challenged her, leaning back in his chair. Olguţa stood up.

"Am I allowed to stand on the chair, Mother?"

"What do you want to do?"

"I want to make a speech... for Herr Direktor."

"Alright. See that you don't fall."

"You look like a statue," Herr Direktor exclaimed, twisting his neck to look at her.

"Don't challenge me, Herr Direktor."

Mr. Deleanu fretted in his chair. He knew the stage-fright of a first try at oratory and Olguţa's first try thrilled him.

Olguţa passes her hand over her forehead, getting covered with crumbs because she had a reminder of a biscuit in her hand.

She spoke unhesitatingly, looking at her uncle: "Dear Herr Direktor, we have been relatives before today because you are my uncle. And I'm not sorry that you are!"

"Nor am I, Olguṭa."

"We are both lucky with our relatives then."

"Bravo, Olguṭa!" Mr. Deleanu applauded.

"We're very lucky, Olguṭa. Take it from me."

"I know, Herr Direktor, ever since I've been related to Fiṭa Elencu… But from now on we're more closely related."

"We're very closely related," said Herr Direktor changing Olguṭa's comparative into a superlative.

"No, I'm only very closely related to father, to mother, and someone else…"

"Who is that mysterious someone else?"

"You'll see, Herr Direktor."

"Don't interrupt her, Grigore," Mr. Deleanu said, to protect Olguṭa.

"No matter, Papa, I can answer him… From today on, you're my brother's father, Herr Direktor. That is why we are more closely related, because two is more than one, and because from today on you are twice related to me."

"Are you glad of it, Olguṭa?"

"Of course I'm glad."

"Let's touch glasses then!"

"Wait, I haven't finished!… I wish my brother to be as lucky with relatives as we two are, Herr Direktor."

"A *bon entendeur*, salut!" Herr Direktor exclaimed, taking her in his arms.

"Bravo Olguṭa! You've earned a ten for your speech."

Herr Direktor seated Olguṭa back at her place, saying: "My dears, it's no great thing to have received a boy! But I see that one can't escape one's fate. God has preserved me from a wife and in exchange, he sends me a mother-in-law!... Let us drink to the health of the youngest mother-in-law on the globe and wish that all the others should be like her!"

...Dănuț had eaten several biscuits soaked in champagne without any appetite. He heard the clinking of glasses, words, jokes, laughter, without listening... So something good had happened. They were all merry because Dănuț has said yes. Dănuț could have said yes or no... He had sat on a chair in the dining room — a high, strangely high chair, like all the chairs of solemn moments — and they had all waited for him to decide... Yes.

Some time ago the dentist had pulled one of Dănuț's teeth out and Dănuț, holding the tooth in his hand, wept, giving it a puzzled, hostile look. At the time his parents congratulated him — as they were doing now — and had laughed as they stood beside the chair of torture... It was strange! A tooth at the time, a yes now, both of them issuing from Dănuț's mouth... And they were all merry! What if he had said no? They would have been sad. Poor Dănuț! He alone was sad... and yet he wasn't perhaps... There was once an emperor who laughed with half of his face and wept with the other half...

Leaning back in his chair, Mr. Deleanu sniffed the Cotnari wine in his small glass and, smiling with ironical melancholy, addressed his brother: "You have greatly defiled our poor Moldavia today, Grigore."

"Every means is fair to reach a good aim."

"No, your criticism was sincere; besides nobody can see the straw in the parents' eyes better than the children. But for myself, my dear Grigore, I have drunk champagne and now drink this Cotnari wine which is fifty-nine years old: it dates from eighteen hundred and forty-eight... And in my turn, I drink to Moldavia where this bitter and mellow Cotnari wine has been made, to Moldavia where hearts arise that are similar to the wine, because they are bitter and mild, and because they are rare. And I only wish one thing: for my child to have such a heart when there will be no Cotnari wine in Moldavia's cellars anymore!"

"Is Cotnari better than tobacco, Papa?"

"Do you want to taste it?"

"If you say so!"

"Let's see."

Olguţa put her lips to the glass, sipped with concentrated attention, and shrugged her shoulders while knitting her brow.

"It's bitter, Papa! Champagne is better!"

Mr. Deleanu smiled. "You're no judge, Olguţa!" he said. "This is for old men like ourselves."

"But tell me, Papa, if it's better than tobacco."

"Of course it is! And it's rarer."

"I'll ask you something then."

"Do."

Olguţa rose from her chair, came near Mr. Deleanu, and whispered in his ear while casting a sidelong look at the others.

"What you're doing isn't polite, Olguţa!" Mrs. Deleanu reproved her.

"Thank you, Papa!... That's how it is when one is having a good time, Mother dear."

"Here you are, Olguţa... And tell him to drink it to you, children."

Olguţa went out with the glass of Cotnari in her hand, stepping like an acrobat on the rope.

"For Moş Gheorghe?" Mrs. Deleanu asked.

"For who else?"

Mrs. Deleanu smiled. "We'll soon be childless," she said with a sigh. "Grigore takes Dănuţ, Moş Gheorghe Olguţa. Monica alone is ours... Let's get up."

"We'll stay here for a while longer, Alice," Herr Direktor protested, pointing to his half-full glass.

Herr Direktor and Mr. Deleanu were left by themselves in front of their glasses.

"When are you leaving, Grigore?"

"Tomorrow."

"And when am I to bring Dănuț?"

"In about a week."

"So soon?"

"School will begin soon."

"And the law-courts."

"Everything begins. I must prepare him: he must have a uniform, and I must also take him around Bucharest."

"Alright... To our health!"

"Cheers!"

Going back to a time long gone by — with a remembrance of sunlight that had turned the leaves of walnut trees yellow — the fragrance of the Cotnari spread in the silent room. And the breeze of autumn from outside entered, encircling the wine, filled with memories.

Mrs. Deleanu had left the dining room with her fingers caressing Dănuț's locks, followed by Monica. Before the door of her room, she stopped.

"Come into my room, children!"

"With his head bent, a silent Dănuț went on towards his room. He stepped in. The door was closed. Mrs. Deleanu's hand abandoned by Danuț's curls remained for a moment in the air with fingers spread out, like a leaf detached from the branch, and away from the fruit, it was protecting... It came down."

"Do you want to come in, Monica?"

The little girl took hold of the sad hand, pressed it as hard as her childish strength allowed, and entered the room with a down case look directed furtively towards Dănuț's room.

Two moments of silence close to one another, hand in hand.

Mrs. Deleanu lay down on the bed with her eyes closed; Monica sat on the edge of the bed.

Monica's eyes were set on Mrs. Deleanu's petrified face. She felt as if she ought to hold her breath so as not to make any noise.

After a time Mrs. Deleanu's lashes quivered... and two tears slid along her cheeks. Holding her breath, Monica bent down and shyly kissed Mrs. Deleanu's hand. Mrs. Deleanu gave a start.

"You were here, Monica?"

"With you, aunt Alice."

"Little girl... go to join Dănuț... I'll try to get some sleep."

Monica went out on tiptoe. She stopped in front of Dănuț's room and knocked gently.

"Dănuț," she whispered, bending an ear...

Pressing the handle gently, she half-opened the door.

"He's sleeping!... Poor Dănuț."

When the door had been closed, Dănuț opened his eyes; he didn't smile.

Monica entered the girls' room alone.

In three rooms, three minutes of silence were considering life.

Coming back from Moş Gheorghe's room with an empty glass, Olguța burst into the dining room. Profira jumped up from the chair, her mouth full, like a bulky schoolgirl caught eating by the teacher in class. Anica looked down, hiding the biscuit behind her with the revealing gesture of smoking schoolboys.

"Good appetite! Come along with me, Anica!"

Profira waited for them to leave. As soon as the door closed, she came alive, like the statue in an allegorical tableau after the curtain has come down… She bent down, picked up the biscuit dropped by Anica, and swallowed it.

"Listen, Anica." Olguța said sternly." "Have you only eaten or have you also drunk?"

"I didn't even have the time to eat, Miss Olguța," Anica complained, showing her empty hands.

"Good! You must hurry if that is so before Profira eats everything. Wait, don't go. I have a job for you… And I'll give Profira something to do also."

She frowned as she pondered and quickly opened the door of the dining room.

"Profira!"

"Oh! You've startled me, Miss."

"Go and tell the vine-keeper to give you muscadine and to choose the best."

"Who'll clean up here?"

"Anica can eat biscuits too! Go and eat grapes. Come on, quick!"

Profira sighed and went on her errand… taking another biscuit out of her apron pocket.

"Listen carefully, Anica!"

"I'm listening, Miss."

"You are to go into the Turkish room where uncle Puiu is. You'll knock gently. If he doesn't answer you are to knock loudly… Show me what you will do."

Anica walked to the dining room door… and got in.

"Anica, are you playing with me?"

"I forgot, Miss Olguța!"

"Do what I told you to do!"

"Yes. I knock gently…" Tap-tap, she knocked with her finger… "And if he doesn't answer I knock loudly." Bang, bang, she thumped with her fist.

"That's it. And if he does not answer even then, you run in, bang the door, slap your mouth with her hand and say in a very loud voice: 'Goodness gracious. I thought you were in the dining room.' Got it? You must make a lot of noise, to wake him."

"What if he gets angry, Miss Olguța?" Anica asked, hardly able to control her laughter.

"That's not your business. You'll tell him that Miss Olguța wants to speak to him."

Waiting for Anica, Olguța was pacing with her hands behind her back more and more quickly, like somebody inventing dialogues with short retorts. At times she would stop, put aside the dark strands of hair that covered her forehead, and start again.

"He said you may come."

"Was he sleeping?"

"No, he was smoking?"

"Good. Now go and eat everything there is on the table. Don't leave anything for Profira!"

"Are guests welcome?" Olguța asked affably as she entered Herr Direktor's room.

"Very."

"How are you, Herr Direktor? Am I disturbing you?"

"You? My friend! How could!... What wind blows you to my quarters?"

"It's nothing much, Herr Direktor. I've come to see you, to have a talk…"

Herr Direktor raised himself, rested an elbow on the divan, and secured his monocle in his orbit.

"Are you paying me a visit?"

"Of course… What a beautiful dressing-gown you've got. You're as elegant as a lady."

"That's how bachelors are, Olguţa."

"Why only bachelors?"

"Because they have no wife! To make up for it, they have a beautiful dressing-gown."

"And the married ones mustn't have one?"

"No need. They have a beautiful wife."

"And if she's plain?"

"They solace themselves. No. well, they sigh!… But why don't you sit down? What can I offer you — a cigarette?"

"You're cheerful today, Herr Direktor!"

"As always…"

"Today is not as always."

"Right you are. Today is a red-letter day."

"For you?"

"Also for Kami-Mura… and for everybody. Haven't you seen?"

"Why did mother cry then?"

"How do you know she cried?"

"I noticed."

"Alright. She cried because she's a mother."

"Nonsense! If that is so she should cry every day!"

"She cried because she was glad, Olguţa."

"No, Herr Direktor!"

"That's what I think."

"I am going to tell you why she cried: it's because my brother is going away."

"My dear Olguţa, your mother has realized that Dănuţ should study in Bucharest, and she decided it — as Dănuţ has also decided."

"Why did she cry then?"

"That's how ladies are, Olguţa. After they decide to do something, they cry and get over it."

"It went against the grain for her, Herr Direktor?"

"Tomorrow, Olguţa."

"Alone?"

"Yes. Dănuţ is coming with Iorgu in a week."

"...I'm glad." She seemed to breathe more freely.

Herr Direktor stroked her locks.

"You're a good girl!"

Olguţa looked her uncle straight in the eyes as she asked: "Herr Direktor, are you severe?"

"With who. Olguţa?"

"How do I know?... With your clerks in Bucharest?"

"Of course. Otherwise, things wouldn't work."

"And what do you do when you are severe?"

"Oh well... I speak sharply, I frown... and if they don't obey, I dismiss them."

"And if my brother won't obey?"

"Dănuţ obeys me!"

"Who knows? If he does some foolish thing?"

"I'll talk to him."

"And if he does another foolish thing?"

"Ahem... We'll see!"

"Ahem... Herr Direktor, have you ever beaten anyone?"

"Perhaps! I can't remember! When I was a boy..."

"But do you like beating people?"

"No, Olguța. It's nasty and savage."

"So you won't beat my brother?"

"Beat Dănuț! God forbid!"

Olguța took a deep breath.

"Thanks you, Herr Direktor. I knew. You're stern but kind... Will you allow me to look into your suitcase?"

"Go ahead."

"Close your eyes, Herr Direktor... Put your hands over your eyes... Now tell me what I am going to do."

"You'll have a Cologne shower!"

"I'm glad you haven't guessed! You haven't got a headache today, Herr Direktor?"

"Thank God, I've got off scot-free."

"I'm so sorry. I wanted to give you a rub-down."

"I do have a headache!"

Cologne water gushed forth. Olguța's palm went round quickly, spreading it over the rough, cropped head, while her lips blew as hard as they could towards the crown.

"Like it, Herr Direktor?"

"Splendid! The North Pole seems to have moved over to my head! But more gently or I'll get a sick headache now."

"No matter, Herr Direktor! I'll give you another rub-down. It's a red-letter day today."

"For my head!"

"And for other heads, Herr Direktor," Olguța added, rubbing in desperation.

There was such a transparent disintegration that it looked as if it were not within autumn's range — and there was also a vast gentleness in the light — like something long gone by...

Dănuț went down the steps of the veranda with his hands in his pocket and with sloping shoulders. Catching sight of the soccer ball which had been forgotten in the yard, he remembered having played with Olguța, also that his knee had been wounded not so very long ago — and it seemed to him that the steps he was descending were not those he had ascended, that the yard was not the same, that Dănuț was not the same. As if the steps he had ascended at the time and had now descended had been the steps of time and the veranda of his parents' house.

He closed his eyes...

Very often, especially at the end of the holidays, Dănuț would dream that he had experienced a misfortune. And the misfortune always came to an end when he opened his eyes. And Dănuț was happy, his heart full of smiles detached from the fear of sleep. So the misfortune of sleep had made him consider a misfortune like a threshold you stepped over — opening a door as you open your eyelids — to enter another room, a room of light, with mirrors for smiles only and windows only for sunlight.

...He opened his eyes. The soccer ball was the same, sky-high and endless; school-time was beginning, his departure was drawing near; Dănuț was small and alone.

So they had driven him out of the house... He didn't feel like crying. No. He sighed.

Dănuț would have liked the sky to get small, very small and to come down, very low down, just like the cover of the little table on which Mrs.

Deleanu would occasionally work out a puzzle or read a book in the win-
tertime. And below the small, low down sky, as Dănuț wanted it, he would
have liked to have a carpet lit by the flames of the stove, and a sleepy cat…

On the table, there was also a lamp with a lamp-shade. Under the table
you could see mother's foot in thin slippers, motionless or rising sideways
when mother was at a loss, or beating time with the tips when mother was
cross. Dănuț would sit under the table, of course, Olguța was outdoors,
playing in the snow. But Dănuț needed no other games. Where he was, the
world was as small as a dollhouse. There was nothing in the world except
the legs of the table. In the middle were Dănuț, mother's slippers, and the
cat. Dănuț knew what mother did because he could see what the slippers
were doing. He knew when she smiled when she frowned when she got
cross. After a time the cat would purr. And there was such a silence! The
warmth of the stove when it reached there was soft and sleepy… It was
there that started the tales with Tom Thumb… It was there that Dănuț had
fashioned a small world, with men as small as letters, with animals the size
of capitals and cottages never bigger than a book of tales so that only fairy
tales could get in. Dănuț alone was a giant, but what a decent giant!… It was
pleasant there! It was Dănuț, but what a decent giant!… It was pleasant
there! It was Dănuț's homeland, lighted by the fire in the stove, which
seemed to be the sun of carpets where children sleep and cats dream…

They had driven him out.

How high was the sky! How big the earth!

He set out for the orchard at a slow pace… What had happened in Ivan's
knapsack? What wind had withered, shaken down, and put to flight the
emperors, Prince Charming, the tales…? Was Ivan's knapsack empty?

Dănuț was walking alone. Nobody accompanied him. The armies that
always marched in his wake or which waited for him ahead had vanished.
A desert stood before him, a desert behind him. He had been driven out of
the house and there was school-time ahead.

"Where he was, the world was as small as a dollhouse.
There was nothing in the world except the legs of the table."

Ivan's knapsack was empty, and heavy because life's sorrow had got in, replacing the sorrow of fairy-tales, with the doleful, deathlike oppression of autumn over forests.

On the way to the orchard, Ali caught up with him, fawning.

Ali alone loved Dănuț. And when Dănuț had left, the two of them would be alone: Dănuț in Bucharest, Ali at Medeleni.

"Dănuț!"

Monica was running to catch up with him, her plaits dangling behind.

She caught up with him in the orchard. She was panting.

"I'm so sorry you're leaving Dănuț!" she confessed, her eyes on the brink of tears. She had taken him by the hand and was looking big-eyed at him.

"What have I done to you all? What do you want of me? Why won't you leave me alone?"

He wrenched his hand away from Monica and set off, estranging himself from his family in the autumn twilight.

"What have I done to him?" Monica murmured, covering her face with her hands... "Poor Dănuț!"

And because Ali alone was following Dănuț, Monica, although dismissed, set off after Ali...

Sweet and bitter fragrances, peppered scents, faint perfumes, indistinct, hardly felt breaths that could not be made out...

A ray of sunshine, the breeze from the stubble fields, from gardens and tilled land, the fruit and leaves hanging from the branches, the tree trunks, the earth, the fallen leaves and fruit, and the wilting blades of grass all blended their fragrances.

Spirits floated between the trees and rose from the grass and the wind, and the fall of the leaves caressed griefs that did not pucker any brows and a laceration that had not been perpetrated by any hands.

A departure was being prepared everywhere, but nowhere could be seen the cheerless trunk of departures or the woman sitting on it, trembling with cold, with knees and elbows drawn close together, covering her eyes so as not to see, so as not to weep.

But autumn?

Monica had hidden behind the trunk of a magnificent apple tree. The ripe apples above her bent the branches, burdening them, as earrings with too weighty precious stones do the ears of little children.

From her hiding place, Monica kept company with Dănuț secretly.

She was tired. That is why she knelt.

Dănuț sat motionless on the bench under the walnut tree. Monica could only see his head, which he bent over the oak table. The sunlight fell right over him, burnishing his curls.

Leaves, sunspots, and dark walnuts in their dark green husks fell on the oak table. An age-old book with pages of walnut leaves burdened by sunlight seemed to have come to pieces. And the bent head of a young faun was dreaming...

If a tear from Dănuț's eyes had glittered in the sunlight, Monica would have dared to come out of her hiding place. But leaves alone fell from the walnut branches.

Dănuț's mind had become so estranged from Dănuț's body that the murmur of his lips was the murmur of a child who could hardly speak. The smile alone was perhaps Dănuț's own, though it might have been the smile of the sunlight of his cheeks.

Meaningless verses that in the past borrowed the artless charm of lips which could laugh but could hardly speak came to his mind. They had been taught to him by a peasant nurse who recalled the verses of her childhood. Dănuț was three years old at the time, wore a dress, like Olguța, and could not pronounce his r's. He would recite the lines in Mrs. Deleanu's arms and on finishing he would get sweets and kisses. When put to bed, he would whisper the lines until he fell asleep.

He could vaguely hear his mother's voice from the bed that was faintly lightly by the shaded lamp, urging him to sleep. And he would go on whispering under his breath, smiling because he alone knew the sequence of it. And smiling, he would fall asleep.

…Walnut leaves fell one by one or several of them together on the oak table.

Last spring the trees were in bloom; now there were no blossoms on them; yellow leaves fell from them, giving a dry rustle. Perhaps that was why the verse which left that sleepy smile on Dănuț's lips — the smile of a three-year-old — and which was meaningless now, came off his lips so sadly, torn as it was from the past.

A moist coolness rose from the orchard as the shadows grew longer. Monica had crossed her hands on her breast: she was trembling. Dănuț was thinly dressed too. He might catch a cold. She stood up and rubbed her sore knees. She made her way back, hiding behind the tree trunks. She stopped to look: Dănuț was motionless. She ran as quickly as she could to bring Dănuț a sweater.

…When you're very sad you feel like sleeping. You feel like laying your head on the knees of someone who loves you, or if you have no one and are alone, to lay it on your palms… Yes. You feel like sleeping when you're sad and you want to forget… But when you're awake? You're sad and can't fall asleep again.

Dănuț sighed.

…Why were the leaves falling?... Because autumn had set in… Were the leaves dead?... No. The leaves were falling; they died on the ground because autumn had set in… Autumn…

Were the leaves falling or did they want to fall?... As autumn had set in, what business had they on the branches?...

When autumn sets in, the birds fly away and the leaves fall...

If Dănuţ had been a leaf on the walnut's branch and autumn had come, what would he have done?... All the leaves about him would have fallen and he would have been left ever lonelier — as he was now... Yes. And he would have hurled himself from the branch... and the wind would have carried him away and would have mixed him with the other leaves; who knows where it would have flung him... and nobody would have known about him...

...When you're very sad you feel like sleeping to forget...

A strange thought was approaching Dănuţ, from outside as it seemed; so strange a thought that Dănuţ's eyes opened wide, but they were blind as one is in the dark when fear approaches, heart-gripping fear that strangles one's heart...

There was a tall bank at the end of the orchard — as tall for Dănuţ as the branch from which the leaf hurled itself down was for that leaf... The leaves float, slide down, and settle down gently... The nuts fall and break... Nuts have no blood. If they had, the blood would trickle over their shell... as it does over a man... A man with a broken head... a sad, unfortunate man...

"Dănuţ! Dănuţ! Where are you, Dănuţ? Where's Dănuţ?"

And the cattle keeper would have found him down the bank with a broken head, streams of blood running down the cheeks... Dănuţ dead? He dead?...

"Me?"

"Impossible!" a remote thought around him like the eastern horizon and murmured.

...Everybody is in mourning. They walk behind Dănuţ's coffin... They weep... Dănuţ himself feels weeping because he also walks behind the coffin.

"Dead?"

Alone in the coffin? Alone in the grave? In black earth?... At night, when ghosts come out? And alone!

"No. It's better to go to school."

Dănuţ gave a deep sigh.

...Broken walnuts and the fallen leaves die in autumn. Dănuţ goes to school in autumn.

Monica appeared behind the bench like an icon lighted by the candles of the setting sun. Without a word, she put the sweater on Dănuţ's shoulders... and unwittingly, unwillingly, her thin arms went around his neck and her lips kissed his curls...

Realizing that the arms were not his mother's, Dănuţ sprang up and shook his curls.

"Who's given you leave to kiss me?..."

"Why have you brought me my sweater?"

"So that you don't catch a cold, Dănuţ," Monica mumbled, swallowing hard.

"I'd rather catch a cold. Why do you meddle?"

"I pity you!"

"Who's given you leave to pity me? I don't need pity!"

Ah! The holidays were not at an end. He'll show them! He got hold of Monica's plaits and pulled. Monica's head drew back quietly. A memory shot before Dănuţ's eyes. At the beginning of the holidays, at the time when the apricots were ripening in the orchard, he had pulled Monica's plaits... He had been afraid of Monica... And he had been sorry. How quickly the holidays had passed. School time was beginning! He was going to leave. It was cold; it was autumn.

"Are you cross, Monica?" he asked her sweetly, letting go of her plaits....

He couldn't see her face — only her heavy, fair plaits.

"I'm sorry, Monica. Forgive me... Aren't you cold?"

Monica's head shook to signify a no.

"Do you want us to run together?"

Monica's head nodded to signify a yes.

"You're a horse and I'm driving you. Yes?"

"Yes."

"Heigh-ho, horsey!" Dănuţ's voice was strong and shrill.

The holidays were not at an end!

Awakened from his sleep, Ali spurted onward, arrow-like. Golden plaits in hand, Dănuţ was running below golden leaves. Monica was running before him, her face both weeping and smiling. And everywhere around them was Autumn...

...Long thin clouds had spread from high up in the deep blue sky to the western horizon, like numberless marble steps of fairy tale palaces.

In the glorious light — like torches raised by the courtiers' arms — a black spot appeared and was gone. Perhaps a swallow. And the sunset beyond the world, taking with it the delicate slipper lost by summer on the last step of the heavenly palace, and the melancholy of the princes in love with Cinderella...

***

Monica gave a start in her sleep, murmuring indistinct words.

She was sleeping on one side, uncovered, her legs doubled up at the knees, one of her fists beside her forehead, the other on her thigh — a white childish bareness in the moonlight, seemingly a little statue of overturned flight.

"Heigh-ho, horsey!"

She was running in the orchard, unable to see Dănuţ who was driving her from behind by pulling her plaits.

She was startled; her dream fluttered before her eyes like long, disheveled hair... She rose and covered her feet with the rug.

"Heigh-ho, horsey!" the heavenly voice from her dream murmured.

She smiled happily and lay down on her back. How nice Dănuţ was! What a gentle smile he had! How sweet were his golden-green eyes! His curls had the fragrance of roasted chestnuts. And how quickly he got over his grief!...

"Heigh-ho, horsey!"

Smiling with her eyes closed, Monica turned her head on the pillow, awaiting sleep... and the dream which would again join her plaits to Dănuţ's hands.

***

With autumn's rustle and the chirping of the crickets, the white dance of the moon rippled at the windows.

In the dark, Mr. Deleanu rolled a cigarette and lit it, bending over the edge of the bed.

"You can't sleep either?"

"I'm smoking, Alice."

"What's the time?"

The flame of a match flickered, disturbing the shadows.

"Rather late... It's one o'clock."

Mrs. Deleanu left her bed and put her kimono over her shoulders. She entered Dănuţ's room, pressing and raising the handle unheard. Dănuţ was sleeping with lips half-open. He had uncovered himself. His white nightdress had gathered above his knees, exposing long legs with scratched knees, gently rounded calves, and slender ankles.

Moonlight played on his open palm. Moonlight quivered on his hair and in his cheeks.

Like a page gone to sleep at the feet of a fair lady whose white feather fan lit his sleep.

Mrs. Deleanu covered him, caressed his rounded curls with her finger-tips, and went out walking lightly.

"How is he?"

"He's asleep."

"It's good to be a child!" Mr. Deleanu said, nodding as he crushed his cigarette in the ash-tray.

"Poor children!" Dănuț's mother murmured for her benefit.

The petals of a rose on the bedside table fell with white, uncertain movements — just as young children uncover themselves in their sleep when dreaming.

II. Robinson Crusoe

I t was raining…

The last cart in the gypsies' camp had stopped in the roadway not very far from the gate of the gentlefolks' yard. The thin horses stood as dead, with heavy heads, and the angular cat bound with a string behind the cart meowed feebly.

Under the cart's canvas, which was the color of the clouds, the gypsy women's tattered yellow and red garments and the fiery glints of the golden necklaces could hardly be made out in the darkness, misty as it was with the smoke of pipes, though occasionally pierced by ruby stars.

A woman's voice murmured gently, singing perhaps, as she put to sleep a child or her grief.

Shivering in the drizzle, Anica rested her heart and her spread-out hand on the chestnut-colored palm of the fortune teller. Now spaced out, now quick and mumbled, the words that told the fortune brought with them hope or fear. Anica looked in fear at the fateful finger that sought in her palm the ways of life, the paths of good luck, and the groves of love.

The rain was intensifying, the wind carrying it this way and that. A harsh voice under the tilt spoke sharply.

The fortune-teller took her money and made for the cart, Anica entered the yard with her head bent. Under the oak by the gate, she saw the faint trace of a car tire. Her eyes looked to the misty distance. She sighed. All the roads were blotted by the dense grayness. She shook with a cold tremor and ran into the house. The dogs gathered under the eaves hardly gave her a look.

In that lifeless landscape, the gypsies' cart rumbled on, carrying under its canvas autumn's last fires and colors and leaving behind a grey sky, like a sickly moonlight.

No barking could be heard. The rain alone spoke to itself like a crazy beggar woman.

**

Through the small windows of the attic, streaked by the rain on the outside and wizened by the spiders within, the light entered like a flow of lace long ago thrown in there among the old things. And there were so many things! As the old people had left the house for the cemetery, the attic had filled with everything that had satisfied their habits and strange inclinations, their own or those of their time — rather than their needs.

Fița Elencu's room had been banished to the attic in full like the remains of the plaque-stricken. The capacious armchairs and sofas, with arched legs and restful backs, upholstered in blue silk brought from France, had grown grey with the silence that slumbered in them. The stools from France had grown grey with the silence that slumbered in them. The stools, like turtles with a blue shell, had grown stiff with the weight of time. And all the books of various kinds and various ages thumbed by Fița's dry fingers and run through by her green eyes were lying in cases or were piled up on the ground.

In a corner, strange musical instruments, devised by an eccentric music-loving ancestor, were waiting for a grandchild in whom the soul of the fore-runners would come alive, to revive the muted melodies. Violins of light-colored wood with curbed neck; brown violins the color of burnt sugar with the sinuous neck of swans; violas with the bulging belly of voluptuousness; cobzas, mandolins, and guitars vying with each other in tortuousness and complexity. All of them drowned in silence!

Piles of portraits with black, brown, or golden frames, whether square or oval, of wood or velvet, big and small, gradually taken off the walls of the rooms downstairs rested together on the shoulder of the same forget-fulness; the portraits seemed to be the image of dust and spiders and not of human faces.

There was a smell of wood heated by the high temperature, of dry mold, and the dust of archives.

So that in the attic the fragrance of fresh peaches was fearfully cheerful…

…I was dining like a king before his court. The parrot alone, a favorite, had leave to speak to me. My aging dog always sat on my right; the two cats at each end of the table, waiting for me to throw them a piece of meat…

On reaching this passage, Dănuţ turned the book on its back, put it down on the floor, took a bright-colored peach, and bit noisily out of it.

The happiest man in the world was Robinson Crusoe, such as the glossy picture on the cover showed him to be.

Between his hut — a cave rather — and the palm tree from whose trunk hung a coconut, the sea could be seen beyond the low fence; it was harmless and as pretty as a small cornflower garden.

At the hut's entrance, in the green-black hole, an allegorical spider had woven a negligently polygonal web. From the hut, young grass grew, with the green reflections of still wet watercolor.

It must have been very hot on the day when Robinson had this snapshot taken because over the sugar-loaf cap, which covered his ears and the nape of his neck like a hood, there was a sunshade made of palm leaves with its edges rosy with sunlight, under a blue sky through which the red letters of the title were lined up: Robinson Crusoe. That's how Robinson fancied it: to dress in thick clothes in any weather. The coat of fluffy fur was cut to fit a thin waist… Robinson had a pleasant-looking face; he looked like Santa Claus except for his beard and mustache, which were chestnut. His mustache turned up wittily; his cheeks were ruddy; his beard was nicely trimmed and curls came out in profusion from below his cap down to his eyebrows, like a bang curled with an iron.

In his left hand, raised above his left knee, he held the parrot. Or rather, it was the parrot that supported the hand, because all the fingers, which were correctly lined up, rested on the parrot's greenback as if on a flute's holes; while the four doll-like fingers of the right hand, floated on the back of the goat which stretched its muzzle towards the parrot as if wishing to kiss it or to feed on it.

Robinson was seated on… impossible to see what on. He sat like fakirs on air. At his feet, which were set wide apart and on tiptoe, like those of someone lifting a child on his knees — a spade crossed another implement beheaded by the cover frame. The cats were probably sleeping in the hut or on the hut's roof. The dog had left the cover and was snoring at Dănuţ's feet in the attic. Its name is Ali. A parrot — similar to the one on the cover, but stuffed — was also on watch in the attic.

Robinson's island, with the merry loneliness of the cover picture, had been removed to the attic full of old things. Dănuţ was Robinson Crusoe on Robinson Crusoe's island And it gave him a comfortable feeling.

Robinson's beard on the book cover was full of fragrant drops… because in the attic full of old things at Medeleni. Robinson Crusoe was eating peaches in the company of a sleeping dog and of a stuffed parrot.

***

The papers and books of Mr. Deleanu's two studies — in Iaşi and on the country estate — experienced an ebb and a flow, owing in turn to Mrs. Deleanu's magnetic orderliness and Mr. Deleanu tumultuous outbursts.

At the time of the flow, the room was like any other room, equipped with massive manly study furniture kept most strictly in an orderly and clean condition. At such a time, Mr. Deleanu was not at home or did not work.

At the time of the ebbing, there was everywhere an onrush of many-colored and Proteus-shaped files, reviews, newspapers, copybooks, note-books, sheets of paper, letters, telegrams, receipts, notes, tobacco, cigarette, boxes, and matchboxes, all derived from inside or above the cupboards, from drawers and shelves, and the pockets of all his coats, including spring and winter coats, and from all his dressing gowns and pajamas. At such times Mr. Deleanu was working like Neptune amidst swirling waves.

A telegram arrived that morning from Iaşi had unleashed the ebbing. It ran as follows:

Arrested fraudulent bankruptcy. Warrant confirmed. Please draw up statement indictment Chamber. Urgent intervention. The wife comes with money, information. Don't let me down. Respects Blumm.

A testy pen ran across the sheet of paper. Mrs. Blumm, vehemently banished from the study, was waiting in the drawing-room, wearing her hat, her umbrella and bag in hand, straining her ears to hear and sighing through the nose with grief and a head cold.

A testy pen ran across the sheet of paper. Mrs. Blumm, vehemently banished from the study, was waiting in the drawing-room, wearing her hat, her umbrella and bag in hand, straining her ears to hear and sighing through the nose with grief and a head cold.

Mr. Deleanu lit a cigarette angrily, gave a sidelong glance to the stereo-type motivation of the warrant for arrest… and the oratory imprisoned in the pen burst out:

"It is revolting…"

He crossed that out... He smiled on imagining the spasmodic ring of the hand bell of justice — a justice that was statuary and cantankerous, like all women who don't get enough exercise.

"...It is strange and insulting to witness how easy it is to deprive a man of freedom in a civilized society which shows how easy it is to deprive a man of freedom in a civilized society that shows regard for wealth but not for men. Preventive confinement ultimately amounts to putting one under illegal constraint..."

When Mr. Deleanu worked nobody entered his study, apart from Olguţa, of course.

"I'm bringing you your coffee, Papa... Will I spill it or not?" she asked as she balanced the cup in her hand while approaching her father.

"What you spill is for you."

"Do you want me to keep from spilling altogether?"

"Why?"

"You'll think I've done it on purpose."

Mr. Deleanu sipped his coffee from the cup, Olguţa from the saucer.

"It's so cold, such nasty weather, Papa! One feels like getting ill."

"It seems to me there is nothing for you to do, Olguţa."

Olguţa looked at him from under her eyebrows, controlling a yawn that had suddenly come to her, like a sneeze.

"I have something to do," she said. "I go about the house... but it irks me that the weather isn't fine."

"What can we do?" Mr. Deleanu wondered, his attention divided between Olguţa and the statement.

"Don't bother, Papa. I'm disturbing you. I can see you're busy."

"When will you up, Olguţa?"

"Why, Papa?"

"So that we can work together."

"How nice that would be, Papa! We would have fun all the time and drink coffee!"

"Yes! We'd have a rollicking time."

"But we would also work," Olguța added, raising her eyebrows.

"No doubt."

"You would dictate and I would write, Papa… And when you got tired, I would dictate and you would write!... And you wouldn't need any secretary!"

"I would have you receive the clients."

"The women clients, Papa. I would show them!"

"Right you are! They are terrible. They ought to pay double."

"Is the woman in the drawing-room divorcing, Papa?"

"How did you draw that conclusion?"

"She's sighing, Papa. I can't stand her. She wanted to kiss me!"

"Unheard of!"

"Yes, Papa. What am I?... And what is the matter with women? They keep kissing people!"

"That's their occupation!"

"I'll never kiss!"

"You won't even kiss Father?"

"Of course I'll kiss you. That's different."

"We get on famously, Olguța!"

"A pity you aren't a child, Papa. We could play together! I should have liked the two of us to be brothers."

"We're friends."

"I'm not letting you work, Papa. I'll be going!"

"Where?"

"Into the drawing-room."

"With Mrs. Blumm?"

"Oh well, Papa... You're working and she's sighing. I'll do so many scales on the piano that she'll cry."

"Well said, Olguţa. After which we show her out and dispatch her to the station!"

"That's it, Papa; we'll show her out!"

"And we two will tidy up the study."

Olguţa smiled. She knew what tidying up meant.

"What a father you've got, Olguţa!"

"You shouldn't have turned into a father... But you're alright as you are!"

"To your liking?"

"Yes, Papa... It's as if I had got you as a present from Moş Gheorghe!"

***

The dining room was invaded by colored gossamer, like all seamstresses' shops. Dănuţ's school dowry was being made in the dining room. Being handled by intermittent but ever refreshed hands, the sewing machine was giving out a metal jingle in a galloping crescendo, then stopping suddenly to start again, like a wife that was reproving her husband in impassioned installments.

The ethical and professional loquaciousness of the seamstress brought over from Iaşi finding no echo here had been converted into sullen dumbness belied by the dance of the feet on the pedals and by the red patter of the hair.

Scissors in hand, Mrs. Deleanu, hermetically enclosed in a white pina-
fore recalling those of hospital nurses, was cutting out on the table, an oil-
cloth ruler going round her neck.

Seated sideways near the window on a chair with two cushions, Monica,
her back a little bent, was embroidering initials on handkerchiefs: D.D.,
That is Dan Deleanu. That is how he was to be called at school, according
to the roll.

Monica was embroidering the first D a little smaller than the second,
imperatively smaller because even Monica's hands could not call Dănuț
otherwise than Dănuț.

If people knew!... D.D., that is Dănuț Deleanu... The needle hesitated in
Monica's hands. The truth came out on the bright cheeks that bent over
Monica's heart, like the scent of red carnations... D.D., that is "dear Dănuț."

The two initials were Monica's first love letter.

"Haven't you seen the patterns, Monica?"

Monica gave a start and the handkerchief slipped onto her knees. Miss
Clara, who knew everything, even the place where the patter was to be
found, answered instead of Monica, with a gracious, freckled smile.

"Who has given you leave to kiss me?" Dănuț had said angrily when
she had kissed him in the orchard.

"Who has given you leave to be fond of me?" Dănuț would have said
angrily, had he known.

"Dear Dănuț..."

Yes, we had given her leave to be fond of him?

She smiled... Who knows?...

Perhaps Dănuț would have given her leave to be fond of him...

***

"Little one!"

The piano replied with a deep C.

Mrs. Blumm nodded.

With the little finger of the left hand and the thumbs of the right hand, Olguța had struck a fierce double C in the extreme left of the piano also pressing the pedal. A mountain thunderclap crossed the drawing-room, striking the window panes and the mirrors.

Olguța was planning a douche ecossaise for the client's tympanum. And so the scale ran at a sprightly tempo, the sounds getting ever thinner until, with the pedal help, it turned into a blizzard of piercing vibrations, into a pricking whiz for the ear, from which the right-hand shrillness was hurled back towards the violent left-hand sonorities.

The wailing increased... The sounds tumbled upon each other with the disorderly violence of a brawl in a hooligan tavern.

Olguța lifted her foot from the pedal. The uncurbed scale ceased. The lull was like a fragrance of lime blossoms. Softly, with Jesuit sweetness, the normal scale, like a procession of nuns, made its way into the drawing-room.

Olguța's eyes and ears were on the alert.

But the listener's tympanum had for long got used to irritating sounds in answer to household questions, and also to tempestuous music for which good money had been paid and which made one dizzy... but aroused the envy of the other shopkeepers. Mrs. Blumm's daughter had gone through the piano classes at the Iași Conservatory. Miss Rashella read Fleurs du Mal and played Wagner on the piano.

It did not occur to Olguța that the listener had turned into an admirer. Mrs. Blumm approved of it all and marveled at the absence of notes. Olguța was supposed to be playing by heart. It was great! Like Rashella, but Rashella's notes cost a great deal of money! The little one was like her father. He spoke so well, and by heart too! He was her last hope...

Olguța's arms were tired. She gradually shortened the range of the scales which became equal and monotonous like a morning drill after sleep.

It was cold in the drawing-room. The rain darkened the windows. The light that got in was a blurred white, like a haze...

"What?"

She couldn't believe her ears. She turned her head and looked over her shoulder. Mrs. Blumm had fallen asleep, keeping hold of her bag and umbrella. She had fallen asleep orchestrally: she would sip the air while sighing as if it were hot soup, snore, sigh again, and snort through the nose and the mouth.

Olguța turned her head in digest... She was out of sorts and she had no one to take it out on... Monica was her friend... Humpty-Dumpty... Dănuț was leaving... Moreover, for the last two days, ever since it had started raining, a restlessness had got hold of Olguța's heart: she wished to stave it off and had no means of doing so. Some words she had happened to hear:

"What can be the matter with Mos. Gheorghe? He's got so thin!" the bailiff of a neighboring estate had asked.

"Approaching death, that's what's the matter. It's time too," Ion, Moș Gheorghe's successor at the stables hand answered with a sigh.

"Aren't you ashamed to tell such lies?" Olguța had cut in, stamping her foot.

That had been all. But ever since, she had been afraid of Ion's lies whenever she was alone. And was mad at with herself, at her fear, as if she had thus believed Ion's lies to be true, thus inducing them somehow to come true.

She began to play Mozart's Concerto in A major for piano and orchestra, this time with notes. In music as in life, Olguța had violent likes and dislikes. Mozart's concerto was her friend.

"What do you practice, Olguța?" Mrs. Deleanu would ask her when she saw her in the drawing-room, which was not often.

"I'll practice my concerto!" Olguṭa would answer, expropriating Mozart and the future.

Her concerto sounded melancholic. She closed the notes... Mrs. Blumm was adoring lugubriously... In the house, everybody was working... Outside it was raining. Olguṭa rested her forehead on the keyboard. Suddenly pressed, the keys whined. Angrily, revolting, Olguṭa's foot struck the second — the mute — pedal.

***

Many years had passed over the pages and the attic, since Robinson's dinner in the company of the parrot, the dog, and the cats. Pulpy peaches were smiling in the past; there were only peach stoned now, like small wooden hearts. Ali had grown old in his sleep; he may have died. The parrot with its faded and dusty feathers was silent, being stuffed with the past. The snowy dust and cobwebs had spread grey snowdrifts, old-time silence. At the windows, there was rain, grey rain, in autumn's sky and in the sandglass of time.

Nor had Dănuṭ been spared by the long passage of the years. On his face, though differently from the insipid translation, one could see that Robinson was leaving his island, that he was parting forever from a tale he had lived through for long.

Bidding farewell to the island, I took with me my cap and my sunshade...

Dănuṭ sighed — and resumed his reading five lines above, just as a lover does not wait for his train on the platform but in the waiting room because it is a little nearer to the house of the beloved and a little farther from the last threshold of the parting.

...Not long after...

His eyes read intently "not long after" but the violas and the sweet cellos of melancholy were weeping with a similar long bending of the bow, "bidding farewell to the island…"

…Not long after, the boat holding the promised stores was sent to the island. According to my request, the master also loaded the cases with the clothes of the sailors which the latter were glad to receive…

And again:

Bidding farewell to the island…

Dănuț's eyes, dim with tears, bade a long farewell to the picture on the cover, stained by the tears of joy. Robinson also cried, through smiling. The tears were those of Dănuț and not of the text. At the time he had smiled on the cover, he did not know he was going to leave. Giving his attention to the cap and the sunshade, the translator had forgotten the tears.

The text urgently, implacably, advanced under Dănuț's eyes.

Bidding farewell to the island, I took with me the cap, the sunshade, and the parrot, nor did I forget the money I have spoken about, which having been hidden for so long, had got rusty!

"…On the island." Dănuț's thoughts added, deeming the money happy. There were seven lines left to the end.

…Thus did I leave my island on December 19th, 1686, after a sojourn of 28 years, two months, and nineteen days, having been saved from the slavery of the Moors of Sale.

Didn't he look at the island from the boat until it was out of sight? Didn't he wave his handkerchief?

Dănuț had another look at the picture on the cover. How was that? A sad like on the island? Why was Robinson laughing then? And why did the island around him, which was the color of Robinson's cheeks, seem to laugh?

He resumed:

Thus did I leave my island…

He had laid the book on his knees. He read and cried, wiping his eyes with his hands.

It was a lucky voyage. I reached England on the 11th of June of the year 1687, having been away from my homeland for thirty-five years.

"Thirty-five years," Dănuț's lips murmured in the silence of the attic. And he had taken nothing from the island! Not a stone? Not a handful of sand! Not a flower or a leaf!… Not a thing!

Dănuț closed the book, bent his wet cheeks over the cover, and gave a deep, long kiss to the colored sadness of happiness.

Dănuț's heart was an island Robinson had left, taking with him only his cap, his sunshade, and his parrot.

…The first grade… the second… the third… the fourth… the fifth… the sixth… the seventh… the eighth…; and more grades after that…

Dănuț alone facing an ocean of school desks…

In the attic, there was only what had once been. In the attic was Robinson Crusoe's island. Beyond the attic were the school desks…

Bidding farewell to the island, Dănuț arranged his book in the case of playthings that had been spoilt and of books that had been read, called to Ali, and left the attic… But Ivan's knapsack now opened desperately wide and swallowed up the attic… But Ivan's knapsack now opened desperately wide and swallowed up the attic, the island, the moment, together with the cobwebs, tears, dust, peach fragrance, and the smiling pictures…

That was probably why Dănuț's shoulders were stooping.

He went down the steps, passing from the attic full of old things into the heart of autumn.

"In the attic was Robinson Crusoe's island.
Beyond the attic were the school desks…"

***

Being in haste and unable to find her galoshes. Olguța took those of Dănuț. They were too big for her. She had to drag them through the slippery slime.

When fear chases you from behind and you can't run, the way to traverse causes your breast to perspire and your heart to thump, as nightmares do.

Wrapped in a rubber mantle, her bare head covered with the hood, Olguța advanced with difficulty... She thrust her toes forward as hard as she could towards the tip of the galoshes so as not to lose them... They sank in the mud... She had to strain her calves and pull sideways to proceed on her way.

It was as if she was dragging an iron ball with stone steps at the bottom of a sea crawling with jellyfish...

Kneeling before the icons, Moș Gheorghe was praying.

The silence around the old man that prays is like the sound of a horn far away.

The religious fragrance of sweet basil floated in the air. The slender light in the red glass before the icon shed a red glow on the dark faces of the icons, as the presentiment of dawn reddens the trunks of the dense forests.

Now and again Moș Gheorghe would unclasp his hands that had been joined for prayer and put them against his chest racked with coughing.

God had steadily fulfilled his prayers, and he would fulfill them henceforward also.

It was right that he should cough: because he was old.

It was right that he would perspire and have pains in the chest: because he was old.

It was right that he should suffer throughout the time he would go on living, that he should die as soon possible: because he was old.

Everything that was, was right. He did not find fault with it, he did not complain, he did not sigh. Moş Gheorghe did not want blasphemy in his mind or a whimper to cause God to turn away his merciful face, his lenient ear. Now on the heavenly threshold of death, Moş Gheorghe asked for mercy for other people's failings: his present-day gentlefolk never partook of the sacrament and only seldom visited the church founded by their fore-fathers. Though they were kind, bountiful, and righteous, they had forgot-ten the House of God, the fear of God.

"Forgive them, of Lord, for great is thy kindness!"

God had fulfilled his prayers. He did not pray for himself. Moş Gheor-ghe was to step into the world beyond followed by the eyes of the poor horses which he had looked after and had spared as if they had been or-phans.

He was praying for the child who was as innocent as the dew and as beautiful as the flowers, from whom he was soon to part.

"The old man's young lady!"

Let not the parent's error weigh heavy upon her. Let her life be calm, devoid of pains and bitterness.

Moş Gheorghe's soul lay at God's feet, like a carpet of kindness on which he would have liked his young lady to spend her childhood on earth before the glorified grandfather up in heaven…

Olguţa ran across Moş Gheorghe's yard holding the galoshes in her hand. On reaching the door, she tried to get in. The door was bolted on the inside… She struck the door with her fists. No answer.

She threw down the galoshes and struck the door hard with both fists.

"Moş Gheorghe! She shouted in a peremptory, but trembling voice."

"…What is it, Miss? You're here? In this weather?"

On hearing and seeing him, Olguța took a deep breath. She picked up the galoshes covered with thick mud and recovering her composure she smiled cunningly as she shook off the rain.

"I've come to ask you whether the horses aren't cold, Moș Gheorghe!"

***

Dănuț had wandered through the house outside the rooms without entering any of them. He found no place suitable and was fretful. Reading in the attic for so long had estranged him from everything. He was yearning for Robinson's island; he pitied its loneliness and his own.

The familiar scenery that met him was an actual presence that estranged him from the house, as roughness does when one is sad. Thus, the scent of a woman you have parted from with tears continues to haunt your heart and your nostrils; the melody of any other woman's voice then seems commonplace to you and the delicacy of any other solicitude seems to be rude.

Estrangements, sorrows, and yearnings that are doomed only to find solace and a home in the letters written by hands that are still warm from being grasped by the desired hands, letters of humble lamentations as bitter as the fragrance of the small autumn chrysanthemums.

He entered Mrs. Deleanu's small drawing-room. He saw the calendar on her desk and approached it. It was opened on a black-letter day, the following day was also a black-letter day. They were all black-letter days. It was as if all the red-letter days in the calendar had come to an end together with the holidays and the three leaves…

He entered his room.

The thick clothes recently taken out of the trunks were arranged on the backs of the chairs; they smelt of naphthalene. The cold stove where the wind whistled was sighing and wailing like a peasant suffering from consumption, increasing the cold in the room and its desolation.

And it was still so long until the night that Dănuţ felt like yawning and whimpering. He flung himself on the bed bringing his knees to the chin, putting his hands into the warm sleeves, coiling himself up. He was trying to keep himself company with his own body, as the cats...

Olguţa's head appeared in the doorway, cheekily questioning.

"Ah! You're here?"

"Yes."

"What are you doing?"

"Nothing. Just lying down."

"I came to see you."

What can Olguţa want? Dănuţ wondered. He looked apathetic but was on the lookout within.

Olguţa entered, holding in her hand Dănuţ's galoshes as glossy as if it is made of ebony. She was wearing slippers.

"I'll put them under the bed."

"Put what?"

"The galoshes? Why?"

"Your galoshes. Where do you want me to put them?"

"Put them under the bed."

What could she have done with my galoshes? "What have you done with the galoshes?"

"I've washed them," she explained, bringing them up to Dănuţ's nose like flowers she had just picked.

"Thank you," Dănuţ said, drawing away. "Why did you wash them?"

"It just occurred to me I might. I had nothing to do."

"Did you wash your shoes as well?" Dănuţ asked seriously, rising to rest on an elbow.

Olguţa frowned, but changing her mind, she smiled.

"You went to the attic?" she queried, screwing up her eyes.

"Who told you?" Dănuţ was startled.

"I know."

"Don't tell on me, Olguţa!"

"Don't worry about that!" she assured him, gesticulating with the galoshes.

"Thank you. But where have you been?"

"I went for a walk."

"With my galoshes?"

"With galoshes!" Olguţa was angry. She threw the galoshes under the bed.

"I see!"

"You don't see anything. Listen: do you feel like carobs?"

"Have you got any?"

"Of course."

"Where from?"

"Just answer: do you or don't you want any?"

"I want some."

Olguţa took a spring with her hands over the threshold and landed in her room.

"Aha!" Making the connection between Olguţa's carobs and his galoshes, Dănuţ understood.

"Here are the carobs..."

"Thank you... They're good, very good!" Dănuţ exclaimed. He knew they came from Moş Gheorghe.

Olguţa was smiling. She was flattered. Dănuţ smiled too; he was proud to have been more cunning than Olguţa.

"What if mother sees you without any stockings on, Olguţa?"

"How could she see me?"

"Haven't you got any stockings?"

"I have… but I can't bother to look for them."

"I can let you have a pair!"

"Long ones?"

"Yes. They're for school. I haven't worn them."

"Let me have them. I'll give you other stockings."

"No. It's a present!"

Whenever Dănuţ happened to be Olguţa's accomplice, he would extend to himself his admiration for her doings. The offer of stockings was a moral obligation and payment for flattery.

Olguţa sat down on Dănuţ's bed crossing her legs Turkish fashion, took off her slippers, and looked at her bare feet while waiting for the stockings.

"Can you move your big toe without moving the others?"

"I can't."

"Why do you laugh?" Olguţa asked, frowning, as she demonstrated the acrobatic feat in which she excelled.

"I don't know… Toes are ridiculous!"

"My toes," Olguţa asked threateningly.

"No. All toes."

"You're right," Olguţa pondered aloud, stretching her foot and examining the toes she had spread out… "You feel like laughing when you look at them."

Encouraged by the intimacy of the talk, Dănuţ sat down on the edge of the bed. "I have noticed something, Olguţa," he said.

"Go ahead!"

"You'll laugh… and say I'm talking nonsense!"

"I'll see about that… Have your say first."

"I... believe it's better to be a foot than a hand." He was spacing out the words and his eyes were directed towards Olguţa's foot.

"How's that?"

Dănuţ blushed.

"Say that once again...."

"Just a moment. You say it's better to be a foot than a hand?" Olguţa was considering the statement, while alternatively examining her hand and her foot. "I have never thought of it! Why do you say that?"

"I thought of it at school one day..."

"Come on, out with it!"

"You see... I sat on the bench. It was the arithmetic class. I was dividing the exercise book... and I got confused."

"Of course — mother wasn't with you!"

"So I thought it was better to be a foot than a hand... Because the feet weren't doing anything. They were there in their shoes... and had nothing to do. While my hand was trying to divide..."

"Yes. Of course! The feet weren't doing anything."

"Just what I said. What do you do with your feet? You play during the breaks and they rest during the classes!"

Dănuţ raised his shoulders; he had got excited talking.

"That's all very well, but you walk with your feet," Olguţa objected.

"I didn't contradict you. But don't you like walking?"

"Of course I like it!"

"You see! With your feet, you only do what you like."

"Do you like going to school?" Olguţa queried.

"Oh well, no."

"You see, your feet don't do only what you like."

Dănuţ pondered as he bit his finger.

"Wait a minute, Olguṭa. But the feet don't mind. They don't learn at school."

"That's so. They have breaks all the time."

"Well said. That's what I wanted to say myself."

"Wait. You first said it was better to be…"

"…a foot. Yes." Dănuṭ interposed, gesticulating with conviction.

"It's not so bad to be a hand either! In winter you wear gloves, stay in an overcoat pocket or a mitten… Hands are clever," Olguṭa smiled as she looked at her own hands pulling on Dănuṭ's stockings after having taken Dănuṭ's galoshes.

"If you're a foot, you have overshoes." Dănuṭ was timidly defending his point of view.

"That doesn't matter. Overshoes are ugly and the feet are silly. That's why you can't see them: you hide them in shoes. I side with the hands… Good stockings these! Thank you."

"What would you prefer, Olguṭa: to have your hands or your feet cut off?"

"Neither!"

"Oh well. What I mean is: if you were in a tale and the emperor ordered that you should have either your hands or your feet cut off, what would you choose?"

"I'd turn outlaw and would cut off his hands and feet — and tongue."

"You don't want to answer!"

"Haven't I answered you? He's got to choose. I don't give away any-thing."

Olguṭa jumped onto the carpet. Dănuṭ remained on the edge of the bed, musing.

"Can you imagine how it would be with your head cut off, Olguṭa?"

"Very unpleasant!"

"I can imagine... But it makes one dizzy."

"You needn't imagine it!"

"Have you never thought of it?"

"Why should I think of such a thing? I've got other things to think of. Have you got ahead to think that you haven't got it?"

"I've thought of it... Do you die if your head is out off?"

"Of course!"

Dănuţ did not dare to contradict Olguţa, but he shook his head in doubt.

"...I once looked into the mirror... and I imagined myself without a head."

"You should first have cut it off."

"I didn't cut off... I was looking into the mirror and imagined that the body was outside and the head in the mirror only."

"Oh! But you were thinking with your head. Which means that the thought was not in the mirror; it was in the head."

"In the head that was in the mirror," Dănuţ insisted.

"Didn't you break the window when you put it back in its place?"

"I was afraid, Olguţa. I was looking from the mirror only at my feet. This means that the feet were on one side and the head somewhere else... like two men facing each other, one of them headless. Like this Olguţa."

Dănuţ raised his palms placing them one in front of the other.

"Let's say that the eyes are here on the fingertips. So the right hand is the head in the mirror. You see, I bend my fingers and I see only the feet in the mirror!"

"Which means that you look into the mirror... and see foolish things!"

"You try it, Olguţa. After that, you feel like closing your eyes and falling asleep!"

Olguța was no longer listening. She was watching the orchard through
the window.

Dănuț sighed… He would have liked to tell Olguța lots of things now
that he was leaving. To tell her, for example, that if your head is cut off, you
don't die, entirely. Your head dies! Yes. Your body dies! Yes. But there is
something else: Ivan's knapsack. It cannot die because it does not live; it
doesn't have a body, nor a head. It exists "when you close your eyes." You
close your eyes when you are dead. This means that Ivan's knapsack remains where it is. Consequently, Dănuț doesn't die either because although
Ivan's knapsack belongs to Dănuț. Dănuț himself is in Ivan's knapsack.
When he closes his eyes, he can think of himself as if he were someone else.
Olguța is also in Ivan's knapsack. They are all in it. This means that if Danuț
dies, Ivan's knapsack remains. When Dănuț dies, the knapsack is his. Who
takes the knapsack after Dănuț dies? God… If God wishes, he breathes into
Ivan's knapsack and those in it come alive; Dănuț with them… Yes, but
Dănuț will no longer have a knapsack then. It is God that keeps the knap-
sack. On the other hand, all those that had been in the knapsack belong to
Dănuț because he has brought them to God in his knapsack. And at such a
time Dănuț will be the master outside just as he is now the master inside…

But Olguța won't listen to him.

"Where are the cartridges?" Olguța asked hurriedly, unhooking the gun
from the nail.

"What do you want to do?"

"Don't bother! Given them to me, quick!"

She walked on tiptoe to the window and opened it noiselessly. Autumn's mist filled the room! With rain pattering on it, a crow was balancing
on the small branch, a sure target for the gun.

"Let it be, the poor thing."

Olguța turned her neck back without moving the gun, measured up
Dănuț — with the look gamesters give to those who advise them, when the

game is at its height — turned her head again, aimed and shot. The crow fell. And all the crows in the orchard rose, an explosion of sonorous black turning the orchard and the sky into coal.

Olguța loaded the gun again.

"Why do you pity crows? I shot it in the head. I wanted to see if it lives without a head — like you."

"I don't pity crows, I thought you wanted to shoot a sparrow." The lie brought a blush to his cheeks.

"Did you see that shot?"

"Yes."

Olguța gave a start and raised the gun. "There's another!" she said.

The door opened simultaneously with the gunshot as if arranged beforehand. Mrs. Deleanu drew back, dropping Dănuț's pajamas.

"What's this, Olguța?"

"I'm shooting crows."

"I'll give that gun away."

"It's not mine, it's his, Mother dear!"

"Have it!" Dănuț said with a smile.

"Give it to Mother. Herr Direktor will give a sporting gun."

"Closing the window and go into your room. And you, Dănuț, will you please undress. I'll try your pajamas on."

"I want to see them too," Olguța pleaded as she closed the window.

"Be quiet, Olguța. You devise all sorts of things only just to anger me! The only thing I needed now was shooting in the house."

"If it rains! You sew, Mother dear — what beautiful pajamas! What can I do? I shoot!"

"Why don't you practice on the piano?"

"Certainly not that! What am I? A hired musician? The client snores while I play to her."

Making the most of her indignation, Olguța crossed the threshold and closed the door. She had thereby saved the gun from seizure, for which reason she smiled enigmatically.

Monica had just entered the room with the pile of lyrical handkerchiefs. Olguța's smile made her uneasy for she thought it applied to her. She avoided her eyes and hid the handkerchiefs behind her back.

"I've brought you ten carobs," Olguța informed her.

Monica blushed still more.

"Why are you so nice to me?" She said, her eyes on Olguța's slippers.

"Why do you say I'm kind to you?" Olguța cried out angrily.

Because you're too kind; I don't deserve it.

"That's not true! I won't have you talk that way. You're my friend. Why do you vex me?"

The door opened suddenly to let Mrs. Deleanu in.

"What's up?"

"Nothing."

"Why do you shout then?"

"Shout? Whom could I shout at? I speak loudly… to get warm."

"Get warm without letting me hear you!"

The door closed.

Monica sat down on the bed beside the handkerchiefs.

Olguța concealed the gun behind the stove and came near Monica. On catching sight of the handkerchiefs, she took the one on top and blew her nose before Monica could stop her.

"Olguța! What are you doing?"

"Can't you see?"

"Take mine."

"This one won't do?"

"It's Dănuț's."

Fortunately, Dănuț's handkerchief had only done duty for a musical instrument. Monica folded it and put it back.

"Have you noticed, Monica, that you feel like blowing your nose when you see several handkerchiefs!"

"Because you never have a hanky," Monica said angrily.

"Who's got a hanky? You alone have."

"Dănuț also," Monica protested, pressing the handkerchiefs with her palm.

"That's what you think. He'll lose them all in a week." Olguța assured her authoritatively.

"No, that's not true. Why do you say that?"

"Not true? Mother made so many hankies for him so that he should have enough of them to lose."

Monica looked up, then down. She turned her head to the right, then to the left.

"You see, Monica, when I've got a handkerchief I feel like blowing my nose... and you feel like crying. It's better not to have any."

***

In white flannel pajamas, Dănuț looked like Pierrot junior.

"Isn't it too tight under the arms, Dănuț?"

"No!"

"You'll put on the other pajamas there only when you're cold, Dănuț. It's not good to put on thick clothes when you sleep."

Mrs. Deleanu avoided the word dormitory.

Dănuț keep looking in the mirror. The pajama trousers were the first trousers of his childhood. He touched them again and again in an indistinct fear of feeling that they were suddenly cut off above the knees — where the old border of his knickers was — and so turn into knickers. They had a crease: the washerwoman's homage. The cheeky grace of the knees and calves vanished under the rigid crease.

Dănuț was proud. So proud that he would have wished to have spectators even if they were those of the boarding school dormitory.

"Aren't they too tight between the thighs, Dănuț?" Mrs. Deleanu continued her queries which made the most perfect article of clothing a provisional achievement.

Dănuț shook his head and his legs together.

"No, mother. My old knickers were!" A posthumous accusation.

"Take them off now."

"Let me keep on the pajamas, mother... My legs are cold."

"Alright, Dănuț. As you wish."

Mrs. Deleanu went out quickly. This white flannel suit weighed heavily on her heart.

"Olguța!"

"What do you want?"

"You've forgotten the cartridges here."

"Alright. Bring them over!"

Monica went up to the window to wipe her eyes as if Dănuț's voice coming to them through the closed door could have seen her.

Dănuț made a dramatic halt in front of the door. He felt like laughing. After having put on a mien of dignified seriousness, he entered and held out the box of cartridges to Olguța.

"If mother had seen it! Luckily I concealed it."

"Why do you brag? Mother doesn't touch cartridges. How do you feel in trousers?"

"Ahem!"

"I'll try them on tonight."

"You?" It was a cold shower for Dănuţ.

"Me. Why are you surprised?"

"Girls don't wear trousers!"

"I'm going to wear trousers. I already have riding trousers."

"Why don't you want to wear the kimono?" Monica offered, sacrificing herself.

"Because I feel like wearing trousers."

"Aren't you going to shoot crows?" Dănuţ asked, trying to direct her towards other victims.

"No... I don't want to frighten mother."

"What are we going to do then?" Dănuţ asked in desperation.

"Do you know what? Are you cold?"

"Yes," Monica and Dănuţ answered in one voice.

"Do you want to sit by the fire?"

Dănuţ was surprised: "What fire?" he asked.

"That's doesn't concern you. Do you want it?"

"I do."

"Follow me... Quietly — nobody must hear."

Walking noiselessly like devotees of persecuted gods, Monica and Dănuţ followed the slippered guide in the Indian file.

They had forgotten the worries and the bitterness of that dull autumn afternoon.

Dănuţ was smiling because he was showing off his pajamas and because he was about to undertake a new feat of bravery together with Olguţa.

Monica was smiling because she was with Dănuṭ.

Olguṭa also smiled because the mysterious fire which was going to warm them was simply the kitchen fire…

With the children coming into the kitchen, the look of the range had changed. Instead of the meditative pots of every size now huddled up at the far end, one could witness the white laughter of the maize that was being turned into popcorn. Close to the edge of the range, three big apples were baking under the eyes of the old cook — a sulky trinity of pupils who had not been moved up, controlled by the teacher's eyes and chaffed by younger schoolmates.

Seated on three low stools in front of the hearth, Monica, Olguṭa, and Dănuṭ, whose cheeks were rosy with the heat of the fire, were nibbling on hot popcorn.

"Eh! The deuce take you! I'm coming directly!" The cook was snubbing a nervy pot that had raised its lid in puffing.

The three children burst out laughing.

The old cook never ceased reprimanding the pots, the pans, and the flies. Anyone listening from the adjoining room would have thought the kitchen to be full of dumb men trained by a matron with a man's voice. In the kitchen, the old cook was mistress of everything in it. A zealous and diligent mistress — so bulky that she seemed to have been supernaturally leavened in the vast oven whence the pound cakes issued, opulent and stately like pashas issuing from the Sultan's quarters.

While giving a sidelong glance to the cook half-opened the oven door, looked in knowingly, and closed it.

The heat overflowing from the oven was fragrant.

"There's a smell of gingerbread, Cook!" Olguṭa proclaimed laughingly.

"I've got customers for it!" the old woman declared as she turned around an apple.

The apples on the kitchen range were aging visibly. They sighed and perspired and shed sleepy tears. On the other hand, their fragrance increased, getting ever more summery and intoxicating, like the soul of martyrs burnt on the pyre rising to heaven.

Olguța was in the middle, right in front of the flames which covered her face with gold and copper fluid; Monica and Dănuț were seated to her right and her left.

On the floor, all along with the oven, the cats, male and female, all down and arabesques were purring lazily in the comfortable warmth. A little apart from the cats — was it prudence or dignity? — Ali was sleeping. Most of the flies were benumbed with sleep. And yet quite a few of them still bothered him. Ali's ears — ever on the lookout — slapped and flicked them

In a small basket full of hay under the oven, a mother hen protected her golden chicks. Concealed under some bean, a cricket subtly accompanied the choir reminiscent of spring.

And the kitchen range roared with flames and the wind, as noisy as a village dance.

When Mr. Deleanu entered the kitchen he saw the children seated around a small round table. They were eating baked apples with their fingers. On the table, the gingerbread cut into slices was cooling, instead of the traditional corn mush.

"This is where you were, Olguța?"

"But what are you doing here, Papa?"

"Mother Maria, please tell Ion to harness the horses to the carriage... And now I'll deal with you three!" Mr. Deleanu threatened, frowning as he rubbed his hands.

"Sit here with us, Papa!" Olguța pleaded, soon followed by Monica and Dănuț.

"There's no room for me, Olguța!"

"There is here, beside me."

On her return, the old cook found four guests huddled together on three chairs around the table. She covered her mouth with her hands to conceal her laughter.

"Don't you offer me anything, mother Maria?"

"What shall I offer you, sir?"

"Eh! A cup of coffee... But not such as you serve us, something your size."

"I'll see to it!" the old woman boasted with a wink.

"Bit, Papa!"

Mr. Deleanu bit out of the apple Olguţa held out to him.

"Hmm! It's wonderfully tasty. I haven't eaten such a thing since I was a child."

"I've got an idea, Papa. You tell us something from the days when you were a child."

"Do tell us, Papa," Dănuţ also pleaded.

"I am asking you too, uncle Iorgu."

"The days when I was child... Hmmm...!"

"Have another bite, Papa. You'll remember then."

The flavor of baked apples and of warm gingerbread, the flames of the stove, and the faces of three children who are dear to you are not only a prompting, they are a source of tales and reminiscences.

There were four children around the small table.

A grey rain fell outside, pattering on the windows.

Over the villages, the plains, the forests, the hills, and the towns, the sulky flood of sadness fell, making the leaves moldy, increasing the mud and the coughs, and chasing all smiles.

But the kitchen ruddy with flames and full of children, cats, chicks, and tales floated through the rain and thought of autumn like a new Noah's Ark.

And the old cook's shadow on the white walls was of a biblical vastness.

III. Monica's Doll

There was a fire burning in Dănuț's room, warming the sunlight. Lined up on the floor were shoes, slippers, and galoshes. The bed, the table, and the chairs were white with the linen that was to fill the trunk in the middle of the room.

"Why do you push?" Dănuț murmured as he crouched.

"Quiet... I've told you to keep quiet!" Olguța threatened him, shaking his shoulder.

They were huddled up in the trunk from which the shelves had been taken away; they had the rigid attitude of fakirs. The trunk belonged to Dănuț; the idea to Olguța. Dănuț cursed the idea. Olguța despised the trunk. But Olguța always carried through her ideas.

"I can't stand it any longer. I'll get out," Dănuț protested in revolt.

"You'll stop here."

Dănuț gave a bitter sigh.

"Open it a little at least... for me to breathe."

Olguța very stingily raised the lid. Dănuț filled his lungs with freedom, but had to duck quickly for his ceiling soon came down.

The psychological pressure kept increasing, as it does in a diving submarine.

Voices could be heard from the corridor, where Anica and Profira filled the other trunk — the trunk containing the bed linen — under Mrs. Deleanu's guidance.

Profira groaned as she pushed in the mattress, like Ion when kneading the pound cake. The work was being done by Anica, Profira was working verbally.

Monica dressed in a blue cloth skirt and blouse was beside the trunk, looking into vacancy. She suddenly seized Mrs. Deleanu's hand as if asleep and pressed it hard.

"What is it, Monica?"

"No… Nothing, aunt Alice," she replied with a start.

She closed her fists tight. She was cross with herself and her eyes were hard and angry. She had wanted to visualize Dănuţ and had been unable to. Though she knew him as she knew herself. And she had only just seen him. Then, when Dănuţ had left — and there was only a night before he would leave — she was not to see him at all?

"Impossible!"

What was Dănuţ like?... Golden green eyes, chestnut curls, turned-up nose. He wore a grey velvet suit that suited him so well.

"But where's Dănuţ?" Mrs. Deleanu asked while locking the trunk.

Monica shook her plaits and turned her head towards the door for fear aunt Alice might see that Dănuţ was playing hide and seek in her heart.

"Dănuţ, Olguţa, where are you?..."

"See whether they're not in the room, Monica."

"They're not, aunt Alice."

Monica looked under Danu's bed. Mrs. Deleanu rummaged through the cupboard.

"Kiss your hand, my lady!"

"What is it, mother Maria?"

Ionel Teodoreanu

"I've come to take orders from my master," she said with a smile and a blink. "What sweet shall I prepare for his bon voyage?"

"Do you hear, Dănuţ?" Mrs. Deleanu tempted him as if he were a greedy spirit.

"I'm getting out, Olguţa!" Dănuţ exploded, pushing up the lid.

Tousled, congested, dizzy, the master of the cook and Monica strode over the trunk's edge.

"Oh!" he made a face because he had bitten his tongue.

"What's the matter, Dănuţ?"

"She's pinched my leg."

"That was to teach you where to tread!" Olguţa said in a thundering voice, feeling for the new bump on her forehead.

"Good luck go with them!" the cook giggled, helping Olguţa to get out.

"Make some meringues, cook!"

"Don't Olguţa. It's Dănuţ, who gives the orders today."

"Can't you see he's silent, Mother dear? Dinner time will come before he decides."

"I'm not silent… what I say is… that she should make…"

"Make what? Meringues. You can't say a thing." Olguţa was authoritative and her eyes were riveted on Dănuţ were the hypnotist's eyes.

"Tell us, Dănuţ," Mrs. Deleanu encouraged him. "What would you like best? Vanilla cream? Pancakes with strawberry jam? Doughnuts?"

"Meringues are best. I want meringues with whipped cream."

"Whipped cream? A whipped cream cake," Dănuţ, suddenly inspired, contradicted her.

"Meringues," Olguţa defied him.

"I can see I have two masters! I'll make meringues with whipped cream and whipped cream cake."

...The leafless apple tree at the window was alive with sparrows. Their shrill, unruly uproar sounded so much like the first break of a primary school after the holidays that you expected it to be put to an end by the bell rung for entrance into the classroom.

***

The race began in front of the yard. Monica knotted her plaits under her chin. Dănuț stretched his arms and bent his body to check the elasticity of his muscles, which had been sorely tried in the trunk. Ali barked and fawned around them. Olguța drew a line on the road with the edge of her shoe sole. At the place of the stone which marked Olguța's place, the line was straight but it curved backward on approaching Dănuț's stone.

"I won't have it!" Dănuț protested, looking askance at the cunning line.

"Silly fool! You draw it, Monica."

Monica spared the sole of her shoes. She picked up a pointed stone and consciously scratched a tremulous line on the wet road.

"One... two," Olguța murmured at exhaustingly long intervals as she strained her calves.

"Three!" Dănuț shouted precipitately.

"Back you go! I do the counting."

Dănuț frowned but resumed his place.

"One, two, three."

They set off at a run with Ali ahead of them. Monica was level with Dănuț, Olguța following. Dănuț was looking at Moș Gheorghe's cottage towards which they were heading. Monica was giving sidelong glances to Dănuț beside whom she was running. Olguța followed them calmly as if the two of them had been harnessed to her race.

Monica's plaits came unknotted; she tied them again while turning her head towards Dănuţ. It would have been so pleasant to run with her plaits in his hands in the golden cold. Nobody would have outstripped them.

Dănuţ was panting. He turned his head back. Olguţa looked down and smiled. Dănuţ gathered up his strength and rushed on. He stumbled.

Monica stopped to help him up.

"It's because of you that I fell."

Olguţa ran past him at great speed, her eyes riveted on Moş Gheorghe who was waiting for them at the gate.

"How about it, Humpty-Dumpty?"

Dănuţ sighed. Monica slowed down, sacrificing herself for Dănuţ.

"Did you see, Moş Gheorghe?"

"Like a swallow, my young lady."

"Who's second?" Olguţa inquired absent-mindedly.

"Dănuţ," Monica announced triumphantly.

Dănuţ was unable to speak: he was breathing. In passing, he cast a hostile look at the vanquished girl and went through the gate before her, together with Olguţa. That's the way of the conquerors.

"Who's coming with me to swing?" Olguţa asked while she filled her mouth with dried morello cherries.

Monica waited for Dănuţ to answer. Moş Gheorghe shook his pipe and prepared to leave.

Dănuţ kept quiet. He had stretched out on the bench in front of the fire. A fit of laziness had come over him. He felt like laughing and could not.

"Aren't you coming, Monica?"

"I'm cold."

"I'm going alone then."

"Won't you take Moş Gheorghe with you?"

Olguţa smiled.

"Who'll keep watch over the house?"

"Eh! The old people were seated by the fire. We, the young, will go for a swing."

Monica was alone with Dănuţ. She did not dare to sit on the bench beside him so she sat on a stool close to the bench, facing the fire. If the flames in the hearth could have pierced through Monica's heart, a rainbow would have shone above Dănuţ...

...Prince Charming had done so many feats of valor that the lot of them would have been too much for a library full of storybooks. Nevertheless, he had not had his fill. He had set out towards other lands in quest of new ventures.

In Dănuţ's heart, the hooves of the wonder-working horse were trotting heroically. Was that a mace throbbing? No. It was a fly. Prince Charming stopped his horse. Dănuţ opened an eye: a fly was ambling along on his nose, tickling him. He creased his nose; the fly flew away hilariously. The open eye accompanied it until it settled on Monica's head. Dănuţ closed his eye.

Monica had golden plaits, like Beauty. What was Prince Charming doing when alone with Beauty? Was he pulling her plaits?

No. They were kissing. That was how the story went.

Why were they kissing?

"Monica, do you know why Prince Charming and Beauty kissed each other?"

Beauty knew but her heart thumped so hard that she was unable to answer Prince Charming.

A strange fear seized Dănuţ. It was as if Prince Charming had wanted to take to his heels... How was that? Prince Charming was not afraid of monsters and dragons and he was afraid of a Beauty?

He opened his eyes and held out his hand. He took hold of one of Monica's plaits and pulled it towards him. Monica's head bent back, having no support, it fell on the bench with closed eyes and a face as pale as the fragrance of lilies.

Dănuţ bent over Beauty. Feeling her sweet, warm breath — as if of hidden strawberries — he drew back a little.

The same persistent, concrete fly wandered over legendary cheeks. Dănuţ got over his fear. He chased away the fly with his finger.

"Where shall I kiss her?" Dănuţ asked himself as the tip of his finger went round the outline of her cheeks. He chose the tip of the nose; it seemed to be less dangerous as it was the most remote from the rest of the face.

When Monica felt Dănuţ's lips on the tip of her nose, she unwittingly gave a start. The kiss slid down and fell like a moist flower on Monica's lips.

"Leave me alone!" Dănuţ tore himself away, drawing back his head. "I'll not play Prince Charming with your from now on."

For Beauty, it had not been a game.

***

Dănuţ's room had gradually got empty. Pale sunlight had brightened the inside of the trunk over which a sheet had been spread; golden sunlight had glittered over the linen on the upper shelf; ruby sunlight was declining on the closed lid in between the labels of cosmopolitan hotels.

There were also surprises in Dănuţ's trunk. A gold coin in the pocket of each coat, a silver money box lined with violet and full of silver coins, which was only natural; a box of candies — Velma Suchard chocolate tablets; a box of Marquis tablets; a scented sachet for handkerchiefs… A good part of what was special in the wardrobe was leaving for the boarding school in Dănuţ's trunk, he being unaware of it.

"Open the window, Anica, to air the room."

With its ruddy horizon, pierced by the gruff croaking of the crows, the autumn twilight seemed to be a giant picture of a battlefield covered by defeat. A cold wind was blowing from that direction.

Mrs. Deleanu locked the trunk and tried its locks.

"Close the wardrobe, Anica."

The wardrobe was full of crumpled newspapers, like the cupboard of a hotel room after the passenger had left.

"Good gracious, madam! You're pulling it? Don't, I'll do it."

Mrs. Deleanu was pushing the trunk from the middle of the room towards the wall.

"Don't bother, Anica. You'd better clean the floor."

Profira entered the room with a lighted lamp.

"Where shall I make master Dănuţ's bed, madam," she asked.

"What do you mean? Here, of course... He's not a guest."

"But he's got no mattress."

"Well, take one from another bed."

Mrs. Deleanu cast one more look over the room, after which she looked at the trunk that was ready to leave: it was heavy, as a heart is sometimes heavy.

She turned from the light of the lamp and went out.

Anica and Profira looked meaningfully at each other.

***

Moş Gheorghe was telling them a story from the days when God walked among men accompanied by St. Peter, looked like a beggar, and being dressed like one.

The three of them listened quietly, huddled together on the bench. Moş Gheorghe was seated on a stool facing the children, his back to the hearth.

They heard him rather than saw him for the light had gone down — it had been violet-blue, then purplish-blue, the color of plums — and the windows of the room were small.

The voices of all manner of people were heard by the children: good and wicked people, indifferent and bountiful people. God had come across them all and had gone on his way. And none of the wayfarers had heard the hearts of the three children singing at their ear through the centuries like three silver bells: "Speak to God. Speak to God. Speak to God."

And the tale had continued, as wonderful as the shadow of the beggar-God along white country roads.

When St. Peter spoke to God, Moş Gheorghe stood up and bent his grey head as a sign of meekness and deep submission. And St Peter's voice and his seemliness sounded so very much like the storyteller's voice and manner speaking that the tale brought to the children's mind Moş Gheorghe's presence and smiled to him without seeing him. God's voice, however, did not sound like any voice they had ever heard; nevertheless, it seemed to be a friendly voice.

God spoke a sweet-sounding Moldavian such as it is spoken in the countryside. He whispered — a distinct whisper — and it was so mysterious that three pairs of ears, and also three heads, bent to listen.

…Night was falling in the tale as well as at the windows of Moş Gheorghe's cottage. God was asking for shelter and food at the door of a tumble-down cottage.

"Come in, good people. Do come in. for, thank God, there is room enough. But I have no food to give you for I am a needy widow with three children."

Moş Gheorghe opened the door. Together with the bluish night wind, God and St Peter entered the hospitable cottage where three children whined with hunger. The woman was baking a cake of ashes to delude their hunger.

"...And when the poor woman raised the wretched cake from the fire, what did she see?..."

Wide-open, and candid like the sun, the children's eyes were waiting.

"...a loaf as big as the sun... God had worked the miracle. The poor man by the hearth was God himself."

Silence and darkness.

"Where are you, Moş Gheorghe?" Olguţa cried out loudly.

"I'm here, lassie."

Olguţa passed her hands over her eyes. She had been seized with the fear that Moş Gheorghe was God and that she had lost him...

"Moş Gheorghe!" the voice at the entrance door put an end to the silence.

"It's mother," Olguţa whispered as she jumped off the bench. "Hide, quick. Here! Ready, Moş Gheorghe."

Moş Gheorghe went to meet Mrs. Deleanu who had entered with three little coats in her arms. "Kiss your hand, madam. It's been a long time since you last came to see the old man."

"You needn't worry, others come often. But where are they?"

"There were three kids here with budding horns, but the wolf has eaten them!"

Remembering how the wolf in the story had found the three kids, especially one of the kids, Dănuţ burst out laughing. Other giggles acclaimed the tell-tale whispers. Fumbling with her hand in the darkness, Mrs. Deleanu detected the sources: three heads were huddled together under the table that bore the old books. In the meantime Moş Gheorghe," a smiling Mrs. Deleanu remarked, pointing to the children's stockings. "Yes, my children are good housekeepers. They resemble someone we know."

More peals of laughter.

"Why do you laugh?" Mrs. Deleanu inquired, looking at each of them in turn.

The children laughed because they remembered the funny incidents in the tale about the wolf and the three kids, which Moş Gheorghe had also told Mrs. Deleanu in her childhood, as he explained to her.

A fit of coughing stopped him. With his hands on his chest, a little unsteady, Moş Gheorghe passed into the entrance hall, dragging his cough with him. For a moment the laughter and the coughing could be heard together, like a strange, sorrowful singsong. Then the laughter became more subdued and suddenly ceased. Something strange seemed to have entered Moş Gheorghe's cottage through the dark shadow in the entrance hall beyond the light of the lamp. They all seemed to be waiting for the end of a struggle. The last tears of laughter on the children's cheeks took on a sad line as they slid along cheeks that also seemed to be different.

A black spear came off the flame of the lamp; it rose straight up, watching over the silence and the waiting.

After a time Moş Gheorghe came into the light again.

"Let's go, children. Say good night to Moş Gheorghe, and you Dănuţ, say goodbye to him. As to you, Moş Gheorghe you'll stay at home tomorrow and the day after... until I tell you can go out. Do you hear, Moş Gheorghe?"

Dănuţ gave a low sigh; he had forgotten he was to leave. Monica too had forgotten.

Moş Gheorghe unhooked a small silver icon — the most valuable he possessed — kissed it and held it out to Dănuţ.

"Let God watch over you. May you grow up big and strong... and bring happiness to my masters..."

He spoke hoarsely, looking down.

Unwittingly, Dănuț bent and kissed the hand that held out the icon. Bending lower than Dănuț, Moș Gheorghe repaired the mistake, kissing the small hand of his masters' child.

…Much later, Moș Gheorghe, seated on the edge of the bench, held up his head and looked around the room. There was a smell of soot. The lamp had been smoking for long that the glass was black. Moș Gheorghe nodded, put out the flame, and sat down on the edge of the bench again. Dănuț was leaving… Olguța too would soon be leaving… Then himself…

***

"Why are there three keys, Mother?" Dănuț inquired as he entered the room in Mrs. Deleanu's wake.

Three small keys jingled, captive in the ring of Dănuț's two trunks: two thick, grey ones, and a thin, nickel-plated one.

"Because you have two trunks and a suitcase."

"A suitcase!" Dănuț was surprised.

Mrs. Deleanu smiled.

"Which one, Mother?" he asked, pointing hopefully but incredulously at the blue Morocco suitcase lying on the sofa.

"Yes, Dănuț. I'm giving it to you. Under Mrs. Deleanu's puzzled eyes, Dănuț ran out, pulling the door open… and came back gesticulating, accompanied by Olguța and Monica."

"Olguța will not believe me, Mother. Look, the suitcase that smells so nice. I've told you."

"Of course I didn't believe you! I wanted to see first."

"Do you see now?"

"Yes… But it no longer smells so nice!"

"That's a lie! You've got a head cold," Dănuț said indignantly, as he smelt the Morocco leather with empathetic avidity.

"Don't open it, Dănuţ. You'll do that in Bucharest."

"So I'm not going to see what there is inside?" Olguţa was pouting.

"There's nothing to see."

Mrs. Deleanu shrugged as she opened it. "Looked what there is: hand-kerchiefs, a nigh-dress…"

Olguţa had the eyes of a socialist customs-house officer.

"What's that over there?"

Without waiting for an answer she brought to the surface a Japanese lacquer pencil case.

"Don't touch anything, Olguţa," Dănuţ said angrily while fishing out a leather bag with relief designs.

"Wait, wait! I'll show you!" Mrs. Deleanu sighed on seeing the invasion.

With the smiling resignation of an artist compelled to give an encore, she revealed the contents of the suitcase.

The Morocco suitcase — itself a gift — included so many other gifts that when it was closed the wardrobe had to be opened. For otherwise Olguţa would have said that she persecuted, a rude remark for which Mrs. Deleanu would have said that she was persecuted, a rude remark for which Mrs. Deleanu would have had to punish her, or perhaps she would only have thought that she was persecuted — as Monica also would perhaps have thought about Olguţa. Mrs. Deleanu deemed such thoughts to be more dangerous than a cheeky remark.

Olguţa received a chocolate tablet and the promise of a small knife similar to the one in Dănuţ's pencil case. Monica received an elegant little bottle of *eau de cedrat*.

Dănuţ was walking about the room casting possessive glances at the suitcase in its cloth cover. He was playing with the keys in his pocket with his fingertips, jingling them quietly. He had adopted the habit of all those who carry keys or metal coins in their pockets.

"How's that? Have you forgotten me? Aren't we going to have supper?" Mr. Deleanu was asking the question from the threshold while shaking off the cigarette ashes on the floor.

"Ugh! You've given me poison, Olguţa!" Mr. Deleanu made a face as he munched the piece of chocolate thrust on him.

"Mother has given it to me!" Olguţa parried laughingly. "When you do that, Papa, you look like a tomcat. Do it once again."

"Don't touch the chocolate. That's how you spoil your appetite. And now to supper!"

Due to the children's liveliness, the fire in the stoves, and the gifts received, the eve of Dănuţ's departure seemed to be Christmas eve. You might have expected thin voices to be heard at the windows singing the ancient message:

The star comes into view high up

Like a great mystery

But after they all had left, taking the lamp with them, the trills of the autumn crickets could alone be heard at the windows which were pale in the moonlight.

***

Prolonged delights give rise to melancholy; a guardian angel that's seasick. This time the cause was the whipped cream off the meringues for Olguţa and of the whipped cream cake for Dănuţ. Mr. Deleanu excepted, they were all serious and silent around the table. Monica had hardly tasted the cake; Mrs. Deleanu not at all. Nor had Profira tasted it. But when her eyes met the fold of whipped cream on the ruddy shoots of the cake, they became human, like those of hungry dogs.

"May I leave the table, Mother?" Dănuţ asked, avoiding the look of the cake and Olguţa.

"Yes, you may all leave... Put on your coats and go for a walk outside."

Monica went to Mrs. Deleanu, kissed her hand, and spoke to her in a low voice, looking down: "Please allow me to go to bed, Aunt Alice."

"You're not feeling well, Monica?"

"I'm alright... Only a headache."

"You haven't caught a cold, have you? Alright, go to bed. Take your leave of Monica, Dănuț."

"Why?" Dănuț arrested his steps. He was bitter.

"Because you're leaving very early tomorrow morning. Monica will still be asleep then... Come on, kiss, children!"

...Monica put out her lips, Dănuț offered his cheek.

"I'll never more eat whipped cream cake," Dănuț swore inwardly, drawing his cheek away from Monica's lips, whose breath again reminded him of the unbearable sweetness of the cake.

And, for the present, he kept his word, Monica's cheek going unkissed and blushing under his indifferent eyes.

***

Monica locked the doors. She lit the candle, drew a chair to the wardrobe, and, rising on tiptoe, took from the top of it a little parcel wrapped in tissue paper. She drew the chair back, and instead of undressing, started undressing her doll — the little Monica.

For two nights in a row, after Olguța had fallen asleep, Monica had been making the white silk dress — from the parcel concealed above the wardrobe — which the doll was to put on instead of the black dress it had worn ever since her grandmother had died... until the eve of Dănuț's departure.

"She first put on the white socks and slippers taken from the feet of the doll given to her by Mrs. Deleanu. Monica's fingers trembled when the turn of the dress didn't fit? What if it was too short?"

"Let it fit her, Oh Lord! Let it fit her, Oh Lord!"

Monica buttoned the last button at the back and laid her on the bedside table in the light of the candle.

"She is so pretty!"

Plump, too ruddy, stiff, and awkward, the doll seemed to be the miniature of a young peasant girl in a bride's dress at the photographer's.

"Monica, do you know why Prince Charming kissed beauty?"

Because Beauty was pretty… as pretty as the doll dressed in this white dress.

Monica's cheeks were burning. Her heart was thumping. And she almost felt like crying in front of the doll because she was such a pretty doll.

She looked at herself in the mirror. She saw her dark dress, her dusty shoes and looked down. She hadn't looked at her head.

The doll was too pretty for words… Dănuţ will fall in love with the doll. Monica's breast was agitated as it usually was after a run.

She shook her plaits and began to undress hurriedly. She put on her nightgown, unplaited her hair, took the doll by the hand, and holding her over her own body, looked at herself in the mirror.

The doll had a white dress on.

Monica had a white nightgown.

The doll had fair curls.

Monica smiled and blushed; she took a deep breath.

The doll looked like herself. She had dark eyes, thick lashes, and a dimple in the middle of his chin. She had fair curls, but short ones. Poor little doll. She was unable to provide reins for Dănuţ with her hair.

"But you are dressed so beautifully!" Monica comforted her.

Her heart was lighter. She took the candle from the bedside table and laid it on the writing-table. Everything had been prepared in the daytime:

a penholder with a new pen, ink, and notepaper — not bigger than cigarette paper; it was colored and had a trefoil on the envelope.

On the rule paper, she wrote unhurriedly in a beautiful, impassioned hand:

"Monica loves Dănuț whole-heartedly."

Four old words on a small piece of paper; four tropical, immensely starry skies.

The doll's white dress had one candid secret: a small pocket for the love letter. Monica's heart was like the doll's dress.

***

Olguța and Dănuț were walking side by side in the yard. They found last winter's reminders. Dănuț had detected a skating rink ticket and two acid sweets encrusted in the torn lining. Olguța was kneading a ball of silver paper in which sugared chestnuts had once been wrapped.

The coats smelt of naphthalene. The children's nostrils were red with the sharp, cold air inhaled. Their breath steamed. The earth sounded autumnal under their steps.

The line of the hills bordered the night with floating undulations, like a fall of veils coming down gently down the nakedness of the moon.

Two shadows passed by the gate — incredible blue against the deep silver hue. The dogs rushed barking in that direction. An unmistakably local oath blurted out by a hoarse bass voice gave reality to the scenery.

Olguța stopped suddenly. "You don't know how to fight," she said, raising her shoulders.

"What do you mean I don't know?"

"You don't know!"

"Are you going to teach me?"

"Yes." Olguța asserted firmly.

"Hmm!"

Nevertheless, Dănuț's heart disagreeing with his lips was thumping.

Olguța looked at him with compassionate solicitude.

"If somebody slaps you, what do you do?"

"I slap him in return."

"And if he punches you?"

"I punch him in return."

"And if he punches you again?"

"I also punch him once more."

"And if he takes hold of your hands?"

"I tear them away."

"And if he kicks?"

Taken unawares by the pressing questions, Dănuț answered sincerely: "I run away."

"You see?"

"No, I don't," Dănuț said, going back on his answer. He was furious. "Leave me alone. I know what I have to do."

"Alright, slap me if that's so."

Dănuț looked her up and down.

"Do you want to fight?" he asked. He sounded conciliatory.

"No. I want to show you."

"You won't be cross if I slap you?"

"No. Because you won't be able to."

"You don't say!"

"Try."

"You'll be cross."

"I'll have no reason!" Olguța was smiling.

"Nonsense!"

"Just try."

Dănuţ prepared his hand for slapping, the target being Olguţa's cheeks. When Dănuţ's arm started forward, Olguţa's foot tripped him. Dănuţ fell to the ground, slapping the earth.

"That's a dirty trick."

Olguţa was laughing as she bent down to raise him with both arms.

"Leave me alone!"

He took a few steps, picked up a stone with fingers that shook with anger, threw it at Olguţa, and ran at full speed towards the veranda steps.

"You didn't hit me!" Olguţa shouted behind him. "Coward! Humpty-Dumpty!"

Dănuţ didn't hear her. He was in Mrs. Deleanu's room.

Olguţa set off for the house, limping. The stone had hit her shin bone.

Monica was in bed. Olguţa undressed silently without looking at her sore leg. Before blowing out the candle she gave Dănuţ's door a long look. Her eyebrows came together as she addressed Monica:

"If you're my friend, Monica, don't ever speak to Humpty-Dumpty again!"

The candle was smoking chokingly. Under the blanket, Olguţa was massaging her leg.

Monica had only pretended to sleep. Her lashes were trembling. Not to speak to Dănuţ? She had forgotten to say her prayer because in her heart choirs like those at Christ's resurrection were murmuring, with a golden aura surrounding them:

"Monica loves Dănuţ whole-heartedly."

***

It had always been humiliating torture for Dănuţ to have his nails, and especially his nail skins, cut by Mrs. Deleanu. This time he deemed it a blessing. He had forgotten that the holiday was at an end; that very early tomorrow morning, when sleep is most pleasurable, he would leave home for a very long time; that he was to be a boarder in Bucharest. He had forgotten. Everything was abstract. Olguţa's revenge alone was a fact, although it did not take shape; as if it was someone standing at your back, but becoming invisible when you look back.

Nine nails had become oval and rosy. The polisher was now taking care of the tenth nail. Dănuţ would have liked to have a hundred nails. He could see the pole star fading out as the nail assumed a rosy hue.

But Mrs. Deleanu was lingering. It was she who had decided that Dănuţ should leave for Iaşi in the morning together with Mr. Deleanu and from there go to Bucharest in the evening of the same day.

"You'll be sorry, Alice. Keep him at home for another day and bring him to the station in the evening. Isn't it a pity that he should lose the last day at home for the sake of paying visits?"

"No. He must take leave of his relatives. A day more or less...."

"Alright. You've caught this from Grigore!"

She was sorry now. If the evening train for Bucharest hadn't stopped at the Medeleni station, it would have been easier to prompt him to fulfill his duties, sacrificing a day that would have been spent at home. But under the circumstances...

"Dănuţ... if you want it, if you want it very much, you needn't leave tomorrow morning. You will remain with your mother the whole day and we will go to the station in the evening to join father. Do you want it, Dănuţ?"

"No. I'll leave with father," Dănuţ said unhesitatingly.

Mr. Deleanu was surprised on entering the bedroom. "What? You haven't gone to bed?" he said. "Do you know it's eleven? We'll have to be up before long. Let's go to bed."

With Dănuț's finger in one hand and the polisher in the other, Mrs. Deleanu looked up, opened her mouth to speak, and closed it again: "That's how men are!"

"Come on, Dănuț. We're not sleepy."

His slippers were on the small carpet in front of the bed, the nightdress on the bed. Dănuț had looked for his slippers under the bed and for his nightdress in the wardrobe. Olguța was neither under the bed nor in the wardrobe. Still, there was the door opening into her room.

"I've never had the key, Mother," Dănuț said dolefully.

"What key Dănuț?"

"The key to my room."

"What do you want to do with it?"

"To close the door, Mother... Why should Olguța have the key? I'm older."

"Why didn't you tell me?"

"I forgot."

"How childish you are, Dănuț," Mrs. Deleanu said affectionately. "Here is the key," she whispered, closing the door.

She laughed and held it out to him. Dănuț turned the key in the lock twice.

"Aren't we going to be, Mother?" Being reassured, he dismissed the useless guard.

When he stretched in his bed, he felt something hard beside him under the blanket. He jumped out of bed: it had seemed to him to be a moving thing. He lit the candle.

"Aha!"

Instead of the mouse he had feared, he discovered the doll dressed as a bride.

"Aha! You're making fun of me!" He raised his fist, directing it towards the locked door: "I'll show you! You're laughing, aren't you?" Olguța will get it! A doll in his bed! What was he? A girl?... She should fight if she feels like it. But she shouldn't insult him.

Out of the Morocco suitcase, Dănuț took a pencil-case and out of the pencil case the small knife with sharp blades. He then sat down on the edge of the bed, holding the doll between his knees. And gradually the blond locks, only recently scented with *eau de cedrat*, fell on Dănuț's nightdress, having been cut off with sarcastic intent.

The doll had shed her hair... Wrapped in a newspaper, the blond locks flickered in the blond flames of the woodstove. From his warm bed, Dănuț, now well covered by his blanket, smiled at the flames and the double-locked door.

Under the bed, the doll, which held Monica's love, fresh and delicate like the first May Cherry, slept, having been completely transfigured by the haircut and the goatee and mustache on her by a Hardtmuth No.1 pencil.

***

Dănuț is crying. Olguța catches up with him and punches and kicks him from behind. Dănuț does not utter a word. He knows he deserves to be struck.

"Are you crying?" Olguța asks him as she lays her hand on his shoulder pacifically.

***

"Don't worry, Dănuț. Let's make up."

They kiss each other. Dănuț would like to tell her something... but he doesn't remember what.

The walk through the yard is resumed, but this time they walk arm in arm like a model brother and sister. Dănuţ realizes that Olguţa is his ally and is sorry that he has to conceal something from her. But he doesn't remember what.

"Why should you go to Bucharest. That's persecution!"

"If mother wants it!" Dănuţ says, heaving a big sigh.

"But I don't want it."

...They both run away from home and go to Moş Gheorghe's. It's a fearful night, but Dănuţ is not afraid because Olguţa is beside him.

They arrived there. A strange thing! Moş Gheorghe's cottage shines in the darkness of the night like a moon.

They knock at the door. Dănuţ's heart leaps into his throat. The door opens of its own accord and Moş Gheorghe appears in the entranceway. Olguţa and Dănuţ kneel before God for Moş Gheorghe is God himself.

They kiss his hand.

Olguţa says that Dănuţ is persecuted that they want to send him to Bucharest as a broader and that they want to send him to Bucharest as a boarder and that they have run away home for that reason. God receives them into his house.

Olguţa and Dănuţ sit on the bench. God sits on the stool. Suddenly, an angel appears with Dănuţ's kite in his hand. It is the big kite from the beginning of the holidays, with the cord cut off by Olguţa.

God looks at Dănuţ. Dănuţ smiles a forgiving smile.

Another angel appears with Olguţa's doll in his hand. Dănuţ trembles.

God takes the doll on his knees, passed his hand over its face and instead of the mustached face with a goatee, a smiling Monica appears. But she is hairless.

God puts his hand into the stove, takes a handful of flames, and pours it over Monica's cropped head.

Dănuţ closes his eyes. Has Monica been burnt?... No. So Monica is the doll...

There's a knock at the door. The people at home are looking for them. Olguţa frowns, Dănuţ trembles. God smiles.

What is to be done? They surround the house. Herr Direktor, father, and mother knock at the door as hard as they can.

God doesn't trouble himself about those that knock; he takes a small icon from the nail it hangs on, turns the three of them into little painted saints, and puts the icon back. Let them look for the kids now.

Herr Direktor puts on his monocle and looks about the room.

Dănuţ winks at the two saints in the icon. The Saints laugh and laugh.

Herr Direktor looks at them, sees the icon and crosses himself. The saints nudge each other and frown so severely that Herr Direktor crosses himself again.

They've fooled Her Direktor.

Mother comes up. She looks at them too — rather a long look.

The saints blink.

Mother takes the icon, leans over it — Dănuţ feels his mother's scent — and she kisses Dănuţ's forehead...

"Come on, Dănuţ, get up," Mrs. Deleanu whispered, caressing the forehead of the child with chestnut locks on the day he wakes up in his parent's house.

Although it was nearly morning, it seemed as if the whole house had awakened in the blackness of the night.

The women entered the corridor with lighter lamps, followed by Pricop, the other stable man. Despite the signs made by Mrs. Deleanu and the orders given by her, Ion's and Pricop's boots trot heavily on the floor, endangering the girls' sleep.

Anica and Profira, dressed in thick clothes, with black kerchiefs wrapped around their heads, were still stupefied with sleep.

Dănuț, rather pale in his blue velvet suit with turn-down collar and elegant lavaliere, was looking about him absent-mindedly. He kept chewing with a discontented air; he had poured too much mouthwash into his glass by mistake and his gums burnt.

A draft caused the flame of the lamps to tremble. The trunk containing the bed linen was taken out. Ali entered the house through the open door. Nobody drove him out.

The men took the trunk from Dănuț's room. In the silence full of whispers broken off only by trampling boots, the shadows of the men who carried the trunk were lugubrious…

In the attic full of old things, Dănuț was rubbing out the doll's mustache and beard in the feeble light of the candle. Nothing had changed in the attic since he had parted with Robinson Crusoe. The same smell, the same peace, the same dry and dusty peach stones.

Under the diligent care of the India rubber, the doll's cheeks resumed their feminine complexion. The chin was dimpled again; the lips lost the arrogance of the musketeer smile and became sweet again. The non-existent locks alone recalled the calamity that had befallen it.

Dănuț put his hand around his waist and kept it at a distance to look at it. Last night's dream filled Dănuț's thoughts as he shook his head. The doll in his dream looked like Monica — was Monica. The doll with cropped hair in his hand no longer looked like the doll in his dream. And Dănuț was sorry because he remembered that in his dream God had given him a doll that looked like Monica and his heart had beaten very strangely. Nobody had known, however, because he was ashamed on account of Olguța. Dănuț sighed and made room for the doll in the case full of books beside Robinson Crusoe. In her white dress, alone among so many books, the doll looked coquettishly disconsolate, like a princess in exile.

Dust was henceforth in store for her, like old age spent among strangers. Dănuț closed the lid.

The doll's night began at cock crow and so did his sleeplessness for Dănuț had forgotten to close the glass eyes in which he had melancholically discovered why Prince Charming and Beauty kissed when they were alone...

At the place of honor at the head of the table, the corpulent copper samovar glittered and smoked. Its yellow hips reflected the dining room, the table, and the three people seated at the table, comically deformed — seemingly of the Mongolian race.

Waiting for his tea to cool, Dănuț thoughtfully nibbled the sprinkled cookies that had just come out of the oven, for the cook had got up before them all.

Mrs. Deleanu drew Dănuț's head on the tablecloth with her finger.

Mr. Deleanu sipped his tea with milk and occasionally tried the knot of his tie. He was in a good mood. After a long, uninterrupted, and peaceful holiday in the country with his family — Bucharest...

He got hold of the rum bottle mechanically and poured into Dănuț's glass a little too much... as one pours out from the bottle when the musicians are behind you.

"No, no, no! Not that."

"Let him have it, Alice. For heaven's sake, he's a big boy!"

A *big boy*. Far from flattering him, he found the two words frightening — a black train that took him from home to land him among strangers. Tears fell into the rum-scented tea.

Gradually, purple dawn, like youthful good health, brought joy to the windows. Mrs. Deleanu rose from the table and looked out.

In the prevailing silence, the samovar puffed and whistled like an ironical railway engine…

"Good morning and kiss your hand!"

"Moş Gheorghe! I'm so glad!" Dănuţ's face brightened up on seeing Moş Gheorghe on the driving box.

"It was agreed that you would not go out, Moş Gheorghe!" Mrs. Deleanu reproved him, with a raised finger.

"Yes, it was! But this coat is as warm as the fireside, madam."

All the servants were on the steps. The horses' hooves were dancing. Dănuţ sat between Mr. and Mrs. Deleanu. Anica and Profira tucked in the rug on either side of him.

"A little prince, no less!" the cook exclaimed aloud.

Dănuţ was putting on his leather gloves. Mrs. Deleanu smiled in his place. The horses started off. Dănuţ signaled to the horse and the servants and for a moment caught sight of Monica on the threshold — was he dreaming? — with her hair loose and a too-large kimono, holding her hands over her mouth…

The fields were white with hoarfrost; the sky was purplish-blue; the eastern horizon a tumult of red gold.

Ali was running after the carriage. When he got into the village the shepherd dogs made for him freely… Dănuţ paled. He stood up and, caressing Mrs. Deleanu's hand, asked her to take Ali into the carriage.

"Stop, Moş Gheorghe."

Protected by the driver's whip, Ali jumped into the carriage and huddled up on the rug at Dănuţ's feet. The village was left behind. And the holidays also…

"The air is so pleasant!" Mr. Deleanu exclaimed. "When I think of the stench in Bucharest!"

"Hush! He's asleep!" Mrs. Deleanu whispered as she took Dănuţ's heavy head in her arms.

Dănuţ had fallen murmuring the meaningless verses of his early child-hood.

***

At one end of the bench on the station platform, Dănuţ and Mrs. Deleanu were seated holding each other's hands. At the other end, Mr. Deleanu was hurriedly going through the pile of writs of summons, copies, and excerpts while listening to Mr. Şteflea's explanations regarding the suit that had come under the jurisdiction of the Court of Appeals… From his clients, Mr. Deleanu required clarity and precision — when he decided to listen to them — and these were qualities that Mr. Şteflea lacked. The dialogue between them was a continuous clash between an express and a goods train.

"Well, Mr. Iorga, that's what I thought best to do. How was that? But the whole country will bear witness to it!"

"My good man!" Mr. Deleanu interrupted him icily, raising his eyes from the papers.

Mr. Şteflea wiped his perspiring forehead and sighed.

Mrs. Deleanu was talking to Dănuţ in whispers.

"You will write to mother as soon as you get there… Write everything, absolutely everything you do. Do you hear, Dănuţ?"

She put his lavaliere and his beret right again.

"Mr. Şteflea," Mr. Deleanu said categorically…

Mr. Şteflea bowed deferentially.

"…I'll be in Iaşi until tonight. I'll appoint the day of the trial and see the brief today. You'll wait for me tonight at the train going to Bucharest and I'll tell you what you have to do."

A bell rang dramatically in the peace of the countryside platform. Two peasants got up. Mrs. Deleanu rose too. Dănuţ's hand was holding her hand like a vice.

The train — a long one — steamed into the station, a blot on the light of the morning. The first-class carriage stopped some way beyond the station. They ran in hot taste. Pale, sleepy faces blinked at the windows.

"Come on, Ion." Mr. Deleanu pressed the man while kicking the suit-cases farther into the carriage. "And why aren't you more careful?"

Dănuţ swallowed hard. His legs had been hit.

"Dănuţ, Dănuţ!" Mrs. Deleanu was walking beside the train now on its way, calling to her son.

He could just kiss the hand stretched out to him.

"Mother," Dănuţ mumbled as he wiped his eyes, "don't leave Ali; take him onto the car… into the carriage," he shouted. He could no longer see her.

Behind the train a crow came down between the rails, pecking in the gravel.

"We still have someone at home, madam," Moş Gheorghe said, picking up Mrs. Deleanu's handkerchief.

***

The dining room had been too big for the silence of the three sitting down to breakfast and lunch; Mrs. Deleanu's small drawing-room had been too big for the afternoon silence, with night knocking at the windows.

"Let's go to bed, children."

Olguța and Monica kissed her hand. Mrs. Deleanu did not see them in their room. They parted in the corridor.

There had been a spring cleaning in Dănuț's room. The door that held the Russo-Japanese panoply was open. The smell of turpentine on the freshly waxed floors brought coolness into the girls' room, suggesting indifference.

Before undressing Olguța closed the door. Monica sat on the edge of the bed, looking down.

"Aren't you going to bed?" Olguța asked.

"I will go."

She began taking off her dress with tired movements. Olguța got into bed. Monica said her prayer more quickly than usual.

"Good night, Olguța!"

"Good night, Monica!"

Olguța blew out the candle, Monica stood for a long time between the beds in the dark… She approached Olguța's bed, holding her breath.

"What are you doing?" Feeling a tear falling on her cheek, Olguța gave a start.

"I have betrayed you, Olguța," Monica said, sobbing. "I love Dănuț."

"Of course. You're my friend… I love him too."

***

Fattened with comfort, spotted by round lights, smelling of the leather of the Romanian railways and cigar smoke, the sleeping car groaned and creaked softly along the kilometers traversed.

In the armchair at the end of the corridor, the railway conductor, his cap on the nape of his tunic undone at the neck, was working out his accounts, again and again dipping the indelible pencil into his mouth.

In cabin number 10-11, Mr. Deleanu was playing cards with a colleague from Bucharest. On the small table beside them, a bottle of cherry-brandy was bobbing, and two glasses with the monogram of the "Wagon-Lits" company were singing a crystal tune, knocking against each other.

Seated on the bracket seat in front of the cabin, Dănuţ looked out, resting his forehead on the cold glass. Nobody was telling him "Go to bed, Dănuţ" or "What, not in bed yet?" although it was past the time when children "must go to bed."

"You'll find it difficult to win this game, my good man."

The wheels' rattle and the Wallachian manner of speaking of Mr. Deleanu's partner kept company to Dănuţ's thoughts.

The engine shrieked sharply. The train slowed down.

"We've arrived in Medeleni, Papa!" Dănuţ had brightened upon seeing Mr. Şteflea's familiar face at the carriage window.

" How's that, man? Are your clients waiting for you at railways stations?"

"An idiot that plagues me!"

Cards in hand, Mr. Deleanu raised in the window in front of Dănuţ, gave a few laconic injunctions to Mr. Şteflea, and hurried back to resume his game. Mr. Şteflea stood dazed by the window. Dănuţ was wringing his hands… He would willingly have given Mr. Şteflea Ivan's knapsack if that had been possible. He didn't know what he could tell him. The departure trumpet resounded dramatically.

In despair, Dănuţ took the box of mint sweets and held it out. Mr. Şteflea took it; he was puzzled and held it in his hand, staring at it. The train steamed off. Dănuţ leaned out the window and waved his handkerchief to the station master for a long time. The latter was running after the train to return the box of sweets.

When he was out of sight, Dănuţ sat down on the bracket seat again and began to cry, as if the station master had been his only joy, his last joy, on his bitter way to Bucharest.

A lady had witnessed the whole scene from the doorway of the adjoining cabin. She came to Dănuţ with a chocolate packet.

"What is your name, little one?"

"Dănuţ." He rose to his feet, sighing.

" Bravo! He's your son alright! Like you in every detail!" the colleague said, pointing his finger at the idyll in the corridor.

Three minds followed the same train that night, looking for the same traveler.

IV. "Won't You Puff at Your Pipe, Moş Gheorghe?"

La tante Julie,
La tante Sophie,
La tante Melanie
Et l'oncle Leon...

"Ah! You've got it wrong again!" Olguţa reproved her father, tousling his hair with the palm of her hand.

Leaning over Olguţa's shoulder, Mr. Deleanu was singing in the voice of a hoarse baritone the song he brought back from Bucharest, together with the hoarseness. Olguţa accompanied him at the piano.

"You see, Papa, you sing BGEC instead of BABC. Listen to me."

She started it all over again, humming with closed lips, nodding all the while.

"Again, Papa?! What will mother say?"

Mr. Deleanu put on the face of a schoolboy caught with his homework unfinished.

"Papa, why is it that you're always off when you get to l'oncle Leon?"

"A great mystery!" Mr. Deleanu said, frowning. "I think tante Melanie trips me up!"

Olguţa burst out laughing.

"Oh, Papa!" If you knew who tante Melanie is, you wouldn't say such a thing!"

"How do you come to know her?"

"Well... I can visualize her... You know, Papa, she's got glasses on the tip of her nose and she looks out above them." While she described her, her fingers molded her shape in the air.

"And what else has she got?"

"Ah! She's got a wart... a hairy wart above her lip. And she's as thin as a stick..."

"A stick with glasses," Mr. Deleanu added.

"Wait, Papa! She's got a mustache."

"You don't say!"

"On my honor, Papa! I could swear to it. When she eats hard-boiled eggs the yoke sticks to her mustache. It's sickening! She's so ugly. Papa, tante Melanie is uncle Leon's wife, the poor man."

"That's what I was telling you. She wants to divorce and she has briefed me."

"Don't accept, Papa. Uncle Leon is in the right. Tante Melanie is a harpy. She persecutes him!"

"What's to be done?"

"Let's persecute her."

"Let's sing it over again then."

"Let's."

Once again the soprano and the baritone went through the rhythmic list of aunts.

The morning came in through the windows like a storm of pollen, brightly gilding carpets and mirrors, Monica was seated on the divan by the stove, a book of the bibliotheque rose on her knees.

She gave a deep sigh: "Poor Olguţa!"

Monica had found out by chance the real reason why their departure for Iaşi has been postponed but had promised Mrs. Deleanu, not to Olguţa.

"...et l'oncle Leon."

"Well done, Papa!"

"With such a teacher I'm likely to make good progress."

"Do you know what, Papa? I'll teach you the accompaniment."

"That will be the end of me."

"Come on, Papa... With one single finger."

Willy-nilly, Mr. Deleanu sat down to the piano. Olguţa guiding his clumsy fingers over the uniform keys.

The drawing-room was opened gently. Anica put in her head and waited. Monica came out.

"Has the doctor come?"

"Yes, miss." Anica swallowed hard, wiping her eyes with her apron. "...Madam is asking for the alcohol in the cupboard and for a clean towel."

Holding the towel and the bottle, Anica rushed down the steps. Monica entered the drawing-room with a puckered brow and heavy eyes.

La tante Julie,

La tante Sophie,

La tante Melanie

Et l'oncle Leon...

Mrs. Deleanu came out into the vestibule with the doctor.

"What can I say, Mrs. Deleanu. Today... tomorrow, it's a matter of hours."

"Should we take him to the hospital in Iaşi..."

"It's useless. He won't be able to stand the trip."

"...Take the doctor to the mansion, Anica," Mrs. Deleanu said, passing her hand over her forehead. "My daughter loves Moş Gheorghe, Doctor," she added. "I don't want her to know... We let her believe you're my husband's client come here on business."

The doctor raised his hand and smiled.

"*Voyons!* You needn't worry," he said. "In a few minutes, we'll be the best of friends. *J'en fais mon affaire.*"

On seeing the doctor, the peasants seated on the porch stood up and bowed low.

"Will he go," one of them asked.

"Something to inherit?" the doctor joked, peering at him. "Don't worry. He'll be gone before long."

The doctor went on his way, followed by Anica. The carriage was waiting for him at the gate, with Ion in the driving box.

"You filth!" Oţăleanca mumbled between her teeth, a hostile look coming from her eyes moist with innocent tears.

***

Moş Gheorghe tried to produce a humorous smile from the corner of his lips and eyes; the smile looked sad on his thin face with circles of bitter suffering around the eyes.

Very gently Mrs. Deleanu sat down on the edge of the bench.

"Is there anything you want, Moş Gheorghe?"

"Why did he prick, madam?" he whispered, spacing out his words, his thin fingers fretting.

"Because he had to, Moş Gheorghe. It is health-giving."

"You're kind, my lady... but I think the priest should come."

"Alright, Moş Gheorghe, the priest too will come... if you want him."

The silence was broken by a heavy sigh.

"Does it hurt, Moş Gheorghe?"

The old man's eyes directed towards the bright windows filled with tears.

"...I'll bring her to you a little later, Moş Gheorghe."

The small room where Olguţa discovered after their fragrance the fruit from the Oţăleanca's orchard as soon as she got through the door, now smelt of Iodine, ether, and burnt alcohol.

***

"That's a fine plum-brandy, Mr. Deleanu."

"An old one."

"Old age is good too, sometimes," and turning towards Olguţa, "Here's to you, Mademoiselle," he said.

Olguţa looked at him with myopic eyes and again peered into her book, her cheek against Monica's cheek.

Pretending to read, she whispered: "Have you noticed, Monica? The client shaves his forehead."

Profira took out the tray, looking at the doctor in disgust: he had eaten all the snacks.

"And what do the young ladies take delight in, if you don't mind my asking?" the doctor inquired, sitting down on the sofa beside them.

"*Les malheurs de Sophie*," Monica hastened to give the title of the book as she huddled up close to Olguţa.

"*Les malheurs*? Oh no! With such readers, we must change the title. I propose: *Les honheurs de Sophie*."

He was being witty. He inhaled air through his nose. Olguța frowned.

"So your Sophie is unhappy? Will you let me know what her misfortunes are?"

"Of course," Olguța offered, looking him full in the face.

"You may speak."

"Our Sophie was a little girl just like us," Olguța began, patting her hair to one side to leave bare a pugnacious forehead.

"Pretty, good, and fond of tales," the doctor continued.

"And well-bred," Olguța added curtly.

"A joy to her parents," the doctor concluded.

"How do you know?"

"Ah! I know a great many things. My little finger tells me."

"Yes? Please tell your little finger — which one, the left-hand and the right-hand finger... or perhaps the toe?"

"This one!"

Olguța looked it up with great intention and for a long time.

"Please tell it that it lies and shall have its nail cut off as a punishment."

The doctor's nails were cut — or more exactly gnawed — short.

The right hand's little finger alone was highly privileged, owing perhaps to aesthetic views.

"Hah-hah! Why does it lie, young lady?"

"Because our Sophie was not her parents' joy."

"I can't believe it."

"Just listen and you'll see."

"I'm all ears."

"A gentleman once visited Sophie's parents..."

Mr. Deleanu suddenly sat down at Olguța's feet on the divan.

"Sophie was playing the piano. What was she to do? She got up to receive the guest because she was a well-bred little girl... But the gust wouldn't leave her alone. Instead of talking to Sophie's parents — as grown-ups do — he talked to Sophie..."

"I propose we should sit down to lunch, Olguța," Mr. Deleanu put in.

"Aren't we going to wait for mother?... And so," Olguța continued stubbornly, "Sophie was unable to control herself and told him to his face: Mr. guest, I can't stand you because you shave your forehead, because you smell like a chemist's shop, and because you shave your forehead, because you smell like a chemist's shop, and because you don't leave me alone."

An uncomfortable silence.

The door opened. Mrs. Deleanu came in with faked liveliness.

"Good news! A letter from Dănuț."

"Let me see," Olguța claimed.

"Let's have lunch... And how are you getting on?" Mrs. Deleanu asked the door.

"Admirably. We are already teasing each other. You know: Qui s'aime se taquine."

Mr. Deleanu bit his mustache and sneezed...

A pile of photos gushed out of the penned envelope onto Mrs. Deleanu's plate.

"Dănuț! Look! It's Dănuț!" Mrs. Deleanu rejoiced.

"Let us see, mother."

"With cropped hair!" A closer look at the photo of the fresh secondary school pupil saddened Mrs. Deleanu.

The doctor alone ate the savory omelet.

"Look, mother: there's something written on the back."

"For Monica from Dănuț," Mrs. Deleanu read the words written in a beautiful hand. " Here you are, Monica."

Dumb with feeling. Monica took the photo without looking at it, laid it on her knees touching it with her fingers, swallowed hard and pressed her napkin over her burning cheeks.

"For Papa from Dănuț."

"Eh! Like it radish! Father's big-headed boy!"

"This one is for me: For Olguța from Dănuț."

"Who is that one for, mother?"

"For Moș Gheorghe..." Mrs. Deleanu read quickly, stopping too late.

"Good for you, Dănuț!" Olguța was jubilant. "I'm going to take it to Moș Gheorghe."

They all made long faces. The doctor alone smiled, winking meaningfully at Mrs. Deleanu.

"Wait a bit, please," he put in while munching. Let me have a photo too. Am I not the young people's friend?"

"Here is an omelet," Olguța returned fiercely, pushing the plate towards him.

"That's right. Let's have our lunch." A cold shiver went down Mrs. Deleanu's back.

"What does he write? Do read the letter."

"Mother dear, I miss you all, also Moș Gheorghe and Ali..."

A long pause.

"Let it be, Alice. Everyone will read it after lunch."

But for the doctor, the omelets would have left the table untouched, and the cook would not have been surprised.

"I'm going to take the photo to Moş Gheorghe, Mother," Olguţa declared while giving a fierce look to the doctor who was coming into the
drawing-room.

"..."

"Later, Olguţa. Moş Gheorghe has gone to the forest. You'll go with father when he returns!"

"Are you coming too, Papa?"

"Haven't I promised? We too are going to visit him."

"And we'll go up in the swing."

"Of course!"

"And we'll leave the client here. Won't we?"

"Naturally!"

"Good, father!" Olguţa breathed freely. "I can't stand him," she added.
"Have you seen the way he eats?"

Mrs. Deleanu held Dănuţ's letter out to Olguţa.

"Read it with Monica. There's something about preserve pots," she
forced a smile.

On hearing the words preserve pots, Olguţa gave a start. She took Monica by the hand and hurried to her room, where no fire had been lit because
Olguţa claimed it was too warm.

Mrs. Deleanu began to cry.

"Poor Olguţa!" Mr. Deleanu said, shaking his head.

***

Olguţa was reading Dănuţ's letter aloud; by her side. Monica followed with
her eyes the irregular lines she would have liked to caress and to kiss.

...The boys here make fun of me because I speak with a Moldavian accent. I don't care. What puzzles me is that they tell lies. Tell me, mother dear, do I mispronounce the *tch's* as some of the Moldavians do?

"If I were there, I'd show you!" Olguţa rated the unseen Wallachians, Dănuţ's persecutors.

Monica too flared up, all red with vexation. "But it isn't true, Olguţa. Dănuţ doesn't speak that way."

"Of course he doesn't. The Wallachians are just fools. And they are rather deaf too," Olguţa approved without knowing how Dănuţ had stood his ground.

Monica accepted the homage.

"...As were getting into the classroom yesterday, a boy was saying, pointing to some boys in another class: "They are free, the bay idiots." So I went up to him and told him he didn't know Romanian because in Romanian the subject agrees with the verb so he should have said, "they are free." The other boys laughed and said he was right because I'm a pig-headed Moldavian. I didn't say anything..."

Olguţa disapproved. "You should have..."

Monica defended him. "Poor Dănuţ, what could he have done?"

"Insult him and give him a hiding."

"...but during the Romanian class I asked Mr. Ilie Popescu what is the right thing to say. He said I was right. But I can't understand anything. He says: "They is." Tell me, Mother dear, did he make fun of me or doesn't he know Romanian either?"

"Ilie Popescu, you're a fool. You can tell he's a fool by his name; isn't that so, Monica?"

"Why Olguţa? He said Dănuţ was right."

"You mustn't side with fools, Monica. They are never right."

Since I've had my hair cropped, I feel very cold. And somehow I am ashamed to go about bare-headed! How Olguţa would laugh to see me."

Olguţa looked at the photo in Monica's hands and smiled.

"Poor Humpty-Dumpty," she said. "It is as if his head had been white-washed."

Olguţa resumed her reading. Monica's eyes were glued to the photo. She was listening and looking.

Dănuţ in his uniform with trousers had a position that was typically photographic: one leg forward as if obeying a military command — stand easy! — one hand stuck on the hip, princely fashion, the other, bearing the cap, hanging rigidly along the thigh: his head was thrust upwards. He smiled seraphically to the photographer's unseen hand. Monica's blushing checks took possession of the smile.

The following postscript ended the letter:

"...I too have eaten preserves from the pots in Olguţa's room. They were so good, Mother dear. Such good preserves are only made at home."

"Good, Dănuţ! That's how I would have written as well."

Olguţa admired the masterly rhetoric whereby Dănuţ had combined the confession of the theft of preserves kept for the winter, with praise and flattery for the loser. She didn't realize that "they were so good, Mother dear!" far from being a cunning trick, was for Dănuţ an artless and complete love song.

***

After taking holy communion, Moş Gheorghe had gazed for long at the blue incense floating wavily through the room. After a time he had dozed off. Now he was sleeping on his back. His arms hung heavily on either side of him. His body as well as his face seemed to preserve the imprint of a resigned crucifixion.

Seated on a stool close to the bench, her elbows resting on her knees and her forehead buried in her palms, Mrs. Deleanu was watching over him.

Oţăleanca too was keeping watch, as she did not dare to sit under the same roof as Mrs. Deleanu and was tired of she had stood up for long, she had knelt before the icons.

Lolling on the porch in the fresh air, the doctor was reading a French novel, making reflections that were specifically Romanian.

...At the time she was Olguţa's age, Mrs. Deleanu had received from Moş Gheorghe a gift that was eternal like Jericho roses: the smile of childhood. But for Moş Gheorghe she wouldn't have known it. It was not because her parents did not love her. But Mrs. Deleanu's mother having been greatly shaken upon giving her birth, had mostly lived abroad ever since. Her homecomings, which occurred less and less frequently, brought home a face that looked even more exhausted, a smile ever more tormented and the order for perfect silence, which had been advised by the doctor and had been enjoined by Fiţa Elencu in front of the piles of freshly bought play-things. Costache Dumşa, enticed by politics, caressed absentmindedly and only occasionally with a sigh of regret the head of the shy little girl with whom his name was to become extinct. The staunch guardian of her child-hood in her parents' home had been Fiţa Elencu's eyes, green like a mold destructive of all tenderness. Later, teachers and governesses, again under Fiţa Elencu's direction, had taught her to be mature in her mind, clever, gloomy, and scholarly also in other languages than her native tongue.

Moş Gheorghe had stood her in place of mother and grandfather. He had wiped away as many tears as he had brought smiles and liveliness on the pale face of the little girl that was exhausted with learning and loneli-ness.

She had been the old man's young lady as Olguţa was now, and the old man of their childhood was passing.

Mrs. Deleanu's fingers caress lightly the old man's white hair.

Memories of later days followed the memories of childhood, but they were still bound up with Moş Gheorghe and his cottage.

...At Iaşi a long time ago Fiţa Elencu had intercepted a love letter from young Iorgu Deleanu, who taught her niece philosophy.

"What's this, Alice?" she had asked with the letter in her hand and an acid smile in her eyes.

Her niece's heart had felt the weight of the whole planet.

"Let's see what our teacher has to say," Fiţa Elencu had said as she sat down in an armchair... "'My dear Alice?' Well, well! So my dear niece, a mere servant, a Deleanu of sorts, dares to be familiar with you, the offspring of a boyar family. Good! Very good! Do you know what whips are for, young lady? You don't. Your aunt, who's older than you, will teach you. Whips, my dear niece, are for thick soles, to make them thinner... and more sensitive. And what else does he say? "Dear" a very disrespectful adjective. And what else? "My!" How is that possible! Doesn't it seem to you, my dear niece, that this unconsidered possessive issues from an altogether disordered mind? For it is not possible that the offspring of slaves should dare steal a word that is reserved to the boyars!... My dear girl," Fiţa had concluded, folding the letter as if it had been a most valuable document, "you will come with me to the country and one there I'll call you 'My dear Alice' until you are fed up with love, and don't feel the need to have servants call you that.

Fiţa had kept her word so very swiftly that young Iorgu Deleanu had found a closed door at the house where he taught philosophy. While Fiţa's niece was learning to control her tears at Medeleni under the intent watch of the green eyes, young Iorga Deleanu let them flow freely at Iaşi, getting ever lower marks in his law examinations.

One day, Anca, Moş Gheorghe's wife had come to the mansion.

"Kiss your hand, miss, the old man is bedridden," she had said with a sigh that hid a smile.

Without waiting for Fiţa's permission, the old man's young lady had rushed out. Moş Gheorghe had met her in the entrance hall, gloom mingling with mirth.

Instead of illness — young Iorgu Deleanu.

Moş Gheorghe knew who Fiţa Elencu was and what she could do. And yet he has not hesitated. For a whole afternoon, Moş Gheorghe and mother Anica had kept watch at the window to shield the happiness behind them. For a whole night, they had slept on the porch because in the room the young lady's young man was sleeping a happy sleep, the sleep of youth.'

...In front of the houses of one's childhood huge and benevolent oaks sometimes grow and their rustling leaves and singing nests are ever dearer to you as the days and years go by because in the leaves and the nests' memories live and sing and because their shade is as sweet as love. And if an ax happens to fell them, their fall is the fall of the past and the emptiness left by their absence is a groan of sorrow.

Moş Gheorghe's harsh and whistling breathing could alone be heard in the silence of the small room. Death was felling a gentle oak with the rattling sound of a saw.

Mrs. Deleanu was crying.

When telling a story or pleading, Mr. Deleanu was prey to a southern excitement that made him behave as one possessed. Once, in a law court, hectic with oratory and interruptions, he had gradually left the bench of the defense and was advancing until he had reached the middle of the room, between the accused and the jury.

Unaware of it, he kept dancing his way onward towards the table of the court, until the president rang his bell:

"Allow me, sir, to ask the usher to remove the court's table for you to have more room."

Mr. Deleanu stopped his advance.

"Excuse me, Your honor," he replied. "Truth carries one forward as if to take justice by storm. I thank your honor for having sent me back in good time."

This time the subject of the tale agreed in every respect with the story-teller's temperament. The feast of valor of the three musketeers was not merely a tool; they were interpreted by gesture and attitude. D'Artagnan's sword unsheathed, reduced to the dwarfish proportions of the paper-knife on the desk, had felled so many of Cardinal Richelieu's guards that Mr. Deleanu in good faith swept aside imaginary corpses with his foot, advancing onward. There wasn't a speck of dust on the paper-knife: Mr. Deleanu would wipe the blood from it after every duel.

The lampshade on the carpet proved that it had done duty for a hat during the ceremonious greetings exchanged between the brave Athos, Porthos, Aramis, and the fourth musketeer of the trinity: d'Artagnan of Gascony.

The cup of black coffee was smeared inside with grounds for, although emptied half through the tale, Mr. Deleanu was draining it, musketeer fashion, to sip the delectable wines which during the short halts repaid the four valiant fellows for their labor and strivings.

Monica and Olguța swayed like swallows in their flight as they followed the zig-zag movements of the storyteller in the large room.

"...Porthos sees them but much does he care; he faces four, five, six guards of that scoundrel of a cardinal. With a thrust of his elbow, he throws down the horse and the rider."

A chair fell, giving a cracking sound.

"...He takes hold of the rider..."

The most suitable image of the cardinal's rider was the statue of justice with its ever uneven scales.

"...And he starts flourishing his sword: three guards fall dead two wounded; the others run for their lives."

The last guard — the statue of justice — fell heavily on the carpet, amidst Olguța's applause. Charitable Monica picked up the justice and put it back on the desk.

***

Like the announcement, "Christ has risen," made by the priest and afterward uttered by thousands of voices, the sun's red hue had set the sky ablaze, passing from cloud to cloud, from one horizon to the other.

The courtyard of Moş Gheorghe cottage had gradually filled with peasants. They had come to receive news about the oldest and best of them. Some of them were seated on the ground and others on the porch, some of them stood, silent and solemn as they would have done at the death of a ruling price.

Moş Gheorghe opened his eyes; they were dim. He closed them again. In the silence of the small room, a struggle had begun, though not between human bodies. Moş Gheorghe opened his eyes again. His thoughts moved with difficulty like snowed over carts in the nebulous winter frost.

The doctor checked his pulse. Meeting the foreign face, Moş Gheorghe's eyes turned in another direction. He looked about the room... recognized Mrs. Deleanu... looked about again. Mrs. Deleanu's eyes met those of the forgotten.

She beckoned to the Oţăleanca woman and whispered to her: "Go and bring over Olguța."

Painstakingly, Moş Gheorghe moved his head, bent, and kissed Mrs. Deleanu's hand.

***

Alexander Dumas had written about the adventures of the three musketeers; Mr. Deleanu was telling them viva voce. Starting perhaps from the legal saying *"la plume est serve, la parole est libre"* — the storyteller intensified the novelist's romanticism. Mr. Deleanu was no longer the barrister Iorgu Deleanu: he was the fifth musketeer hitherto unknown, the verbose gallant fellow, Tartatin de Tarascon.

So the musketeers fought whole armies which they negligently vanquished. Galloping at full speed, Porthos plucked out bunches of oaks — or other vegetable giants — which he threw over the heads of the pursuers without the stallion he was riding, which was of the most romantic breed, noticing the addition of thousands of pounds.

D'Artagnan passed through the enemy ranks — like Jesus on the waves of the sea — handling out thundering sword thrusts and Romanian interjections right and left.

And when the four musketeers fought together, the draft of the four swords uprooted the forests. If Richelieu, that scoundrel, had been more practical, he would have appealed to the musketeers' patriotism instead of persecuting them. And then the musketeers — flamberge au vent - would have flourished their swords from dawn till dark, thus impelling all France's boat over the seas and oceans with the Gallic wind of their swords.

The national outlaws now had serious rivals in Olguța's estimation.

Anica knocked at the door several times. As she received no answer she went in.

"...A sword thrust to the left: bang! The opponent parried it..."

Olguța frowned; she had her heart in her mouth.

"...A thrust to the right... What is it you want?" d'Artagnan asked, on seeing Anica.

"Out with you!" Olguța shouted. "Go on, Papa."

"Was the opponent Athos himself?"

"Eh!"

Anica's eyes were glued to Mr. Deleanu who went on with his tale excitedly. Seeing that she was not taken notice of, Anica went over to the desk.

"Madam has sent for Miss Olguța."

"...Porthos's opponent was Aramis himself!"

"Ah!"

"Moș Gheorghe is very, very ill," Anica said aloud.

Olguța jumped up.

"What did you say?" she asked.

Anica had run out. Olguța looked at Mr. Deleanu with a frowning brow.

"What did you say?" she asked.

Anica had run out. Olguța looked at Mr. Deleanu with a frowning brow.

"What did she say, Papa?"

Suddenly awakened, Mr. Deleanu took Olguța's head between his palms, held it tight, and kissed on her forehead. Olguța blinked, wrenched herself away, and rushed out.

***

On seeing Olguța, the peasants in Moș Gheorghe's courtyard took off their hats and stood up. Olguța made her way between them at a run, looking at them as if dazed.

"Moș Gheorghe!" she called out from the entranceway. She was panting.

The Oțăleanca woman followed her to Mrs. Deleanu and the doctor stood up, Olguța looked at them in turns without receiving any answer.

Mr. Deleanu, Monica, and Anica entered on tiptoe. The porch was full of heads. The silence was oppressive.

Olguța's cheeks paled. She went up to the bench along the wall, looking at Moș Gheorghe fearfully, unconvinced. Moș Gheorghe could no longer speak or smile at her. He could perhaps see her faintly with the semblance of a soul that still dwelt in his eyes.

"Won't you puff at your pipe, Moş Gheorghe?" Olguţa asked him secretly, leaning over him so that nobody should hear her.

The old man's eyelids moved spasmodically over the white of his eyes. Olguţa took the pipe from the table that bore the holy books. Everybody made way for her. She put the pipe in Moş Gheorghe's hand, her cold little hand resting a long time on the old man's frozen fingers.

She returned to the table, took the matchbox, and went up to the bench along the wall. She lit the match. The pipe fell from the stiff fingers... The match burnt fitfully in the trembling hand.

The Oţăleanca woman held out the candle and lit it from the match that was nearly out, at the same time putting out the flame that burnt Olguţa's fingers.

"God forgive him!"

"What for?" Olguţa asked beseechingly, with heart-rendering affection...

They all bent their heads.

The grave icons on the walls were silent.

Cold noonday with a sky grown old with gray clouds.

A bell tolled above the village, calling to the attention of the distant sky that a man had entered the earth. On the big lane and in front of the villages' courtyards, there wasn't a soul, except for the very young children — those who talk to the dwarfs, are at variance with the sparrows and are vexed with the trees. The village seemed to belong to the children.

At the cemetery, the peasants with bent heads behind the Deleanu family listened to the mournful bell.

When the service had begun at the grave, Olguţa has taken off her hat. Her dark locks had fluttered in the sharp wind together with the locks of the young lads and the old men.

The priest was old. The cemetery was quiet. The words of the service sounded like those in the old books of the now-empty cottage.

"Where are you, Moş Gheorghe?"

"Let the earth lie light over him…"

The peasants drove in the oak cross at the head of the grave.

Has Moş Gheorghe seen the eyes of his young lady — with dark circles around them as they had never been before — riveted tearless to the grave, their look would have been a heavier burden to him the moist earth that had definitively relegated him among the dead.

"Here I am missy."

Behind the mansion, the burial feast prepared by Mrs. Deleanu, according to the custom, had started.

Olguţa poured out the drink from the ewer into the peasants' jugs. Mrs. Deleanu and Monica served glasses of brandy from the tray carried by the Oţăleanca woman.

Anica, Profira, and Safta — the cook of the men working on the estate — brought the dishes.

The gloomy timidity brought over from the cemetery did not last long. To begin with, the old men talked about their memories. After which, the young people's jokes burst forth, whispered at first warm dishes that followed increased the mirth.

Olguţa frowned. A sharp word made her eyes glow with anger… She made her way to the mansion pursing her dry lips. She stopped before the steps as if she had been driven away. She made for the stable. Nobody laughed there…

…On the box of the motionless carriage that had no horses harnessed to it and no reins, a child cried, holding her hands over her eyes.

And the God of the wonderful tales did not send angels to be harnessed to it; nor did he take hold of the wet fists from behind, putting reins into them; nor did he whisper, smiling gently:

"You drive, missy."

***

"Take a seat, Father."

The priest brought out an envelope from under his surplice.

"Sir, two years ago, Moş Gheorghe — may God forgive him — entrusted to me a paper for you. Here it is."

Mr. Deleanu took the tissue envelope with red seals. On the paper inside it, Moş Gheorghe's hand had written in tremulous Cyrillics. After a brief look, Mr. Deleanu looked at the priest.

"I have nearly forgotten those letters, Father. Kindly read the paper for me."

The priest put on his glasses and read the last will of the man who was no more. Moş Gheorghe began by taking leave of his masters, thanking them for the bread he had eaten in their house and for the kindness they had seen fit to show him. He then gave directions for the use to be made of the money he had put aside. Finally:

"...I, Gheorghe Iernilă, leave my house and household to the children of barrister Iorgu Deleanu, that is to Miss Olguţa and Master Dănuţ. So that my house and land should be a place where they could play after my death as it was in my lifetime. And the Braşov chest which I have as a gift from the late Costache Dumşa, I leave with everything in it to Miss Olguţa. In the chest, I have put together a bit of a dowry bought with my work for Miss Olguţa. And I would reverently and submissively ask you to make a wedding dress for Miss Olguţa from the silks in the chest. For if I had not the happiness to see her a bride, at least this joy I should partake of for much did I love her."

"On the station platform, Mrs. Deleanu and the girls
huddled together around their suitcases,
were silent like a family of emigrants."

Ionel Teodoreanu

In the meantime, Mrs. Deleanu had gone into the study in search of Olguṭa. The words in Moş Gheorghe's will had brought to her mind dialogues from the years gone by, throwing light upon them:

"Cotton print — it's good and inexpensive."

"Silk, my lady — it's expensive and beautiful."

"What for, Moş Gheorghe? You have no marriageable daughter."

"Just to have it... The old man knows what for."

"And may I be permitted — as an old servant of your family and as an old man — to raise my eyes to my mistress, Miss Olguṭa, and to say: 'Do not be ashamed to receive a dowry from a servant, missy, for work and love, are blessed by our Lord God...'"

Mrs. Deleanu alone knew — by a mere chance — that Olguṭa had secretly put on Monica's mourning dress for the burial of the servant who had devoted the work of his years to the purchase of a white wedding dress.

***

The autumn night was wet and bitter as if driven out of the bottom of an ocean.

On the station platform, Mrs. Deleanu and the girls huddled together around their suitcases, were silent like a family of emigrants.

The train pulled into the station an hour late. They boarded it in haste. A man's voice in the unlighted corridor asked, yawning:

"What station can it be, man? When the deuce will we reach our destination with so many halts?"

Olguṭa clenched her fists.

The trumpet gave a short blast. The train set off from the anonymous holiday station to the cities with well-known names.

Note on the Pronunciation of Romanian Words

This note is intended to give readers who are unfamiliar with the Romanian language some idea of the proper pronunciation of the Romanian words which appear in this book. Romanian orthography is almost entirely phonetical, a letter representing the same sound, in all positions, with few exceptions. Here are the letters of the Romanian alphabet and their pronunciation:

a — as *a* in *half*, but shorter.

ă — as *er* in *father*.

â — similar to *e* in *morsel* or *u* in *sullen*.

b — as *b* in *baseball*.

c — before consonants, the vowels a, ă, â, î, o, u, and at the end of words, as *c* in *cat*. Before e and i, as *ch* in *cherry*.

d — as *d* in *dog*.

e — as *e* in *pen*.

f — as *f* in *fire*.

g — before consonants, the vowels a, ă, â, î, o, u and at the end of words, as *g* in *got*. Before e and i, as *g* in *general*.

h — as *h* in *behind*. In groups che, chi, che, ghi, it is mute, showing that c and g preserve their hard sound.

i — as *ee* in *see*.

î — similar to *e* in *morsel* or *u* in *sullen*. Same as â.

j — as *s* in *measure*.

k — as *k* in *kite*.

l — as *l* in *like*.

m — as *m* in *mother*.

n — as *n* in *neither*.

o — as *o* in *comb*.

p — as *p* in *police*.

r — similar to a rolled Scottish *r*.

s — as *s* in *sand*.

ş — as *sh* in *ship*.

t — as *t* in *toil*.

ţ — as *ts* in *cats*.

u — as *u* in *glue*.

v — as *v* in *valley*.

x — as *x* in *excellent*.

z — as *z* in *zebra*.